SHADOWS IN A DARK ALLEY

BY TED S. BALDWIN

BOOK 1

SHADOWS

OF

THINGS

THAT

WERE

Dedicated

To

My Son Ben,

Without whose insights and help, this book could not have been published

Prolog

Ted Baldwin's "Shadows" series of novels is a compelling story about people with haunting as well as hopeful struggles in an America conflicted and divided by the ideal "all men are created equal" and the reality of America's struggles with equality.

First book in the series, *Shadows of Things That Were*, begins in that brittle time between the Great War and the Great Depression. The world was lost. Not the earth, or the planet, or the globe. The world. Classes crashed, empires passed; raw new empires were being built. Nobody knew who they were or how to react, except the very poor, for whom life had not changed, and the very rich, who just got richer.

But nothing stays the same. The Great Depression and WWII turned America inside out and created shadows of new freedoms and opportunities for America's Black population. Luke Powers grew up a Black American through all this. He experienced the prejudice and horror of being Black in the Jim Crow south, the brotherhood and terror of fighting in WWII, and the ultimate hope that post-war changes in America might give his people the opportunity to achieve the dignity and societal equality they deserved. This story is both troubling and inspiring with strong characters and action you will find leaving you wanting more.

Contents

CHAPTER 1

A Light in the Dark

It is that brittle time between the Great War and the Great Depression. The world was lost. Not the earth, or the planet, or the globe. The world. Class crashed, empires passed, raw new empires were being built. Nobody knew who they were or how to react. Except the very poor, for whom life had not changed, and the very rich, who just got richer. Into that chaos came the scream.

The sound of the scream was uncommon, even there, where a common sound was the sound of a scream. In such a place as this, where brutality coexisted with tenderness as a way of life, the sound of human pain rarely gave much cause for alarm or curiosity.

However, on Magnolia Street a sound of joy might command some attention. On this day that sound was of both joy and death. It was of such intensity that people heard it up and down the block. So unusual was the temper of the sound--even to the world of the ghetto--that for one imperceptible moment the people on the street and behind Magnolia's ancient doors, seemed to pause for their own hearts to skip a beat before going on about the drudgery of their day. Some small few, those closest to the Powers' house where the sound had originated, paused longer as though waiting for something more, something even more violent.

It was June 1925. Magnolia was one of a thousand streets all alike, streets without the glitter of the times in America; streets devoid of cars and flappers; streets bustling instead with bandanaed women and ill-tempered muscular men; streets of home brew and heroin, and of crime committed without fear of being caught since there was little law enforcement present. These were streets where love and love—making tried to smother hate and violence, streets with ragged children and trashy gutters. As they are today, these streets were streets of the ghetto.

Little distinguished Magnolia Street from countless others. It was store fronts and tenements, an occasional makeshift school splashed with graffiti, and churches. But Magnolia was a little different. It had houses, not just tenements. Few of its families were fortunate enough to live alone in one of those houses. The houses on Magnolia were built of wood by the Whites during Reconstruction, then abandoned to the Blacks after forty years with no paint or maintenance. The Whites moved to brick or stone or fled to other towns. These were strange looking houses on narrow lots, each almost like half of a house. They resembled one side of a Northern Victorian duplex built with shades of French and a touch of the old plantation home. The front porches and upper balconies ran down the side, three feet from a neighbor's front porch across a common walk. Their clapboard siding was warped and twisted. The cracked windows were of ancient, distorting panes. Maroon or brown or red or yellow curtains covered them. Smells rich and human emanated from these windows as they lingered on the breeze and settled on the streets.

North of Magnolia was the city. To the South and East was Georgia as Georgia had always been with its red clay earth and lush vegetation. New corn and cotton and peanuts once again robbed the soil. Black and poor White backs bent to pull one more crop from an earth exhausted by two hundred years of crops leaching wealth from it.

The only difference between the Blacks and the Whites working the land was that with few exceptions the Whites owned it and prospered from the sweat of the Blacks. The Blacks gained little more than the day's meager nourishment and a life shortened by hopelessness and hunger.

The White man seldom thought of this as anything but the natural order, as anything but fair, almost just. He saw it as his due as payment for the South being raped of her riches while Georgia burned to the ground over six decades before. Yet these Whites considered themselves good Christians. They were always sure to collect and distribute their old clothes, old furnishings, worn out or useless belongings as "charity" for the Blacks working their land.

These Whites had done the same for a fee that was exorbitant when compared to actual value, with their cast-off houses in cast-off neighborhoods in Atlanta. And the ghettos were born. On one of these streets called Magnolia the scream had come that June day in 1925. It was when for a breath or two something happened in this house worth remarking about. On the twenty—fourth, that scream broke through a second-floor window and a woman died giving life. That was when and how Luke Powers was born.

Luke was not the firstborn. He was in fact almost not born at all, for his mother struggled to take care of herself during the pregnancy. Luke came after four other siblings, who were now cowering with heads down in near silence on the shabby balcony outside the bedroom door. Although they had seen death before, this was different. They had lost their mother. They did not really understand. There was no unusual comprehension of life and death inherent in their souls, just normal human needs and emotions which conflicted within them. It made them mute. Only the puffiness of recent weeping on their faces or the knuckle-bearing grip of little Black hands pressed around their knees told of their grief.

Although Eldon Powers loved and had pride in his children, he had never dared hope, really hope, that they could move out of the ghetto. But with Luke, only less than half a day old, he could see, he knew, he was positive, that this child would. He could not define or verbalize why he knew. He just did. Looking into the eyes of his own parents, he knew that they shared this feeling, and that made the pain a little more endurable.

Over the weeks leading through the hot summer toward fall, Luke began to affirm his father's intuition. Luke seemed to progress faster than the others had. This growth was not so much in pounds gained as awareness, not so much in motor skill as perception, not so much in physical strength as mental agility, not so much in handsomeness as magnetism.

/ / /

At two, Luke was all over the house, into every nook, dark corner and on the lap of every visitor. The questions asked and the responses given by this inquisitive child amazed and delighted adults, who sought his company and his attention. Even in a crowd, he seemed to give this attention to each individual.

At six, the pattern continued, but the world was different. The changes happening cast shadows on Luke's life but as shadows do also hinted at light beyond. The Great Depression had begun and the meager resources of those who were already poor were all but gone. Feeding one's family became almost impossible as dust ate the cotton, and truck farms blew away in the wind of poverty.

For the Powers household, these things brought about a change to their family. Brotherhood among the Blacks being what it is, the Powers opened their doors without second thought to homeless cousins, aunts, uncles, and even destitute strangers.

One old soul came from the outside world as a traveling participant in a minstrel show. While too aged and sick to continue on the road, he could still weave words into legend and fairy tales. He could talk for hours of his parents and their enslavement while he was a youngster. This old minstrel inspired Luke to tell stories that would spellbind folks. Luke repeated what he had heard from his ancient mentor. He discovered and nurtured within himself a charisma others recognized. Luke's sharing in this large family circle also taught him inexorably and forever the power of brotherhood and love.

At six Luke started school, such as it was. Those in the ghetto fought for and jury-rigged their schools. Often adult peers taught one or more classes in opposite corners of the church. These peers had little or no formal training, but they had life experience. They shared from the community table and lodging for this contribution.

When Luke was eight, Eldon Powers disappeared. His grandparents told Luke that his Daddy was on a long journey and would not be back. Somehow Luke knew that Eldon was dead.

Luke's grandparents were sure their lie had worked, because Luke seemed to accept that his father was on a "trip." Luke smiled with this news. Touching the hand of each, with a quick hug he was off. The front screen door slammed behind him.

"Now, where's that boy goin'?" Harriet Powers questioned in a shaky voice. She started toward the door.

A soft "Leave 'em be" stopped her with a finality in its deep resonance. Eldon Powers, Sr. understood that they had not fooled Luke. Harriet did, too. She hugged her man and her silent tears turned to wails and sobs. Her grandson's insight had brought to her the reality of her son's death. The emotional avalanche which had been building inside her exploded under the mountain of grief where it lay buried. Anger and frustration with a life that could allow this to happen cooled and only tears followed.

CHAPTER 2

Retreat to the Alleys

Confused and stumbling, Luke cleared the front porch as the door slammed behind him. He looked wild-eyed up and down the street. He did not know where to go. He did what any eight-year-old in a panic would do. He ran. Luke reached the end of the block. In front of him was the corner store. He looked around, then went in. *Maybe this man will know where my Daddy is,* he thought. *Maybe he will know what happened to him.* He went up the storekeeper behind the counter. "Sir," he said, "do you know where my Daddy is?

"T'was them Whites what killed him. Kill a man t'save a chicken. Shoot a man, like he weren't no man at all. Them Whites." The storekeeper vented more matter of fact sorrow than anger in these words, as though through this knowledge, he could answer the question, "Why?" But for Luke, it answered another question which had burned in him since he began school. That question, "What is White man?" now had an answer: "The enemy."

Two weeks later, Luke was exploring his new home. He had been gone for a week when he came back to the old house on Magnolia to find so much changed, including himself. Luke had set out to discover for himself the White man who had killed his father. He had traversed Magnolia and Peachtree Streets, uptown into Atlanta. He traveled mostly at night like his daddy had done. He hid in the shadows of alleys or behind the checkerboard shadows under lattice-faced porches during the day. More than once he cringed to the snapping of a dog just outside such a porch, squirmed away from a packrat in whose path he lay or skittered from shadow to shadow to melt away from an approaching form.

But usually in such hiding places, Luke watched and learned. He watched strange looking children of cream color with blond hair laugh and play ball, skate or fight among themselves. He watched panted legs over shined shoes or scruffy work boots walk by his porch havens. These were topped with strange voices and stranger accents. Luke saw bare, smooth White legs perched on high heels click past, sometimes carrying nauseous smells of dirty bodies masked by cheap perfume.

But Luke saw almost no bare feet. They all had shoes, even the children. This menagerie of legs from another world all had shoes. When Luke realized this, he took his cold, brown and dirty toes in his grimy little hands. "Who'd want 'em" he asked himself. "Who would want them!" He wriggled his toes into the powder-dry red clay-laden soil under the porch and knew that it was he who wanted them.

When in the shadowed alleys, Luke gained a different perspective. In his own blackness, he went unnoticed. His small form was but one of countless shadows in those dark alleys of the White man's world. For other daddies had died, too, and mammas. The back streets of Atlanta in 1933 crawled with little children, some Black, some White, but all grey with dirt. Those children competed with the rats for daily bread. From these alleys Luke saw White flesh masking misery or anger. Sometimes he saw the White man dressed in fine clothing but usually he saw him in frayed, old and ill—fitting remnants of a better time. He saw loneliness, even in groups. He saw hunger and greed, and crime committed in the name of hunger or greed. He saw winos and the weak and weary succumb to defeat. He saw children with looks of innocence, others with looks of ancient men. He felt a tentative kinship, still thwarted by residual hate, fear, sorrow and his own loneliness. During those days he did not speak to another human being. Nurtured by a sorrow akin to the sorrow he was watching, he needed to have that sorrow soothed by the gentle touch of a friend.

When the idea came that Whites were like him, Luke consciously began comparisons. Other than skin, eyes, hair, what differences were there? They usually had coats and all had shoes. He suddenly felt naked and cold and wished to have shoes, too.

So the picture of White man as enemy slowly shifted. Pushing it was a growing image of White man as human. Luke became angry all over again at his father's death. He grasped again the words of the storekeeper. He realized that the White man was at least fed and clothed no matter how poorly, while he was nearly naked and starving. Sometimes in such thoughts those around him went unseen by him, as he often was by them. This was because they were there in the shadows. Then suddenly a small voice reached through the shadows to him.

"Hey!" The sharpness of the voice behind Luke spun him around as his hand grabbed at the handle of a trash can lid to whip it up in front of him, or at the intruder, or clattering to the pavement. As he eyed his beholder, he instead settled the can lid somewhat warily to his side. The small boy that faced Luke was about his size. He was a White boy in shoes and coat with a cap parked at random on his red hair.

Lord, his eyes are blue, thought Luke, but no sound came from him. He did not strike out at the boy. He did not run or remember to close his mouth which had dropped open as though to widen his black eyes to better see. Time suspended both boys as each drank in the other searching for a flicker of danger. None seen, they looked for a flicker of friendship and initially seemed to settle on the reality of color, a barrier supposedly unbreachable.

Slowly regaining his wits, Luke began backing off while never taking his eyes from the White boy. He tightened his hand on the handle of the can lid. His body began to turn independent of his head which, as though locked tight in gripping hands, remained still. They both stood open-mouthed with dark eyes and blue eyes fixed on each other.

Without warning, the White boy lurched toward Luke and threw his arms out as though for Luke's throat. Luke whipped the can lid away in his spin to run. But the boy just fell face down and blood stained the pavement around his head. Luke stopped. He turned again to look. The boy was prone, motionless. The din of the wallowing trash can lid was like a coin spun on edge but losing speed. It settled in a quickening cessation of wallops to quiet. The city sounds of the street half a block away took over again. Nothing moved in the alley.

Luke looked around to make sure of this, then eyed the coat and shoes. He crept closer. He could hear breathing. He could see the short, quick rise and fall of the boy's back. Closer, kneeling, he reached out one finger and gingerly touched the boy's face. No sound, no movement, no response came to acknowledge him. He touched his own face, then that of the small, prone figure once again. They felt the same.

Suddenly Luke experienced a wave of confusion. Why was this White boy his enemy? Why were they not brothers? So far, everything about the boy except coloring seemed very much like Luke's own brothers. It was then that Luke fully realized how lonely he was, and how alone. He sat down beside the small, unconscious stranger who was his only companion, and cried softly. He felt exhausted, cold, hungry and alone, painfully alone.

Only four days had passed since Luke's flight to the city. But he was not the same Luke who had stood before his grandparents the moment before he had received the news of his father's death. He was not the same Luke who slammed the front door for a quick escape or sought comfort from the storekeeper or watched White people from the shadows. He was not the same Luke who reacted with such fear a short moment before when another human being, a supposed enemy, appeared to lunge at him and instead had fallen to the filthy pavement and trickled blood as red as Luke's into the splotches of mud in the alleyway.

It was a different Luke who now saw the prone person in front of him. Through teared and blurry black eyes, he saw small, White fingers close over his hand, spread on the pavement beside the inert form that had just been the catalyst in reversing his life. Luke jerked his hand away instinctively. Then he gently returned it to cover the hand of the other boy. A well of joy at the responding presence of another overcame his fear. The change which had begun in Luke with that act was welcome. He did not know if this White boy was a friend. But he was certain that the boy was no enemy, no threat. *Maybe an ally?* He thought. He decided to see.

"What happen, y'all Okay?" Luke looked into the boy's eyes that began to reveal their blue through the haze of returning consciousness.

"Thanks for not leaving me", said the boy. "I was afraid I might be alone again. Wanna be friends, Boy?"

Luke dodged the question. He was not ready to answer. Yes, he wanted a friend, someone to talk to, be near, share with. How could he so quickly assume this boy to be a friend when he had just been fearful and angry with Whites? But suddenly, too, he wanted to be home. He did not want to be with a strange, sick kid from another world he was just beginning to accept and did not fully understand. But he was not sure he could find home. The boy's offer of companionship was drawing him. Still, he hesitated. "Why'd y'all fall? Why'd Y'all come after me?"

"I never. I don't think. Guess I don't know. I'm hungry. Are you?"

"Yeah. Maybe that's why y'all fell. I had a aunt what fell lots'a times when my daddy weren't home with something t'eat. At least that's what Gramma say was the matter with her."

"I know where we can get lots of food, all the food we want. What's your name?"

Luke hesitated. He was afraid to give his name, afraid the boy might turn on him. But he finally tentatively responded. "Luke. Where's this food? How come y'all ain't been gettin' it, then? How come y'all so hungry that y'all fall when you knows where all this food is?"

The boy slowly turned onto his back and propped himself up on his elbows. Luke noticed that his shoes had no toes, and the boy was without socks. Luke felt a little better, a little more equal, a little closer to the boy. "What's your name?" he said.

"I'm Freddie. I can't get at the food by myself. We could get it together if you'll help me, though."

"How?" Luke still mistrusted the boy. But he knew that this mistrust belonged to the past, to that other Luke not gone ten minutes but gone forever. He would need to risk trusting this boy if he wanted a chance at getting something to eat. Luke thought he might have an ally that accepted him. He found himself ready to return that acceptance if not friendship. Luke lifted the boy to his feet, wiping the bloody scratches on his face while seeking more detail on the boy.

"How you come to be alone here?"

"Ma and Pa's gone. Dead, I guess. Wanna get the food?" Freddie had turned, weakly pulling on Luke's arm to turn him, too, toward a blackened and crumbly brick wall about twenty feet deeper in the alley's shadows. He pointed. "That's the backside of this store, see. It's full of food. My Ma used to take me in there when I was a little kid. We'd walk by this alley up yonder and I'd quick look down here. That's how I know this here is the back."

"But how we get the food?" Luke's puzzled look made Freddie laugh with the pleasure of his secret and the chance to share it.

"There," pointed Freddie, directing Luke's eyes toward a window about eight feet up. A dusty line showed broken glass where the sun penetrated to catch the pane's jagged edge.

"How we gonna get up there?" Luke's wandering eyes answered before Freddie could respond. He grabbed the empty trash can. Together they rolled the can to the wall under the window and turned it upside down. Luke climbed up and reached for the window. "Can't catch it, Freddie. Boost me," he whispered back over his shoulder.

"Can't" replied Freddie, who was wavering as though he might again pass out. Luke jumped down from the can and shot his arm under his new friend's, hugging Freddie to himself to keep him on his feet. But Freddie's head rolled to Luke's shoulder and his sagging weight toppled Luke backward to the pavement. Freddie sprawled over him. *Oh Lord, Freddie,* thought Luke, and all the misery returned. But the warmth of Freddie's limp body, the rise of his back and his hot, stale breath on Luke's brown neck calmed Luke.

The moment passed. Luke summoned strength and courage from within himself and the life force of his companion. He rolled with Freddie to ease him onto the pavement. Luke stood up and faced the opposite side of the alley. There he saw a long plank lying alongside the building. He rolled a second can under the beckoning window, bridged the two with the board, and struggled a third can to the top of the rough scaffold. He clamored up one can, then the second. Taking a quick look back at his companion, he stretched toward the window with increased urgency. He had to get Freddie some food.

Luke touched the window but could not pull himself up. He looked around for something else and spied an empty fruit box down the alley. Five minutes later he was inside the building. Ten minutes after that he was pouring a warm Coca Cola down Freddie's throat. An hour later they were lying on the bare floor of an abandoned tenement. They had satisfied their hunger. In their innocence they lay face to face and arm in arm, Black and White. Trustingly, they slept amidst the litter of their shared bread, fruit and candy feast.

The alley was darkening in the next afternoon's fading light when Freddie and Luke busily rebuilt their way toward the yawning window to plenty. With Freddie's strength returning, his shoulders proved quicker and easier to Luke's bare feet than adding extra layers to the rickety scaffold. Grabbing the windowsill and placing his foot on top of a squirming Freddie's head, Luke caught the edge of the window across his waist and slithered through to the stacked boxes on the other side. Stealthily, he lowered himself to the floor and began filling his pouched shirt front and his pockets with the most convenient foodstuffs he could find.

Suddenly a "Hey! You! Boy!" resounded in front of him, as the bare light bulbs silhouetted his little Black body against the greasy whitewashed brick of the storeroom interior.

"Gotcha, nigger," snarled the man and suddenly Luke knew how his Daddy had died. Luke cowered against the wall. The man loomed over him, glaring down at him from under bushy, scowling brows. "You goddam thievin' Black beggar!" he shouted. "Know what I do to niggers like you? I cut off your ears is what, and your toes and hands, so you'll never steal from decent White people again. Then I cut out your tongue so's you never tell what's happened to you."

Luke kept terrified eyes pasted on the threatening red-white hulk before him, easing, easing, easing nearer the boxes leading to the window. Without warning he screamed, "Freddie!" and scrambled for the boxes as the man ripped at him, tearing the bare threads of his shirt apart. Luke kicked his way up the boxes, spilling those behind him on his attacker as he went.

"Luke," came a panicky cry from the small and dirty White face in the window. A short, thin arm shot through the portal to the clatter of falling cans just outside. Black and White fingers locked together in a checkered chain of small-boy terror. The pair slipped back through the dark hole and headed for the pavement with Luke crashing headfirst into a tumbling Freddie's stomach.

With not even time to groan much less cry, they scampered and stumbled to the head of the alley and took off running. Each alternately passed the other, pushed the other, dragged the other in tow. They vanquished any thought of slowing down when they heard the scream of police whistles behind them. A sudden onslaught of grabbing hands reached for them as alerted strangers tried to stop their forward charge. They were saved by the slippery sweat of their terror, which caused both the incessant rhythm of their running feet and frustration for those whose hands might stay them.

Eventually they realized that the whistles had stopped. They slowed, paused, hands on their knees, choking in their exhausted panting. Flushed and sweating, their brown and white skin alike looked red and streaked with muddy trails of moisture pouring from their furnace hot faces. Still leaning over, they spontaneously threw arms around each other and joined in a deep, heaving sigh.

Then without warning, Freddie jerked himself free. He slapped his hands on Luke's shoulders and shoved him to arm's length. He screamed a maniacal "No!" The scream was so full of fear and pain that Luke was startled into speechlessness. Now that they were clear of danger, had Freddie suddenly realized that he was hugging a Negro in plain view of the world? Was this how the life-saving sharing of the past two days would end? Luke's defenses rose and anger fought with the fear dominating his sweating, twisted face.

"You're bleeding, Luke. Geez, you're bleeding all over yourself. Oh, help! Help!" Tears rolled down Freddie's cheeks to mingle with the sweat frozen there by the chill of fear, and as violently as he had pushed Luke away, he suddenly drew him to himself and sobbed heavily over Luke's shoulder.

Luke began to cry. He felt no pain and could not see his wound because Freddie was in the way. *Where, where,* he thought, *am I bleeding? How did I get hurt?* Pushing Freddie from him, he cried, "Pull away so's I can see too."

Freddie slowly released his grip and stepped back, pointing at Luke's chest. Luke's head did not move, but his big black eyes slowly rolled downward so that only white was showing. He saw nothing. He began moving his head, placing his fingers to his chest, and with sudden discovery of the deep red and wet blotch there, snapped his chin into his neck in a new panic to discover just how he was hurt.

A wave of nausea swept him as the dark, cold substance oozed between his small fingers. Then he looked at Freddie and began to shake. Small, white teeth appeared in abundance across his shining wet face, as he slipped to the pavement in almost hysterical spasms of uncontrolled laughter.

Freddie dropped to his knees with a look of frightened bewilderment screaming, "What, what?" and guiltily felt the infection of Luke's laughter tugging at his lips. Luke tried to suppress his laughter long enough to form the word, but could barely restrain his wild howling. He choked in a gasp of air and screamed, "Tomato!" and busted out again into laughter accented by squinting, watering eyes.

Then Freddie too collapsed to the pavement in spasms of mirth or relief or vented emotion, saying over and over again "Tomato, tomato, tomato", and laughed harder with each repetition.

This silly, boyish reaction broke the tension of the experience. It exposed to each the depth of the other's feeling for him and solidified an unspoken sense of brotherhood strong enough for a lifetime. Most important, it caused them to miss the real blood marking them here and there. Superficial wounds and scrapes collected like trophies pronounced their victory over their pursuers. They could not know, nor could anyone, what great benefit to Freddie had been missed because they had escaped. They did not know that the experiences of the week were the prelude to and the shadow of future events which would change their lives irreversibly again and again.

From there, only moments passed before two very small, very close friends walked up on the porch of the house on Magnolia Street. Seeing the familiar sights of his own neighborhood after the chase, Luke knew how to get home, so he went. And where Luke went, so did Freddie.

Within another hour, the two youngsters were sitting with Luke's family and sharing a large pot of weak soup. They had been hugged, stripped, scrubbed, doctored and dressed by gentle hands and whipped and badgered by the sharp tongue of Luke's grandmother. But they heard none of the chatter. They were intently relating their adventures to Luke's four brothers, and to anyone else in the crowded household who would listen. As for the other boys, they could not even begin to understand how Luke could bring home a White boy after a White man had killed their daddy just days before. What Luke and Freddie said before dinner Luke repeated for all of those who had missed it during the meal. Luke now knew that his companion was also his friend, maybe even his best friend, for Freddie had found him food, cried when he thought Luke was hurt and laughed and joked and told stories with him just like he was a brother.

It would be years before Freddie knew that his parents were looking for him. The police who had pursued them had been looking for Freddie. The boys had escaped to a future vastly different from what either had expected.

CHAPTER 3

Home and Away

For three days the two boys shared laughter, diminishing discomfort from their various cuts and bruises, and bed and meals and secrets in a late autumn interlude of eighty – three-degree sunshine. For three days, Luke's brothers remained silent and edgy, waiting it seemed, for Freddie's whiteness to take over. They plotted among themselves how they would "take care" of Freddie and get Luke back for themselves.

Though food remained sparse, the two friends took little notice, for at least it was there and they could spend lazy days doing the little things boys do, instead of creeping down alleys or cowering under porches.

As Luke expected, without even thinking about it, his Grandmother was color-blind and took in "Mr. Freddie" as though he were her own. Luke's very special accounting of how Freddie had saved him from the foul demon in the warehouse endeared the entire household except Luke's brothers, to the blue – eyed, freckled Freddie. Eventually even Luke's brothers softened their sour looks although they belittled the story among themselves.

Once Freddie washed, they discovered that he was covered with a multitude of freckles and his brownish hair was red. His wide smile matched Luke's in boyish appeal, even with one of his two front teeth broken because of his adventures in the alley.

Except for growing quieter when he approached or whispering at his passing, the rest of the neighborhood showed little notice of the White boy. They had too much love and respect for the Powers family to do more. Yet they seemed not to be knocking on the front door with their accustomed frequency. Other youngsters with whom Luke had been growing up seemed to shy away. This confused Luke who saw little freckled Freddie not as White, but as a friend, a brother closer to him in age and shared experience than any of his natural brothers.

Luke could not understand the unspoken feelings in the neighborhood. Obviously, Freddie was White. Whites regularly abused most of Luke's neighbors. It would not be reasonable to ask any of them to cast aside their hate and fear without first giving them sound reason to believe in Freddie not as White, but as a human and brother. He worried about this and discussed it with Freddie, who could not understand the feelings Luke was trying to communicate. He had never hated and feared the Black man or been his victim.

Luke at last realized that if Freddie were to continue living with his family, he must bring about a change in how the neighborhood viewed the boy, and Luke set about trying to fashion a plan to show Freddie's value, trustworthiness and friendship to the folks on Magnolia. He knew he had to do it with words. He knew that words were his single most powerful resource in achieving what he wanted or needed. Aside from the fascination for words and his recognition of their power in print which had caused him to drink in every book he could find, he had long ago discovered his own ability to use them to embroil, fascinate, persuade, or inspire those around him. It was this ability which he plotted to use. He would use logic, emotion, loyalty, curiosity and pride. "Forget Freddie," He would say. "Let me tell you what it's like out there and I'll weave a tale leaving me nearly dead at the hands of starvation, cold, exhaustion. By the way, I made it home. This kid I met, he helped me".

"Always talkin' 'bout that Whitey, that big-shot nose in air Whitey. Ain't you ever goin' shut your mouth 'bout him?"

"Y'all think we dumb or somethin'? Y'all think y'all can use them big fancy words with us an' we bow down an' do what y'all want?"

"Yeah. Truth is, y'all soundin' kind'a White yourself lately, with your uppity talk and seeing the friends y'all choose and all."

"Y'all so all-powered in love with whitey, why y'all don't go live with them? An' take that little red-faced bastard with you. He ain't welcome 'round here, an' neither is you."

It flabbergasted Luke. He had never been so challenged. He realized that where he had thought they did not understand, it was he who failed to understand the depth of their feeling. All he wanted was for them to accept Freddie among them. He was not hoping for an ending to the war, only the welcoming of a valuable ally.

Was his logic shrouded by the shadows of their prejudice? Was it not clear because he still possessed some of his own that made his logic into hypocrisy? Was his emotion but tempered shallowness? Can mere words of pain and starving delivered to the pained and starving hold weight? Had using loyalty made Luke appear to have turned on his own people as something they felt Whites prone to do? Were they speculating on how soon Freddie would turn on his "new brother" and go back to the old proven and more expedient or comfortable?

Luke wondered if his biggest mistake, however, had been to challenge their pride, for having next to nothing else, they guarded that with fierce, and often angry intensity.

The other children insulted Luke and argued with him in a way for which Luke was unprepared. He had seldom had what he said challenged. He responded in shock, then anger. He began returning insult for insult and turned his own pride into arrogance which spilled like acid over the turmoil of his adversaries.

In the houses, folks could hear voices rising above the din of the street. They were not the voices of shouting boys at play, but angry voices where anger had no place because each depended so much on the others for survival. All other noises seemed to disappear as folks inside and out turned their ears to this storm raging among them.

Front doors cracked open and eyes peered out to see the commotion. Tired mothers stepped to their porch rails and watched their youngsters in verbal battle with one small child. Murmurs like, "I knowed it'd come to this . . .no right to bring no White boy here . . . getting' what comin' to him" came from nowhere and everywhere.

Freddie appeared on Luke's upper porch to see what was happening. Realizing that his friend was in danger but not knowing that he was the cause, he raced through the house and down into the street to help. He shouted as he approached the swelling crowd of boys. This proved to be the wrong catalyst for calm. Instead, it became the cause and Freddie the target for the initial thrown stone. Freddie was suddenly cowering and bleeding under an onslaught of cobbles and broken brick from the old, red street.

For all of his pride in words, Luke could summon only "No! Stop!" which did nothing against the anger now being vented in front of his grandfather's house.

Luke's grandmother raced indoors in terror to root out her husband. She knew something must be done immediately or both boys might be killed, and others killed or hurt in the process.

"Eldon, Eldon, come quick! They're killin' our Luke". Luke was in fact down. He had thrown his body over Freddie's to shield him from the barrage. Crying with rage and fear and confusion, he plaintively turned his face to the mob and his round eyes commanded and pled that the stoning stop.

Eldon Powers bound to the front door to halt the murderous crowd. He found none, for a quiet and dejected and tense Black circle encompassed the two small boys. Only an occasional sob or whimper came from the circle's interior. Then the sound of shuffling feet rippled through the circle as it swayed and parted. From its center came two small, contrasting figures, limping, bruised, streaked with tears and blood, and supporting each other.

Luke's grandfather cleared the steps and lifted one boy, then the other, under his arms. Flashing a look of total sadness and disbelief upon his friends and neighbors, he bowed and shook his head as he disappeared through the door. Although a soft knock on the door pursued his heels, he walked to the closest bed and laid the boys on it. While Luke's brothers surrounded the duo and his grandmother fetched water, clothes and bandages, Eldon Powers went to the door to face the intruder.

"What y'all want, Atkins?"

"I come to say I's sorry and to see if they's okay."

"Course they ain't okay. They's frightened and stoned bad. No tellin' what be broke. I hopes you an' the rest is happy at what your boys done to them two babies there in the street. My Luke's only eight. That White boy ain't much over ten. What do they know 'bout hate, except what we teach 'em? Y'all take that Luke. Y'all want that kind o' leader t'grow to be a man what recall that a White boy save him an' the Black boy stone him? What good he goin' to be to our people with that kinda' memory? What y'all thinkin' about y'all do such a thing when y'all shoulda been whalin' the tar outa your young'ens for what they doin'. I don't like havin' that White boy here no more than ya'll, but he just a boy, an' he were hurt with no place t'go. Since when we turn any child onto the street in this community? Where's your pride, Man? Sweet Jesus, where your sense o' what's right?"

Eldon stopped, breathless and drained, and sad, deeply sad at what had happened and what was happening then. He wished with all his heart that Freddie had never come there, but found that wish absorbed in other wishes that life were other than it was, that poverty were not his lot and domain, that his son had not died leaving five boys for him to look after in his old age. He was tired, so tired, and felt so completely burdened and helpless.

"It was his eyes."

"What was whose eyes? What y'all talkin' 'bout?" Eldon suddenly realized that the whole crowd of men was at the foot of his porch, sharing in the apology. The children were gone, but he could hear their cries following the whap of Black hands on their bared bottoms, as their mothers conveyed in another way the unforgivableness of their actions.

"It was his eyes. I never saw nothin' like it. They stop us cold. Flat. In mid-air, I swear. They was like fire an' ice. They told us we was wrong and suddenly we knowed we gotta stop our young'ens. I can't 'splain no better. I just know I ain't never forgettin'. That boy special, Eldon. Y'all is right. We wants him on our side."

"What y'all got, Atkins, is one on the side o' man, White or Black, if the man is right. If y'all is right, then it your side he be on. Just y'all remember, 'cause that's the way Luke boy is. We's always knowed that since the minute we laid eyes on him the day his ma die. We knowed. Now y'all do, too." Luke's grandfather turned and entered the house leaving the crowd standing there for how long he neither knew nor cared. He went to Luke and Freddie and there he stayed until the two boys were well asleep.

The boys spent the next day indoors. They were much too sore, too tired and too frightened to venture into the late October street. The balmy sunshine of the days before degenerated under the cover of night to purplish haze and wet wind that slapped the old windows. The trees issued a haunting scrape against the weathered siding. The weather suited Luke's mood. In its sobriety and solitude, it led Freddie to feel a sense of rejection he had not known with Luke before. "You mad at me, Luke?" he finally asked, but got response only in a wistful, vacant glance. "Come on Luke. Tell me what I did. What're you mad about?"

"Nothin' Freddie. Just leave me be".

Freddie would not accept that. He had already learned that Luke could be almost caressed into a good mood just by getting him to talk. But Luke would not respond this time. He felt that he had let his friend down, allowed him to be hurt and humiliated, and had been humiliated himself by his own words. In his childish way, Luke vowed to never again speak unless spoken to, and then to respond in the briefest manner possible.

Luke's grandfather noticed the mood, too, but tried to ignore it. But Luke's steady rejection of Freddie's overtures finally moved Eldon to speak. Not wanting to chance rejection for fear he would not have a second chance to bring Luke out of it, Eldon spoke instead to his other grandchildren. He was sure that Luke could hear all that he said. "Y'all know what stopped them boys? I know, an' I can tell y'all, it ain't somethin' y'all goin' see every day."

"What was it, Grampa? Was it y'all?"

"Nope. T'weren't me. T'weren't me a'tall or nothin' I done. Was done before I got there. Truth is I wouldn't a knowed myself if those very men had not own up to the reason. T'was Luke himself. He stopped all them boys, mad as they was an' throwin' brick bats an' all."

"C'mon, Grampa, how he do dat? Dat ain't likely. I mean they had 'em.

"But Luke got'em in the end, didn't he," Eldon said.

"I figured they just tired o' the thing. They'd just had all they wanted."

"Y'all figured wrong, Boy. They was stopped. I seen Luke stop y'all just the same way, I seen him get y'all t'do exactly what he want y'all to do, many times, just by how he looks at y'all."

"Yeah. I know the look y'all is talkin' 'bout," the boys agreed.

"Lord, I was proud of that boy out there in the street. What he done. Why, without a thought for himself he done throwed himself across his friend t'shield him. He used them eyes of his where his words weren't workin' t'stop that mob cold. I tell y'all, it a smart man knows when to use a pistol and when a buck shot is best. Luke, he knows what weapon t'choose, and if he happens t'pick up the wrong one once in a while, that don't matter none, 'cause he got sense enough to quick throw it down an' pick up the right one real quick."

Eldon went on talking to the boys about Luke, using him as an object lesson to teach them the strategy of controlling what others do. But Eldon carefully selected each utterance to reinforce for Luke his pride in the boy, and to help Luke understand his own actions and the forces within him a little better. He emphasized the rightness of what Luke had attempted, and talked of the courage it took to try.

///

By the time Harriet Powers got home from her new job, Luke was still achy, but much of his old self again. He was eager to hear how his grandmother's day had gone, for Harriet's job was a major blessing for the entire family. A lady for whom she had worked some years before had returned from New York with a new husband and had immediately called upon Luke's grandmother to keep house and run errands for her. She was paying a dollar a day, and Harriet could be home by seven and have Sundays off. She had jumped at the chance. Six dollars a week would buy a lot of groceries.

But six dollars a week would not easily feed twenty People. Because of the depression, many of the folks were being cared for by the Powers. It was this and the afternoon before which caused Harriet Powers to approach her employer with a proposition which she now prepared to present to the two youngsters. She interrupted their chatter to speak with them, but they usurped the impact of her message with a pronouncement of their own.

Harriet Powers was tucking in all the boys. Luke and Freddie shared his parent's big double bed with Luke's four brothers. Luke gave his grandmother a big hug and said, matter of factly, "Freddie and me are going back to school in the morning, Gramma, if y'all says it's okay. One thing we both learn yesterday, is we need more learnin'."

"Oh well now, Chile. I don't know. That'd be fine, of course and Lord knows y'all needs your schoolin'. That's a sure thing. But I is not so sure about y'all goin'. I means here, now. I means, what with Freddie bein'---"

"White", piped in Freddie.

"Well," Harriet continued, grateful for Freddie's words. "It's a problem. We done seen that, and near lost y'all while we was seein' it."

"But, Gramma. Freddie's real smart. He's been five years to a real school. He can read and print real good---"

"And write, too, Grandma Powers." Freddie was determined to help Luke win this one.

"And he even knows his numbers," added Luke. Y'all should see what he can do with timeses---"

"I knows, Darlin'. But that ain't the point. Freddie done said it himself. He's White. And that's just fine, if he lives with White folk. But Freddie's different than most of the folks round here---"

"I ain't. Me and Luke knows I ain't."

"Inside maybe y'all ain't, Son, but on the outside y'all like an orange tryin' to grow on a pear tree. Sooner or later, no matter how hard y'all is tryin', y'all ain't gonna make it. Y'all LOOK different, see. They don't know y'all, but they know lots o' people that look like you what ain't done right by them. They don't not like y'all because y'all is y'all, but they ain't gonna forget y'all's White, an' they ain't likely ever gonna cotton to that."

"It don't matter, Gramma. We be best friends.

"Sweet baby, y'all gotta understand. Its fine y'all be such friends an' all, but, Honey, some other folk that should'a seen didn't see it yesterday. There are other Folks around here like your daddy, sufferin' and even dyin' because of what the White folks is doin'. They have troubles with White folks and ain't likely to understand how y'all is feeling."

"But Gramma, Freddie and me can tell how he saved my life in the city and---"

"Ain't gonna make enough of a difference to spit at. No difference a'tall. But never y'all mind, Honey. An' y'all neither, Freddie, 'cause I done talked with your grampa, and we've worked out a plan. An' I spoke with Miz Sloan where I work at her house, an' we worked out a plan. And I'm gonna tell y'all what it is, if y'all just hush an' listen for a minute.

"I'll tell 'em, Woman. You done beat around it long enough. Weren't no need to say all them things about White folks with little Freddie right here, even if they was true."

"Can we go to school tomorrow, Grandpa? Can we?" Luke was up on his knees bouncing slowly up and down on the old mattress. He leaned into the bounce and appeared ready to topple over on his face. But there he stayed and there he bounced as he waited for the reply. By now the other five boys were sitting up looking at Eldon. They were wondering if the plan would include them, too.

Luke's enthusiasm was affected. It was his last-ditch effort to get his Grandparents to relent. But in fact he had no hope. He already knew the answer was "no". He had easily figured out a "yes" would have come from his Grandmother with little fuss. But there seemed about to come an answer for which he had not thought to ask a question. Maybe there was hope, after all. Just in case, he kept up the act.

Eldon looked suddenly sad and stern as he prepared to respond. All those dark eyes were on him now. They were accented by one set of bright blue that shared Luke's expectancy. No one but Harriet knew what the answer would be. The answer came as a question. "How'd y'all like t'live in the country, Boy?"

Luke was momentarily taken aback, but quickly got his mind back on the track. "Can we go t'school there, Gramma?"

"Sure you can, Son. Maybe it'd be an even better school. Maybe even as good as the one Freddie done went to. Think y'all would like that, Boy?"

"How's come we movin', Grampa? I like it here. How we gonna get to the country anyway?" The questions were flying from all six excited boys, who in unison with Luke were now each on their knees, rocking the old bed with their anticipation as they waited for an explanation of the impending adventure.

"Well, uh, Luke. We ain't. Y'all is."

The sudden creak of the bed disturbed the absolute silence as all six boys rocked back on their haunches in six different states of confusion. Freddie started crying first.

"Said it all wrong, Eldon. Now look how y'all got'em upset," Luke's grandmother quickly said as she reached for the shaking White boy among the dark.

Luke said nothing. His brothers suddenly harbored the realization that it was always for Luke. This last big letdown turned their admiration for him to resentment of him and their Grandparents. "Daddy wouldn't o' done that for Luke and left us here. He wouldn't."

"And what about me?" said Freddie. "I ain't got no one and no place. Why can't I go? Luke! Tell 'em to let me go with you."

"Now wait a minute, all of you. I ain't finished my tellin' this thing. Now, like I was sayin', your Uncle LeRoy is bringin' his wagon tomorrow or the day after to fetch y'all, Luke. Y'all is goin' to live with him for a spell."

"But, Grampa, why can't we all go?" Luke sensed what his brothers were feeling. He knew exactly what Freddie was experiencing because he himself experienced the same sense of aloneness for a week.

"Fact of the matter, Boy, is that nobody can go but Y'all. Your brothers ain't goin' 'cause they older and got strong backs for what work we might pick up. But with your daddy gone, Y'all got to go. We knew it would come to this the day he died. There just ain't 'nough to go 'round. We can't get the food an' all that your Daddy done got. Y'all. see an'---"

"But Gramma is working. Y'all just don't want me because of the trouble I made yesterday.

"T'ain't true. We wrote your Uncle LeRoy a week ago and been waitin' for him nearly as long as we been lookin' for y'all. Your Uncle's comin' an' that's that."

"An' we get nothin'". That one utterance spoke to the feelings of all four of Luke's brothers.

"Why, boys, what y'all talkin' 'bout? You gets us. With Luke livin' with your uncle, why there's more for us to share. An' y'all can go to school here same as there."

"We don't want no school. We wants to leave."

"Hush your face with that kind of talk. Your daddy would drop your britches and take some tar from your behind with that kind of sass. He left y'all to us an' we is keepin' you." Eldon Powers was getting hotter and hotter with the situation and bringing up the heat in the rest of the family as well.

His wife stopped it. "Eldon, that's enough. Go on. Y'all have said too much. "Course they ain't leavin'. They just upset. Now git! I'll talk sense to them." Harriet Powers talked on softly about why they had to send Luke away. She talked about the farm and his Uncle LeRoy, about how he was mighty rich for a colored, even owning his own place.

But Luke heard none of it. His mind had stopped recording when his grandfather has said he was going alone. Finally, just to be sure, to clear up the chance he might have been wrong, Luke whispered with his head down, eyes up and hands twisting the band of his pajamas into a tight ball. He said "you mean me and Freddie, don't you GrandPa?"

"No, Sugar, just you."

"But---"

"I'm sorry. Freddie's a nice boy, a good friend. But Freddie's White. Ain't no colored going' t'take no White boy in a wagon out'a here on no country road. Ain't safe. Why, some White man sees that, he might just haul y'all and your uncle LeRoy up out of that wagon right off. And do somethin' bad to y'all. Maybe even kill y'all. Hear me? Maybe even kill y'all. They's mean sometime, like that white man in the warehouse, or the one that killed your daddy. Some of them's mean. No, Luke. Freddie ain't going' and that's that."

"But what will happen to me, Mrs. Powers?" interjected Freddie.

"That's the rest of the big news, Freddie. I done told y'all I talked with Miz. Sloan, the lady I works for? Her and her man is real fine folks, only they ain't havin' no children, because they can't. Now they is wantin' children, but Sweet Jesus seen fit to say no to them on that account.

"That's where y'all come in, Freddie. They want y'all. That makes you somethin' special. 'cause they is somethin' special too. Not like most White folks around here, 'cause they come from up north. And when I told 'em what a smart and handsome young'un y'all was, why they all but up and asked could they have you come stay with them. 'Course I told them I have to ask y'all if you wanted them, too, before I could give them a yes to that one, but I knowed y'all would want to go. 'Specially since Luke's gotta go to the country, and y'all not havin' no one but us poor colored folk, and them being such nice folks and havin' money an' all. There, What'd I tell y'all. Ain't that a double surprise for everyone?"

"But we want to go together," the two boys once again implored her.

"I ain't goin' without Freddie, Gramma. I ain't. Freddie and me is together. Please---" Luke was standing now, leaning on the bedstead, plaintive, searching his grandmother's face for some message of sympathy, some sign of relenting. The sympathy he found, but he also saw the stubborn look of a mind made up.

Suddenly both boys knew that they had lost. Luke started getting angry again, started beginning to figure how he and Freddie might slip away in the night and go back into the city. Tonight, he thought. They would do it. After everyone else was asleep. "OK, Gramma. Me and Freddie will go away like y'all say."

Freddie looked at Luke and started to protest. Then he caught the glint in Luke's eye and turned away with a slight smile cracking the cast of his grim face.

"Now that's 'nough talkin' for one night. Y'all little lambs just close your eyes an' go t'sleep an' we's goin' to work it out just fine. Y'all hear? This here plan is goin' t'make us all better off." Grandmother Powers continued to mutter to herself as she slipped to the door. She waved a final smiling good night and closed in the dark from the light beyond the room.

Luke knew that he must act now, for tomorrow would change it all again. But Luke never got the chance to carry out his plan.

That night, Luke's Grandmother took Freddie away to the White family. Luke fretfully slept. He was too exhausted to act on his plan. He dreamed that he and Freddie were actually running away. He felt the motion of his bed, heard the voices, the "come on" and "get dressed." They became a part of his dream, as though he was saying these things to Freddie as the two of them prepared to sneak off through the shadows of his dream.

Early the next morning, a sad and silent Luke eyed the road in front of him, never once looking back toward home and family. He could not believe he was there. He could not figure what had happened. He could remember sneaking off with Freddie. Yet Freddie was gone. His granddaddy had said that his grandmother had taken the boy to his new home, but Luke did not believe it. To him, sleepy-eyed and bouncing alongside a stranger called Uncle LeRoy, this was the dream, or nightmare. At the same time he knew the truth. He hated his grandmother for taking Freddie away and he hated the Whites again for making her have to do it.

CHAPTER 4

Red Clay

As the last house drifted by and the pavement narrowed to two clay lanes, the morning sun pierced the last remnants of the previous day's haze as it crossed the fields and settled in Luke's eyes. He turned his head away to avoid the glaze which was dancing on his shining tears. Uncle LeRoy came into his line of sight. It surprised him to see a man sitting there looking very much like his own Daddy. It was not so much the face of his father, as the expression, the way he would stare away to nothingness, then return to the moment. He noticed that the man was darker than his Daddy. He noticed, too, how different LeRoy looked from what Luke was accustomed to, and realized it was the way his uncle dressed.

There was nothing at all colorful about the way LeRoy dressed. He wore a dungaree shirt and bib overalls with muddy and worn work boots. He had a faded, sweat-stained bandanna tied about his neck that covered the strong muscles which started there and worked their way through his upper back and arms. A deep scar painted a pink line through the dark flesh of LeRoy's lower right arm where none of LeRoy's black body hair grew. His hands loosely held worn, time-blackened reins to the two grey mules. They were huge and bruised, scraped here and there and calloused even along their sides from long years of working in the fields. Nine split and dirty fingernails were all that he had. The index finger of his right hand was half gone from some past misadventure that roused Luke's curiosity.

Despite his rough look, LeRoy aired a quality of gentleness and understanding, of acceptance and strength which caused Luke to warm up to him. Luke's tears dried as he eyed this stranger who seemed less a stranger as the moments passed. He realized that this was his family now. Out there under the glare of the sun, the mask of vapor over the fields blanketed his new world and shrouded his new life in the mystery tomorrow always holds. Yet, he was who he was, and he was feeling some sense of peace and trust in his Uncle LeRoy. Luke began facing his future with a small bit of confidence and anticipation. But he vowed to never forget his friendship with Freddie and the questions and confusion which it had created.

Luke marveled at the relative luxury of Uncle LeRoy's modest cottage. It was unpainted clapboard outside, much as the house on Magnolia in Atlanta, but the glass in the windows was clear, the screen in the front screen door whole, the porch straight and scrubbed. Inside, a cheery whitewashed main room with a big red brick fireplace surrounded his Aunt Crystal, a woman whose robust appearance belied the name given her as an infant.

"Luke, Honey!" she exclaimed. "My, how y'all do look like yo daddy, rest his soul," tumbled quickly from Aunt Crystal as she moved to embrace her handsome eight-year-old nephew. "LeRoy, get his things an' put 'em in his room. Come on, Chile, let's get some food in ya'll."

The kitchen smells pulled at Luke as much as Aunt Crystal did. His mouth opened wide at the array of fruits, hot cookies and home-made bread laid out on gingham napkins to cool on the planked table dominating the center of the room. Aunt Crystal poured a tall glass of milk, popped a handful of cookies on a plate and set it down in front of her nephew. As an afterthought, she snatched an apple up and added it to the plate of cookies. "Reckon that'll hold y'all 'till dinner," she said. "Now tell me all about yourself."

Crystal Powers was a large woman with grey—streaked, straight black hair pulled back at her forehead and partially covered by a red polka dot bandanna. Her brown, soft arms folded across the edge of the table. They cushioned a large bust that looked deceivingly as though it had suckled twenty children. The fact was that after two stillborn boys, Crystal had born no more children, nor had she ever nursed any. Crystal's eyes were wide set in a broad face that God had made to properly contain a very broad smile while leaving room for the dimples. Those dimples deepened when she laughed.

And she laughed often at the tales Luke was spinning. His usual talent of storytelling enhanced the quality and adventure of the life he had led to date. Luke somewhat self—consciously skimmed the surface of his adventures of the last two weeks, responded with his mouth full to questions about the rest of the family. He squirmed at references to his "poor, departed daddy, rest his soul" and thought about finding out about his new home.

His Uncle LeRoy's appearance interrupted the conversation. LeRoy took Luke to a ladder off the back porch and pointed up. "Y'all sleeping up there, Boy. Now go on an' get your things put up. Then I'll show you about the place.

Luke climbed the ladder through a hole cut in the porch ceiling into a low attic about six feet high at the apex. LeRoy had nailed cardboard and tin to the rafters in a mosaic pattern. He had spread nearly new linoleum on the floor. A dresser and small mirror stood at one end of the attic room next to a small window out of which Luke could see the fields of LeRoy's farm with stands of woods beyond. A small table and chair stood in the middle of the room. An old iron bedstead occupied the far end. It was covered with a colorful, if faded, quilt on a straw — filled mattress. A rag rug occupied the center of the floor. All in all, it was the nicest room Luke had ever seen. He looked around at his Uncle, whose head was just above floor level as he stood halfway up the ladder watching his nephew.

"Who am I stayin' with?" Luke queried.

"Why, with yourself. Just yourself. This is your room now. Me an' your Aunt Crystal ain't blessed with no young'ens of our own, so, from now on y'all gonna be our young'en."

"You mean there ain't nobody else gonna be up here with me? I ain't never slept by myself in a bed before. Where's y'all an' Aunt Crystal gonna sleep?"

"We sleep in the back room in the house."

Excitement replaced the last vestiges of Luke's sorrow and trepidation. He could not imagine his own bed, his own dresser, or even needing one, and his own, private table, too. He let out a joyful yelp and ran toward the ladder to follow his beckoning uncle in exploring the rest of the place.

The tour of the twenty-acre farm was a blur of trees, water, vegetable patch and chicken coop, with chatter from Uncle LeRoy absorbed almost by osmosis if absorbed at all.

The next couple of weeks were much the same. Just as Luke finally mastered the small farm, a trip up the creek running below the house led to the discovery of a pond on the south edge of a stand of wood. Luke found neighbors on other farms, and children working in the fields alongside their parents. He was surprised at the lack of interest shown by these folks in much besides their toil. He could not understand why this place did not seem to excite them as it did him. When he asked his Uncle, LeRoy mumbled something about the hard times being worse for the folks working the White man's land and changed the subject.

Sundays, the family went to church to hear an enormous man spin words into frenzied magic for a congregation almost in a trance brought on by the weaving motion and ups and downs of the preacher's body and voice. To Luke, this man was magical at spinning a tale, and he lost the message as he studied the man's style.

Day by day the blur blended to routine, and routine became a life pattern, and that life pattern a shadow of the future. Surrogate parents of this small orphan of such bright promise carefully balanced a routine of school, chores and church. Luke grew more and more articulate with passing time. He mimicked the eloquence of the preacher, adapted his word forms to match those of the Whites with whom his uncle came in contact and mastered the words and thoughts in the few books he could borrow from the feeble little school.

Aware of his nephew's thirst for knowledge, LeRoy negotiated, parleyed and begged, hat-in-hand when necessary, to get his hands on anything with printed words on it. An old Sears and Roebuck catalogue from a White man's garbage pail, a copy of Homer's Iliad with no cover which he had scavenged while cleaning out the judge's library, hot sex paperbacks from behind the saloon and local cat house, the Bible. To Uncle LeRoy, who could do little more than make an "X", it was all the same. But to Luke, the world was opening up. Even more important, the White man's world of mystery was becoming very clear to him. This was not only from the reading with which he was being supplied, but from the letters he continued to receive from Freddie, in answer to his own. This exchange had begun on Luke's very first night on the farm, in his own room, at his own table and chair. He had to tell Freddie about his good fortune.

Dear Freddie,

I was really sad when you was gone today when I get up out from bed. I am here on the farm now. I have my own room, my own table and my own bed. its neet but I wish you could be here too. My ant and unkle are nice. we got lots of food. she makes cookies and bred all the time.

your best frend luke.

Rit me bak.

CHAPTER 5

A Citadel of Sorts

When Elsie Offenbach married Colonel Howard Sloan in the Spring of 1931, she had not known of his impotency. Nor, for that matter, had he. A man in his late thirties whose meteoric, if political, rise in the Army had impressed all manner of people. He had spotted 29-year-old Elsie at a minor State Department reception, and for the first time in his life considered adding something to his living beyond rank and status.

As for Elsie, she did not quickly respond to the Colonel's overtures. The widow of a Wall Street tycoon, she had married in her late teens, as did so many Southern women before the Second World War. She had followed her husband to New York and the money of the twenties stock market boom. Her life had nearly been destroyed two years before when her husband followed his fortunes out of a Wall Street window, leaving her alone with very little money.

If Elsie's husband left her anything, he left her a few connections in high places. This enabled her to use her talent as a hostess by acting as one at receptions for the powerful, and she began within the year to build a clientele among ambassadors and wealthy bachelors who needed not only to have parties and gatherings organized but conducted for them.

She sustained herself during those years with dreams of the large brick Southern Colonial, with a cool veranda over-looking a yard full of happy offspring upon whom she could wait, whose hurts she could tend and whose talents she could nurture. That dream died when the market crashed in 1929.

She earned a living as a hostess with charm and grace in Washington where government money and embassy events were plentiful. She felt close to no one. It was from this bitterness that the loneliness lingered a full two years after her husband's death. It was with this bitterness concealed at a party that she met for the first time Colonel Howard Sloan.

She soon discovered that he too was also a Southerner, having been raised in Charleston, where he attended the Citadel. Howard came from a family of Southern military gentlemen and was able to attribute part of his rise in rank to his father's influence among Army power and Congressional leaders. Part however was due to his own political maneuvering, his commanding appearance on the parade ground and his somewhat enhanced record as a young lieutenant in the closing months of the World War.

Howard knew from experience that sometimes with no justification, except by the smell of victory in the air, officers received accolades for the daring of their men. So Howard was decorated for valor and proceeded in his political way to make the most of his false glory. He worked hard at his façade of strength and cultivated his casual command appearance. In so doing, he appealed even more to Elsie, who desperately needed someone to lean on, to love her, to be strong for her. She was tired of being lonely and working to be strong for herself.

Howard combined political intrigue with his apparent strength and facile charm to win the rank of Colonel years before his peers. He applied these same talents to winning the heart of Mrs. Elsie Offenbach. He heaped an abundance of affection, praise and gifts upon her. He listened as she slowly untangled the confused feelings with which she had lived since her husband's death. He succeeded in concealing his boredom with her story behind a sympathetic facade.

He played at sharing the building of a new set of dreams unsurprisingly similar in nature to those crushed on the street of Manhattan two years before. Elsie became so blinded by Howard's attention and her need to communicate her feelings that she did not really take the time to discover who Howard really was. Neither his shallowness nor his bigotry came through his charming and commanding visage. Elsie happily and quickly accepted Howard's proposal of marriage when it came, and Howard patted himself on the back for catching one of Washington's most eligible women.

Their wedding was the social event of the Spring, an event at which even the Vice President made an appearance bearing an unusual gift of linen embroidered in the corner with the Seal of the President from the Great Man himself.

However, the greatest gift in Elsie's mind was the orders to report to Atlanta for duty near there. Howard had maneuvered these orders to prove to Elsie his intention of making her dream come true. It was for Elsie a beautiful day and a beautiful dream recommenced. But the normal finish of a wedding day was denied them as Howard had feared it would be.

That night in the small resort hotel outside of Richmond where they stopped, the handsome and commanding Colonel Howard Sloan sat shaking and naked in the bathroom. The door was bolted to his new wife, whose silent tears he could almost hear through the door. He simply could not consummate the marriage.

Elsie broached the subject the next day, suggesting very gently that perhaps the excitement, the drinking, the food, had just tired him too much and that indeed, once they had settled in their new home, things would be different. She could recall many times when the tensions of her first husband's work had affected him the same way. Sloan seemed somewhat comforted, although Elsie thought she detected a sense of disbelief within him even though he smiled, squeezed her hand and agreed with her. He thought, *Perhaps if I really try to love her, it will be different.*

But it was not.

Nor was it through the months occupied with moving into and refurbishing the grand house in Atlanta. Her training helped her put forth a bright face against her misery. The genuine love she had for her husband combined with her growing awareness of his fear and increasing bitterness made her gentle, encouraging, and understanding. At no time did she push him. At all times did she make herself available, attractive, provocative. He often moved to her feeling himself growing excited in her presence, only to be overwhelmed by his own anxieties at the last minute.

After nearly seven months they both were convinced of his real impotency. A falseness and strain developed between them which neither of them fought to conceal. Elsie began to care less for the house, found herself instead eating in a nervous way, failing to keep her personal appearance as she always had. Howard found more and more reason for his work to keep him from the house, which was to him but a monument to his impotency, containing as it did six empty bedrooms originally conceived by them as being filled with children. Now the house seemed a tomb of his sexual inadequacy, a stark reminder of his long-suppressed feeling that he was not a man.

Finally, because she cared no longer for keeping the house herself, Elsie sought a housekeeper. When Harriet Powers applied for the job, she had no idea that this Mrs. Sloan was the Elsie Jarvis whom she had cuddled as a little girl, or the Elsie Offenbach at whose wedding she had served so happily. But there Elsie was, in need of a maid and, obviously, much more. In a teary embrace, Luke's grandmother was hired.

The job proved a godsend to both for a variety of reasons. First, the money was more than important; it was critical to the Powers' family survival. Also, Harriet was again near a person whom she knew and loved, shortly after the loss of her own son. And that person needed her. Unknown at that point to either of them, Elsie's problem and the problem soon to be dropped into Harriet's lap was, when combined, a solution for both.

On the sixth day of their reunion, Harriet came to work looking tired and distracted. Her eyes reflected tears and worry, her usual demeanor and bustle slumped to foot-dragging carelessness. For the first time in months, Elsie's self-pity was surpassed by feelings for the needs of another and she reached out to help this long-time friend who had so faithfully helped her so many times in the past.

"My dear Harriet, you do look troubled today. I declare, please come sit. Let's have some good old fashioned woman talk and see if we can't find some solution."

"Oh, Miz Elsie. I is troubled. I got me a pack o'trouble like I never have before, and Lord as my witness, I see no way for it t'end."

"What is it, My Dear?"

"I done got me a White boy at my house, an' he ain't got no place t'go, and the menfolk on the street is hatin' him and yesterday done even stoned him, and my Luke come home with him t'other day and done got himself stoned right along with him, not two weeks after his poor daddy done got his self killed, and like as not them boys is gonna get themselves killed too and---"

"Wait, Harriet. Slow down a bit and let me sort this all out. You say Luke is home?"

"Yessum. He come home 'bout three day ago, maybe four, all tired an' hungry and torn an' dirty, a-draggin' this here boy with him. Breathlessly and with hesitation, Harriet began recounting the events of the last several days, leading up to the events of the night before. As she continued the saga, her speech became more natural, but her countenance less contained, and several times she stopped to force back the tears she felt welling up inside.

Ironically, Elsie's eyes seemed to be brightening as the story progressed. She paid less and less attention to the detail of the saga and more and more to any reference to Freddie. "Tell me, Harriet. What's this boy like?"

"Oh, Luke is just 'bout the finest, sweetest---"

"I'm sure he is, Harriett. But I was more wondering about the other one."

"Like I say. He's White."

"Yes, Dear. I gathered. How old is he?"

"Don't rightly know for sure. Ten maybe. Or eleven. Luke did say he have five years of schoolin'. When do White young'ens start to school, anyhow?"

"At about five. What's he look like?"

"Ain't no bigger than a bug. 'Bout the same as Luke I guess. Mighty thin and got them freckles on his face, with hair 'about like yours except maybe a little darker. And the bluest eyes I ever saw."

"Does he seem smart? How're his manners? Does he do what he's asked?"

"Oh, Yessum. He just as quiet an' nice as y'all please, and mighty devoted to my Luke too. He ain't lookin' for no trouble from them rowdies, neither, but when look like Luke gonna have trouble with 'em, he right there aside his friend t'help."

"You know, Harriet, I might just have a solution to your problem. I might just know some good White people who would dearly love to have just such a boy." Harriet Powers brightened considerably at the words and raised her eyes to Elsie's. The look that greeted her told her immediately who Elsie had in mind. Suddenly, full communication bonded the two women in a moment of shared joy, rare between any two people but strangely more common between people of different backgrounds, for such moments are then not shrouded by feelings of competition.

"You wants him?" She stated, asked, pleaded, granted permission and concurred in three words. And it was settled.

About three the following morning, having already spent the better part of the night convincing her husband to accept a child she already loved sight unseen, Elsie was pulled from restless sleep by a persistant if quiet rap on the door off the kitchen below their bedroom window. "Howard, there's somebody out there," she whispered.

"How do you know?" he grumped from under his eyelids.

"I hear them knocking."

"The wind."

"No! It's someone at the door. Go see."

Howard Sloan felt himself being bumped by Elsie's plumping rump. He grumbled in resentment of that weight gain, and the hour, and a long day tomorrow and the uselessness of it all. The idea of meeting a prowler on the stairs occurred to him as he elevated his long body to a slightly bent and definitely sagging vertical position, reached for his robe and stumbled in the dark toward the bedroom door. The months of strain had taken much from Howard Sloan too. The appearance he made at the door in the dimly lit kitchen, whether from that strain or the hour or both, forced his visitor to slip backwards silently into the shadows.

"What in the hell do you want at this time of the night," gruffed out the sleepy man.

"I is Harriet Powers, Suh, and I is sorry."

"I don't care if you're President Roosevelt! It's three in the morning, for God's sake. Now, get out of here before I call the police."

"But Suh, I is Harriet Powers. I just got to see Elsie."

"She's in bed." But Elsie's voice bounced loudly down the steps and into the kitchen.

"Who is it, Howard?"

"Some nigger woman with a kid. I'm sending them packi-–Oh, Harriet. Yeh. Elsie! C'mere." But Elsie was already bounding down the stairs as though she had just finished a fourteen-hour nap and was ready for six sets of lawn tennis.

"Harriet", Howard continued, "what are you doing here this time of night? Come in come in. Sit down. I see you brought the boy. Elsie, look! It's him, the boy. . ." Howard became more unintelligible, embarrassed and flustered as he chattered himself into silence. But his dragging, defeated countenance was somewhat supplanted with curiosity. He looked hard at the boy in Harriet Powers' arms. Freddie was small, but hardy and well formed, compact, with pale lips and a pug nose. His shock of red hair was much brighter than either had imagined, based on Harriet's description. Freddie looked not a day over nine, maybe younger. His small hands and bare feet and handsome sleepy head were scrubbed red and clean. A large reddish-brown smear on his cheek bespoke the abuse he had taken. It was counterpoint to a jagged but closed cut on the jawbone on his left side. His ears tended to stick out a little too much. His mouth appeared slightly too wide, and one particularly large freckle adorned the right nostril of his blunt little nose. Howard softened toward him quickly.

Elsie had taken Freddie from Harriet Powers' arms. Having set him up at the table and not knowing what else to do, she was getting him some cake and a glass of milk.

Freddie was wondering what was going on. The last thing he remembered was he and Luke making good their escape. *Luke must have brought me here,* he thought. Then he realized it had been a dream. It was a long time before he knew that Luke had strangely shared the dream, thus causing both of them to be fooled into their new and separate lives.

"Where's this, Aunt Harriet?" Freddie surprised himself at the sudden use of the endearment, but a smile from Harriet's lips told him she approved.

"Why, this here's the surprise I told y'all 'bout. Now I know I was gonna bring you here in the morning, but me an' Eldon figured it best you come now."

"Are these the folks?"

"They is. This here Mr. and Miz... Oh, I's sorry... Colonel and Miz Howard Sloan. They ain't got no children and you ain't got no Mamma and Papa. Now ain't that just perfect."

Freddie started, realizing that Howard Sloan was staring at him, and that Elsie was stroking his neck. He turned and looked back at her and saw in her face such pleading need that he could not protest. He did not know what to do so he said, "Where, uh, can I go to sleep, now?"

The Sloans looked at each other, at Freddie then Harriet and found their looks returned. All four folks smiled broadly, then began a titter which expanded on each other's into a belly laugh all round. It was done, and to each for their own reasons seemed done well. As far as they were concerned that night, Freddie was home to stay. They showed him to the room made up the evening before in anticipation of his arrival. Whether it was real or he was pretending, they never knew, but to hear them tell Harriet a few moments later, Freddie was sound asleep and peaceful the minute his head met its new pillow.

CHAPTER 6

A Surrogate Image

Freddie twisted his body and rolled from his stomach to his back. He looked for the peeling wallpaper above him as he rubbed the sleep from his eyes. The room seemed unusually bright that morning, with the sun filtering its way through the window in a strange way. In place of the peeling paper and sagging plaster, Freddie saw pure white.

He rolled his eyes to right and left. Where lath boards should show, a delft blue paint adorned the walls. The window was not where it had been the night before, and there was a sheet over him, wrapped and tangled around his legs. He began turning and pulling at the bedclothes as he looked to the other side of the room. There was the window emitting the unfamiliar light. But the ragged and yellowed window shade was not there. In its place was a handsomely draped window, with small panes reaching from ceiling to floor. He focused on it and realized that it was no window at all, but two doors of glass.

Still drowsy with the remnants of sleep, Freddie swung his feet to the floor and realized he was in only his underwear. Someone had undressed him while he slept. He jumped back into bed and pulled the covers over him. He looked around for Luke or Aunt Harriet. No one was there. Then he remembered. With a mixture of sadness and anticipation confusing themselves in his brain, he lay back on the bed. Propping himself up on his elbows, he took in the room again.

He discovered three other doors besides the French doors. Wrapping the sheet around his middle, he eased his way across the carpeting to one of them. He turned the knob and inched it open. Faint noises greeted him from the other side, including voices whose familiarity was very vague. He closed it quickly and pushed the lock lever. *I don't wanna see nobody yet*, he thought, and approached the second door with a little more caution.

Pulling it open, he discovered a gleaming ceramic tile bathroom, with a black-and-white checkered floor. Across the room was another door. He crossed the floor and just cleared the door from its frame. There he saw another room, nearly empty except for some boxes and a sewing machine. Fearing suddenly that they might discover him there, he quickly closed the door. Then realized he needed to use the bathroom. He bolted both doors and dropped the sheet to the floor.

Then Freddie recalled the reasons and methods for being there. In snatches, he remembered the faces of the people in whose home he found himself. He felt uneasy, dispossessed, out of place, alone. He thought of how he got there. He remembered his parents, the alleys, Luke and the Powers' home.

///

Freddie had awakened one morning some weeks before to find himself similarly alone. There was a note from his parents saying that they would return the next evening. It was not unusual. The depression cost his father his job, and sometimes they would take a day or two to travel to another city where they had heard of work.

But as the days passed and his parents did not return, Freddie experienced fear, cold, loneliness, and finally hunger. In growing degrees, these things haunted him, especially the fear. Initially confident that his parents would return, he stayed home. Although there was little food in the house, it was enough to keep Freddie satisfied for nearly a week, during which he maintained a constant vigil for the return of his family.

As the week progressed, Freddie became more and more concerned about finding them and more afraid that he would not. The food supply grew lower until one day there was none. The house grew colder as the week passed. The two candles Freddie had located waned along with his hopes, until like those hopes, they remained only as wax, melted down then hardening on the surface of the scarred kitchen table.

Finally, Freddie went out in search of his mother and father. Finding no trace of them, he found instead deeper cold and more piercing hunger. Each night he returned to the little house as his only shelter until the day the landlord took that from him.

Freddie came home just as he had every night for nearly two weeks, tired of looking, hungry, and ready to fall into his bed. Approaching the house, he caught sight of lights in the front room. With wildly leaping heart, he rushed up the steps and slung open the screen door. He grabbed the front doorknob and pushed as he turned it. Somebody had locked the door. He pounded and kicked at it, yelling "Mamma!"

Hearing strange voices and footsteps on the other side of the door, he stopped to listen and wait. Through the door's frosted glass panel, he saw a shadow approach. Suddenly a strange man threw open the door and his dark, brooding face greeted Freddie.

"What the hell you think you're doing, kid? Don't come pounding on my door like this."

"Where's my folks?" Freddie got out before constriction in his throat stilled his voice.

"If you mean the Hendersons, they moved. We rented this place today. It's ours. Now get, before I call the cops." The door slammed, and the shadow through the glass melted back into the lighted room.

Freddie stood looking at the closed door, trying to absorb its implication. He could not accept the finality of it. These people knew his last name. They must know his parents, maybe even where they were. Screwing up his courage one more time, he knocked gently, then knocked again. After two or three minutes the shadow grew once again, and the door opened.

"Now what?"

"Sir," Freddie gingerly began, "Do you know where they moved, please?"

"How the hell should I know? They just moved. I don't even know them. What's it to you, anyhow?"

"I'm their — uh, I mean —." Suddenly Freddie thought better of exposing his loneliness to this scowling threat. "I just wanted to know."

"Didn't you call them your folks? Are you their boy?"

"No! No. I gotta go now. Gotta get home. My folks'll worry. Thanks, Mister." As he talked, Freddie backed down the steps. Suddenly he remembered the day his neighbor's mother died and how some man took his friend to an orphanage. Freddie did not want them to take him. He needed to find his parents. But even as he thought this, he feared it was useless. Freddie suddenly turned and leaped the two porch steps. He spun to the left as his feet hit the sidewalk. He raced down the street into the night.

From then until he met Luke, the world remained threatening. It was an indifferent enemy in whose shadows he lurked while seeking their relative safety. Through dark nights he stalked, partly to keep warm and partly to find food. Then he stumbled upon a row of abandoned houses. He took up residence in one of them for the seemingly endless days that followed. He was afraid that this place too might house other occupants by the time he returned. He was always careful to leave nothing behind as he began his nightly search for food.

Once, while he hid in a room during the day, he heard voices very near. Fearing jail or an orphanage, he left that night to find lodgings in one of the other abandoned buildings.

He grew weaker and slower every day as he moved out into the night world. But he located a familiar store and a familiar alley, and if he could just reach it, food. He determined that he must risk some daylight if he were to figure out that way. Then he found himself face to face with a Colored boy about his size.

///

Freddie returned to the present. He flushed the toilet without thinking of it as he remembered his adventure again with Luke. Leaving his sheet lying on the floor behind him, he unlocked the bathroom door and stepped back into the bedroom. Feeling secure behind locked doors, he ventured to the door yet unopened. *It has to be a closet,* he thought, and so it was. An old pair of men's boots and some hunting clothes were tossed in the back corner. There was nothing else there. Freddie turned to look for his own clothes but found nothing.

Geez, they got my stuff, thought Freddie. He headed back to the bathroom and the sheet. He needed to find something to put on. He had to get out of there. He had to go find Luke and Aunt Harriet. He started toward the hall door, determined to locate his clothes undetected then sneak away. Freddie eased the lock off and slowly turned the knob. Cracking the door about an inch, he pushed his eye to the opening and peered into the hall, listening intently.

Voices suddenly filled the void, and Freddie jumped back to slam and lock the door. But stronger arms than his pushed it open in front of him, blocking him. Freddie stepped back and trampled on the dragging sheet. He nearly pulled it clear of him as three adults burst in the room and filled it with smiles and good wishes.

Embarrassed by his near exposure, Freddie blushed and scowled, then grinned as the warm greeting registered. He crouched to regain privacy and wordlessly gathered the surrounding sheet. Squatting, he wrapped the sheet around him. He blushed deeper at the laughter now spewing forth from the threesome standing over him. The Black one knelt and reached her hand toward his face.

"Morning Freddie," said Harriet. "How'd you sleep, Chile"

"OK, I guess. Don't rightly know because I was asleep."

The threesome laughed again while "Isn't he a dear?", "Good-looking boy" and similar endearments passed between them.

"Come, Freddie, let's get you dressed. You must be absolutely famished."

"Yes, Ma'am. But where's my clothes?" came from within him and escaped from his toothy grin. He looked at the other two. They appeared as strangers, yet vaguely familiar feelings of comfort and attachment to them stirred within him. *They're the folks I met last night*, he finally recalled to himself.

"Howard, bring Freddie his clothes." Howard Sloan stepped back into the hall and grunting, heaved a heavy armful of boxes and bags which he deposited on the bed.

"There, Freddie. Pick and choose what you want to wear. We went shopping this morning while Harriet stayed here with you. Hope they fit." Howard stepped back from the bed, gestured at the boxes as he spoke and rejoined Elsie and Harriet. They stood there looking.

"Uh, I should get dressed?" queried Freddie, who was now standing once again in his protective shroud.

"Of course" piped in Elsie. "I want to see you in your new things."

"But you, uh---"

Sensing what Freddie was trying to say, Howard turned to the women and with a gentle nudge edged them toward the door. "Don't overwhelm the boy, Elsie. Give him a little room to breathe. Now, go on downstairs and leave him to get dressed in peace." Howard turned back as he moved out the door behind the others. He pointed at the bathroom and smiled again. "Grab yourself a bath, Boy, and take your time. Getting better acquainted will keep a while longer." With that, Howard closed the door and Freddie was alone again. But he was not as lonely anymore.

CHAPTER 7

A Shadow of the Future

"Freddie! That you?" Elsie trotted down the long hall from the kitchen as Freddie closed the front door behind him, shutting out the early but considerable scents of the Georgia springtime. He stood taller than when he had arrived six months before and was at last filling out the clothes he got on his first day. He dropped his books to the polished side table and returned the greeting.

"Yes, Ma'am. But I gotta rush. The guys are going to walk across town. They've been telling me about a swimming and fishing place out there. It's the first good chance to use that pole Uncle Howard gave me for Christmas." Freddie kept his momentum toward the stairs as he talked. Pausing at the foot to finish his sentence, he waited poised with one foot on the bottom tread for Elsie's response. It surprised him.

"He's not your Uncle Howard now, Freddie, and I'm no longer your Aunt Elsie."

Sudden misgivings caused Freddie to tense. He became alert and fringing on the defensive at the threat of still another change in family, another loss, or word that his parents wanted him back. But Elsie continued. She gently placed her hand on his and leaned close. "Call us Dad and Mom. The papers came. You are ours now, and we are yours. The adoption is official!"

Tears of joy and love welled in Elsie's eyes as she pronounced the news. Freddie backed around the banister and threw his arms around the neck of this gentlewoman who so welcomed him into her heart. "That's not all," she continued. "Can you stand more great news all at once?" Elsie pushed Freddie to arm's length so she could look right into his face. "You'll never guess what."

"What could be as perfect as this, Aunt Elsie? Mom! I mean Mom". Freddie laughed and Elsie joined him.

"I guess it will take a little getting used to," at that, she said, "but it sure sounds good. Oh, Freddie, you just will never know what your coming to us means to us. We just sometimes can't stand the joy." Freddie was getting a little embarrassed. Even though he had grown to love Elsie Sloan, he was always a little uneasy at her overzealous expressions of devotion. It looked to him that Howard was trying to convince himself that he loved Freddie. They seemed unsure that they had his affection and were looking for him to express it to them the way they did to him. He could not bring himself to do it. He was practically twelve and not inclined any more than any twelve-year-old toward what he referred to as "mush". Further, he still held a part of himself in reserve. He was resolved to never again suffer the pain he had endured during the weeks before entering this house with these people. He changed the subject, or rather put it back on course.

"What's the other news, Mom?"

"We're going to have a baby." This startled Freddie.

"You said you couldn't! How can you? You said ---"

"I know, Dear, I know. But now, we can. It was your coming to us that made it possible. I can't explain it any better, but it's happening."

"Don't blame it on me, Aunt Elsie. I haven't done anything."

"Yes, you have. You have given this house a feeling of love we never had before, and babies come from that."

"You mean you don't, didn't, love Uncle Howard?"

"Oh, yes, dearly and forever. But we needed you to make it, oh, I can't explain it. It's just that now it's happened. You will soon have a little brother or sister. Isn't it wonderful?"

"It's okay, I guess." Freddie pulled away from Elsie, his face flushed with confusion which he was trying not to show in his voice, and he bounded up the stairs to his room, his sanctuary, the place of his things, his letters from Luke, his one place to be alone and undisturbed in his thoughts. Uncle Howard had seen to that, giving Elsie instructions to leave Freddie alone when he was in his room, to knock and be invited in before entering.

Howard understood Freddie's early need for privacy, time for him to contemplate and sort out the elements of his new life. He had laid down this rule early. Freddie had less and less retreated under this protective mantle. But now, aware of his confusion, and of the hurt he must have just laid on Elsie's shoulders, he was glad to have it, glad to be alone. He knew he should turn right around, head back downstairs and tell his new mother he was glad, that he was proud to be called "son", that he was excited about having a new baby in the family. But he could not. He was not sure that he was happy about any of it at this moment.

He was suddenly jealous of the yet unborn child. He feared that it might take away from him the Sloan's affection which he had cautiously accepted as he reached for belonging to someone. At that moment, it seemed cruel that his triumph of belonging and a threat of being cast aside should be almost within the same breath. No, he could not go downstairs. For that he felt a guilt which added further to his confusion.

Freddie threw himself on his bed and stared unseeingly at the now familiar white ceiling above him. As it often had in the past, Freddie's mind began creating scenarios of the future. But these images were dark and foreboding for almost the first time since he had collapsed in front of Luke so many months ago. In sympathy with his feelings, late afternoon shadows began creeping through the room. They reached then covered his bed. Soon the white ceiling disappeared from view in total darkness. Freddie drifted into a fitful sleep, never aware of his friends who had rapped on the back door on their way to the fishing hole. He was never aware of the tearful and hurt new mother who had sent his friends on their way by saying Freddie was not feeling well.

Instead, he dreamed of a tiny body with a big head who screamed his wants and took everything away from his unnatural and now unloved big brother. He dreamed of Elsie and Howard moving him to a cot in the attic so that the new darling could have his beautiful room. He dreamed of the child wearing all his new clothes which miraculously always fit although they were still a little big on Freddie.

He dreamed of being punished when the baby with the big head and loud mouth did something wrong. He feared being yelled at for eating too much when the baby was still hungry. He dreamed at last of waking up and finding the closets empty and the family gone, and of growing cold and hungry and searching the streets to find them. He dreamed of finding loneliness instead, of finding no one he loved. He dreamed of getting hungrier and hungrier until he collapsed, hit his head and screamed with the pain of it all. That scream woke him up. Fitfully coming to a sitting position in the dark, he caught the shadow of a man outlined in the open door to his room.

"What is this, Freddie? What happened? What has made you so unhappy? We thought you wanted to be our son. Why have you reacted like this?" Howard Sloan was moving toward Freddie slowly, voice low and a little shaky. His arm was outstretched and reaching. He sat alongside his new son on the bed and wrapped his uniformed arm around him, squeezing. Freddie flinched, pulled away, looked into Howard's eyes, and leaned forward for Howard to hold him tight again.

But the moment passed. Howard had picked up a signal of rejection. He stood up. "Very well. When and if you feel like rejoining the family, we shall be downstairs." He stomped out and closed the door behind him. Freddie rolled over on his bed and wiped the tears from his eyes on the pillow.

Freddie was not sure how much time passed before light through the doorway awakened him. He roused himself at the bright intrusion and turned toward the light. Howard and Elsie both stood at the door, looking at him. Elsie spoke first. "Freddie," she said as she flipped on the light, "We absolutely must talk."

Howard moved into the room behind Elsie and sat near the foot of the bed. Sensing the hurt and disturbance within his new parents, Freddie sat up against the headboard and silently prepared to listen. Elsie reached for the chair in front of Freddie's desk, but Howard stood quickly and moved it over by the bed. Elsie sat down too heavily for her weight, as though countless pounds of sorrow were weighing on her. Her expression confirmed this to Freddie, who suddenly felt compelled to say something to ease that pain. He had a hard time bringing out the words to express what he felt. He was fearful that they might misunderstand what he wanted to say. He did not want to hurt these two people whom he loved so and feared losing. Finally, he began. "I'm sorry, Mom. I'm sorry, Dad. I love you, you know I do. I did not mean to hurt you. It's just that it all happened so fast. I just want you to . . .you to . . . I don't want to. . .it's just that a baby might---"

"I think I understand what you're trying to say, Freddie," interrupted Howard. "Your mother and I have been talking in the kitchen for hours."

"What about?"

"Mostly about you," answered Elsie. "We understand the pain and loneliness you have gone through. I have lost a husband. I have been lonely, too. But we can't live in fear of the past. We cannot live with its shadow over us. It is now and what is coming that is important. And what is now and what is coming is that we love you and always will. You brought to our lives a joy we had never known. You are such a part of us now that we cannot imagine trying to go on if you were not here."

"But the future holds more than that, Freddie," continued Howard. "It holds added life and sharing to this family with a new baby, and maybe more after that. This is something for all the members of this family to enjoy, and that includes you. Now we figured you might feel unwanted or threatened when you found out about the baby. That's why we waited until now to tell you. We knew nearly two months that this would happen, just as we knew that our first son, you, would soon be officially ours."

"Then you . . .you still want me?"

"Always, Dear Freddie," responded Elsie, who leaned forward and placed her gentle hand on Freddie's knee. "Because we want you here and love you so, we did not tell you. Because you are just as important to us as any natural child we may bear, we continued with even more happiness the process for your adoption after we found out about the baby. We so very much want you to share this with us.

"But," continued Howard, pointing his finger at Freddie and speaking softly, "whether or not that happens is up to you as well as us. You must try to understand. We have given you food, clothing, a nice room with nice things. We sent you to school, doctored your scrapes and bruises and tended your winter colds. We always try to let you know what you mean to us. But many times you seemed to take all of this with a kind of disbelief. It's as though you thought you needed to grab while the grabbing was good for it would not last."

"I didn't mean to." Freddie's eyes were shining and smarting with emotion as he listened and felt the need to defend himself.

"I know you didn't, Honey." Elsie shifted to the bedside then and gently laid her hand on Freddie's cheek. "I know. We both understand that you have a right to be fearful after what happened to you before God sent you to us."

"Sure we do." Howard leaned forward and pulled at Freddie's foot through the covers. "But what we are trying to say is that is all in the past. That each of us has pain and mistakes in our past. We also understand that each of us has done things that hurt others and probably will again. We may do them because of our past, which is the poorest of reasons, or just because we are inconsiderate, or because we have suffered hurt and the others did not know."

"That's right, Freddie." Elsie sat back in her chair and folded her arms across her swelling stomach. "But when that happens, or even before it happens, we must try to talk to one another, understand each other, make room for each other's feelings, for that is the true basis of love. If we can accept one another and like one another for the imperfect humans we are, that sense of love will grow.

"And that is the real security, the real guarantee, the real freedom and joy we can share. It is not the food, the clothing, the shelter. It is the love with which we gave them that makes us want you to have whatever you need. It is the sensitivity born of our love for you which has helped us to understand your needs so we could show our love to you."

"I think I understand," said Freddie. The forgiving and conscious effort they showed him overwhelmed him and thrilled him. Even Howard made him feel wanted. At that moment he did and felt more at home and more secure than he could ever remember.

"If you really understand," said Elsie, "then you will understand also that we will have this baby, that we will love this baby as much but never more than we love you. Love expands with each new child so we will not love you less to make room for the baby. We will love you more, for sharing grows love and we will all have someone new with whom to share."

Freddie slid from the bed and put his arms gently around the neck of his new mother. He still had doubts. He still did not fully understand, nor fully believe what he had heard. He still thought of the child as a threat to his own position in the family. But he knew that he must accept it. He knew that he had no choice and he loved them. He felt good about being called their son and about being able to call them Mom and Dad. So he gave in to trust and decided to wait and see. "I'm hungry, Mom," he said.

"I'll bet you are!" bellowed Howard, and squeezing Freddie's neck in his powerful hand, he forced Freddie to his feet and gently pushed him toward the door. "I could do with a little something myself. Elsie, why don't you whip us up a snack?"

Easily On her feet without the burden she had carried into the room, Elsie walked lightly to the door saying, "I've got just the thing" and she was gone except for the soft sound of her feet on the stairs.

With his hand still on Freddie's neck, Howard impulsively spun the boy to him and squeezed him tightly. Then he pivoted Freddie back toward the door and slapping him on the rear propelled him down the hall toward the stairs after his mother. Howard stopped to watch the boy move away. Taking a quick look back into the room and sighing into a whispered chuckle, Howard clicked off the light and closed the door.

CHAPTER 8

Old Shadows, New Fears

Freddie could not help but think how right he was. He was alone in the house except for Lillian, his new little sister whom he was babysitting. He speculated on all that had happened and what it meant to him since her birth nearly a year and a half before. During that time, he became convinced that she received the better half of all that his parents had to give. *At first they fooled me*, he thought. *At first I believed what they said. All that stuff about love and sharing. Crap. They just wanted me to help keep the place clean and keep the kid when they wanted to do something else. And she gets anything she wants. I get nothing anymore. "Freddie do this. Freddie do that. Freddie, are you watching the baby? Freddie, have you finished your homework? No, Freddie, you can't go out. You've got to watch the baby." I'm sick of it.*

Secretly, Freddie knew that some of this was not true. But he could not help believing the way he did. He knew why he felt that way but had difficulty in admitting it. It was hard to reconcile what he believed with what Howard and Elsie had explained to him concerning love. It directly contradicted the way Howard treated his Aunt Harriet. Freddie loved and trusted Aunt Harriet almost as much as his stepmother. He resented Howard's cold, superior, condescending treatment of her. He could not understand how his stepfather could haughtily demand so much help from Harriet and still treat her the way he did. It was the opposite of what Howard had told him on that night over two years before.

As Freddie thought about it, he remembered vaguely the way Howard, then a stranger in the middle of the night, greeted him and Harriet when they first arrived. His cussing, his gruffness and the hostility in his voice had caused Harriet to back away from the door and Freddie to feign sleepiness to avoid having such abuse also heaped on him.

He recalled the day when he overheard Howard tell Harriet that he was cutting her wage. "Can't afford it, with the baby coming," he said. "Besides," he added, "it's unseemly for a Colored to get the money you're making. I don't understand what possessed Elsie to pay you that much, anyhow. A good White housekeeper doesn't make much more." Shocked, Freddie had left the room.

That was the first time Freddie had seriously considered leaving. It was a week before the baby came and Elsie was having a difficult time. She was usually in bed when Harriet came to tend to the house, and Howard gave Harriet instructions each day before his driver picked him up to take him to the Army Post.

Freddie tried to understand his stepfather's attitude. He blamed it on the anxiety Howard was feeling with Elsie's difficult pregnancy. When the baby came and Elsie recovered her health, the household relaxed once again. He remembered sitting at the kitchen table doing his homework. Christmas was coming and Howard and Elsie were talking in the other room about the holiday. Eager to hear something secret, he stopped to listen.

"I have arranged passes for the entire garrison," Freddie heard Howard say. "They will all be able to be home for the Holiday."

"My, that's wonderful, Howard. But who will cover the post?"

"Oh, there are a few good men, and two lieutenants plus Captain Hargrave. Their homes are all too far away, or they don't have families, and they have volunteered to stay."

"Will that be enough?"

"No. Of course not. But fortunately we have the Colored help. They're mostly useless but I'm keeping them around for KP and things like that."

Freddie spun back to his work. *That isn't right*, he thought. *Dad shouldn't do that, just because they're Colored.* Thinking he ought to say so, Freddie went into the living room where his parents were talking.

"Dad?"

"What is it, Freddie? Your mother and I are talking."

"I know. I couldn't help but hear what you just said. Do you think that's fair?"

"What's fair? The men all volunteered. And what are you doing listening in on a private conversation, Boy?"

"I was studying and just heard you. What I meant was, is it fair to keep the Coloreds there just because they're Colored?"

"What are you talking about? Would you rather I restricted our own people?"

"It seems like maybe some should stay. The Colored men have families, too."

"Their families are not as important. They breed them then leave them. If I let them have the holiday, they will probably just get drunk and not see their families, anyway. Also, they'd probably be late getting back. Then they'd be in trouble with the Army. You don't want that to happen, do you?"

"But---"

"And since when, my high and mighty friend, have you been so concerned with how I treated the Coloreds? I notice you let that nigger mammy your mother hired wait on you any time you need something. I don't see you looking out for what's fair to her!"

"Neither do you, Dad. You cut her wages when she has twenty people to feed."

"Don't talk back to me, Boy. As for the wages---"

"Howard! When did you do that?" Elsie was on her feet with a look of surprise on her face.

"While you were ill, Dear. I knew with the new baby coming we would need extra money. Freddie, have you been listening in on my private conversations? Who do you think you are?"

"I just happened to hear."

"You will not 'just happen to hear' any more of my private conversations, do you understand?"

"Howard, he meant no harm. Leave him be. Now, why didn't you tell me you had cut Harriet's wage? Why that poor woman has barely enough to keep her---"

"She's got enough. They live on anything, anyway. I'm not responsible for her having twenty children. She should have been more careful."

"She doesn't have twenty children. Christ, Dad, they're Luke's brothers and others who have no place to go. You've never been down there. You don't know what it's like."

"Don't tell me I don't know what it's like or isn't like. I grew up here. I tell you if they weren't so lazy they'd all have jobs. I constantly have to push your Harriet just to get an honest day's work out of her."

Elsie jumped up and said, "Howard! You know that isn't true. Why Harriet is a life saver around here and you know it."

"I don't wish to discuss it further. And you, Boy, watch your tone and language. Now get back to your schoolwork."

Freddie left the room fuming and deeply offended by the blatant prejudice his stepfather displayed. He learned to hear but ignore it from his friends, but he could not tolerate hearing it from the same man who had talked so much of love.

As Freddie sat down to his books again, Howard's voice reached him one last time, with words he was not to forget. "This started out a simple conversation about Christmas, and that kid ruined it. Who does he think he is? If it wasn't for our generosity, he'd still be on the street, or in some institution. I will have to teach him to appreciate all we've done for him." Freddie listened more intently, easing out of his chair and toward the door to hear better.

"But, Howard," his stepmother was saying, "look what he's meant to us."

"That was before," countered Howard. "Now we can have our own children. He'd better just watch it, that's all."

"Howard Sloan. Don't you ever say such a hateful thing again. He is legally and in my heart our son!" Elsie turned and started from the room, passing the kitchen door as she did. Freddie saw her flushed face. The tears of anger and hurt in her eyes fell away in the face of horror as she locked her eyes with his and realized that he had heard it all. "My God, My God," she breathlessly uttered and almost ran from the room. Howard sat there. The room became quiet. In the kitchen Freddie caught himself quivering, his throat constricted. Hurt poured like sweat through every gland. He heard the bang of his stepfather's pipe on the glass ashtray. In a moment the strong smell of burning Prince Albert filtered through to him. The air in the other room became clouded with Howard's smoking. Freddie heard the newspaper rattle. *Damn him,* he thought. *He will read the newspaper and smoke just like he always does, just like nothing has happened.*

///

Freddie sat in the middle of the floor helping Lillian build up and knock over houses of blocks. Freddie reached the conclusion that the conversation he overheard was the beginning of the end. He realized that they might jerk the secure home he enjoyed from under him. He would have to be silent and very careful. *I'll take care of Lillian, he thought, and keep up my studies. I'll give the bastard no room to criticize. If I can just hang on four more years, I'll be eighteen and I can earn my own way.* Freddie reviewed in his mind how he must behave. He always came back to taking care of Lillian as the way to keep himself needed so they would not kick him out. He knew he had an ally in Elsie because she loved him. He also recognized that his love for her was the main reason he stayed. He watched the infant girl giggle and chatter before him. Her deep, mysterious blue eyes search him as though she knew what he was thinking. He realized that he loved Lillian, too. Through her he really appreciated what love was. With the love of those two and the love he would give them, Freddie felt safe for the time being. And he was for nearly two more years.

///

During those two years much changed in the Sloan household which caused Freddie to be both more hopeful of permanency and more fearful of rejection. The Great Depression deepened. Like his stepparents, he was dismayed to learn of the cut in pay for all military personnel. The house became less and less well tended. It would have gone into real decay without his constant effort to be indispensable. Almost daily he spent time repairing it.

A second baby came that further strained the family finances. The Sloans fired Harriet and closed part of the house. They pulled Lillian's infant clothing from storage and re-used it for her new little brother. He seemed to gain Elsie's full attention to the exclusion of Freddie.

Under the pressure of tending two small children without help, Elsie had less time for Freddie while she became more demanding of his time. All the while Freddie approached sixteen and experienced changes in himself, his strength and his interests. Giving up limited free time to help keep the household together became more difficult for Freddie but his sense of need demanded it. He resented the trap that forced him to live in a house where he viewed himself as a virtual slave. He wanted to be with friends. Lately those friends tended more to be girls, and new and inexplicable emotions and physical impulses welled up in him.

He struggled with the feelings but had nobody he was able to discuss them with. He poured out what he was experiencing to Luke in longer and longer letters. This became his only outlet. But the replies he received to his letters were fewer and fewer. Although he could mail his letters to Luke, Luke's replies always came hand to hand through Blacks as they traveled through the countryside toward Atlanta. Once there, Harriet secretly brought them to him. Now that she was not working for the Sloans, she made a special trip to the Sloans to deliver each of Luke's letters. She hid them in a chink between the bricks on the back porch.

For several weeks, Freddie did not get a letter from Luke. Freddie was certain that there must be at least one waiting for him at the house on Magnolia, and he was concerned that he had not heard from his best friend. He knew that Luke was nearly thirteen now. He perceived through the change in tone in Luke's letters that Luke's thoughts and feelings were also beginning to change.

Arriving home one day hoping to find a letter, he found his disappointment particularly acute. It was a late spring day and Freddie was having a difficult time with his feelings and his maturing body. There was a special girl whom he could not get out of his mind. Her presence caused him to feel that old constriction in his throat, and some embarrassing feelings welled up in his body. He wanted, needed, to talk to someone about what he was experiencing.

Because he was so quiet with his friends and so distant in the face of their prejudice, he could not talk to them. They considered him odd because he did not join them in the jokes floating around about the size of a Colored man's privates or ripeness of a Colored "jelly roll." He was sickened by it. He refused to subject himself to ridicule from those he knew called him "nigger lover" behind his back.

Freddie could not converse with Howard. He did not talk to him about anything. Elsie was out of the question. She was much too busy and probably would not understand his feelings, anyway. As far as Freddie could see, only Luke would listen and respond with understanding. Still there was no letter.

Freddie went into the house. Quietly he fixed himself a sandwich and pulled a Coke from the refrigerator before sitting at the kitchen table. He could hear no noise in the house. He listened carefully. As it always did when the house was so quiet, his mind returned to the old fear of being deserted and alone. The fear no longer sent him into a panic, for he was nearly a man and almost self-sufficient. Yet he knew he would not like being alone again. He did not want to, and always felt a twinge at the thought of that happening. He pulled himself with a slight dread through the house, half expecting to see empty closets when he knew he would not.

As he often did, he found a note from Elsie telling him she and the two little ones were shopping. She left instructions for him for the work he should accomplish before dinner. On impulse, Freddie let the note slide from his hand to find a place under the small table in the hall. He turned and grabbed his light windbreaker as he passed through the mud porch off the kitchen. He headed toward Magnolia Street, the screen slamming behind him. *She'll think I didn't find it,* he thought, *and figure she'd left nothing for me to do.*

When Freddie reached Harriet's home on Magnolia Street, there was a long letter from Luke. Excited to receive it, he still made time to hug his Aunt and bring her up to date a little before settling down to read. He finally opened the letter.

Dear Freddie,

I guess you must be kind of mad with me for not writing you in so long, but in truth, I've been awfully busy. Uncle LeRoy and I have been planting in the gardens and fixing the fences, and what with school and the reading I do in the evenings, there just doesn't seem to be much time. Not that I don't think of you. I can hardly wait to get your letters. Your life is so much more exciting than mine. The best--- I guess the only--- thing exciting in my life beside my reading is the pond. I still try to fish there every chance I get, and often take my book with me. It is a good way to get my reading in without being interrupted. I've learned when to get there and when to leave in order to avoid the hunters, and, of course, they mainly come in the fall, anyhow. Last week I caught the biggest catfish I ever hooked. It had to be 17 inches long, and it fed us good that night, all round.

Grandma says she's not working with your family anymore. Sorry to hear hard times are getting to you, too. I was reading in your letter about your trouble with your stepfather. You really should not blame him, you know. Most White folks, although they are decent and God fearing, look on us the way he does. It's just the way things are. Maybe we can see things change a little before we have kids of our own. But your stepfather isn't likely to change much. You might as well learn to accept him. I guess you have, really, because last year you were writing about leaving home, but you haven't mentioned that in a long time.

Big news on this end. I'm nearing my 13th birthday. It will be here in about six weeks, just after school's out. Now, Aunt Crystal and Uncle LeRoy haven't said anything, but some of the boys tell me of big doings when they turned 13. And this winter I was at Joel's house (you remember me telling you about Joel, in the next farm over. His Daddy's in the penitentiary for lifting vegetables from a White man's wagon. They nearly killed him before they sent him away.) Anyway, I was there when his mamma and lots of relatives sprang a big surprise party on him. Can't figure where all the food came from, times being what they are, but there sure was a load.

We ate like I never did before, not even at the summer socials up at the church after Sunday service. So, I expect there'll be something brewing on my birthday, too. Do you think you could talk your stepparents into letting you come on down here for my birthday, and maybe spending a few days? I kind of think my Grandma and Grandpa will be coming, although no one's said that either. Still, they been coming for a visit most every summer, and that seems as likely a time as any, especially with Grandma not working now, so they are free to come and go as they please.

I sure hope you can come. I guess you're looking forward to a birthday, too. Sixteen. Doesn't seem like you could be three years older than me. What's it like being so old? I hardly even know the 16 or 17-year-olds around here. They won't have much to do with the littler kids. Of course, we all go to school together, what with only one room for the bunch of us. But they kind of sit off by themselves, and during recess, instead of playing tag or something, they are off by themselves or hanging around the girls. I've never met the girl that could keep me away from what I would rather be doing. Doubt if I ever will. Although, you know, I don't always play the games during recess, either. Depends on what I've got to read. . .

It was a long letter and it took Freddie a long time to read it. Throughout he searched for hints that Luke was feeling what he was feeling, looking for the changes in himself which Freddie had already discovered. But the references were not there. He could see the constant improvement in Luke's writing, and could not help but be amused at his storytelling and rambling. At the same time Freddie felt a growing gulf between them. Freddie knew it was not a break but a gulf of maturity which he figured time would take care of.

Ironically Freddie thought that he could not wait three years for Luke to catch up to him. He felt sure that if he could talk to Luke he could explain what he was feeling. He could talk to Luke because Luke was so sensitive to the needs of others. *Maybe he could help me understand myself,* he hoped. However, he knew that talking to Luke was impossible.

Near the end of the letter, Freddie felt Aunt Harriet's eyes on him, and looked up to hear what she had to say. She had been sitting patiently patching Eldon's other pair of pants while Freddie read. But then she spoke, mid-stitch, while he marked his place in the letter and listened.

"Been watchin' your face, Chile," Harriet said. "Got some strange looks while you readin'. Luke say somethin' to make you frown?"

"No, Ma'am. Not really. It's more like what he didn't say, I guess."

"What's that?"

"I don't know. I suppose I never thought before how much younger he is than me. He talks on about things I've even forgotten I did, and he's doing them now. When we first met, we were about the same size. Now he talks about boys my age as being big kids. I wonder how big he is?"

"Tell y'all the truth, he's gettin' on up there. Still he's got some growin' to do before he matches y'all, that's for sure. Truth is, I ain't seen'im since he left some five years ago. 'Spect he's grown a passle since I last laid these tired old eyes on him."

"He says you might be going on down to see him around his birthday. That right?"

"Now how's he know that? That's supposed to be a secret. Yessuh, me an' his granddaddy is headin' out 'bout the second Sunday in June, just after church. Folks here goin' hafta watch out for themselves a few days, 'cause we's headin' down to see Luke."

"Are his brothers going with you?"

"No. Can't. Seems like the onliest way to get there is in Brother Hawkins' wagon. He's picking us up at church and carrying us the other half day to the farm. It'll be late afternoon before we get there, an' ain't room in Hawkins' wagon but for the two of us besides the tradin' goods he's carryin' down that way."

"Then there's no chance, say, that I could go with you I mean, Luke said in his letter he sure would like for me to."

Harriet studied Freddie a while. She knew what he was asking was nearly impossible, yet she recognized the minute she had opened the door to him that something was troubling him. She wondered why he did not try to discuss it with Elsie, but she had decided long ago not to try to figure why White people do what they do to each other, but to just accept it. Still, she thought, this boy needs to talk to someone, and maybe that someone is Luke. Even as she thought it, she knew it would not work. The wagon was just not big enough for the three of them plus Hawkins and a load. She thought she might instead see if he would talk to her.

"What's botherin' y'all, Mr. Freddie?"

"What, Ma'am? Nothing, Ma'am. I'd just like to see Luke, that's all."

"But y'all knows that can't be unless your folks was to carry y'all down there in their automobile. 'Sides, I done watched y'all grow, and watched my boys grow, and theirs too. I knows when a boy's troubled. Now tell me."

The gentle, matter of fact, almost detached quality of Harriet's voice, the dimming light of the late afternoon and Freddie's need to get it out where he could deal with it worked on him. Harriet nudged and chided and poked at him with words. She explored and worked on the leads he offered. She read his eyes as she rattled on about things she helped all the boys in her family to understand. Then Freddie hesitantly began to talk of himself.

At first he spoke of the frustrations in his family, of the feeling of being trapped and worked then ignored, of the coldness between him and his stepfather. Before too long, he was discussing his lack of close friends at school. He skirted the reasons for it out of concern for hurting Harriet.

He eventually started talking about the girl who so excited and confused him. Harriet was the first person to whom he mentioned her. Once he began, he poured out the detail of her dress, her walk, the way she looked, especially the way she looked at him. Harriet sat quietly and patiently. She listened in the half-light, helped the conversation along only through an occasional grunt, a quick smile, half frown or a nod of the head. As she watched and listened, Freddie sorted it out for himself. He did not realize that she was not talking at all, but simply letting him find his way as he talked. Without her saying so, he could feel her love, her sympathy and the understanding she communicated by the way she responded.

Freddie felt better and better, for even though he had no answers her presence and understanding made him feel less alone, less unique and stronger. Then he knew he would be able to find the answers he was looking for, even for the very private questions about which he had not dared to talk.

Suddenly, Freddie knew there was nothing more he was comfortable in saying. He knew Harriet understood that he was growing and needed to sort out the new thoughts, emotions and feelings of that growth. To express it directly would be redundant and embarrassing. He changed the subject abruptly. "Gosh, Aunt Harriet, I never even finished Luke's letter. Just one more paragraph."

So, Uncle LeRoy is at last giving me a little time in the late afternoon as long as I get my chores done. I like the routine, the work and the relaxation at the pond afterwards. Sometimes I miss the time at the pond, when we go to town for trading and supplies. But not today. Today I'm taking part of my time to write to you, so don't be mad that I haven't written in so long and take care of yourself and try to come visit me in June. I'm closing now. No real time left for fishing today but it's really warm here for the first of May, and I expect I'll strip and take a little dip in that old pond before dark. That's something I've really come to enjoy this spring, even when it's not so warm. If you come this summer, maybe we can go together. It's practically all mine. No one else hardly ever goes there. Write soon.

Your best friend,

Luke

CHAPTER 9

From the Book of Life

"Luke!" Aunt Crystal stood at the front door of the cabin with hands on wide, aproned hips, shouting into the wind for her wandering nephew. Murmurs of the celebration planned for when he finally got home rose and fell from within the small house.

But Luke was lying by the pond in the heat of the mid-June day, and did not hear. Lathered by the humidity, fishing line in the water, book in hand, his thoughts were not on the book or the line, but on the special day and how birthdays seemed to be a mixture of sadness and delight.

That's true today, he thought, and noticed little water drops appearing on the page of his book. He returned his attention to it. The book was not new. His Uncle LeRoy had given it to him nearly three years before. But he understood little of it when he had read it and put it aside for others before finishing ten pages. Now that he was older it made more sense, and Luke found it exciting in a way strange to him. He wondered heatedly if he would ever feel what the characters were feeling, do what they were doing. He also wondered what his Uncle LeRoy would say if he could read, and knew about the contents of this little dime novel which he had innocently handed a ten — year — boy.

Luke felt exceptionally warm and excited, which was surprising for just lying under a tree on a late June Georgia day. He was sweating on the book and his hands were leaving wet imprints on the pages. Luke realized that he was experiencing some of the sensuous and arousing feelings about which he had been reading. Suddenly embarrassed, he threw the book aside.

I think I see why this birthday is so special, thought Luke as he examined what was happening to him. He considered the changes in himself he had been wondering over during the last several weeks. The attendant emotions, rapid growth, changing voice, pitch and oscillation of his mood, all heightened Luke's awareness of self as an individual. They increased his fervor for his studies as he struggled to bury and deny the strange feelings. He wanted to hold the solace and hope that words had always provided him. But he was facing those changes now. They filled him with anticipation and sadness for this, his thirteenth birthday, was also the thirteenth anniversary of his mother's death.

Suddenly a torrent of emotion grabbed Luke. It pulled him inside out in the conflict between expectation and regret, fear and hope, hate and love. Luke stood up among this whirlwind of feelings. He was afraid of them but half enjoying the new sensations. He flung his pole aside in conflicting anger and joy, and jerked down the straps of his coveralls. Dropping them to his bare feet, he leaped forward into the chilly pond.

A change in the atmosphere about the pond broke through Luke's meandering mind as he lazed belly—up in the cool water. Seeking to soothe his emotions in the cool retreat to childhood freedom it offered, he sensed that he was no longer alone.

Sinking and rolling to his stomach, he poked his head up and cast a quick glance about the pond and into the woods. He expected to see signs of approaching hunters and their dogs, a sight which had sometimes caused him to scurry bare-bottomed into the weeds This time, however, there was no White hunter. There was a girl. She was not coming through the weeds or the woods. She was standing by the pond itself right beside Luke's britches. He had nowhere to retreat. He sank his dark body deep into the cloudy water and mouthed a furtive and feeble "Hey" across at her.

"Hey," Aggie replied. "You is Luke Powers, ain't you?" Aggie took a step closer and leaned over the water. "I been sein' ya' in church near every week for a long time now. What y'all doin'?"

"Nothing. Just swimming, that's all. Where'd you come from?"

"Over yonder is my folk's place. I come here alla time."

"All the time? Get on, Girl. I haven't seen you here before."

"But I seen you. I been watchin' you here for weeks. Y'all sure a strange boy. Never knew one what would always be a-pouring over them books like you. And, Lord, y'all talk like a White man."

Luke felt suddenly uneasy. The coolness that the water brought disappeared as his inner furnace heated him up. "For weeks, you say? What else did you see, I mean, how much or___"

"Y'all know. This your fishing pole? That's a nice pole. I got me one, too. "Cept I's not allowed to fish here, on account of the dogs what chased me back awhile."

"Too bad, Girl." Luke's normally strong voice cracked with irritation.

"Oh, now, don't y'all be mean. Come on out and sit a spell."

"No. Go home. I can't, I mean . . ."

"Can't? How come?"

"Just can't. Now git!"

"No," grinned Aggie. "I likes it here and can stay if I wants. Besides, 'can't' ain't no answer." By then Luke was thoroughly flustered and Aggie thoroughly enjoying herself. She turned, looking over her shoulder to see him. She tipped her head slightly forward so that her thin dark brows shadowed her black eyes. It was her most practiced look of mystery and it stirred Luke as it reminded him of the bawdy book lying in the weeds. He looked toward it.

"What you lookin' at, Boy?" Aggie followed his glance to the book. "Oh my, Luke. Your book is gettin' all dirty there. Let me get it for you."

"Leave it be, Girl! Git! Go away!"

"Name's Aggie, not Girl. And it ain't no trouble at all. What's it 'bout, anyway? I never could get the hang of reading words."

Luke felt a shudder of relief that slightly dampen his inner fire. When he remembered his own state of nudity the fire roared again. Luke shouted, "It's not about anything special. Now just go away!"

Aggie dropped the book at Luke's tone but continued to taunt him. "Y'all sure do talk like a White man. Got 'bout as much respect for a poor Colored girl as a White man does, too. Imagine shouting like that. Shame on you, Luke Powers. I say, shame on you. Now come on out'a there and apologize."

"Git, I tell you! Git!" Luke was confused and angry. He directed his anger at the girl as well as himself. No one his age ever bested him but despite all conscious efforts at control, he continued to feel hotter in the cool water. He was sure he would be sick. "Go on," he shouted. "I want to get out"

"Go on, then." But she replayed his last words in her mind and detected the agony lying behind Luke's voice. She knew her teasing was not being taken as such. She feared he might really be angry, perhaps angry enough to harm her.

Then Luke's words confirmed his anger "If I get out now, I'll whip you good, and take you home and tell your mamma what you've been up to."

Still Aggie felt safe enough for one more taunt. "That's what ya'll say. But you be there with nothing on but your beautiful Black self, so ya'll ain't likely to be coming at me. But Okay. I gonna turn around and show you my backside, so's ya'll can climb out of there and get decent."

"Don't you dare, Girl." Aggie turned as Luke sank backward into the water, glowing a reddish brown beneath his scowling brow.

Aggie could not quit her taunting even as she had turned her back. She kept faking a look over her shoulder, forcing Luke to jerk back down in the water and grow more and more agitated. At last she said, "You ain't got nothing I ain't seen a hundred times. I got me two brothers, ya' know. Besides, if y'all gonna talk White, I'm gonna watch you until the sun goes down, or maybe 'til the White man comes with his dogs and guns."

Luke exploded. "I hope he does, and his dogs chase you up a tree like a coon, and he comes up and shoots you out of it, and he sells your skin up North, and they make a coat out of you, and every time the owner wears it other Whites will say, 'Where did you get that ugly black coat?' and your owner will say, 'Why this is a nigger skin coat,' and you'll be a slave on some White man's back just like your grandmother was, except you'll be a dead slave." Luke was shouting, waving his arms for emphasis, standing in water only to his knees. He completely forgot his modesty in his reversion to the less modest demeanor of an infuriated small child. His embarrassed rage was nearly uncontrolled.

But Luke's modesty was uncompromised despite his abandonment of the shielding waters, for Aggie was already tearfully racing toward home. Her first encounter with her future ended in the terror of Luke's childish if fruitful imagery.

By the time he reached the bank, Luke's shame and rage had turned inward where it dissolved into a low depression while he dressed. He felt shamed at his tantrum. Dragging the fishing pole carelessly and forgetting the book completely, Luke half focused his cooling eyes on the weeds and red clay beneath his wet and mud-caked feet and headed home.

Chapter 10

From the Shadows to the Light

"Luke!" The call of his name with just a bit of edge to it reached Luke's ears and quickened his dragging feet as he approached the edge of his uncle's land. *How'd she find out so fast,* thought Luke as he shouted a reply and beelined toward the front of the house.

"Where you been, Chile? I declare I done call you for the best part of the afternoon. Your uncle wants you in the house. And wipe those feet."

Luke avoided his aunt's searching eyes as he approached the steps. His bare toes caught the worn wood of the first step and slapped his foot back to the dust — padded earth. Luke pitched forward and struck his hands flat on the lined old porch boards and barked his shins.

"Owe" Luke whimpered as he stumbled and lifted his five — foot — six frame to the porch. His toe banged the stair riser one more time as a final insult to his clumsiness, itself something he lately seemed more inclined to do than not.

"Boy, git in here." Uncle LeRoy propped the screen wide with one strong Black arm and motioned for Luke with the other. Aunt Crystal gave Luke a little propelling nudge to get him through the door.

What greeted Luke was anything but what he expected during his journey home from the pond. His grandparents were down from Atlanta for the first time since he had left there five years before. They stood in front of him with wide, white grins bursting from their worn, Black faces. "Happy Birthday," guffawed Eldon Powers as his wife's sturdy arms engulfed the boy. She squeezed him too hard then abruptly shoved him backwards. Her big fleshy hands snapped him up short before her just as his grandaddy's broad, flat palm caught him between his bony shoulders.

Now Luke felt nothing but joyous surprise. The hurt, shame, disappointments and resentments of the day dissipated; the feeling of loss for his mother simmered somewhere in some other Luke. This Luke grinned widely as the "My how you've grown" routine concluded.

As the moments passed, Luke became more aware of differences in the room and of the other people there. Drawing his first solid breath since stubbing his toe, he drank in the room with the realization that he was at its center, where he was at his best. His old assurance and charisma grabbed hold as he graciously greeted and charmed his teacher, neighbors, the preacher he had been studying with for five years, and his friends.

All the while his eyes flicked across the room incorporating the other changes that had taken place. There was a makeshift table of barrels and boards. The fine white cloth borrowed for the occasion was nearly invisible under the food laid on the table. It was a feast like none Luke had seen before. There were savory stews, spareribs, sausages, pork chops, fried chitlins, pig's feet and tails. There were candied yams and ham, baked beans and fried chicken, steaming soups, rice and potatoes, green beans with bacon, black-eyed peas and juice-sucking corn bread. There were sweet smelling morsels of this and that the origins and odors and tastes of which were as foreign to Luke as a White man's parlor. At the center of this feast stood a giant chocolate pan cake with real frosting of powdered cane sugar and lard. As Uncle LeRoy watched the boy's every motion, he caught each moment of discovery as though it was a signal of major importance instead of a nearly imperceptible twitch.

"Open it, Boy, we're ready to eat." Luke's hand reached toward the package, but it met him halfway, born along in Uncle LeRoy's hand. This was the final two feet of a journey begun in LeRoy's mind months before when he first got the inspiration which led to this special gift.

Luke took it. He looked to his uncle's anticipatory gaze, threw a glance toward each expectant stare in the room, then ripped the covering from this, the first real birthday present he ever received.

"It's a book," exclaimed LeRoy. "It's about some great and powerful brothers and sisters what help make us proud we are Colored." LeRoy rattled on about the book as though he had read it, even though everyone present knew he could not read.

As much as Luke wanted to dive right into the book, he always enjoyed his status as the center of attention and was ready to hear praise after the difficult and confusing day. So he thanked them all with high enthusiasm, then ate and chatted and recounted the past with his grandparents. He entertained his friends and relatives with stories from long ago in Atlanta.

Toward dusk, most of the food was gone. The men went to the stump liquor with full bellies all around. The whole day drifted around in Luke's mind as he considered the praise he had received. He recalled his earlier confusion and remembered the shame he felt for his outburst at the girl Aggie. Confusion overwhelmed him again, and a hint of depression replaced the euphoria that the party had generated. He returned to the table and reached out to take the book. *Doubt I'll ever be half as good as these folks are*, he thought. *I can't even be kind to another person. It's all 'me' with me.*

Self-deprecating thoughts continued to pass through Luke's mind as he thumbed the pages of the book and caught names like Charles Richard Drew. He read that Drew was not yet famous to any but his own people and still seven years from being called the father of modern blood banks. More familiar names like Booker T. Washington and Frederick O. Douglas jumped out at him while the name of the current and only black West Point cadet, Benjamin O. Davis and other rising Black Americans emphasized the potential there for a Black person with the character and intelligence everyone seemed to attribute to him.

Yet Luke could not help thinking of these people as beyond him. Surely they never experienced the depressing shame and sense of hypocrisy which he was now feeling. Because of the way his encounter with Aggie had occurred, he could not go to his uncle or grandfather to talk about it. He did not understand what had happened to him at the pond, or why he had reacted as he had.

As dusk settled, Luke drifted toward the screen door and into the cool evening. He crossed the porch to the first step and sat there, the book at his side. His hands propping his chin, he vacantly eyed the impending darkness. A moment later his grandmother sat beside him. Arm across his shoulder, Harriet squeezed him gently but firmly and began working to soften or solve the problem he bore.

"What y'all doin' here by yourself?"

"Nothing."

"Come on in yonder with the folk. We be havin' a grand ol' time."

"I'll come in a bit Grandma. You go ahead."

"What's on your mind, Boy. You can tell your grandma."

"Nothing."

"Sure it's nothing, with you acting this way, just setting there with your chin between your legs. Fess up, now, just between us."

"Really, Grandma, nothing." Luke was feeling the pressure from his grandmother to talk about his feelings and similar pressure from within was pushing him toward it. Since he felt shame himself, he was afraid she might be ashamed of him if he told her.

Harriet changed her tack, attempting to make him see indirectly that his feelings were normal, healthy, and universal among children reaching for adulthood. She kept probing. "Nothing" she murmured again under her breath. "MMM-MMM. I knows sometimes 'nothin' means something what ain't clear enough in y'all's head to talk about. Now, don't it, Luke?"

"Uh, Grandma, really, it means nothing's the matter."

"Luke, Boy, this is your Grandma. I been raising boys for near fifty years. I'se watched and rocked and patched up their hurts in both body and soul. I know when somethin' is wrong and expect I even know what."

"Humph!" Luke wished he could just get up and go into the yard, away into the lengthening dusk, but he was afraid of hurting her. "Wish you'd tell ME then", he snapped. "It'd be news, I'm sure."

"Ain't no sense in giving sass to your Grandma, Boy. Just worried over you is all and thought it might help a bit if ya'll get it out."

Luke looked at his grandmother and saw in her eyes the offense which he had tried to avoid giving. He felt even worse. Damn, he thought, I even hurt the people I love the most. Me and my famous mouth! It's gotten me in more trouble today. Continuing to condemn himself inside, Luke offered an apology to his Grandmother, raising his arm behind her and returning the squeeze of affection.

"You're right, Grandma. I am kind of down. It really is nothing special," Luke said. His words belied his inner turmoil, and he hoped his grandmother would leave him alone to deal with it. But he wanted to speak. He wanted to talk about it with someone, and could think of no one else with whom he would feel comfortable in doing so. Luke hoped that his Grandmother understand what was bothering him. Still, he was not ready to risk speaking out.

Luke inched toward talking in third person terms, about the age into which he was moving hoping to glean from his Grandmother her best counsel without compromising his shameful secret.

Reading right through his vague references to his feelings, his grandmother replied, "You know, I seen your daddy and your brothers get themselves in the same kind of fix about your age. You're growing in mind and heart. Now your daddy and your brothers made mistakes, and they done had their troubles. I know you got yours, too. That's part of it. Lord knows I got mine. It ain't the troubles what's important, it's how y'all face them and deal with them. I know my Luke. Whatever you got facing you, you will get over it and keep on growing to the finest kind of man. Why, I knowed that the first time I lay these old eyes on you."

"I love you, Grandma, and I'm not saying this to hurt you. But you're wrong, at least about me being so fine. I'm nothing. I'm no good. Everybody thinks I'm so terrific. All my life as far back as I can remember, everybody has been telling me I'm special, I'm a leader, I'm their hope. Well, I'm not, and I'm not sure I want to be. I am not sure I wouldn't rather be just me, just ordinary. Everybody expects so much of me. I'm just a kid. And I can't do it. Why can't I make mistakes like everybody else?"

"Y'all can, Luke. Y'all can. That's what I'm trying to tell Y'all. Why them great men in that book you is holding done made plenty of mistakes and had plenty of misery too, just like the rest of us. It ain't the mistakes, it's---"

"I know. It's the way I handle it. How I own up to it. Well, I'm not strong enough or brave enough, or whatever it is you think I am, to just say 'I made a mistake and I'm sorry'."

"Y'all ain't sorry about the mistakes you make?"

"Yes. I am. I don't want to hurt anybody. I just can't say it."

"Why, Luke, just the other minute y'all said it to me. Why do y'all say you can't say it. I don't understand why."

"Because saying doesn't change things. The mistake is still there. If I hurt someone, it's done. The hurt is there. Just saying 'sorry' and walking away means nothing."

"It's a start. And sometimes, it's enough."

"Not often."

"Then you show you're sorry. It takes a big man to own up to his mistakes and do something to correct them."

"That's what I'm trying to say. I am not that big man you keep trying to tell me I am. You haven't seen me in five years, Grandma. How can you know who I am? I'm just a kid. I don't want to be a man yet. It hurts too much."

"Son, you ain't no kid no more. Y'all gotta face that first. Out here, in these times, y'all gotta grow fast. Y'all may not yet be that man I know y'all be some day, but you ain't no kid, either. No 'kid' feels what you feelin' right now. No 'kid' is as tall as you. I hear the man in your voice. I see the man in them muscles y'all sporting' these days. And I can easily see you are feeling some man feelings on the inside, too. Y'all gotta face it, then maybe those feelings won't confuse y'all the way they been doing."

"What do you mean, 'man feelings'? I look at Uncle LeRoy, so burdened and strong. That's man feelings. I don't---"

"Luke, Okay. Let me see if I can explain. When we little, most things is done for us. When we got troubles and wants, we goes to our folks and we tells 'em we want this or that, and they either says no, or they says yes, or they says maybe. Whatever they say, we knows that's the way it's got to be."

"I know that, Grandma."

"Now let me finish. As we grows, we finds one day that we ain't takin' 'no' for the answer all the time. We finds ourselves thinking for ourselves and reasoning things out different from our folks. We try to tell them our side, our feelings about this or that. And good folks, why, they listen and they try to help us know that if we want to choose our own way, we gots to be accountable for the way we choose. We make a choice and it's a mistake, we got to stand up and make it right."

"Like Uncle LeRoy does."

"Exactly. Like your Uncle LeRoy. But then we grows a little more, and we think about things that ain't just our wants. We think 'bout things outside ourselves, things like how other folks is feelin' and why. Things like how folks treat other folks. Now one reason we always know you special, is because y'all been able to do that almost since the day you came to us. Y'all know that's the truth, Luke."

"Not anymore, Grandma. Anymore, it seems like all I do is hurt other people."

"I knows, Honey. And that's natural. That's what I'm getting at. See, the next step in your growing is looking at yourself to see if you is kind or mean, smart or dumb, strong or weak. It's too bad but true that just when you starts that self looking, your body ups and changes on you. Had me a puppy once, him just weaned. Small enough to fit in the flat of this old hand, he was. I babied that critter, feeding him milk and scraps, teaching him not to mess on my clean floor. After a week or so, he got kinda spunky, and began exploring around the house, up and down the stairs, and eating like you wouldn't believe,

"That's what puppies do, Grandma. I don't see---"

"But it was what happened next that counts. Why, that puppy started growin', and I mean growin' so fast that come each morning, he'd growed so much since the morning before, that he'd plum have to learn all over how to mount them stairs or what he'd fit under. 'Cause what he could do yesterday, he couldn't do today, and what he couldn't do yesterday, he suddenly could do today, which weren't no guarantee at all for tomorrow."

"And?"

"And seems like all qrowin' critters, including young boys, is sort'a like that puppy. Comes a time when they be just growing too fast to keep up with themselves. Still, time goes by, they finish all that growing on the outside, and finds out they been growing on the inside too. Those that accept who and what they is, and learn to make the most of it, kind of like that puppy who made such a fine dog, those what learn makes fine men."

"But I know what kind of person I am. I am selfish. I see it. Just like when I hurt your feelings a little while ago. I do things like that, without meaning to, but it seems like all the time I am making Uncle LeRoy mad at me, messing up my chores."

"But don't ya'll see, Boy? You're just like that puppy. Every night he went to bed thinking now he knows who he is and what he can do. Nobody can tell him different. But every morning he tries it, and finds he's got to start all over. How can ya'll say you know who you are when ya'll's changin' so fast? Now admit it to me. Ya'll's changin' every day, ain't you?

"Yessum."

"Now that puppy, he keep trying. He ain't giving up just because he falls on his face when he tries today to climb the same stairs he was leaping up yesterday. He just backs off, takes it slow, and starts again. See, there is something inside that pup, and inside you, that ain't changing. Those things may come out a little stronger, but they ain't different."

"Like what, Grandma?"

"Like your natural goodness, that helps y'all know when y'all done wrong even if y'all can't make yourself make it right. Like your being able to see the goodness and hurt in others. Like the courage y'all showing right now by being willing to say out loud that you make mistakes, and that y'all feeling selfish."

"But I am selfish."

"It ain't selfish ya'll being, Luke. Its self-looking. It's trying to find who ya'll really is. Like I say, with your body and soul demanding so much of your thoughts just to keep up with itself, it's no wonder you're more interested in you than anybody else. Main difference is, ya'll see that. Most don't. Too many folks getting' to be your age tend to think it's the rest of the world that's crazy and they is just fine. They is lonely and hurtin' like you. Instead of havin' the courage to say to themselves they must change to grow, they say, 'the world is mean to me. I will learn to be wary, to not trust, to put others down first. I will get mine and protect mine and the devil with them selfish people.

"Those like that never grow up, Luke. They are still thirteen years old in how they see the world around them. They never did get the courage to say, 'I been wrong.' They is starting wars, cheating folks, looking down their long noses at folks that is different than they is. They is wearing sheets in the night to hide from themselves while they hurts others. Yes, Luke, there's lots of folks like that. But you ain't one of 'em, and you knows it. Truth be, most folks is just strugglin' to get on with it, trying to find somethin' worth somethin' in a world that has a lot of hurt and evil in it."

"Put like that, Grandma, I guess I'm not like that. Still, I keep on doing things I know are wrong even as I do them, but other people seem not to know I'm doing wrong and they keep telling me how good I am. All I'm saying is that I am not as good as everyone keeps saying. I've learned that for sure. And it really gets to me to hear them talk any more. I want to shout at them, You don't know what you're talking about! Fools! Look at me, how I deceive you. Hate me! Go on, I dare you! Hate me."

Harriet paused at this. She opened her mouth to speak, then fell silent for a moment. Crickets sounded in the darkening woods, and they could hear the gayety of the rest of the family from the other side of the screen door. Finally, she spoke again. "That's only because you ain't liking yourself right now. And that's only because you ain't sure who you is, on account of you is changing so much. Now, those things you say you've been doing wrong a long time. They may seem wrong now that you is old enough to understand and know better, to think them through for yourself, but that don't make them all that wrong in the past, when you and what you was is what other folks said was. Does that make sense?"

"Kinda. You maybe mean they weren't wrong, just childish?"

"That's it. Childish."

"And now I should start deciding for myself what's right or wrong for me, and not listen to what others say about me?"

"That's part of it. But there's still lots you can learn from others. You need to listen and think about what other folks say. Test it in your head and heart against your instincts. Like I said, you got fine instincts. Use 'em. Don't come down on yourself when you make a mistake, for like you say, you ain't perfect. But use them instincts to avoid mistakes by thinking about things before ya'll act, and to correct them or make amends when they do happen. Y'all seeing some things in yourself you want to change? Change 'em. And don't go feeling sorry for yourself. Y'all have too much to give go wallowing in the 'poor little me's'."

"Now, just pick yourself up, Luke. Listen to that preacher in there a little more and talk things out that confuse you with your Uncle LeRoy. He understands. Read that book and get yourself educated. I tell ya'll Luke, it's near lost for folks like your granddaddy and' me. Time done pass us by. But ya'll have a chance. Take it. Maybe your children will really be free.

"Because being free in the outside comes first from being free on the inside. And y'all got the ability to be free on the inside, because you have the instinct about life. And more, you can help others understand, so even if y'all ain't perfect, if y'all share the gifts the Good Lord gave you, maybe you can help make others be truly free, too."

Harriet's love for Luke and the simple wisdom of her words pulled at him. He had never heard her go on like that before and thought to himself it must have been something she had wanted to say for a long time. He began to feel that she was right. He turned to her as she spoke, first in response to her hand tugging at his chin, then to the pull of her eyes grabbing at him from out of the dark, then to the magnetism of the words themselves. Her form had separated from the black void around her and became as distinct and meaningful to Luke as her words. The moon now was casting a blue glow on the landscape, further enhancing her silhouette as a kind of shadow vibrating in the dark of the night with her truths and her love of him. Opening up his heart and drawing on the fresh resolve he summoned from her words, Luke could say but three words of his own. "I will, Grandma." And his tone told her he meant it.

Then she surprised him. "Good, Boy. I knew you would. Now ya'll can start by apologizing to that girl you yelled at so bad down at the pond this afternoon."

"How'd you know about that?" Luke was nonplussed.

"Why Honey," said Harriet, flashing a big smile and knowing eyes, "I is your Grandma, remember? Besides, ain't that the 'nothing' you said was bothering you? Ain't that what y'all been trying to tell me about all evenin'?"

Luke smiled in amusement and amazement. He now realized that his Grandmother really saw him for what he was and respected him fully as an individual in all his strengths and weaknesses. She understood him, but for the life of him, he never would figure out how she knew about Aggie.

"You're amazing, Grandma. And you're right. Jeez, you're right. Come on. Let's get back in and have some of that fun they're tossing around in there."

The two of them rose and turned to go up the steps. As they did, Harriet once more put her arm around Luke's waist, once more pulled him tight to her big, firm side saying, "Just one more thing I got to say. Don't come down on yourself when you make a mistake. Don't be afraid to love yourself. Jesus done say, 'love thy neighbor as thyself.' What he means is that in loving yourself you learn what love is. Once you've got that, share it. So don't go feeling shame for loving and admiring yourself; just be sure you love others the same way. Why, when you look at it like that," she said with a grin, "even the White man can be loved. And when you learn to love them in a giving way, you have a better notion of what loving yourself means, which then helps you love others even more."

Harriet's 'Just one last thing' led to another, and the two ended up settling down in the old porch swing with still more talk, touching again on the early years in Atlanta, being young and growing up in a wandering, exploring, intimate family way. As they talked the rising moon changed the cast of the landscape from blue to a strange reddish silver.

The chattering crickets and bellowing bull frogs by the creek to the rear of the house interrupted and brought them back from the past and the future into the present. There the laughter from inside once again moved them to action, and they got up with a look at the yard and the trees then each other. Smiling, they walked tall and arm in arm through the screen door.

Somehow, Luke felt like a man just then, one ready to accept himself and be proud. As he entered the room and felt eyes on him, his Grandmother's talk came and went through his mind. He straightened his shoulders, widened his grin, opened his flashing black eyes and started talking. After that, the room quieted to his perceptive storytelling, and he was fully Luke again. In his own heart and mind and body, he liked himself better and sensed that he was a more mature, stronger Luke than the boy who had been so upset just a few hours before. It made him proud to be thirteen, and proud to be who he was.

CHAPTER 11

Seeds

Freddie got home from visiting Harriet again long past supper and long past dark. He expected his stepfather to be fuming. He hoped to tiptoe through the kitchen and up the stairs to his room before he was noticed. But luck was not with him. As he stepped gingerly and softly through the kitchen door, Howard's voice accosted him.

"Well, Boy, nice of you to drop by." Freddie knew Howard's sarcasm was a prelude to big trouble. If Howard just scowled, he was safe for the moment. If he started yelling at him, it would last a few minutes and Howard would stomp from the room. He would still be upset and all care must be taken to avoid him, but at least he would be off Freddie's back. If he icily ordered Freddie to sit, Freddie knew bad news was coming. He would be facing increased chores or loss of yet another privilege.

In these moments Howard's pompous military manner gained full force with his adopted son. He often had Freddie stand instead of sit. Freddie faced him in an almost unconscious position of attention. When Freddie took this most uncomfortable position, Howard would deliberately insult him by ignoring him. Instead, he sweetly heaped attention on his two natural children.

Things had changed dramatically in the household since he had last visited Harriet. The intolerable state which had existed since his stepmother's sudden death during childbirth often drove Freddie back to see his adopted Aunt Harriet.

Freddie knew that visiting Harriet was taboo. He knew that Howard had an underlying dislike for Harriet because she was Black. This loathing was ingrained in Howard's intense prejudice against all Black people. Freddie went to considerable lengths to disguise his relationship with the Powers family, for he knew that his stepfather bitterly resented the closeness which Freddie had with them.

Howard considered that relationship personally offensive and demeaning and he frequently told Freddie so. At the same time, he declared that no true child of his could ever lower himself so. He insisted that he allowed Freddie to remained in the house solely because of his own charitable temperament. Often, he sarcastically expressed shame in and contempt for Freddie and Freddie lived with it. He knew he must stay for the two remaining years before he could legally join the Army. He also recognized the primary reason he had endured the awful suffering of the last year. It was the supportive and motherly affection which Harriet Powers gave him, and the prospect of visiting her when things turned awful. He almost always found a letter from Luke at the Powers', and a loving person to help him sort out his feelings.

The last time he had gone it had been easy. His stepfather had been in Washington on business. A neighbor lady had been engaged to look after the two little children because Howard no longer trusted Freddie to do so. That had hurt Freddie. He had deliberately and conscientiously nurtured his relationship with them not only because he loved them, but as a tool to make himself valuable to the household. This helped assure that he would be able to stay until he finished high school. Now even that was gone.

///

The visit to Harriet this time was different. It had nothing directly to do with Howard. Freddie had committed an act which he believed would have disastrous consequences. Though but seventeen and still in school, he had gotten a girl pregnant. He was terrified. He knew nowhere else to turn but to Harriet. Instead of heading straight for home to complete his chores immediately after school, he had wandered around the city trying to think of a solution for the problem. He came up with none which would avoid a major conflict with his stepfather. In his meandering, he eventually found himself in front of the Powers' home on Magnolia Street.

As always, Harriet Powers was quiet and supportive and listening, offering advice only when Freddie seemed to run out of words. The advice she offered was more in the manner of simple questions and quiet direction. This helped him think through his options and consider solutions compatible with his values. She never condemned. Freddie realized it was this which had brought him back to Harriet Powers' door with the most difficult problem he had ever faced.

For Harriet's part, she would not recommend marriage. She reflected on her own values and realized that his were different.

Were Luke in such trouble she knew exactly what would happen. Either she or her daughter-in-law Crystal, or perhaps the girl's parents would take in both mother and child if possible, but at least the child. They would make raising it a family responsibility to assure that the youngsters who had in passion and ignorance brought the child into the world would have at least the opportunity to finish growing before they had to take on the full responsibility of parenthood. But then there were not as many taboos in the Black culture against intimacy itself. It was considered natural and therapeutic. She believed that the White man condemned Blacks for this attitude and at the same time allowed himself to accept the idea that sex was dirty, backroom, to be hidden.

As far as Harriet was concerned, the involvement in sex should be taken on with as much a sense of responsibility as any other act which might have implications for the lives of people beyond self. At the same time, she could not fathom why the Whites had created such a set of guilts about sex and a White child born of unbridled and irresponsible passion should for the rest of his or her life bear the burden of the parents' indiscretion.

But she knew that such reasoning would not appeal to Freddie. She felt certain that she knew what he would end up doing before he even began to consider it himself. She was sure that he would ruin his life and quit school to marry the girl right away, squelching any chance that he might have to gain the decent education which his stepfather had begrudgingly promised him.

She also felt that his combative relationship with his stepfather might prove the only excuse that Howard Sloan would need to renege on that promise. She feared Howard might toss Freddie out of the house to find his own way in a world full of unemployment. Without even a high school diploma and with a wife and brand new baby for which he must care, Harriet believed he was in very serious trouble.

The unknown factor was the parents of the girl. What would be their attitude? Would they accept the child? Would they, like a Black family, accept not only the child but the outcast father? Would they provide support in the near future to help guarantee that the distant future would hold promise for their daughter and grandchild? Or would a puritanical prejudice overcome their love and good sense causing them to join Howard Sloan in a senseless conspiracy to shove the transgressing couple and their helpless infant into a world for which they were unprepared? She probed Freddie to try and find this out. She was determined, if needed, to intercede in finding a suitable home for the child just as she had done for Freddie some years before. As Freddie left, she made sure she told him that she would help.

The visit itself had lasted for hours. Although against Freddie's excitement and amalgam of emotion it had seemed like minutes. He was surprised to find darkness when he went outside and began running toward home. He knew that he was in trouble. He wondered all the way home why he was hurrying toward the furnace blast of anger he would receive from Howard. He was keyed up, excited and disturbed at the prospect of being a father. Harriet had raised optimism in him that it would work, but he was deeply concerned as to how. He was very much in love with Martha in a seventeen-year—old way. In his naivety he was sure that she was just as much in love with him. Harriet's assurance that there were ways and there was hope buoyed him but it disturbed him that those "ways" were yet undefined, still unsettled.

He knew that he must weather the difficult bombasts he was facing that very night and get back to Martha and her parents as soon as possible with some reasonable and practical solution to the problem. Right now, his problem was more immediate. It dealt with the overwhelming challenge of simply avoiding the full wrath of Howard's displeasure at his having not done his chores. Freddie did not realize how much more than that his encounter with Howard Sloan was about to involve.

/ / /

"Or," continued Sloan in his most dripping of sarcastic manners, "don't you consider this to be your home anymore?"

"Yessir." Freddie thought resorting to the military manner might be appropriate in response to Howard's sarcastic vehemence.

"I see. Are you sure? I would have thought a stud bastard like you would have felt more at home in a whorehouse, lying with that cheap pig you knocked up."

"Sir?" Freddie was totally taken aback to discover that Howard already knew. His planned defenses were shattered. He recognized that Howard had the upper hand and that he would probably be on the street before he even had time to plan with Martha what they were going to do.

"Is she another one of your nigger friends? I can't imagine any decent White girl letting a nigger lover like you near her."

"Hey, Howard, Watch it!" Freddie's defensive posture was disintegrating into an overwhelming and powerful anger. The abusive and degrading treatment he had endured at the hands of his stepfather during the last several months culminated in the intolerable filth this man goadingly spit out.

"Hey, Howard. Watch it," Howard mimicked. "Is that the best defense you can offer for unlicensed sex with some little whore? Get good stuff, did you? Better get rid of the kid, BOY, because with your sense it'll probably turn out to be an idiot, or a pervert, or worse, be born a nigger out of sympathy with your friends."

"You son of a bitch! You dirty bastard!"

"My, my, my." Howard was sporting his most wicked smile and enjoying this encounter immensely. "Look who's calling who a son of a bitch. My mother didn't desert me like a dog. And speaking of bastards, are you sure you have a mother? And what about the little bundle of licorice you are about to bring into the world? Now that's what I call a bastard."

There was no defense, Freddie knew. He had but two choices. He could leave now and be at the mercy of the street, or he could stay and be at the mercy of this man. Some choice Freddie thought. He wondered again how Howard had found out so fast. It dawned on him that he and Martha had agreed that their parents must be told soon, but he had not figured on telling them this soon. He had wanted to develop at least a tentative solution to the dilemma before confronting Howard with it and had told Martha that. But Freddie knew that he could not blame her. After all, it had been he who had left so quickly after school. She probably panicked and went straight home to her mother. Her mother had, of course, called Howard. All thus seemed lost.

"I absolutely renounce you as my son. See what I have here? Your adoption papers. I think I've wanted to tear them up ever since you pushed me away the night we got them. Nobody does that to me. Well, then. Watch me now". Howard started tearing them up but paused at Freddie's words.

"Please do, for I am ashamed to call you Father." Freddie's sudden, low, calm tone intimidated Howard like shouting and begging never would. He was not used to being addressed this way and certainly not used to the commanding presence he saw in his adopted son. He wanted the tearing of the papers to hurt. Obviously, it was not going to. Freddie's tone conveyed such quiet and absolute contempt for him that he quickly realized that destroying the papers would please this despised intruder. So instead of tearing them, he countered, "You, you are ashamed to call me, me your father?"

"Absolutely. I have despised you for years and hold you totally without respect."

"ME, who has fed you, has clothed you, has---"

"Used me as one would use a slave. You have mocked and maligned me instead of trying to understand me, have condemned my every action as slovenly, have offered me the love of a father, then jerked it back tauntingly when I tried to accept."

"It was you who withdrew from me. It was you who had no respect. It was you who kept alive the feeling that you did not really belong to us."

"If that is true, Sloan, then why did your own wife love me? She actually shielded me from your insensitive and unreasonable outbursts. If in fact it was I who would not accept the structure of this family, why did my stepmother and I have such a close bond?"

"She was a fool when it came to you."

"Maybe, but then it was not she who could not spawn children before I came along, was it? It was the big, tough Colonel, wasn't it."

"Shut your filthy mouth!"

"You don't like the truth? You're jealous of the fact that at a mere seventeen I have proven better in bed than you ever achieved before the age of forty? Phony! You resent me because I remind you that you are basically impotent in bed and in life." Freddie was amazed at his own words and his own strength. He found himself recounting to his stepfather all the loathsome thoughts of him he had had during the last six months. He knew that the most severe blow was the reference to Howard's temporary impotency, and he pushed it, pushed it hard, until Howard countered.

"You don't know what you're talking about. Shut up. We were just not ready for children before you forced your way in, that's all. Didn't I get your stepmother pregnant three times? Didn't I?"

"Yes, you bastard. And you knew it was dangerous the last time, but you had to prove yourself a man, didn't you! You had to kill her, didn't you?"

"I might just kill you, Mr. Big Shot! Or I might just kick you brainless and throw you into the street, if you don't shut up."

"Go ahead. A man of your narrowness and low mentality will often resort to violence, especially against women and children, to get what he wants. You've proven that often enough over the years."

"I never laid a hand on you!"

"I sometimes wished you had. It would have been over sooner, and the pain would have quickly gone away."

"What do you mean?"

"I mean, Colonel Sir, that you punished and browbeat me constantly to the point where if I had not had Mom and Harriet Powers to work it out with, I probably would have killed either you or myself long ago. The punishment you inflicted on me by just hating me so openly was the worst kind you could have given."

"If you hadn't been so hateful."

"Call me what you want. Your attitude created a conflict in this house. The tension you created made the last poor years of your wife's life as miserable as mine. You pinned her in the middle, between the two of us."

"You are at fault. It was you that---"

"It was me that nothing! I was just a kid, remember? Or have you used me for your personal slave for so long that you've forgotten that I'm human? No. It was you. You, the father, the head of the household, the commanding officer, the leader. It was you who froze the atmosphere with your military frigidity. You who tried to play the emotions of your two little babies off against my need to be loved and accepted by you.

"You who remained unbending and cruel to all of us, who insulted and mistreated and finally fired the one woman in the whole world who had given your wife real help and companionship while you were strutting around like a wounded peacock unable to fornicate."

Howard Sloan was dumbfounded. He was speechless. He had been totally whipped down by a teenage boy. What surprised him and ultimately defeated him was his discovery of Freddie's courage in the face of his own wrath. He found that he actually had affection and admiration for the boy! It was in the confusion of this discovery that he vacillated in choosing a response to the onslaught. He had thrown away the advantage he had held at the beginning of the dual and lost the day.

Yet for some reason he felt he had won. Something in him felt alive as it had not since his wife's death. He felt a contact, albeit violent, with another person, a surrogate member of the family, but a member none-the-less. When at last he could speak, even his own words surprised him. Howard leaned back and said nothing. Freddie could see him thinking, considering, calming down. "Some of what you say may have some truth in it."

"You're damn right it's true."

"Alright, Freddie. Alright. I let you have your say. Let me have mine."

Freddie sneered a superior, victorious sneer, as though allowing the final plea before the passing of sentence. But he remained quiet, and Howard continued.

"As I say, some of it may have some truth in it. I suppose, though it is hard for me to say, that I might have at times been somewhat impulsive because of anger and hurt that I suffered. What is important here, Freddie, is not what happened, but what is happening."

"Meaning what?"

"Meaning that although it's violent and hateful, you and I have finally communicated honestly with each other, back and forth, for the first time, I believe, in our lives."

"Not for the first time, Sloan. Not as far as I'm concerned anyway."

"Tell me, Freddie, when was the last?" In all the honesty he knew was critical at this point, Freddie could not think of one.

"Let me tell you what was really in the back of your mind all these years, Freddie. Now, you have accused me of some terrible things tonight. I have said some of them may have some truth. Do you have the courage to hear what I have to say, and the honesty to admit it if I am right?"

"Do I have a choice?"

"Certainly. You are a self-proclaimed man and father to be. You may leave whenever you wish." Howard knew he had Freddie right where he wanted him. He knew Freddie would listen, because he thought he knew why Freddie had put up with the abuse all those years. But Freddie fooled him again.

"Then I will leave. I have not proclaimed myself a man, but at least during the years while I shared your roof I have done everything I could to make myself useful and wanted and really loved. I can see that I have failed on all three counts. I will be gone within the week."

"Where will you go?"

"I don't know yet, but I'11---"

"Stay."

"What?"

"Stay. I do not like you, Freddie. I openly admit that I resent you, your attitude toward me, your secretly staying on and sucking up to my wife, your early pretense of loving me so I would adopt you. I know all that and do not like you for it. But, well, strangely, I love you and always have, since the moment Harriet carried you in."

"You . . .love me?"

"Take my word for it, it's harder to say than believe. Why do you think I have resented you so bitterly all these years? I wanted you to love me back but knew the day the papers came that all you really wanted was the security that I offered."

"But Howard, you misread me. I admit that I pulled back. That was because I was terrified that I might lose your love to a natural child."

"Like a self-fulfilling prophecy, wasn't it, Freddie?"

The impact of the last exchange now left Freddie nonplussed and speechlessly on the defensive. Only now he realized there was nothing to defend. They had both been so wrong. It had happened. But as Howard had said, it is what was happening then that mattered. And Freddie had to think of his future which was so complicated by his relationship with his stepfather. And it was further complicated by the coming of a child and possibly a wife into his life.

"I'11 stay," he said, "but only until we sort this out. I have some tough decisions to make, and I don't need to be on the street trying to make them. And maybe in the meantime we can learn to at least get along."

"Perhaps. To start with, I withdraw what I said about Martha. I was being deliberately cruel, not to hurt her but to hurt you. I would like to help if I could."

"Maybe someday, Howard, but not now. I have opened myself to you before and been hurt. I can't have that happen to me now. Maybe it is best I leave."

"No. Wait." Howard looked 1ike he had just had a brilliant inspiration. "Do you want the child?"

"Of course. I guess. I don't know. I always loved children, but--"

"But what?"

"I'm not sure I'm ready for all that. If only it could be delayed." Freddie had with this statement played right into Howard's scheme, and Howard jumped at his chance while Freddie was confused and looking for answers and a way out.

"It can."

"What? How're you going to delay a baby?"

"I am not talking about the baby. I am talking about the responsibility. I don't mean you would not be helping to provide for the child. But you would not have to be a father until you're ready."

"If you're going to suggest that I move Martha and the baby in here, forget it."

"Not at all. What I am going to suggest is that Martha stay home with the child. If they will not have her, she could move in with your mother's sister in Macon. She is not known there and could deliver and raise the child without shame."

"And what do I do, stay here under your shadow, knowing how you feel about me and what I've done?"

"Actually at this point I don't even know how I feel about you and what you've done, so that is a poor argument. And it's a poor excuse for having you stay here, too. To be truthful, Freddie, you need a vacation from me as much as I need one from you. And you need time to be yourself in new surroundings with some semblance of stability and discipline. Plus, I think your leaving might help settle your brother and sister down a little. I have been worried about them ever since your mother died. It has become especially difficult to deal with them since you and I have been going at each other so regularly."

"Then what do you propose I do?"

"I will simply keep my promise a little early. I will send you to a prep school. You know I went to a military academy before going to the Citadel. It is not far from Macon, so you could see Martha occasionally. I will pay your tuition and expenses as necessary, and, well, I guess I could provide some support to the baby."

"And if Martha decides to stay in Atlanta?"

"I will still provide support for the baby. You have but three semesters to go before you graduate. You can decide during that time what you want, whether it be college, marriage, or both. You and Martha can grow up a little. You can get away from here so you can find yourself. It all makes sense."

It did seem to make some sense to Freddie who despite his feelings for Martha, was frightened and looked forward to the idea of escape from the whole nightmare in which he was living. "I guess I need to talk to Martha and her parents, Howard. But it might work."

"Why don't we both talk to them?"

"If you want, okay."

"And Freddie? This may sound silly but, I used to wonder, that is, why you call me Howard. Didn't you ever want to call me 'Dad?"

"A long time ago, yeah. I guess I even used to dream about it."

"And now?"

"Not now. But maybe sometime. Maybe."

///

Dear Luke,

By the time you get this letter, I will probably be on my way to military school. I am leaving just after Christmas vacation, not even finishing the first semester of the school year here in Atlanta.

I almost don't know where to begin telling you about all that has happened to me in the last few weeks. I have had a reconciliation of sorts with my stepfather. We don't say much to each other these days, but at least we are leaving each other alone, and at least he is keeping his promise to send me to school. (Although I am not sure a military school is what I had in mind.) Still I am super glad to be getting out of this house and away from the heavy load of chores, the tension and all. You can't imagine what it's been like. The understanding Howard and I have reached isn't because he just decided to be nice for a change. Truth is, I kind of got myself in a little trouble. A few months ago, I wasn't sure you would understand, but your last few letters have been so different; you seem to have been feeling some of the very things I have. I mean about girls and all. What my trouble is, is that I got a girl pregnant. How about that? Can you believe I am actually going to be a father?

I love her, of course. I mean, it wasn't just a one-time fling, even if we did just do it once. And one day I want to marry her and take care of her and the baby. But Howard has convinced me and her that my going away is the best thing now. He is even going to pay for the cost to deliver and support the baby. Fantastic.

Martha (that's my girl) is going to stay with my Aunt in Macon the next year, until the baby is born and all, then she will probably move back with her folks until I graduate. But that's not for sure yet. They took it pretty hard, but I hope they'll come around in time.

Maybe once I'm set in school, I will be able to get over to see you at long last. I sure will work for it, I guarantee you. Of course, I will have to spend part of my holidays in Macon, and I don't know yet either how much time off or how much spending money I will have. We'll see.

By the way, keep this thing about Martha totally a secret. If the people at school find out, that's the end of my military career right there.

Got to go now. I'm meeting Martha in a little while, and we have a million things to do.

Your best friend,

Freddie

CHAPTER 12

Aggie

It was a balmy autumn afternoon in Southern Georgia. Tall pines and spruces in rows to the west stretched toward cumulus clouds puffing across the delft blue above. It tinged the sky with hints of yellow and orange and red. The afternoon sun rays skimmed the treetops, glittered and bounced off the pond's cooling surface and raced to the hardwood stand just beyond, ricocheting its intense green light toward Luke.

Luke himself was feeling rather than seeing this Georgia panorama. Propped by his favorite tree to the south of the pond, he raptly concentrated on the letter from Freddie in his lap. He read and reread it with amazement and a mixture of concern and admiration.

Beads of sweat dotted his upper lip and clung to the dark down beginning to appear there. Luke back-handed the moisture away and went on reading. The moisture reappeared, and he wiped it away again. The third time, Luke swiped at his brow too. He withdrew from the letter long enough to realize that he was sweating. He folded the letter along well-worn creases and turned his head toward the lowering orb to the West. He stood up and peeled off his rather ragged sweater, thinking to strip and swim.

"Hey Luke" came a gentle small voice behind him."Hey Aggie. What are you doing here?" Luke was genuinely surprised to see Aggie. Not one word had passed between them in the four months since she had almost tearfully rebuffed his clumsy apology in church. Luke believed then that she would seek him out again. He saw in her wet eyes a reflection of that sense of attraction to him which Luke observed and accepted from most whom he met. Despite her behavior, he knew that Aggie accepted his apology and eventually would approach him again. He had been thrilled at the prospect. Without fully understanding why, he thought of this next meeting often during the ensuing summer and early fall. Now with Aggie's soft greeting to a Luke well into his thirteenth year, Luke understood better the special friendship of a girl and thought her beautiful. Aggie was beautiful. Nearing thirteen herself, she too had matured. Her sleek black hair was still pulled to pigtails tied with bright ribbons. Although her face was still soft and round like a little girl's, she was different. She was slightly taller but still nearly a head shorter than Luke, who had grown another two inches since his birthday. She was perhaps a little too thin but Luke noticed that the straight boyish shape of her body was giving way to her growing femininity. The front of her bulky old sweater was just raised by tiny breasts. Luke did not recall finding this exciting in the past. But now he caught himself glancing at those small mounds. Then his eye searched the hint of a curve at her waist and he turned away with a touch of self-consciousness. But the feeling was mixed pleasantly with a warm tingle in his spine and groin and a slight constriction in his throat. As he turned to cover his shy reaction he repeated, "What are you doing here by the pond? I thought you said you're not allowed here."

"I's been over to Aunt Lilly's gettin' some eggs for my mamma and happen 'long this way home. I seen y'all sittin' there an' thought t'stop an' say 'hey'."

"I'm glad you did. You're not mad at me anymore?" Luke was about half swinging around the base of the tree. He was eager for something to do with his hands and anxious to appear less excited than he was. He was not at all sure it was working.

"I ain't mad. I was mean that day, too, teasin' y'all like I was. But y'all was so funny there in the water with yo' britches here on de bank."

"You nearly caught me again, Girl."

"What you say? I can't hear you."

"I said, you sure caught me that day didn't you?"

"Oh. Yeah. I sure 'nough did."

Luke flushed again. Trying to figure out why he had said that, he turned to sit. He waived the letter at her and said, "I've got to finish this. You'd better go home before your mamma gets worried."

"I's goin'. What that y'all got?"

"It's a letter from a friend of mine in Atlanta."

"All the way from Atlanta? Glory be. Can y'all read it?"

"Of course I can read it, Girl."

"Why y'all always call me 'Girl'? Name's Aggie."

"I know that."

"Then why y'all call me 'Girl'?"

"Don't know. I like to."

"Well, name's Aggie and I'd be pleased if you call me that."

"Fine. Go home, Aggie."

"Y'all read books, too?"

"Sure. Don't you?"

"Can't read."

"Not at all?"

"Oh, 'course I can, a little. I ain't never been to de school, but I learned my ABC's off'n de list of the folk what's in the preacher's back room of the church."

"How come you don't go to school? How do you expect to amount to anything if you don't learn?"

"I tries. Got too much to do at home t'go to the school."

"Shucks, Girl, uh, I mean Aggie, I got chores, too."

"Ain't chores I be doin', Luke. I mean, ain't chores what help that White man and his ol' farm. Why I should clean that ol' shack what he own an' let us live in? Iff'n we makes it better, he goin' take more of the crop for rent. Same if we grows more crop. He just take the difference an' we ends up workin' twice as hard for the same amount. 'Least dat's what my daddy keep tellin' mamma."

"I don't believe that, Aggie. Surely you must be trying somehow, to, well, I---"

"My mamma, she don't believe it either. She always workin' workin' workin' and what'd it get us? Ain't no more food. Ain't no better clothes and dat shack is worse all de time. It 'bout to fall down, I swear. I ain't doing nothin'. She ain't no better off an' neither's us. The White man takes it all, anyway."

"Then you should have time to go to school. That way, you could have it better when you grow up."

"Y'all a fool, Luke, for all your fancy talkin'. Ain't no better 'round here so long as she waste her time workin' while de White Man's in charge. 'Sides, I done told y'all I's too busy for school. I has my little brothers t'look out for so Mamma can waste her time working. An' iff'n I ain't got time to go to school how I gonna learn? Y'all goin' learn me?"

"Don't have time. You should go to school. It isn't much, not nearly so fine as the Whites have, but if you work hard and do extra, you can learn."

"No. Can't go. Guess I'll grow up just a poor ignorant Girl. Can't even get help from a boy what already knows."

"I can't teach you, Aggie. I've never taught anyone."

"Oh, fiddle. I hears y'all goin' on after church meetin', makin' things sound so interestin'. If y'all ain't lyin', then for sure y'all teachin'. Same thing."

"No, it isn't. That's just story telling. Teaching you to read and write is a whole different thing."

"Y'all thinks I's too dumb, doesn't y'all?"

"You mean, 'don't you'. If you really want to learn, you'd better start by using the right English."

"I uses it right."

"No. You talk like a poor little picaninny."

"Ain't no picaninny. I's nearly a woman."

"Then, it's about time you started talking like one."

"How I goin' do dat' less y'all learn me?"

Luke smiled at Aggie, liking her spunk and determination and appreciating the word battle in which, he knew, she had just trapped him. "Okay," he said, "we'll try it, but only for a little while. We'll see."

Aggie leaped forward and threw her arms around Luke's neck, giving him a big hug and a rather wet smack on the cheek. She released him and was standing back in her original spot almost before he knew what had happened. "Oh, thank ya, Luke. Thank ya. Y'all see. I's gonna make Y'all proud."

Luke stood there immobile, savoring and mulling over what Aggie had done. He felt pleased with himself and a bit too warm. "Sure" was all he replied.

"Lawd, it gettin' late. I's best be gettin' home a'fore my mamma worry. See y'all here tomorrow?"

"Sure".

With that, Aggie left. Luke knew it was time for him to go home too. He hesitated then stripped and hit the water to finish what he had started just before Aggie arrived. Although the sun was getting low, the autumn air felt warm and Luke felt flushed. Floating in the pond, Luke thought *I've got this swim coming. I need it.* He thought of Aggie and laughed to himself as he dived for the bottom.

By the time Luke swooped up again to avoid the muddy sediment under the pond, Aggie was near the sharecropper shack which served as her home. She paused as the afternoon waned around her, holding carefully the worn basket full of eggs which would feed the family its scanty evening meal. *Mebbe Mamma have 'nough flour an' fat for shortbread or biscuits,* she thought, and a picture of biscuits and gravy in her mind added to her hunger. She began moving again, watching the shanty seem to grow bigger as she narrowed the distance between them. Aggie saw her two younger brothers playing in the dirt in front of the porch. From the corner of her eye, she saw the outhouse door closing. From behind the shanty just visible around its warped and weathered siding, a few raggedy shirts flapped on a clothesline. Aggie could not see who was taking on the wash but surmised it to be her older sister. *Duraine always gots t'be helpin' Mamma,* she reflected. *Can't she see it ain't no use? An' who Mamma gonna get t'help when Duraine up an' marry Aaron in de springtime? I ain't. Just look at us. A body can see it ain't no use.*

Aggie looked down at herself. The ragged smock was the only thing she wore. Her mother said underclothing and shoes were a waste of money in the summertime. "Best save 'em for winter, Chile," she had warned. "Ain't no tellin' what hard times is bringin' dis year."

"Lawdy," Aggie almost laughed. "Iff'n dis ain't hard times, iff'n life ain't hard times, what is? I swear. Looky that house." She studied it. The shanty had stood the pressure of one growing family after another for more years than Aggie knew. Its present load was six human beings now gathering with the day's end for its scant shelter and scantier meal. There were also two dogs and various critters. They had invited none of these animals to join the family, but they still shared the shanty.

Cast off linoleum scraps covered the floor of the shack's one large room to cut the draft coming between the wide planks. They could see dark reddish earth first thing in the morning and last thing at sundown, when the sun was low enough to push its rays beneath the open underside of the cabin.

Aggie could not fathom how this hovel had stood so long with so little sag on such rickety stilts and she did not care to. Instead, her mind's eye switched to the old wardrobe, worn wood chairs and hanging oilcloths which both divided the cabin into rooms and helped furnish them. To any White man Aggie believed the shabbiness of that place would say, "No account niggers." Aggie was sure they would never look beyond that. If they had, they would have found those linoleum covered floors to be spotless, bed clothes ragged but clean, rafters daily dusted, and the whole house clean. But Aggie recalled no White man ever looking and reasoned that they were not inclined to bother. Aggie thought every White man knows how shiftless and dirty niggers are.

Aggie suddenly realized that she was seeing the shack in such dismal light for the first time. She realized a sense of both anticipation and hopeless misery she could not recall having experienced before. She remembered how excitedly she had skipped home after leaving Luke at the pond. She had been eager to share the news of Luke's offer to tutor her with the family. But oppressive reality outweighed that small hope. How she wished she could really believe there was a way to escape the despairing poverty in which she feared she might drown. *I gots t'hang on to dat boy*, she thought. *I gots t'make him like me good 'nough to learn me. I gots t'get away from dis.*

Aggie did not realize how important that quickly made resolution would become. Nothing of substance in that "get away" formed in her head as something to replace the share crop existence. Because Luke said so, she knew that something better was possible. But she did not even know what "better" was. She had never had it.

Throughout the evening and on into the night Aggie dreamed of that "something better", and of Luke. She dreamed of learning, of sharing. She dreamed of Luke's strong, handsome body and magic words. She dreamed of that new, undefinable life he might represent. Still, in the backwash and neglected sharecrop patch of her life, reality continued to do what it had always done. It interceded and fought against any hope. This time, however, a little of its sharp edge was perhaps dulled by transient, forming, and formless thoughts and images of Aggie's coming dreams.

Ironically, this small easing of reality's burden ended when first light accented rather than relieved Aggie's feeling of hopelessness. She had dared in the dark of the night to raise her mind's eye to something better. In the daylight the boundaries to that envisioned horizon returned. They were in the form of a frame of split rail and ragweed and the border of the cotton patch owned by the White man. She believed that the White man owned her family too. He trapped her family on those meager acres while Aggie knew that White men were in full control of her destiny and did not even know she existed. They did not even consider her family to be human. Aggie could no longer handle the conflict between this reality and the embryonic aspirations which had formed since her talk with Luke the previous afternoon. The pull of and need for some hope was too strong. Long after the glow of the moon had been submerged in the dawn's yellow and blue light, Aggie, without even knowing it, began creating in her mind a new world. This inner world was secure and formed around her a growing, glowing image of a young boy on the next farm over.

///

That afternoon, Luke was again sitting under his tree. The sun was again playing its color game through the trees and across the water. But Luke could not seem to get involved with his book. He would read a sentence, look around, and read the same sentence again. Like Aggie, he had not slept well the night before, thinking as he was about teaching her. When he drifted off to sleep, he would soon wake himself up again by dreaming about teaching Aggie. About two hours before dawn, Luke talked with himself and admitted that he was looking forward to the teaching.

He felt strangely drawn to Aggie, and it flattered him that she had asked him to be her tutor. Luke started daydreaming about being a great teacher. Strangely, Aggie was always by his side to hand him a book, a pencil, a piece of chalk, while the class oohed and aahed at his every word.

So most of the day Luke was tired and dreamy. Uncle LeRoy seldom saw Luke like that. He knew when he did that it was best to take over Luke's chores and send him off to do whatever he did all the time down by the pond. Luke offered a grateful glance and wide smile to LeRoy upon being granted his afternoon of freedom and scooted to the pond a full hour earlier than usual.

Yet once there his normal pursuits did not seem inviting. He would almost always swim the sweat away first, but today he did not dare for fear Aggie might be early. He often swung by to pick up a friend or two, but today he did not want them around. He wanted to be alone with Aggie and he did not want his friends to know it. He preferred that his friends knew nothing of either his friendship with Aggie or his promise to teach her. So he waited alone and in silent daydreaming while occasionally skimming a flat rock across the pond.

Then she was there. Aggie surprised Luke even though he was looking for her. She always seemed able to surprise him, to just appear. "Hey, Luke. I sees y'all brung some books."

"Hey, Aggie. Yeah. Here." Luke started to hand the books to Aggie, then thought better of it and laid them in the grass. He sank back down beside them. "Does your mamma know you're here?"

"Yeah. I told her y'all was goin' be here, and she say it okay as long as y'all is stayin' with me. She think a whole lot o' y'all, Luke. My, y'all sure does make an impression on folks."

"Never mind that. Are you ready?" Luke was nervous and eager to get into the more neutral territory of the books. Aggie was making him shy by her presence. She kept looking right at him. He squirmed. "Come on," he covered for himself. "We're wasting time."

Aggie slipped down beside him and let her shoulder touch his. She quickly brushed his cheek and, as on the day before, retreated before he could respond.

"Quit, Girl. If you're going to do that, I'm damned if I'll teach you anything." Luke was flushing, trying to look serious while he smiled to himself.

Aggie reared back and looked at him with wide eyes in feigned indignation. "Oh, what y'all say. Shame, shame on Y'all. Anyway, I's just sayin' thanks. It don't mean nothin'. I's thinkin' y'all afraid bein' kissed by a girl."

"No I'm not. It's just that's not what we're here for. Never mind. Come on. Let's start. Read that word." Luke opened the now well-worn book that his Uncle LeRoy had given him for his birthday. Luke had read it so often he knew most of it by heart. Without thinking, he expected Aggie to follow as his eyes raced from line to line.

"Can't."

"It's 'Peter'. Can't you read at all?"

"I told y'all I can't. Ain't y'all got somethin' easy for me to start with?"

"I guess I could find something, but not today. I'll bring something tomorrow."

"Peter who?"

"What?" Luke loved the way Aggie could seem to pick up the thread of something discussed moments before and, without preface, continue with it as though nothing had been said in the interim.

"Peter who? Y'all say that word is Peter. Peter who?"

"Peter Salem. He was a Black soldier all the way back in 1775, a minuteman fighting with the Massachusetts militia against the British before the Revolutionary War."

"What dat?"

"What?"

"The Revlushun War."

"It's Revolutionary. You don't know that either? It was the war fought when the Americans won freedom from England."

"England?"

"Yeah. Another country across the ocean that used to rule us."

"Like the White man do now?"

"No. The White man doesn't rule us, not exactly, anyway."

"This country, England. It like Africa?"

"Kind of. But Africa's a whole continent."

"I's confused. Let's start somewhere else."

"I didn't know you knew so little. I'm sorry. But you can learn. I can teach you some other things, too."

"Luke?

"Yeah?"

"Was dem dat was fightin' for de freedom White folks? Was dey fightin' de colored folk? Or t'other way 'round?"

"Actually, they were both White. "

"Y'all say! That don't make no sense."

"War seldom does, Aggie."

"I ain't talkin' 'bout de war. De White man can kill his whole self off for all I's carin'. What don't make no sense to me is why Peter Salem fight with de White man. Dey make him fight?"

"He volunteered. He was a free man. Lots of our brothers and sisters were free, then. And lots of them fought right alongside the Whites for independence from England.

"Then how come we was slaves? An' how de White man have all de good things now an' we is made to live like trash with what he don't want no more? It don't make no sense."

"I know, Aggie. You see, back when the United States was part of England, Negroes came to America mostly as indentured servants."

"What dat?"

"That means somebody paid for their passage and they worked for that person a few years to repay him. Peter Salem did that. He was the servant of a guy named Grosvenor during the Revolution and served in the Army with him for seven years."

"When we get to be slaves?"

"It didn't happen all at once. One of the big problems with indentured servants was that just about the time their masters had them well trained in a trade or as house servants, farmers or whatever, their indenture would be over and they would be free to start a life of their own. Both Negroes and Whites would do this. But then the guys they were working for would have to get someone else. They had to train them and stuff. Then they'd be freed, too.

Finally, someone thought of getting Negroes from Africa. Of course there were slaves before then, too. The book says Negroes were being sold in Virginia as early as 1619. Some of these early Negro slaves later earned their freedom. Some of them even became wealthy and owned slaves of their own. Also, some White men did not believe in slavery."

"For real?"

"Yeah, really. But they mostly lived in the North."

"I didn't figger dey was from 'round here."

"Actually, some were. Some Southern White men set their slaves free long before the Civil War."

"But I been thinkin' we was allus slaves, before dere was dat war dat set us free."

"There were some. But the widespread acceptance of the use of Negro slaves only lasted about sixty years."

"Iff'n we be free, then how come we still so poor? How come de White man own all de land? How come we only have de stuff he don't want no more, an' he get de rest?"

"Aggie, that's just not true. Not completely, anyway. My Uncle LeRoy owns his own farm. My Granddaddy owns his own house in the city."

"Dey ain't many what can say dat."

"I admit it's more like you say. Still, we have brothers and sisters who are college professors, scientists, preachers, politicians, statesmen, writers, doctors."

"Ain't many. I never hear of 'em."

Luke got wound up in talking of the brilliant men and women to whom most adult Blacks looked as a hope of better things to come. He tried to relate a sense of history and heritage and unity to Aggie.

But Aggie's entire world until then had been a few acres of truck farm and fear. She could grasp but a small part of the revelations Luke poured forth that late Autumn afternoon. However, she fully grasped the special qualities of this boy with whom her first encounter had been so painful. Her earlier attraction for him began growing toward something more while the words he spoke subtly joined into the faint images of the dream she had begun the night before.

Their chatter wandered from the past to the present, from others to themselves, and finally to just Luke, who talked of the past and of his father and Freddie. Aggie was astounded to hear of Luke's continuing friendship with a White boy. But Luke continued as though such a friendship were natural and common. He continued to talk about the storytellers from his younger years and of the preacher and his wise Grandmother. He talked of his ambition to be somebody important like the men he was reading about in the book his Uncle LeRoy had given him.

As the sun finally faded to an afterglow, Luke quieted. He realized that while he talked, Aggie came still closer, and was now sitting with her head on his shoulder, her hand over the top of his, both of them with a hand on the book in his lap That strange, fearful yet delightful sensation, which had angered Luke at his first meeting with Aggie, crept over him again. This time, he did not become distraught or confused, but only a little restive, feeling a sense of adventure, a tinge of fear. He did not know quite what to do. He thought he should get up but enjoyed being where he was and whom he was with.

For Aggie's part, she knew exactly what she was doing, in a naïve but not quite innocent way. She experienced a warm glow in her own body at the tension in Luke which her close contact revealed. At the same time she felt a shiver in her spine. A welling choke in her throat made it hard to breathe, and she knew she must get up or she might spoil things. "Luke?"

Luke uttered a "Yeah" and needed suddenly to clear his throat and head.

"I's gotta go now. Mamma's goin' worry if f'n I's home too late. It near dark."

"Yeah. You coming tomorrow? I'll bring that other book, I promise."

"I be here." The two children were standing now, dusting and pulling their clothes straight. Impulsively, and for the second time, Aggie stretched up and forward to catch Luke's cheek to her lips. But Luke turned to her for a last word just then and their lips brushed. Luke froze.

"See ya," laughed Aggie and with a quick dancing skip she was gone. Luke stood there a moment longer, not moving at all from the exact pose of the quick kiss. In a wild, excited joy, he stripped his coveralls and cartwheeled to bottom up in the cold, dark pond. He whooped at the wet chill on his flushed brown body and the warmth in his heart.

CHAPTER 13

Awakenings

Dear Luke,

I really do appreciate your letters. Aggie sounds really great. Feels neat to kind of be in love, doesn't it? Wish there was someone around here I could really talk to. Not that I'm not making friends, but I can't really talk to the other cadets about Martha. If word ever got back to the Commandant, I'd be out for sure.

Guess what? I'm a father. Martha had a baby boy, which is the real reason I'm writing this letter. I just had to tell someone. It was over a week ago, but the only way I could find out about it was for her to write me. She is going to stay in Macon a while longer, I guess.

She says the baby has red hair just like mine. . .poor kid. We haven't even decided on a name yet. She wrote me and asked me to name him, but I told her she should choose.

They never let me out of this place. The only way you can get to go is to go home for the weekend or a holiday, or something. And I've no place to go. Howard sold my stepmother's house and was transferred to Hawaii, of all places, to a place called Hickham Field, where he is in supply. Cushy, I guess. It must be really neat there.

Anyway, that was the only place they would let me go, so now I spend all my time here. I don't know yet what I'll do this summer. I almost never hear from Howard, so can't figure he'll want me there. Somehow, I doubt it. Besides, I am not sure I could stand spending the summer with him.

I might be able to talk Howard into writing the commandant and giving his permission for me to spend the summer with my Aunt in Macon. That way, I'd be able to see Martha and my son. But Howard is not anxious for the Commandant to even know I have an aunt there. He doesn't want anything to mess up this arrangement so he might have to take me back, I'm not sure I would go back anyway. I'm nearly eighteen now. One more year and I'll graduate.

Keep writing me, Luke. You're the only real friend I've got. You and Martha. I sure miss her.

Your best friend

Freddie

Luke finished the letter for the fourth or fifth time. He wanted to write right back and tell Freddie to come to the farm for the summer. He wanted to tell him more of Aggie and all they had been enjoying together for the last several months.   When the weather got too cool to be comfortable by the pond, or Luke had too much to do with chores and school to meet Aggie in the afternoon, Aunt Crystal and Uncle LeRoy all but turned the front room of the cabin over to them, retiring in the evenings to the kitchen so that Luke and Aggie could continue their studies together. Luke thought Aggie was making remarkable progress and he kept working on her over the winter to get her to actually attend the school with him. He finally exacted a promise from her that she would try it after summer.

Now that spring was with them again, the two of them had been drifting back to the pond more and more and were managing to spend the last hour of most school days by its familiar waters reading and talking and growing with each other. On Sundays they rarely went there, for much of Sunday was taken with church and after church socials. Often they would have dinner together at Luke's, where the food was better and more plentiful. Aggie seemed to prefer the Powers' company to that of her own house.

But there were Saturdays. Saturdays were different. Luke was usually able to get his chores out of the way by early afternoon and he was always at the pond when Aggie arrived shortly after three. This long afternoon together became their favorite time of the week. Luke's Aunt had come up with something for him to swim in and they spent more and more time in the pond together as the weather warmed. They still found time to fish or talk and teach and read together. Recently they would kiss and hold hands with restraint and timidity. Their feelings deepened daily, their mutual dependency growing with equal steadiness.

/ / /

Aggie arrived at the pond to find Luke strangely absent for a Saturday afternoon. Luke had a growing burden of chores as the planting and weeding season had progressed, and some early vegetables were already ripe for harvesting.

This occupied most of his morning. In the early afternoon LeRoy had announced a trip to town to sell off some of the vegetables and get the season's canning supplies.

By two thirty Uncle LeRoy had loaded the wagon with the last of the truck farm products and a large crate full of various small wooden toys he had carved during the long winter evenings. He was ready to go. "You Comin' with me, Boy?"

"I don't really want to, Uncle LeRoy. I thought I might go to the pond this afternoon."

"You're spending too much time at that pond, Luke. Besides, this time of year, and Saturday, too, you're likely to be seein' the hunters down that way. Come on and go to town with me. You ain't been to town in quite a spell." Luke could see that his Uncle's mind was set. Resigning himself to the trip, he climbed up beside LeRoy in the old wagon.

Dawson was more like something from the past than 1939. Some sections did have painted houses, paved streets and sidewalks of brick. A few signal lights methodically popped up the stop or go signs to the few cars to be seen on the streets.

But most of this was in the White part of this Southern Georgia town. Just coming up from under the depression, that part too looked worn and somewhat neglected. The lumber mill had only been hiring again for about a year. The sparse cotton crop of the last several years had all but closed the once busy depot of the Southern Railroad. One freight per day was now stopping there with perhaps a passenger train pausing for five minutes once a week to take on water and the few Whites with money enough to travel to Atlanta, Savannah, or Charleston.

The part of town Luke and LeRoy entered was worse yet with more roads of dusty red clay than concrete or crushed stone. Few if any had the smoothly laid brick of the larger Georgian towns. Porches of the small stores lining the business street, on stubby stilts of dark weathered and rotting wood, were planked unevenly in ancient Southern pine now splintering and loosened under the constant bombardment of years of bare Black feet treading on their wide, soft grain.

The grey buildings were much like the porches except that the wind and rain and sun were totally responsible for the warped and bleached barn siding on the storefronts. Tired from eighty years without care they clung tenaciously to their studs as though in desperation to rise above old age and fulfill a destiny of protecting their worn human counterparts from the ravages which continually threatened them.

An occasional White man would venture here. Those with money sent their hired Blacks. The poorer would come themselves hoping to bully the Black storekeepers into an unreasonable bargain or steal from the shops and wagons on the street. Few Southern sheriffs would believe a Black accusing a White of such a thing and any Black knew that such an accusation might well end with a lynching.

Through cunning and care, the Black man with goods and services to sell usually managed to fool the occasional White intruder into taking his most inferior offerings. They held the best for the Blacks who relied upon them to feed their families, help clothe them, or lay in other necessities for which they may trade, ask credit, or occasionally spend hard cash.

"Hey, LeRoy. Y'all got your youngen' with y'all today, huh? That boy's growin' now ain't he?" LeRoy jumped down from the wagon to the clay street in front of the store, drew the feed sack over his mules's muzzles and called to Luke to help unload. A quick nod and smile returned Ol' Tom's greeting. Ol' Tom was the chief clerk and owner of this general merchandise store at the east end of the street. It was closest to the line which divided the Black community from the poor White and industrial sections. A mixture of storefronts, sawmills, small weaving mills and a nail factory, warehouses and worn houses were a buffer between the Blacks and the better educated, more affluent Whites uptown. Ol' Tom's store featured a greater variety than most along the block and even sported Dr. Pepper and Coca Cola coolers on the front porch. Candy, home remedy and tobacco counters ran along the rear wall in front of the storeroom. Most of the better off Blacks such as farmers like LeRoy, folks like the preacher, the one Black doctor and the undertaker did their business with Ol' Tom.

But a good third or more of Ol' Tom's business came from the poor Whites who could not afford the finer merchants uptown, and from the bootleg that passed under the counter each day. Ol' Tom acted as a conduit from Black and White home brewers to bootleg drinkers of both races. He knew he was secure in his bootleg operation as long as the Sheriff was his biggest customer.

Ol' Tom's wife took in washing, ironing and sewing. Any work she got from the White women she usually had to collect from their back door and haul back to the store herself.   Still, the business plus the washing and the whiskey kept Ol' Tom and his wife relatively prosperous.

Ol' Tom had the reputation of being fair and neutral. The services he offered to both Blacks and Whites tended to make the store a haven from trouble. This day, however, was going to be different.

Luke continued unloading the wagon while LeRoy began the chitchat and exchange of community and family news which generally preceded the bargaining for the value of the exchange.

Ol' Tom popped a Dr. Pepper from the cooler, opened it and handed it to Luke with a quick, "Here, Boy," and a smile. Stepping inside he drew a jug of whiskey from behind the counter. While checking to make sure no one besides LeRoy was watching he poured two quick ones and offered one to LeRoy. They tossed off the brew and continued to barter.

Luke stood to the rear of the wagon leaning on the wheel nursing the rare soft drink. An occasional White man passed. A group of Black boys came around the corner of the store and clattered and shouted their way across the porch. They cleared or clopped down the steps on the other end and disappeared down the dirt alleyway between Ol' Tom's and the next building. Luke watched after them for a moment, took the final draw on the Dr. Pepper, and turned back toward the wagon to finish the unloading.

"Hey! What're you doing? That's my Uncle's stuff." Luke discovered a stubbly-bearded, red-eyed and disreputable looking White man standing by the wagon devouring a tomato and filling his shirt with more from the basket on the wagon's street side.

"Shut up, Boy. I take what I want. You no account niggers don't need it, don't deserve nothin' anyway." The man leered at Luke, daring him to say anything but "Yessuh, help yo' self', Suh." But Luke did not say it.

Instead, he stepped to the man and grabbed at the tomatoes, intending to return them to the basket. The reek of rotten teeth and alcohol staggered Luke for a minute. Unthinking, he uttered, "Filthy White trash" under his breath, but the man caught the words, familiar as they must have been to him. He shot his hand out and grabbed Luke's shirtfront.

"What'd you say, Boy?" He pushed his face into Luke's, his nauseating hot breath turning Luke's stomach. Luke turned his head away. "Nothing," he said. "I didn't say anything." Elkins lifted Luke to his tiptoes. Again Luke's face was pushed into the nauseating, stench-filled mouth. The bloodshot squinty eyes peered into his, reading the fright beginning to show there.

"You take it back, you dirty nigger trash, or I'll break you in two."

"I didn't do anything, Mister. Really. Please. I just said those tomatoes are my Uncle's."

"Your Uncle's, huh? You want 'em back, do you? I'll show you, you uppity Black little bastard." The man started taking tomatoes and shoving them into Luke's face and ears and rubbing them across his wooly black hair. "There now. You got your tomatoes. Now I'll get mine." The man shoved Luke away, jerking him up short as he released his grip to let Luke fall backward into the dirt.   He placed a worn, heavy hunting boot on Luke's outstretched leg and stomped down while again loading his own shirt with tomatoes.

Luke screamed out loud with pain just as Ol' Tom and LeRoy came running from the store. Black men, women and children were standing there motionless with eyes glazingly burning but shielding their helpless anger. Whites were poking each other, throwing in obscenities and taunts and guffawing heartily at their own wit.

"Mistuh, Suh," shouted LeRoy. "Leave de boy be. He ain't meanin' no harm. Help yo'self to de tomatoes too. I's glad fo' y'all t'have some. But please, Suh, leave---"

"Elkins!" The man straightened tall and spun around at the command from the source of the booming voice behind him. A giant White man in uniform stood there red faced and glaring. His sheriff's badge glinted in the afternoon sun. His right hand rested on his pistol and pulled his shiny black holster belt at an angle just below his immense belly.

"What's going on here?" he bellowed.

"This boy, he got uppity with me, and I let him know what's what. That's all, Sheriff Pulver."

"Okay. You've let him know. Now get. I don't want this kind of trouble in my town."

Ol' Tom and LeRoy both knew Sheriff Pulver did not give a high hoot what any White did to any Black in almost any part of town. But they also knew that the sheriff wanted no trouble from any source which might draw attention to the store and threaten the bootleg operation he had going there. Ol' Tom's relief at the approach of the sheriff had been justified.

"I told you to get!" commanded Sheriff Pulver.

"What about my tomatoes?" a drunkenly brazen Elkins persisted. "That old nigger said I could have 'em."

"That true, LeRoy?"

"Yessuh, Sheriff Pulver, Suh." LeRoy knew that if he contradicted Elkins, more trouble was bound to come, either now or later, when the Sheriff had gone. Right now, all he wanted was to get Luke out of there.

"Then what's your boy doing bothering this White man? Don't you teach your youngen' the proper respect anymore?" Pulver knew full well that Luke had not done anything but needed to find a scapegoat for Elkins in order to cool the White man's anger.

"Yessuh. Goin' punish him good, too. Luke! Get yo'self up, Boy, an' 'pologize to Mr. Elkins here, Go on. Get up."

"Sorry," murmured Luke, trying hard to stand tall on his throbbing ankle, his head and shoulders stained by smashed tomatoes.

"Sorry, what!" sneered Elkins, the mean grin exposing his broken and rotting teeth.

"Sorry, Sir," snarled Luke. He turned to limp off.

"I's sorry, too, Mistuh Elkins, Suh. I's goin' t'whip him good when I gets him home. Don't y'all worry 'bout dat. He goin' learn his place. I promises dat, I does."

"Take your tomatoes, Elkins, and get out of my sight," bellowed the sheriff. Then he turned to LeRoy. "You get that boy out of here. I don't want to see either of you near my town again until you learn proper manners." Turning and shoving Elkins in front of him, Sheriff Pulver started up the street.

"He took the whole basket, Uncle LeRoy."

"I know, Boy. Next time, y'all better just let 'em have what they want. Y'all is better off in the long run that way."

"But it isn't fair."

"No, it ain't. But that's the way it has to be, Luke, if we're to be allowed to live without trouble. That's the way it will always be."

"Maybe. Maybe not. Maybe it's going to change too."

"Ain't no use talking like that, Luke. Leastways, not here, not now."

"But what about the book, Uncle LeRoy? What about the hope?"

"All them brothers and sisters in the book ain't change a thing for the likes of us, Luke. It takes a lot more than a handful of folk to change things for the likes of us.

"And the White man. He runs it. And he ain't about to let Coloreds get enough education to see what could be, and get together to make it happen. No, Son. He owns most everything worth owning, including the law and the government. Except for a near worthless parcel here and there like mine he even owns the land. And if he takes a notion to take it all, he can do that too. That includes mine. Because like I say, he owns the law.

"I don't need that kind of trouble, Boy. So you let them have the tomatoes and things like that because we can grow more as long as we've got the land."

"Amen to that, Brother LeRoy," chimed in Ol' Tom, who reappeared from inside the store with a bucket of water.

Lifting it high, he dumped it directly over Luke's head. "There. That'll cool y'all some an' get rid of most of that tomato. Take another Dr. Pepper with y'all now. Y'all'd best be on your way."

"I'11 settle with y'all later, Tom," said LeRoy as he climbed into the wagon. For the most part the crowd had disbursed by the time LeRoy had claimed his seat. Luke was having trouble pulling himself up. He sank back in pain.

A couple of men were unloading the wagon and slipping in the supplies LeRoy had ordered. One of them stepped around and boosted Luke into the seat. They all knew that Sheriff Pulver would be back any minute to make sure LeRoy was gone as he had ordered.

Finally, Luke and LeRoy were pushing the mules hard to get the wagon clear of town as soon as possible. Luke was tense and tired and angry. He was as angry at LeRoy as at the White trash who had caused it all. He was angry at the fat sheriff who had saved him because even the sheriff had treated him like dirt and allowed Elkins to openly steal from them. Most of all he was angry at himself. His smooth tongue had failed him and he had been humiliated and had allowed his Uncle LeRoy to be humiliated. He would not forget. And he would not accept LeRoy's resigned pronouncement that things would never change. They had to change and he was determined that he would help bring about that change.

"How's your foot, Boy?" Luke was roused by the note of apology and concern in LeRoy's voice, and tried to sound calm in response.

"It hurts a little, Uncle LeRoy.   Seems swollen some. It'll probably be all right."

"That's good. I was afraid he might'a broke it."

"It's okay. Uncle LeRoy?"

"Yeah, Luke?"

"I don't think it has to be this way."

"I know y'all don't, Boy. An' I hope y'all is right. But for the here and now, that's the way things are. And while we're about it, there's something else y'all should know. Y'all know that our folks all think y'all is special, going to be a leader someday. Y'all is smart and educated and talks good. Y'all is quick and young and good looking."

"Maybe. I didn't feel all that smart back there."

"But y'all is. What y'all needs to know is that the White man can see that just as well as the Black.

"I suppose so."

"He ain't gonna admire y'all for it. Truth is, he'11 hate y'all for it. If y'all is really smart, y'all will act dumb in front of White strangers. That's what he expects y'all to do. If y'all don't, he'll fear   you, cause secretly the White man fears that the Black man will one day rise and rule. He sees a Black man showing that he's capable, he fears him more."

"Good. Let them."

"Y'all don't understand. The White man has power. If he fears y'all, he'll hate y'all. If he hates y'all, he'll bring his power down on y'all. He can use the law or ignore it to do whatever he want to y'all, even see you killed. Then what good is all your smarts and learning and high hopes?"

"But then how can we ever improve our lot?"

"Bide our time, play the game and stay together until we're ready."

"When's that?"

"When there are enough Lukes in the world and a really great and brave leader or two, they'll step up and pull us together into a force to be reckoned with. Even then it won't be easy. A lot of folks will be hurt on both sides. A lot will die. But the change will come. Mark time, be patient and keep on getting ready. But don't let a little thing like happened today kill that challenge before y'all are ready to take it on."

Luke sat quietly thinking of what LeRoy had said. He had heard it a thousand times before in a thousand different ways. But now with his hurting ankle and humiliation still with him, it made more sense. It made more sense than anything he had ever heard. After this afternoon he was certain that he wanted to accept that mantle of leadership which he had recently wanted to reject. *But only when I'm ready,* he told himself.

He rubbed his ankle and watched the dancing shadows in front of the wagon, as the sun sank lower behind them.

Luke remembered Aggie and wondered if she had gone to the pond and was still there. He was anxious to sit quietly with her to tell her of the adventure of the day and feel her out on his latest decision about his life and what his uncle had said. He nursed his swollen ankle and fidgeted on the seat of the buckboard as the mules methodically plodded their way toward home. He decided he would go to the pond as soon as he got home to see if Aggie was there.

CHAPTER 14

Premonition and Pain

Aggie had been waiting by the pond for over an hour. She watched for Luke while having dreams of Luke, and of Luke and her together. That dream opened up for Aggie possibilities fed by the stories which Luke told her of a life and lifestyle for which she had never dared to hope. The dreams were still not specific, but a mixed set of images of the things she would like to have. They included the places Luke had described for her in the vivid detail which he knew only from reading. It included things for them to do and greatness for Luke to achieve, for she knew he would achieve greatness. In these dreams she saw herself somehow as the observer and not the participant. In her dreams she was always there by Luke's side, holding his hand and so her position as a mere observer did not bother her.

So engrossed was she in these dreams there by the pond that she was startled to realize that hours had passed and Luke had not come. The dream evaporated and the familiar sounds of the pond intruded upon her ear. She strained to hear the first sign of Luke's approach. But she heard neither the usual spaced-out thump of his long strides nor the faint tune he always whistled without realizing it. She thought he had forgotten.

Yet they looked forward to these Saturday afternoons so much that she considered that impossible. So she began imagining things which might have kept him away. First, she assumed the truth that his Uncle LeRoy had taken him to Town. His courage to go to Town was something she admired in him. She thought she could never bring herself to go with him. But she could recall no mention of extra chores or a trip to Town for this day. She thought maybe he was hurt. She pictured him cutting himself with an axe, or breaking a limb, or falling down the ladder from the loft room of which he was so proud, but which she had never seen. Fear for him took over her imagination until the worst fear of all slipped its sinuous fingers around her mind. The realism of her thoughts caused her to flush and shiver. *He must*, she thought, *have had some trouble with the White man.*

Then it all made sense to her as her mind put together the pieces. She reasoned that if he was injured on the farm, he would send someone to the pond to tell her. So he must have gone to Town. She knew Luke well enough with his vision of personal equality and his talk of a White friend to know he would approach a White man as an equal. She knew that was instant trouble.

She thought she might cut back across the field and up the creek to the Powers' farm. But she was afraid, for she would have to cut across White land to do that. That was something she never did unless she was with Luke. The casual way Luke did this impressed her. He was always saying the Whites would not mind. But still it frightened her. She worried about him each day as she moved to the pond in fear that he would run into trouble on his way there too.

This brought to her mind another possibility for his tardiness and she was overwhelmed with a vision of him lying gut shot in a corn field unable to get help. Again she started to rise and invade those forbidden fields to search for Luke in the corn. But she could not do it and when she realized that she could not, she was ashamed at her own timidity. She was certain that the White man would catch her if she tried alone. She was sure they would accuse her of stealing the corn and probably shoot her.

She could put on the lowered head and contrite shuffle act as well as anybody. By so doing and traversing the center of the road and never even nearing a field, she could feel safe. But could she actually cross the field? Aggie was too terrified of the White man to attempt that alone. She had seen, or imagined that she had seen, too much in her life to think it safe. Worried and ashamed, she waited for someone else to come tell her if Luke was safe, if all was well.

The sun was getting lower. Aggie became concerned about being at the pond alone at dusk. She decided to go home and see Luke in church tomorrow. But Aggie knew that would not do either. Her fears would not be relieved until she was certain that Luke was all right. So she continued her frozen vigilance. A kind of numbness came over her mind, softening the edges of her fear for herself and for Luke. The sun continued to retreat. The day neared its end.

Then it was the time she usually left Luke and started for home. Even aware of this she could do nothing but continue the watch. Her only company was the rising tide of bullfrog bellows, the incessant screech of crickets, and her own fear-filled imagination.

In self-protection against the ensuing dusk, she conjured up pictures of a strong and handsome Luke bounding in his coveralls through the tall grass and cattails toward her. The image seemed so real that she looked toward the fields expecting to see him just there. She could see the wide smile, the strong but tender jaw, the smallish ears, Luke's neat and not too broad nose and the twinkle of his magnetic eyes. She pictured his brown, lightly muscled arms, bare feet which both made her laugh inside and told her by their size that Luke would be a tall man. She felt again the touch of his lips on hers. She imagined his arms around her with his body pressed against hers tightly and his magic words and the heat of his groin exciting her mind and heart and body. So involved was Aggie in this fantasy that when she heard noises she assumed it was Luke. She felt good, and safe, and relieved. But it was not Luke.

Luke was in fact on his uncle's farm painfully trying to help unload the wagon and turn the mules into their small corral. LeRoy was explaining Luke's condition to a flustered Aunt Crystal. He told her they must do something drastic to settle Luke down or there would be more trouble. They finished their work just as dusk pushed the shadow of their small outbuilding to the edge of the house and the kerosene light in the kitchen grew brighter through the back door.

"Uncle LeRoy. I have to run down to the pond for a minute."

"Y'all can't run on that ankle. 'Sides, it's too late for that tonight, what with dark almost on us. Come on in the house."

"But---"

"Luke? LeRoy?" Aunt Crystal's voice from the kitchen interjected, "Dinner's on the table."

Luke protested. "Uncle LeRoy. Aggie's down there waiting."

"She's long gone home, Boy. Your Aunt done call us for supper. Let's go."

"It'll just take me a minute. I've got to be sure she's okay." Luke was shouting back over his shoulder as he limped toward the creek, favoring his swollen ankle.

"Luke! I say 'No'. Y'all come back here. NOW!" LeRoy knew he was wasting his breath and turned to his wife on the back porch. "Lord, Honey, what're we goin' to do with that boy? He don't listen no more, and he is always in trouble of one kind or other."

"He's just growin' up, LeRoy. He'll be all right."

"Ain't goin' to be alright if he keeps talkin' back to the White folks, that's for sure. He came near real trouble today. And now he's headin' across the White's land at this time of day, on the same day when all the White folks surely know about what happened by now, and that good-for-nothin' Elkins being drunk and mean and all. I best go fetch Luke and bring him back."

"I expect you're right. But y'all be careful yourself, LeRoy Honey. And since y'all are goin' anyway, why, check the pond just to be sure that little gal has gone home, too."

"I will, Woman. Y'all keep supper in the oven. We'll be back directly." As an afterthought, LeRoy pulled an axe handle from the outbuilding before starting down the creek path.

"What's that for?" shouted Crystal after her husband. But she got no response.

///

After leaving Sheriff Pulver, Elkins put on a swagger to go with his prize, and slammed through the doors of Kitty's Eatery, a misnamed hole in the wall where men and women of Elkins' vintage congregated.

"Whatcha got there, Elkins?" asked another disreputable everyone called Bubba.

"I got me some prize tomatoes off one uppity nigger," bragged Elkins. "Get me a drink, Kitty."

"What you payin' with?"

"Why, with tomatoes, Kitty."

"I don't need tomatoes, and from the looks and smell of you, you don't need no drink."

"Shut up, Woman. I took all the guff I'm takin' today from that nigger and nigger lovin' sheriff. Keep on me and I'll smack you like I did that boy.

"Whop him good, did you, Elkins?"

"You bet, Bubba. Laid him right out in the dirt. Teach him to get uppity with his betters."

"Oh, I saw you. You sure were brave," came a voice from the back of the room. Harvey Johnson was in the crowd when Elkins began manhandling Luke. But, he had no fondness for sharing space with the law, so he disappeared at the coming of Sheriff Pulver. "I mean, it impressed me. Why, you only had twenty years and sixty pounds on him. Took a lot of guts to knock down that nigger brat and steal his tomatoes. You're quite a man. And what a prize for so huge an accomplishment: A handful of overripe tomatoes from some nigger's garden, probably fertilized with nigger shit."

Rage edged its way up Elkins' body at the taunting. "Shut your face, Johnson. For your information, his uncle gave me the tomatoes. And besides, I'll knock around any goddam nigger I want."

"As long as they're smaller than you?"

"Any size, you sonofabitch."

"How about that, Boys. He'll knock around any size nigger he wants."

"Yeah," piped in Bubba, his face in his beer, "and knock up the ones he doesn't knock around."

"Right, Bubba. Because, sure as hell no White woman would ever lay with the likes of him."

"What'd you say, Johnson? I'll have you know I get all the White women I want."

"Ain't likely there's a White woman in town could stand your smell, Elkins. You see, only the jelly roll, being just as dirty, don't mind."

"Take that back, you bastard."

"What's the matter, Elkins? Truth hurt?"

"Shut up! Kitty, I said gimme a drink." Elkins was upset, but not enough to risk a fight with either of his taunters. Instead, he turned his anger on the woman, and tested his false bravado with the demand for whiskey. But Bubba and Johnson knew they had him on the run and would not let up. "Give him a drink, Kitty. He deserves it for being so brave." The sarcasm dripped from Harvey's words. His back to his tormentor and seeing Kitty reach for the bottle, Elkins struggled against the impulse to rise again to the bait. Instead, he downed the shot Kitty poured him, slammed the glass down on the bar.

"Another!" he demanded.

"One per nigger, Elkins," laughed Bubba, "Which means you've already been overpaid, seeing as how that was only half a nigger you let back talk you."

Elkins grabbed the glass and threw it at Bubba, then whipped a tomato at him and reached for another. Kitty's arm shot across the bar and grabbed his wrist. "Hold it, Sucker. Don't go wreckin' my place, hear?"

"Leggo, Slut! I'm gonna kill em."

"Here" cooed Kitty. Suddenly changing her tactic. "Take this and go off somewhere and cool down." She pushed a full pint bottle in front of Elkins' face. He looked at it, around to his taunters, and back to Kitty.

"Ah, Hell," he said, and tucking the bottle in his hip pocket, swaggered toward the door. "It ain't over, you know," he tossed in as balm for his humiliation and left.

"You and Bubba owe me for a pint, Harvey," Kitty pronounced.

"Keep his tomatoes, Honey. We ain't payin' for nothin'."

///

Staggering half sideways and off track, Elkins kept muttering his bitter profanities against Luke and all Blacks as he stalked an unsteady course toward the Powers' farm. Though the country was familiar to him, the setting of the sun and rising state of drunkenness caused his path to arch wide to the left, bringing him on a collision course with the pond.

Elkins stopped just after passing the stand of hardwoods edging the east side of the water. He stumbled forward a few more steps to get his bearings and turned to look for his direction. It was then that he saw her.

"Another nigger brat," he thought and staggered toward her. Aggie was standing with her arms wrapped around herself, facing the pond with her head back and tilted to the left. She swayed slightly from side to side as thoughts of Luke caressed her mind. Then Elkins reached out and grabbed for her arm. She turned, calling Luke's name and shrieked as the loving apparition of Luke's gentle face disintegrated into the drunken monster she now beheld.

"Now hold on, Girlie. Ol' Elkins ain't gonna hurt you. Just point me to the Powers' place."

"Let go," cried Aggie, pulling hard backward as revulsion wrestled with terror inside her.

"My, ain't we a pretty little nigger," slurred the staggering brute. "Just gimme a kiss, Sugar, and point me towards ol' LeRoy's. C'mon, now." Elkins jerked Aggie to him and pushed his rotten mouth toward her as he pressed her head backward. She turned at contact to feel his rough lips and stiff whiskers bark on her soft, brown cheek. She screamed again.

"Bitch!" cried Elkins. "Give me a kiss or I'll have all of you, I swear."

Aggie jammed her hand between their faces and dragged four long scratches across Elkins' cheek. Groaning and cursing, he shoved Aggie away. She turned to run as she screamed again. Elkins snatched at her, fingers holding the left shoulder of her dress. It tore, but that only slowed her.

Elkins' other hand slammed into her right shoulder and he spun her around. Both hands went to her neck. He started squeezing. "I ain't good enough for you, huh? Just like that nigger Luke, you ain't respectin' your betters. I'll show you something you'll respect, and ain't likely to forget neither." Using his free hand, Elkins loosened his pants and let them slip to his knees. "See this here, you fresh little jelly roll? Bet you ain't seen nothing so delicious and White. You respect that, don't you Honey?"

Aggie's widening eyes beheld more than her ears where only one word had penetrated. That word was Luke, and her mind raced in new terrified directions, searching for some clue as to how and why this creature knew Luke's name. She watched her assailant's arousal in frozen terror. Her mind whirled with the images from the fears for Luke and herself that she had been creating since arriving at the pond. She wished she had taken to the fields, was home, dead, anywhere but there.

Suddenly she realized that dead she soon may be. She felt his grip break from her throbbing neck. The searing pain of his fingernails scraped down her chest. The agony of rough hands grabbed and squeezed her small breasts. The damp heat of blood welled up from the scratches creeping down. She screamed at the rending of her dress and the chill as it fell away, leaving her protected only by thin panties. More filthy words than she knew issued from the foul mouth, words her mind did not know, others it could not comprehend through her fear.

"Looky them little tits, Whore. Bet you do this all the time," panted Elkins as he pushed forward. He shoved his hand into Aggies panties and ripped downward as his hot stale stinking breath putrefied her terror and churned her stomach. Without warning, she threw up all over them both. Elkins boiled and cursed violently again. He threw Aggie to the ground and pounced on her. He jammed his knees between hers. She eyed the White ugly face above her and forced her eyes and mind and body shut to rigid tightness. She lay stiff to wait for the assault.

/ / /

Luke limped gingerly through the tree stands and fields between him and the pond. He crossed the wandering creek several times in a familiar beeline toward his favorite spot and Aggie. He paused breathless and hurting several times and reached down to press at his swollen ankle. He started again. Shortly he eased from a fast walk to a slow limp. His ankle was hurting worse with each passing minute. He sat on a rock by the creek, rolled his cuff up and immersed the foot to the calf in the cool, soothing water. It was then that he thought he heard a scream from the direction of the pond. He stood with his head cocked slightly and moved again. Another scream hit his brain and the resounding signal to his feet numbed the returning pain. Luke shot forward toward the pond. Aggie was the only thought he had.

Coming out of the pine stand to the small clearing near his favorite tree, he saw Elkins, exposed and near raving as he shoved a naked and screaming Aggie to the ground. As Elkins squirmed between her knees and poised for the assault, Luke pushed the ground away and behind with all his strength. He charged through the near dark, head down. Elkins started to thrust just as Luke hit. He threw all his weight into the raping hulk and knocking him sideways. Pants still half down, Elkins lost control of his drunken body and flipped over, bounced on his shoulder and lay prone on his back, naked from the waist to the knees.

Further thought of Elkins fled as Luke winced with a stabbing awareness of the pain in his ankle shooting up his leg to push under his stomach. Nausea, sweating, faintness overwhelmed him at the onslaught, but a new and unfamiliar pain in his heart overcame these. He dragged himself beside Aggie. He reached his hand to her face, gently turning it to him.

"Aggie?" he softly murmured. Unconsciously his hand reached behind him and grabbed the cloth of her torn dress. He pulled it over his body and draped it across hers. "Aggie," he said again, this time a little louder reflecting his fear and pain. But her eyes shifted in her head, toward him.

"Aggie. It's okay. He didn't do it. I stopped him, Aggie. I stopped him." Luke was crying the words now. His gentle tears and gentler reassuring words, to calming away her terror, gave Aggie control and voice once again. Opening her mouth, she screamed wildly and gushed forth sobbing. She threw her arms around Luke and squeezed so hard she left three neat blood lines down his chest and bib, transferred through the remnant of her dress from the deep scratches Elkins had scraped on her chest.

"Ain't that sweet now," growled Elkins, who was standing over them threatening once again. "This here your lover, Sweetie? This here the stud you prefer to White meat? C'mon, nigger Boy. Show me how you do it to her."

Luke scooted backwards, hands and thighs in the dirt. He was afraid to stand on his ankle but was determined to lead this White horror away from Aggie.

"C'mon, Boy. Do it. Hey, ain't you Luke?" Elkins lurched forward and dropped to his knees in front of Luke. "Well, Jesus Christ. Look what's been delivered unto me. If you ain't the same smart-ass little nigger from town. Come back for more, have you? Ain't no big shot sheriff here to protect you now, Boy. You better do what I say. Take 'em off. I want to see if niggers is hung as good as they say."

Luke did not move. He did not take his eyes from the ugly face. He did not blink. Praying silently that the power of his icy hot stare would hold Elkins in abeyance just a few more seconds, he willed as large a wad of saliva in his mouth as he could garner.

Elkins leered and kept talking. "You know what they say, don't you, Boy? They say a nigger's a good stud cock, bein' hung so well. Let's see how you do it, Boy. That'd make your little nigger there like you better'n me, me being White." Elkins leaned forward to rip away Luke's overalls. As his hand touched Luke's bib and tugged, Luke spit as hard as he could right into Elkins' face. Elkins reacted, pulling himself up and back.

Luke dragged himself backward toward the pond. Elkins wiped his greasy sleeve across the saliva covering his mouth and nose. His eyes burned back at Luke's intense black gaze. Opening his mouth to speak, Elkins let his hand fall and it struck the bottle in his pocket. "Now, you filthy bastard," he yelled. "I'll give you what I should have this afternoon. If you won't use it, damn you. I'll cut it off." Smashing the bottom out of the bottle, he thrust it in front of him and charged at the downed and battered boy.

Aggie bit her hand so hard as the charge began that Aggie drew blood. Eyes still fixed solidly on the menacing form of his attacker, Luke rolled and fell back as Elkins thrust the bottle toward his middle. The sharp edge sliced through the side of Luke's overalls, drew a quick red line on the side of his brown buttocks and slammed into the dirt with Elkins sprawled over it. Luke looked down at him. Elkins did not move, but his eyes stared back with a strangely empty stare. Blood oozed slowly on the ground beside LeRoy's boot. The axe handle hung at LeRoy's side, hair and blood clinging to its butt. "Luke! Luke! Y'all okay?"

"Get to Aggie, Uncle LeRoy. Aggie, Aggie." Luke was waving a pointed finger toward Aggie's prone body. Quickly, LeRoy moved to the girl, took his shirt from his back and wrapped her in it. She blinked. He smiled a thankful, tender smile. "She's okay, Son. Just passed out. We'll get her home now."

"What about him? Is he---"

"Dead? Looks to be."

"Oh, God." Luke was looking at the dead man. He wondered at how mean he still looked, lying there staring back at Luke with those cold, unblinking eyes.

"I'll take care of him, Luke. Hey, what's this?" LeRoy realized that Luke had begun to cry. As he moved to the boy, the sobs became convulsive and uncontrolled. LeRoy lifted his nephew to a sitting position and cradled him in his arms, saying over and over, "What' this, what's this? Why it's over. It's over, I tell y'all. C'mon now, Son. Shh. What's this?"

Finally, Luke got enough control of himself to say, "He tried to rape her, Uncle LeRoy. He tried to rape her."

"Did he actually do it?" LeRoy questioned, knowing full well before Luke spoke that he had made the attempt.

"I stopped him." Luke's voice was suddenly guttural and deep like a man's, and full of vengeance.

For the first time, LeRoy fully appreciated of the strength within this thin boy, and the power of the feelings he had for Aggie. *Thank God he has 'em too,* thought LeRoy, *or else he would've stayed home to eat, and that little girl of his would be dead for sure by now.* He rocked Luke back and forth as he thought. As Luke spoke he felt Luke pushing him away, turning him back toward Aggie. "I'm all right, Uncle LeRoy. See to my Aggie."

"I'm gonna get y'all both home. Can y'all walk?"

"Yeah. I think." Luke struggled to his feet and dizzily stepped forward. His ankle gave way and he collapsed to the ground. LeRoy reached down and wrapped his arm around the waist of one, then the other of the two children. Lifting them to their feet, he started home. In a few minutes LeRoy was panting severely and nearly dragging Luke. Aggie pulled away from LeRoy. She moved behind the man and the boy and slipped Luke's other arm over her shoulder. LeRoy stopped and lifted Luke a little higher, pulling the boy's arm over his own shoulder as well. In this way, through the dark and across White man's fields to which Aggie gave not one thought, the two of them brought Luke home.

///

With Crystal tending Aggie, LeRoy got Luke to bed and hitched the wagon. He threw a rope and a gunny sack into the back. Then he called for Aggie so he could take her home.

As she came out the back door, a worn and sad little Aggie climbed the ladder to Luke's loft for the first time. Creeping silently to the groaning form in the bed in the room she had thought of so often, Aggie leaned over and laid her head beside his. "I love you," she whispered to his sleeping face.

"I love you, too, Aggie." he replied, fully awake. A fresh tear re-stained Aggie's just washed cheek, but this was neither of fear nor terror. After all that had happened to Aggie this night, her last tear was one of happiness. She climbed down the ladder and out into LeRoy's wagon and soon was in the arms of her own mother.

A hollow, bubbling, gurgling sound was all the testament Elkins got for a eulogy. After he wrapped him in burlap and tied him tight with the rope, LeRoy heaved him into the pond. He was a lone Black man in the middle of the night who had just killed a White man. He looked at the pond which was the favorite place of a Black boy Elkins had tried to kill and a Black girl he had tried to rape. LeRoy watched him sink, shook his head and hoped this marked the end. Somehow, he knew it did not.

CHAPTER 15

Lesson I, Lesson II

The seasons came and went with small notice and came and went again in Southern Georgia. Life changed little for most. The Whites verged again on prosperity as a new decade entered, and more Blacks pulled away from starvation. But the Whites still controlled the world and the Blacks still feared and resented them. There were exceptions.

Whites like Elkins still roamed drunk and penniless. They survived on prejudice as a point of pride in a self whose whiteness lent the only glimmer of imagined superiority and self respect. When that failed as false assumptions often do, they drank their courage from a bottle, and boasted of false achievement. They sought out "niggers" to harass, just as they always had. If they had not had Blacks, they would have found someone else just as Hitler had found the Jews at that same time half a world away. For that is the way of some men, regardless of their color or religion.

For each of these, there are tens of thousands content to live out their lives in a quiet struggle for happiness. They seek to assure that the way things are is the way things stay as long as they themselves are comfortable and secure. From each ten thousand of such are a few who will grow with life and prosper by understanding it. Through personal drive or circumstance or both a few of those will rise to greatness or near greatness. Most however will remain anonymous while still moving humanity along a little.

Such men and women exist today and will tomorrow. In all of this, humanity must have faith. That such people existed in 1941 is a certainty for this is history. Anyone can read in books about those who achieved fame for their contributions. Soon forgotten are those whose contributions were less spectacular if no less remarkable within the framework of their lives and circumstances. One such man was LeRoy Powers.

As a Black man in a White world, LeRoy was remarkable because he managed to keep his own farm in a depression. He was remarkable because as the depression lessened, he not only prospered but was able to buy land from a White man. He was unusual because he accepted leadership in his small community without thought of reward or power. He sought to ease the burden of those whom he led. His most important contribution to humanity, however, he felt to be his raising of Luke.

Luke seemed headed for greatness. Luke possessed magnetic charm, intelligence and quick judgment, compassion and the ability to be assertive on principle or to seek justice. Though these things seemed inherent in Luke, he was but sixteen. He was not fully a man. The depth of his compassion, the breadth of his judgment and broadness of his intelligence were far from fully tapped. They were only really appreciated by his Aunt and Uncle and Aggie, especially Aggie.

Aggie knew and loved Luke far beyond normal for a fifteen-year-old girl. Luke taught her to read, tried to teach her of the world as he understood it, broke the mystery of numbers for her, attempted to show her that not all Whites were bad and not all Blacks were good. In Aggie's simple way of thinking, life was the here and now, a holding-on experience. Change and growth were something one realized had happened, either with satisfaction or regret. They were not normally something to be planned. Yet Aggie enjoyed the dreams Luke shared with her in intimate detail in his gentleness, or boastful bravado in his strength. She knew that she would follow him no matter where those dreams carried him. With him as her strength, she could carry on in her own world of the moment. She was fully confident that Luke would fill each moment with protection and joy. She knew that once she had Luke as her husband she would never again have to face or fear the real world, the White man's world. She was certain Luke was strong enough to do that for them both. It was the constant in her life which sometimes allowed her to accept change.

But Aggie could not understand why Luke still believed the White man to be good. Had not the White man killed his father, almost killed him twice, tried to rape her, almost carried LeRoy away for murder after discovering a body in the pond?

Aggie often thought about that day. Although she did not witness the confrontation with the Sheriff, she found out about it later from Luke. Like him, she spent several days in bed after their ordeal. But Luke heard the whole exchange with the Sheriff from his loft and recounted it to Aggie as only Luke could.

"It was Sunday afternoon, Aggie. I had been asleep most of the day and finally waked up to the afternoon sun shining across my face through the window at the end of my room. By the heat in the room I knew it must be another gruesomely hot day. I almost called for Uncle LeRoy or Aunt Crystal to come open a window but I decided to get up and do it myself.

"I tried to sit up but couldn't. Lord, Aggie, you wouldn't believe how they had me trussed up. My whole middle was a giant white stripe of bandage. What wasn't under tape was under pain and ache. Every joint was stiff, sore or swollen. I figured if I could just swing my legs over the side of the bed, I'd be able to hobble to the window. No luck there, either."

"Because of your ankle?"

"Right. Every time I tried to pick it up, it throbbed even more. I pulled the covers away and found it in a cast. I swear I don't remember the doctor coming. But Uncle LeRoy says he had come that morning and suspected a hairline crack in the ankle bone and some busted blood vessels were causing the swelling. Uncle LeRoy didn't tell the Doctor about all the walking and running I'd done to get you away from that no account White trash."

"Oh, Luke. I'm so sorry."

"No. No. Don't say you're sorry. I'm okay. It's just that we had to let the doctor think it was broken so bad by Elkins, you see, because as far as anybody around here is concerned, I went to bed as soon as we got home from town. Uncle LeRoy and Aunt Crystal stayed right with me clear through until the doctor came. Covered as I was with dirt and tomatoes when we left town, who's to say I didn't get this cut on my rear right there, if anyone was to ask."

"Did anybody?"

"I'm getting to that. Anyway, I was just about to call out for someone to come open the window when I heard a car. Knowing absolutely nobody with a car, I figured it must be a White man."

"A White man? In a car? Right there on your farm?"

"Stranger things have happened." As he often did, Luke was enjoying weaving a story web from a simple incident and he was eager to build the punch line in his tale. In an exciting chain of embellishments, he described how he heard the fat sheriff approach the house. He told of the expressions he conjured on his Aunt and Uncle's faces, and of the shuffling and sparring which led to the actual accusation. Uncle LeRoy flatly denied the accusations and insisted that the sheriff knew he was a gentle and honest man who respected all Whites as his betters.

The revelations by the sheriff were that Elkins' body had floated to the surface of the pond. The evidence of a struggle, the blood and the wagon tracks leading to and from the road which passed very near the Powers' farm all pointed to trouble for the Powers. LeRoy countered that the road passed by nearly every farm in the district, and coincidentally, through the center of town.

"Finally," continued Luke to Aggie's rapt attention, "The fat old sheriff pulled out his second to last card. He slammed the very rope and sack Uncle LeRoy had used to wrap the body in right down on the table in front of them and accusingly questioned them as to ownership. Ol' Uncle LeRoy stood there with a blank, questioning look on his face, and with his best mimic of the poor, dumb but honest nigger, said, 'Why, Suh, I ain't got no rope like dat. Dat too fine a rope fo' Black folk. Dat look like a White man rope t'me.' I tell you Aggie, the sheriff must have been livid. He shouted back, 'What about the sack?' LeRoy had replied, 'But Suh, dey's zillions o' dem sacks, an' mo'. I ain't knowin' who dat 'ticular one belongin' to, no Suh. I's sure it ain't me.'

"Well, Aggie, despite these denials, I could almost smell the sense of victory on the sheriff. I couldn't smell any fear from LeRoy, though. Strangely, I heard Aunt Crystal humming in the kitchen as though nothing at all out of the ordinary were happening. But then the sheriff pulled off his coup d'état."

"His what?'"

"Coup d'état. Big card, kind of. It's French."

"Oh, Luke. You're so smart. What'd the sheriff do?"

"He pulled that bloodied axe handle out of the bag. Seems Uncle LeRoy had left it lay there in the mud. 'This ain't your axe handle, either, is it LeRoy,' he said. LeRoy came right back with, 'What I needs wif dat thin'. Why, it look new t'me, and I ain't got but jus' one ol' axe, an' it done got a good handle on it already. Dat mine? Lawd, Sheriff, Suh, I ain't no rich man, what can 'ford to have spare axe handles jes layin' here 'n dere.' Honestly, Aggie, I could hardly keep from bursting out laughing. LeRoy was pouring on the 'nigger talk' so smoothly, you would have thought he really talked that way all the time.

"Anyway, the sheriff knew LeRoy was guilty, and LeRoy knew he knew. The trick was to keep playing innocent, keep reminding the sheriff that LeRoy was a gentle and honest and respectful Black, and hope that the sheriff considered that Elkins to be less trouble dead than alive. Nobody but the sheriff had made the connections between the evidence and LeRoy. When it boiled down to whether or not the sheriff could just walk away or would arrest my uncle on the circumstantial evidence, it seemed to be whether Uncle LeRoy could prove he had been home all night. That's where I realized I could help. I called to Aunt Crystal in my most pathetic, weak voice, saying my foot hurt terrible, and I had had nothing to drink since I got back from town yesterday afternoon and I went straight to bed."

"Why'd you do that?"

"Well, to change the subject and start an alibi for Uncle LeRoy. I figured if I could convince the sheriff that I had been there in bed and tended to by my worried Aunt and Uncle all night, he might change his mind about LeRoy's being guilty.

"LeRoy picked up on what I said and knew what I was doing. He played right along and shouted back at me, 'What Y'all say, Boy? I's been bringin' ya'll water up an' down dat ladder all de night long. Why, I'd jes done managed to git uppen de ladder when Y'all ask fo' yo' fust drink.'

"The sheriff interrupted with, 'What's this? What's goin' on?' to which LeRoy answered, 'Why, Suh. Yo didn't know? Dat Elkins done stomp on my boy's ankle yestiddy and broke it clean. He couldn' walk and it hurt somepin fierce all de night through, 'til finally we go on out dis mornin' afore breakfas' an' drag Doc Etters down here fo' a looksee. He say it broken, all right, wif a bruise like y'all wouldn' believe where de boot come down. It be a shame, a shame I say.'

"Well, Aggie, then the sheriff wanted to see. I hadn't figured on that. I thought we'd been discovered. Of all people, the sheriff would surely know that the rest of the cuts, bruises and scratches all over me was more the work of a tussle by the pond than from simply being knocked down in the street."

"Lord, Luke, what'd you do?!"

"Well, that fat old sheriff started up the ladder, just huffing and puffing and calling for me to come down there. Of course I pleaded that I had a broken foot and couldn't move an inch from the bed. He said he thought I was lying just like my Uncle, and I heard rung after rung creak under his weight. I stuck my encased foot out from under the covers and let it hang slightly over the edge of the bed. I pulled the blankets up to my head to hide the rest of the bandages on me. I don't mind telling you I said a little prayer. Well, the Lord was smiling on us all that day, Aggie, to make up for the day before, maybe, because that old redneck sheriff came on grunting and huffing and puffing until his immense body was about halfway through the trapdoor, then he stopped."

"Why'd he do that?"

"Dear Aggie, you would not believe why. Because he got stuck, that's why."

"Stuck? Did you say stuck?" Aggie laughed out loud and a wide grin spread across Luke's face. He continued.

"That's exactly right. All he could see was my big white cast just hanging there over the side of the bed. I thought to moan a little for effect, but figured I'd better keep holding my breath in case I started laughing. I heard that old boy curse under his breath, and then what surely was the ripping of his shirt as he squeezed his way back through the hole and tried to gather his dignity."

"What'd he do then?"

"Why, he was too chagrined to argue, and having seen the cast and who knows why, really, he just muttered something about not believing a word of it. He told Uncle LeRoy to stay away from town for a while and waddled out to his big sheriff's car and left."

Aggie clapped her hands together in delight. Luke said, "I could hear my Aunt and Uncle sighing and giggling to themselves. I myself laughed out loud at the stupid fat redneck being stopped from finding the truth just because he was too fat to reach it. I've got to admit, though, that a good part of my laughter was relief."

Luke laughed at Aggie's delight in the story, and afterword, the two of them often made jokes about the whole thing. Both hid pain which haunted their thoughts concerning the uglier side of the event by telling just such jokes. Luke viewed the experience as a learning one, however, and not necessarily as Black versus White. He knew Elkins was trash and was drunk when he attacked Aggie. But he had not experienced Elkins' heavy body being forced upon her. The horror of that memory stayed only with Aggie.

So it was different for Aggie. She hated and distrusted Elkins as a White man more than as a drunken rapist. The emotions she felt concerning that night were more associated with White men for whom her general feelings of fear and hate grew from day to day. She strengthened her image of Luke as her savior and protector by his actions that day. They grew to a point where Aggie became even more dependent on Luke to supply a framework for and substance of the fantasy life Aggie was creating so she could cope with her fears.

Sometimes she would dream that Luke was gone. She would awaken in terror, as though all the Whites from whom she imagined Luke was protecting her were charging in to avenge themselves for Luke's unforgivable intelligence and cunning. This was something she knew most Whites feared in any Black man. After such a dream, Aggie would cling even more worshipfully to Luke. Luke himself welcomed such devotion and gladly fulfilled the role of protector Aggie demanded of him.

Awakening

As the season moved toward summer, Aggie clung even more worshipfully to Luke. Luke himself welcomed such devotion and fulfilled the role Aggie demanded of him. He continued to teach her and interpret the world for her as he saw it. He tried to break through her fears to show her humanity as a mixture of good and bad, weak and strong all across the color spectrum.

She would nod her understanding but did not always believe. Luke knew that she did not and probably never would. This saddened him deeply, and he constantly renewed his resolve to relieve her of her fears. He did his best to protect her from them. So Luke kept trying. He delivered logical or emotional oratories on the subject as though he were a preacher.

Aggie was not the only one aware of Luke's growing preaching abilities. There were his Aunt and Uncle whom he entertained with one discourse after another night after night over the supper table. There was the preacher himself who worried that Luke may be a little too tolerant, a little too idealistic in his view of Whites. Like most of his congregation, the preacher handled Whites with cunning and care but seldom openly. This was to him a key to the survival of his Colored congregation. He believed that Blacks must camouflage their intelligence, worth, pride and true skill if they were to get along in the White World. He knew that the Whites would often just as soon kill an "uppity nigger" as look at one. He knew a secret most Blacks had not realized. The Whites feared them, too.

Luke began to understand this first when he met Freddie. This slowly helped Luke see the similarities between Whites and Blacks. By being who and what he was, Freddie helped Luke see Whites as individuals. From this, Luke reasoned that to view either Whites or Blacks as a homogeneous group was dangerous and inaccurate. It was a breeder of the fear and hate which existed below the surface between the two races. He knew that ultimately dealing with this stereotype was key to conquering prejudice before they could achieve peaceful and equal participation in a common society. So he continued to preach his philosophy of individual worth and to practice a lifestyle of equality.

It was this "equal terms" approach which most worried the preacher about Luke. His experience told him it was a rare White who could view or accept a Black as his equal. Even those Whites who would help the Blacks at some personal risk usually considered themselves separate and superior.

The Preacher knew that despite his intelligence and grasp of humanity, Luke could not or would not face this. Luke's attitude was definitely an inspiration for those brothers and sisters with whom he came in contact. They did not always accept what Luke professed regarding the equality of all humans as something the Whites would inevitably accept. But they still drew hope from his words, strength from his attitude and courage from his forcefulness. It was this very hope that encouraged Luke to accept and find worth in each of his brothers and sisters regardless of their opinions of themselves. It was this hope which encouraged them to seek him out and cultivate his friendship.

This did not always hold true for his friends and family. They based their own view of the world on more direct experience than thought. Those old enough to be his parents or grandparents often responded with skepticism about life and mankind. They were old enough to have known most of the pain and degradation to which their people had been subjected. This was true even though they had seen a few special members of the Black race rise above their burdens to greatness.

They were convinced of two things when it came to Luke. First, they knew he had the qualities of greatness. Second, they hoped that this greatness, when combined with that of other Blacks yet unnamed, might raise some future generation from the bondage that forced them to suppress talent to survive.

The preacher knew how the congregation felt about Luke and he shared their hope. He believed in the uniqueness of this handsome and commanding boy. So when Luke exhausted all the resources of the six grades in the local Black school, the preacher worked with Luke's Uncle and teacher. They found for Luke a wealth of reading, mathematics and social commentary material. Luke's thirteenth birthday present was only the beginning. The Preacher made himself available repeatedly to discuss the readings with Luke. He repeatedly found the depths of comprehension and understanding his pupil displayed to be far beyond his own. Far from resenting this, the preacher marveled at it. Sometimes he became the pupil instead of the teacher. Some thoughts expressed by Luke even became the basis of sermons.

On one such occasion, the Preacher used one of Luke's ideas to deliver an especially forceful and inspiring sermon on accepting mulattos as brothers. Luke thought they represented the ultimate blending of the races. After church, one parishioner said he did not really agree but thought the message inspiring for a people seeking equality. Then the man added, "Sounds like y'all been talkin' to that Luke Powers again, Reverend. We sure know it when y'all does. Y'all is a powerful speaker yourself, but with his thinking behind y'all, y'all is downright inspirin'."

This flabbergasted the Preacher. It was Luke's thesis which he had preached. Luke had presented the idea as a kind of metaphoric illustration of equality of Black and White within certain contexts. Symbolically it represented a touch point, a linkage from which they could discover future commonalities. Luke often did this through the stating of the obvious, such as blood and physiology. Sometimes he used less obvious but common emotions such as the need for deity worship. His premise was that both races directed this need toward the same God. The mulatto example was the most symbolic he had offered, and the Preacher marveled at its freshness when expressed this way. So he had used it. That usage revealed to him not only that his congregation knew when he was using Luke's ideas but preferred them to the sermons based on those ideas to his own.

Still, the Preacher worried about Luke. Not that Luke was straying, in fact he was steadfast in his growth. Not that Luke's ideas were dangerous, for although they were, he thought he could control that. What bothered the Preacher was that Luke insisted on living his ideas as though they were reality. Again, the Preacher knew that a Black could not do so in the presence of Whites. Yet Luke's dangerous assumption that he and they were equal caused him to discount events like the Elkins incident as only the act of a drunken bully. He truly believed that the same power and influence he thought he held over Blacks he could exercise with Whites. The Preacher and LeRoy had contrived to keep Luke away from Whites during the two years since the Elkins incident, so Luke's testing of this belief had been more by intellect than experience.

Luke received reinforcement of his ego from his peers, the congregation and particularly Aggie. This erased any doubt that he could handle himself equally well with any group regardless of color. That was basic to his view of life. The preacher believed it was not conceit but humility which made Luke feel capable of dealing with Whites. In viewing all humanity as equal, he viewed himself no better or worse than anyone.

So the Preacher feared that Luke was on a collision course with the overwhelming reality of the true way to coexist with the Whites. If the Whites noticed Luke's views or his methods of expressing them, the Preacher felt sure that this collision would occur. This would threaten the bright hope Luke had for himself and the Congregation. Even more disturbing, the Preacher knew that if they lost that hope, the Congregation would be far worse off when that hope shattered than they would have been if Luke had never brought that hope to them.

The fact was that Luke had enormous influence over the Congregation. The Preacher felt responsible for both Luke and this influence, for he had tutored and encouraged the boy. He was unsure what to do about it and often found himself preoccupied with the dilemma.

Ironically, the comment received after church the day he preached Luke's metaphor of the mulatto opened his mind to a possible solution. He decided to talk Luke into becoming a preacher. He mulled this solution over. He talked with LeRoy Powers and Luke's old teacher and constantly warmed to his crystalizing idea. He thought it would be relatively simple. Luke often spoke of his desire to preach. For a long time most members of the Congregation assumed that this would be his vocation.

Lately Luke softened his belief that he could lead his people from their current bondage by changing the Whites' general attitude. The Preacher perceived this change shortly after the general community became aware of the Elkins affair. But the Preacher knew Luke could apply all his talents to the vocation of preaching. He believed that the ministerial and teaching side of the calling would appeal to Luke's romantic notion of leading Colored people from the shadows. He hoped that concern for and responsibility for his own congregation might help Luke see the dangers under which they must live. He might recognize that those dangers existed for him as well. Finally, the Preacher reasoned that if the time ever came when the Congregation accepted Luke's ideas, he would have the stature, education and respect necessary for him to assume a leadership role. The Preacher hoped that through ministry, Luke may arouse in the people an appreciation of their own self-worth. He believed the strength this would give him would hasten that prayed for day of equality.

One problem remained. Luke was shying away from being a preacher at the very beginning of his most formative years. Luke apparently now assumed that he would not even go to college, for that was far too expensive. He had expressed the thought that he might continue his self-education and teach, lead or as he had put it one day, "charge through history as the conqueror of bigotry." But preach? His adolescent pipe dreams had not included such pursuits for a while now, and the preacher did not quite know how to convince Luke to choose the vocation.

As he frequently did, the Preacher approached Luke's uncle with the problem. "Trouble is, Brother LeRoy, how am I going to convince him? He knows he's smarter than me and thinks himself wiser, too. And in some respects, he is. But he's still just a boy, with a boy's idealistic vision of the future and life. He has an unbound sense of his strength and little appreciation of his own mortality. For all his reading, he hasn't been two miles from here in eight years. What does he really know of the world? What of the world, therefore, can I use to persuade him to preach?"

"Well now," mused LeRoy, "I been watching and helping this boy grow for eight years, and I'm here to tell y'all there ain't but one thing to do if y'all really want to show him the Light. After that, it's up to him. If y'all do what I say, and it works like I'm thinking and he has the faith for a true calling, why I expect y'all have got yourself a preacher-to-be."

"And if it doesn't?"

"Then, why he's near a man, and he will have to do what a man does. That is, he'll just have to find his own way."

"What is this thing you think we've got to do, Brother LeRoy?"

"Why, y'all got to get him to think it's his idea. If he takes the bait, y'all might even try and talk him out of it. But not too hard, now."

"That might work at that. But what're we going to use for bait?"

"Why, let him do what he likes to do best, anyway. Let him preach. Make up some reason why y'all can't one week and tell him how y'all'd be mighty grateful if he could do it for you. Y'all know Luke will never turn away a chance to do a body a favor."

"You want him to actually preach, on a Sunday morning?"

"Yessir. Why not? The folks will just love it. He'll see that they do, and that's the bait."

"I don't know. It might not work. Or it might take more than one time."

"That's OK, isn't it? Y'all are getting the preaching done and helping Luke at the same time. Why, it might even become a habit with the boy, something he'd sorely miss if he had to quit it."

"I see your point, Brother LeRoy. It might be just the thing at that." The more the preacher thought about it, the more he liked the idea. "When should we do it?"

"Let me tell y'all. A week from Sunday that boy's going to be sixteen. Now, what nicer birthday present could y'all give the boy than to let him climb up in that Ol' pulpit and talk his fancy talk to all the folks?"

"Mighty slick, Brother LeRoy. I can see how you come to do such a good job raising that boy. So you're saying that if he gets the feel of preaching, of having all those people and be their counselor---"

"I don't know about counselor, but I know my Luke. If he does in that pulpit what I think he'll do, why, just a little nudge at the right minute will make him say he might want to preach again. He might even say he want to be a preacher. Then all we've got to do is tell him how smart we think he is to think of that, and what a fine thing he's doing and what a grand preacher he'll surely make."

"Let's do it."

"I'm right with y'all, Brother. Right with y'all."

The first thing Luke did when he heard the news was to tell Aggie. Then began the most confusing ten days of his life. For the first time someone challenged him to make an intellectual statement beyond his extemporaneous postulating with the preacher or Aggie. Now he had a chance to say something important to the whole Congregation.

At first he thought of things he could say, styles he could use to impress the Congregation with his powers and command of the language. In his youthful way, he daydreamed of their accolades and wonderment at the prodigy among them. He considered the glory which might be his. But when he shared these arrogant boasts with Aggie, he caught a glint of disappointment in her eye.

"What's the matter, Aggie?"

"Luke, Honey. I know you're smart. So do the folks at church. You don't need to impress either me or them. Everything I know, even the way I speak, you taught me. I know you're strong. I know you can speak well. Lord knows you've wrapped me around your finger with your wonderful words for years. Remember what the Bible says? 'The greatest of these is love.' That's 'Love' not conceit. I don't want you to tell me how good you are. I want you to tell me how good I am. I don't want you to tell me of your ambition, I want you to tell me of my hope. You didn't used to be so conceited. You didn't used to be so stubborn, so always right. Sometimes simple folks like me can be right, too, you know."

"I'm sorry, Aggie. I know that."

"The preacher hasn't asked you to do this to glorify yourself. His compliment to you is in his asking. He is sure that you have something to say to the people which will mean something to them, which will help them, which will give them some of the feelings of pride and worth and hope of which you have so much."

"What are you trying to say, exactly, Aggie?" Luke was becoming very uncomfortable at what he was hearing. His adolescent pride and ego were being challenged. Yet he had to admit to himself that at least there was some truth in what he heard. Aggie continued.

"Just, well, just that most of us don't have your vision, your sense of the needs of others, your ability to find the root of a problem or condition and tackle it. These are your greatest gifts from God, not your words. And He didn't give you those gifts to use for your own gain. He gave them to you so you could help the rest of us get a little joy from the meager life we have. At least that's what I think. As to your fancy words---"

"Why do you keep saying that?"

"Because your words are fancy. Most of us are inspired by your ideas but still do not understand some of your words. You express your ideas in grand words that sometimes have no meaning for a lot of us."

"I didn't realize. I'm sorry, Aggie"

"I think, Luke, and I don't ever want to hurt you, but I think sometimes you use those words just to impress people. And you usually get away with it. But not with me, Luke. Not anymore. I always used to be impressed with what you said. But now, knowing you like I do, I can tell when you are really saying something important to you and when you are just saying words to hear their sound. I think maybe some others may, too. They might forgive you because you are so young. But I cannot, for I love you and I know you are better than that. I think you are letting yourself and your listeners down when you talk that way."

Luke was hanging his head, staring at the ground, listening intently to Aggie's wisdom for the first time in a long time. It pleased him that that Aggie had the wisdom she was offering. It surprised and impressed him. He respected her for it and for her courage at saying it. It made him love her even more. "I hear you, Aggie, and you are right. I am a selfish fool."

"I didn't say that."

"But it comes down to it."

"No. It comes down to sometimes you do foolish things. I have done foolish things. I have had foolish ideas, silly dreams. You have come to me and helped me see them for what they are. So I come to you now and---"

"But you don't let go of your most foolish dream, Aggie, your attitude about Whites. I am afraid, so afraid that it will get you hurt."

"Yes," replied Aggie, "Just as I am afraid that your attitude about them will get you hurt. That is one we will both have to work on. You have not convinced me you are right. Although I pray you are, I do not believe the Whites will ever consider us their equal."

"But we are and---"

"I'm not arguing with you there. You told me once that it is not what 'things' are that count. It is what they are perceived to be. And Whites do not perceive you to be equal."

"That's partially true. That is why I cannot understand how you can feel the way you do about Whites. Your perception of them is just out of line with the facts."

"It's not out of line with the facts as I see them. It's not out of line with my family barely existing by working from sunup to sundown on some White man's land while he keeps getting richer and richer off our labor. It's not out of line with my being deliberately chased as a small child by the White hunter's dogs. It's not out of line with my nearly being raped by a White man."

"But those are isolated instances. That Whites did them is incidental."

"Maybe so. But the fact remains that those so-called isolated instances are the only times I have ever had direct contact with Whites, or that Whites have come into my world. I never yet met a White who one way or another wasn't out to take from me or hurt me. No, Luke. It is your perception that is wrong. You perceive yourself as an equal, and you are. But to perceive them as seeing you as an equal? Take another look. Show me."

"Then what am I to believe? On what am I to hang my faith? What hope is there?"

"Only that we can be happy together, from day to day while it lasts, Luke. That is our hope. And that someday things will change for us."

"Oh, Aggie, you're so wrong. We can be more. Others have done it before us."

"Yes, Luke, you can and probably will. But you will be hurt, deeply and permanently hurt in the process. I don't know if I can stand that."

"I won't be, Aggie, I promise. I won't be."

"We'll see. I don't think you can promise that. But I don't want to think about it anymore." Aggie felt the crack in her dream world beginning to show. It was that same fissure she was always covering over, the one that came out at night in her nightmares. She quickly patched it the best she could and turned the subject back to the sermon. "About the sermon, Luke. Give us a message with something to reach for, a reason to hope. Give us a simple message about hope that we can understand. And don't go preaching down to us."

"I wouldn't. Geez, Aggie."

"You wouldn't on purpose. But you might if you didn't think about it. I'm asking you to think about it. Your Uncle LeRoy is a simple Black farmer, but he has had the wisdom to see the promise in you. He and your Aunt love you so much that they sacrifice and risk so you can become educated and use that talent. If we are all human therefore all equal, doesn't that include you? Is everybody, White or Black, equal to each other, but below you?"

Luke looked at Aggie, his eyes glazed with hurt and confusion. Was he really so bad that she felt she had to keep pushing and pushing her thought? Was she really so afraid he would dishonor himself? She was partly right, and he was angry with himself for having felt about the sermon as he had felt. But he needed to think through what she had said. He felt he would have come around to the approach of which she was speaking.

Suddenly Luke was angry at her lack of faith in him. In self defense, he allowed his hurt to join with that anger and turn it to a juvenile rage. Luke looked at Aggie. His eyes burned with that rage. They burned through her face to the dust of the reddish Georgia earth behind her. Then, fists clenched and reddish-brown veins standing in his neck, he walked away from the one person besides himself he loved most. He felt hate for the way she had made him feel about himself. He felt self-loathing for that hate.

Luke slept little that night. His anger had turned inward again, much as it had the first time he had met Aggie down at the pond. His thoughts turned to that time, *nearly three years ago come Sunday a week*, he thought. The gentle words of his Grandmother returned to him. "Love thy neighbor as thyself." Her words and Aggie's comment, "The greatest of these is love, not conceit," tumbled together in his thinking. He thought of that thirteenth birthday, and the ensuing three years since then. He thought of how his Grandmother should be there to hear him from the pulpit, and he was afraid that she would never be there again. He wondered, *what would my poor dead Grandmother have thought of my arrogant outburst.*

Look at it as self-love, he imagined her saying, *then you can learn from it how to love your neighbor*. He mused at this simple but profound idea. Recalling his Grandmother's words, he remembered how they helped him accept his own shame, forgive his own weakness and find the courage to do what he must do. *And again*, he thought, *what Grandma said gave me direction. Her wisdom is simple and profound, as is Aggie's. Their wisdom was proved today to be far greater than mine.* Suddenly he knew that Aggie was right, and it fully justified her fears about his sermon. He had thoughtlessly acted like a supercilious hypocrite, so impressed with himself for "deserving" the "right to preach" that he had forgotten the great responsibility it placed on him. He thought of the great honor it laid before him. Now in retrospect, he was not at all sure he deserved that honor.

He mixed among these thoughts the fragments of Aggie's plea, "Give us a simple message of hope." Having let go of his immediate anger and shame, he considered what allowed him to have *his* hope. *Wiser and older, weaker and younger, taller and stronger people than me have so little hope. It's almost as though they live so completely under the shadow of the White man, so completely in the dark in the shadowed alleys of life,* he thought, *that, having never seen the sun, they don't know it's there.* He saw the color of his people almost symbolic of that shadow. He compared the narrowness of the life they were forced to lead to the dark alley he had cowered in as a small child having recently lost his father.

Remembering that, he recalled for the first time in years the feeling of fear and hopelessness he had had. And he thought of Freddie. He knew that Freddie would agree with Aggie. In a new way, he came to appreciate the depths of feelings of hopelessness within the congregation. And he knew what he would say. Placing himself in their shoes, in their bodies, in their souls, he knew what they needed so desperately to hear, to believe. The message he was to deliver began forming in his heart and organizing in his brain.

CHAPTER 17

Old Shadows, New Hope

Aggie watched Luke walk away from her. His strong brown back rippled with angry muscles. They worked their way down from the back of his neck, under the pronounced blades of his shoulders. They continued down his spine into the beltline of his coveralls. The dusty light soles of his feet flashed at her from beneath his pant legs. His long strides carried him away from her. She sighed deeply and sagged under the weight of her despair. Aggie had never dared challenge Luke directly and in such a personal way. She hoped she knew him as well as she thought. She hoped he would turn inward when he became angry as he usually did. She prayed that he would search for blame or solution within himself. She was afraid he might build resentment toward her criticism that might damage the deep love and relationship which these two youngsters had nurtured together for so long.

Approaching fifteen, Aggie was herself more than a child. Long since developed physically as a young woman, her mind and soul were also developing rapidly. She carried a deep sense of justice that conflicted with her deep fear that there was none. She continued to harbor a fear of men. She often thought about her own father. Years before he broke under the weight of providing for so many on so little. He rejected further involvement with the women of his family because they could not carry a man's weight in the fields. He considered them an intolerable burden. She knew he carried heavy guilt for this feeling until he finally buried that guilt beneath a front of total contempt. Leaning on stump liquor to hide his self-condemnation, he became mean. Aggie frequently witnessed her father's rage as he beat Aggie's mother before his cowering children.

The hunters, Elkins, the landlord and her own father were to Aggie but typical of men. Each represented a direct threat to her peace, to her survival, and to those she loved. She rarely thought of Luke without marveling at how different he was from such men. His calm and loving way and the tenderness and patience he continuously showed her helped balance her perspective on men. From that small thread she allowed herself to hope that through Luke, she was safe from the ravages of men and especially White men.

Then Luke assaulted her with his proud and selfish fantasizing over the sermon. When she saw the look in his eye and felt the power of his self-importance, Aggie suddenly was as frightened of him as she was of most men. It dawned on her that she had been relying on Luke heavily from a vision she had held of him since they met. She knew now that this was the vision of a child. She could see that neither she nor Luke was a child anymore. Luke was becoming a powerful and talented man of ambition and pride. The question in her mind was whether he could discipline and direct himself in a way that he might also remain gentle, loving, giving, possessing of those qualities which she most admired in him.

Aggie understood that these were the qualities for which she loved him. Her sense of security lay in his inherent power, for this represented protection from a hostile world. Yet she knew that without his understanding of her nature, without his gentle acceptance of her as she was, he would be transformed from protector to threat. This is what had frightened her into speaking so boldly. She surmised quickly that if Luke were to keep the essence of his boyhood character as he moved into manhood, she needed to use the little power love gave her over him. She needed to make him think of what he was doing, what direction he was moving, how he must tame then use the talent and power inherent in his large and handsome frame.

Turning to walk home and resume her duties with her two brothers, Aggie was unsure whether she had succeeded in making Luke look at himself or whether she had cut too deeply. *Perhaps he might twist my words to mean resentment or jealousy and come to reject or even hate me*, she thought. *Anything else I say now would just make things worse. I must trust him now to be the man he should be but still have the quality of the boy he was.* Aggie went on home. She prepared to wait him out. *I must wait for him to come to me, no matter how indirectly, and show me his decision, which I know will be through action, not just words.*

As she moved into the yard and approached the broken down cabin, she paused as she spotted the rear of the landlord's new convertible around the side of the house. *As if today had not been bad enough*, she thought in self pity as she crept to the opposite side. She stooped near the lonely paneless window emitting sounds of conflict from within. She listened.

"Come now, Gloria" The Landlord was speaking and as usual he addressed Aggie's mother with a tone of contempt, disbelief and condescension. "I know it has been a good Spring. Why the rains have been just about right, and there's been plenty of sun. You really expect me to believe that you have had a bad early crop?"

"'Tis true, Mr. Allsworth, Suh, for my man ain't been well dis year, and we'uns just didn't get de crop in de ground as early as we has been."

"Well now, I suspect I know what's ailing your man, Gloria. I suspect your man's been treating himself to a little too much from the jug, and just got lazy about the planting. Now, isn't that right?" Aggie cowered back. She knew that what Allworth had said was exactly right. She and her mother and sister had feared the landlord's visit since March when the ground had sat unturned. Her father had gone off somewhere doing whatever men do when they disappear from their families for weeks at a time. *How I hate men*, she thought, then listened as her mother was speaking again.

"But Suh, I's sayin' dat ol' crop is just slow. I done never seen such a slow crop. But for all it slow, it got quality. It Gonna bring a good price. We be payin' right on time next time. Dat for sure."

"One crop's like another, Gloria. You know that. You can't pull enough from this crop to pay me and feed your family, too. And I suspect you will feed your family first, won't you?"

"Oh no, Suh. Why, de land's de thing, Suh. We appreciates yo' lettin' us use it, and we knows our place. We's payin' y'all first, afore anythin' else, fo' sure. Come one mo' month, and we be payin' you de half year we is owin' an' right on time. Y'all'l see."

"How can you stand there and say right on time, Woman, when now is the time when the rent is due? All right, Gloria. I'm not a mean man. I know you have a lot of mouths to feed. I stayed with you during the hard times, so I guess I can't rightly dump you now."

"Oh, thank ya, thank ya, Mr. Allsworth, Suh, I promises we pay by de end of just one mo' month, I knows we can."

Aggie knew they could too, unless the crop was ruined. She resented this man's condescending tone in granting his sparse benevolence to the family. He took at least half the crop money up front. He expected the same or more each year from the worn-out land. But he never lifted a finger to make it better.

Luke had taught her of new fertilizers and farming methods which his Uncle LeRoy used to reclaim lost land in the last few years. But she had seen none of this on her place. *It's his land,* she thought. *We just work it. If he'd put a little into it, he'd be better off as well as us.* But she knew that made too much sense for a White man to comprehend. So she resigned herself to another hungry summer as the late and lean crop went first to pay the landlord his fifty percent. He set the amount some twenty years earlier when the land still produced a reasonable crop.

Aggie heard Allsworth shuffling across the floor followed by her mother's heavy footsteps. Her mother opened the door for her hated visitor. Sliding to a squatting position, Aggie waited until the sound of Allsworth's car faded across the dusty field. Then she rose and went toward the house. Feigning innocence, she asked her mother what the man had wanted.

But as Aggie turned the corner and mounted the porch, her two younger brothers, Sammy and Jason, came from behind the outhouse where they were hiding.

"What he want?" they chimed together. "An' where y'all be all de day? Y'all wif Luke? How come y'all didn't take us? Y'all say we can go see Luke wif y'all t'day. Can we'uns go now?"

"Hold on, Youngens." Aggie smiled as she pulled the two forward and hugged them. At eleven and twelve, Jason and Sammy seemed small to her. She suspected their meager diet would keep them from ever being large or particularly intelligent. Still, with the way they had pitched in to get the crop planted, Aggie knew they were strong enough to hold on to the land for perhaps one more generation. She dared not project beyond that. "Luke's busy this afternoon," she said. "Besides---"

"But what dat White man want? Is we havin' t'move? We hear him say he ain't got no rent yet."

"No, Sugar." Aggie soothed Sammy, stroking his wide-eyed face. "But we have to work harder to make sure the crop's a good one, or I'm afraid there won't be much to eat this year."

"We done good helpin' so far, ain't we, Aggie?"

"Yes, Jason. And I'm proud of you. But come on. Get yourselves out back and wash up some. I have some thinking to do. Now scoot."

Aggie wanted desperately to tell Luke of the landlord's visit and to ask him what they should do. But she found herself still wary of facing him. Loneliness overwhelmed her. The hairline crack in her dream, which had been threatening to reveal tomorrow to her all day long, widened in that loneliness. It allowed the shadows of her fears to creep through the passages of her mind. It crawled down her spine and tingled the nerve endings of her fingers. Then it lodged in her heart and throat and stomach. She was afraid the boys would see her fear. She needed to be alone.

The fear remained for days. Aggie became more and more sullen when she did not hear from Luke. The fear of having lost him became more and more like the reality she had always feared. The pieces of her dream world gave way to the real world around her. She saw her mother with real eyes for the first time in a long time. She saw an old woman, although her mother was not yet forty. She saw the same future for Jason and Sammy. She could hardly bear to look at them all.

Finally, Aggie left the house, and looking back at it with new eyes, she saw that it was falling down. She traversed the fields and saw dust and weeds where there should have been crops. Promise to the landlord or not, she realized that no one was working them. Not enough was growing to even pay the rent. And her fear deepened. The reality she saw nearly overwhelmed Aggie. She could not stand it. She grappled with her own mind. She moved away from all the pain she was suffering and retreated into her fantasy world. No longer could she stand to see the shattering reality surrounding her.

For days, Luke kept reappearing in her unconscious wandering. Her dreams of better times and safer, more secure images finally blotted away all the hurt. At last she reached the pond and her sanctuary. She reconstructed the image of Luke and her as two children learning from each other. She took comfort from the hopes and passions they shared. She visualized all their past pleasant summer afternoons by a small and hidden pond in the lowlands of Southern Georgia.

Aggie sat by the pond with her feet in the water dreaming her dream. She felt the peace and joy she used to feel with Luke *before*, she told herself, *he grew up and went away.* She heard him say "Hey," as he used to when they would meet. She felt his gentle arm surround her and marveled at its strength for such a lightweight child. She looked at that arm now and knew that it was real, that Luke was there. She knew that he had come to terms with himself and what she had told him of himself. He was no longer angry. He was again her Luke there by the pond. She would live as she had lived, a day at a time, protected by Luke's love.

With that very real feeling welling up inside her, she turned and faced Luke. He was smiling. "Been a long time since we met here at the pond, hasn't it, Aggie?"

"Luke. I'm glad you found me." She buried her face in his bibbed overalls and cried softly.

"I've been looking for you for days, Girl. But you have really been on the move. Every time I went to your house, your Mamma would say you were out somewhere. I checked everywhere."

"Why'd you come here?"

"No place else left."

"Luke?"

"What, Aggie?"

"Do you still love me?"

"Aggie, I love you more than ever. I know what you said to me could only have been said by someone who really loves me and understands the conflicts within me. I admire you for saying it. It needed saying, and it helped me understand myself a little better. And by the way, it helped me find what I want to say, come Sunday."

"Oh, Luke, tell me."

"No, Darling. I'll tell you Sunday, if you want to come and hear. Right now, all I want to do is hold you close and make up for missing you so much."

Luke pulled Aggie tight against him and brushed her forehead with his lips. With that gentle kiss, something new and delightful like a quiet breathless surge passed between them. So hungry for the repossession of her dream, Aggie knew what she had to do almost before Luke knew what he wanted of her. Raising her small, soft brown hands to the downy stubble of Luke's chocolate chin, she pulled his lips toward hers. Her melting eyes fastened onto his and generated heat in their depths as he leaned closer with his mouth parting to greet hers.

As their lips met Luke felt a slight wave of confusion, a gush of teary love, a strange sense of wanting beyond anything her body had provoked before. The backs of his eyes, tops of his ears and tight black knots of hair on his head tingled with anticipation of what was happening and about to happen. The chilling, heating tingle slid down his neck to his shoulder, where it pulled the strap of his coveralls with it. He knew that Aggie was pulling that strap, that she wanted him as he wanted her. That thought transferred the full force of the heat building inside him like a shot through his heart to his loins where he felt himself pushing against the tired fabric of the old denim he always wore.

As though he was standing outside himself watching, Luke responded to Aggie's advance. He moved closer to her without thinking about it. Knowing fully and exactly what they were doing, they stood apart linked only by their eyes and the shaking tips of their fingers. Each pushed from the other's shoulders the straps which kept their clothing in place. Each with growing confidence unfastened the fasteners, unbuttoned the buttons of the other, until as vibrant shadows against the glowing evening sky, they stood a foot apart. They stood silhouetted for each other as God had made them, hungry for each other as God had made them, eager to be as close, and as one as God had made man to be with woman. Together, eyes again locked on eyes, but with a new urgency and sense of abandon, Luke and Aggie, now man and woman, sank to the red and moist bank of the Georgia lowlands pond.

After, in a long and silent moment they listened to each other's breathing. The feel of each other and the soft earth beneath their bellies cooled the aftermath. Cheeks in the clay, each watched the other with wet and joyous watchfulness, and each knew that at least in spirit they would never again be two separate people. Luke rolled gently to his side and faced Aggie. He placed his hand on her and stroked her. She smiled and began stroking Luke's cheek, his chest and his stomach. Then Luke pulled back. "Aggie, are you hurt? Did I hurt you?"

"No, Luke. I love you." She felt him sink back and released him. She sat before him, placing her hand on his shoulder. "Why? Why did you ask that?"

"You're bleeding."

"I know. I am supposed to the first time, Honey."

"Oh." Luke felt a little foolish, a little naked and yet a little older, a little wiser. He flushed. "Let's swim, then come back."

Aggie laughed at him, then with him. They jumped to their feet and padded quickly to the cleansing waters where they played freely and naturally and excitingly until they realized that it was dark. They mounted the bank and Luke pulled Aggie's wet body to his. She felt his closeness, but the other, older feelings were in the way. A flash of the last time they were at the pond wended its fleeting way through her consciousness. "Luke, Honey, Tomorrow. It's dark. I don't like being here in the dark, remember?"

Without answer or hesitation, Luke swung away and reached for Aggie's clothes. Suddenly shy, Aggie held her dress in front of her and Luke, feeling a kinship feeling, turned his back to her and climbed into his overalls. When he turned around again, Aggie was dressed. "I better get you home before your Mamma gets upset with the both of us, Girl."

"I would have thought, considering what has just happened, that you would be about ready to give up calling me 'Girl', Boy."

They both laughed, and linking arms, headed for Aggie's cabin across the fields.

CHAPTER 18

Ashes and Rings

"Aggie! Luke!" Aggie's mother was standing with Sammy and Jason on the scrubbed, worn stoop in front of the cabin. No lights were on inside. A strange orange glow lighting the east silhouetted the house as they approached, but they did not see Gloria or the boys until they were practically on the stoop itself. Gloria startled them with her sharp words. When they could see her clearly, what startled them even more was the sharpness in her face. "Y'all get in de house, Girl. Luke, yo' Uncle LeRoy was here not a half hour past. He be out lookin' fo' y'all. He say iff'n y'all come dis way, I 'sposed t'send y'all home. Dere's trouble a-brewin' dis night, an' from de looks o'things dere in de east, dat trouble comin' here."

Instantly, Luke knew what Gloria meant. He did not need the awesome glow bathing them orange when they stepped into the yard to tell him. He had seen it before. *Night Riders*, he thought. With a quick and worried look at Aggie, he headed out of the worn yard and bounded over the rickety split rail fence. He jogged deliberately down the sloped field toward the stream and its protecting cover of trees, through which he slipped home the back way so he would not be noticed.

The Congregation spent the next three days in hurried activity. They hid the few valuables they had, like family keepsakes, shabby linens and small caches of hard money. Some they buried in potato cellars. They hid some in tree trunks or wrapped them in gunnysacks and dropped them in fresh holes dug in the soft earth. The entire Congregation was sure that night riders would come again. Word spread from farm to farm of the misfortunes of some. The men spent part of each day sifting through the ruins of the night before. They rebuilt where they could and abandoned what they could not. The women took in the children of others or welcomed back a sister or daughter long since married and on their own. Before the three days saw the dreaded arrival of Saturday night, the night riders burned out eleven families.

Luke and Aggie saw each other only for snatches because, like the rest of the Community, they each concentrated on tending to the needs of others. Constantly fearful, Aggie kept her brothers hidden. She added the children of others to the hiding places each day. She sought at every turn a glimpse of Luke. She feared at every turn that some white-robed, masked demon would swoop upon her and end forever her dream just as it seemed to be restored and better than she had ever hoped.

Finally, the dreaded Saturday night came. They darkened all farms. Black faces sat silently by blackened windows in watchful fear. They looked across barren or fertile fields, green grass or red clay, through tall trees or across low bush. Each had his or her own thoughts, in his or her own world. They knew how poor they were and prayed that the night riders would spare what little they had.

At last Aggie was with her Luke at the Powers' farm and her fear eased. However, an uneasy wonder replaced it. By a gentle squeeze of his moist hand, Luke calmed Aggie's sudden flashes of alarm at this sound or that light. Aggie was there only because her cabin was full of the homeless. There was no room at home for her and her brothers, whom she had brought with her. LeRoy's cabin, too, was laden with blankets strewn on the floor. His small outbuilding was now housing a family of six. He had staked his precious animals deep in the woods where the undergrowth and threat of snakes would keep the night riders away.

The glow in the sky signaling the beginning was long in coming. The crickets inhabited the night and announced its presence to the world. Hot bodies and cold sweat mixed with deep or short breath in the darkened and sightless cabin interiors. For each, that dark and those sounds were comfort and protection. Their shelter was each other, together. What safety they felt was undercut by fear of the fire which they all were sure was coming. That fire might well trap them in their flimsy sanctuaries. They felt certain it would feed their nostrils with the smell of searing flesh before the night was through. Aggie's fear mounted at the thought. "Why," she wondered. "Why?" She reached one more time for the small bodies of her brothers and the other children. They shivered at her touch.

"Luke?"

"Hush!"

"Why do they do it? We've done nothing to them."

"I don't know. Maybe they're afraid, too."

"What've they got to be afraid of?"

"Fighting."

"Fighting what?"

"Germans."

Aggie did not understand and fell silent. Luke believed he had identified the main cause. In that June of 1941 when he was less than one day from his sixteenth birthday, Luke Powers knew with the absolute positiveness of his youth what was coming and what he would do. But he voiced no more explanation to Aggie. He was more concerned with surviving the night than the holocaust to come. In silence among friends, he kept his own counsel and waited. Jason crawled over to him and, putting his face an inch from Luke's, stared at him with terrified eyes. Luke pulled the boy to his lap, and soon Sammy joined them. Aggie and the other children were there too. They all huddled together and continued the silent and terrifying vigil until dawn.

That dawn came as an eerie bright as though through light fog. But there was no fog. The air hung low with smoke and the putrid smell of charred flesh. Each family looked around and each found things whole and safe. Each wondered then, why the smell, why the hazy sun. And each prepared to go to church to give thanks for being spared and to hear Luke Powers preach on his sixteenth birthday. They knew the night riders would not be back right away. They always quit after Saturday night. Sunday was even more the day of hope when the night riders had ridden. And it was at last Sunday.

Even with the telltale scent on the wind, neither Luke nor the Congregation foresaw the significance of that Sunday. They did not know yet about the blackened tragedy and forlorn despair signaled by that breeze. Nor did they until the first of them arrived at church.

What words now? thought Luke. He stood where the pulpit had been, his bare feet in the still warm, powdery grey-black ash of the small church. It was now but a sooty memory. The rest of the Congregation stood before him mourning their loss. They had lost of their church. They had lost their Preacher. The only thing left standing was the charred cross of the Klan standing in the burnt ground. This proved that they had lost it all because of an incomprehensible outburst of violence from white-hooded cowards in the name of the very Christ they called "Sweet Jesus."

As with most senseless tragedy, it all happened fast. That second Saturday night in June 1941, the hate and fear filling the hearts of Blacks and Whites alike for five days had exploded in violence. Yet remarkably, no one but the Preacher died. *Perhaps*, thought Luke, *that was why the violence had not continued.* The Preacher's sacrifice had seemed to satisfy for the moment the thirsts hidden beneath the pure white cloth shrouding their oppressors.

During the entire week before, news of Nazi Germany had filled the airways of the Whites, though few Blacks even knew of the existence of the Nazis. Luke knew. He had been reading and digging to find out ever since rumors of German atrocities toward Jews had reached his ears over a year before. He imagined frustration and desire to act, rousing the hate among the Brotherhood. Still, he could not envision their wrath being generated out of sympathy with the Jews. No, he reasoned, they must have another target. Secretly they envied Hitler's radical methods of dealing with racial inferiors. He assumed that, considering their inherent fear of Blacks, they wished to align themselves with Hitler's ideology. Luke reasoned with a wry half smile that the most dangerous among them must surely be those whose blood was just a little tinted with Black from somewhere in the past. Those must fear that Hitler would find out and they would be publicly shamed and executed, along with their families. Luke thought such frustration and hate must have an outlet, a target.

He knew they could attack his people with impunity and that Hitler would approve. He pictured someone, in a frenzied meeting of frightened and roused Whites, suggesting that "niggers" were like the Jews, inferior beings they needed to eradicate. Consistent with their fear of Blacks, they might even think the Blacks were secretly working to bring about the downfall of the Whites, their subjugators. Luke strongly believed that this was the fear that was the basis of most White reaction to and treatment of Blacks in that awful year. He knew this fear had grown stronger with each year since Reconstruction. So subjugating and eliminating Blacks was not a new thought. Now Hitler gave them a new excuse to act on their fears. The logic was clear in his inexperienced mind. He could almost hear members of the Brotherhood supporting the argument after so many nights of not catching a single Black in the engulfing fires. He could imagine them suggesting that the Blacks were not home because they were gathering at the church to plot and plan and organize.

Luke was certain that burning the church was born of this belief that fueled a mob mentality. He pictured in his mind the few White faces he knew. He saw them disappearing behind faceless white masked creatures whose numbers swelled in their anonymity. He pictured them mounted on horses or in the backs of pickups, beat down old Fords or mule drawn wagons, pushing, surging, stomping and crowding forward. He imagined torches blazing, hearts and groins throbbing at the renewal and frenzy of the ritual. In his mind each was totally lost in the identity of the Klan. Like a rapist just before orgasm, the act was now the thing, the only thing that might satisfy. Nothing else mattered. Their motions and sounds were involuntary, instinctive, driven from each by a force too powerful and too old to be squelched, controlled or denied by the bodies they possessed.

Luke could almost see in his mind the torches and the marchers. Their profanity and lewd stories excited them to become a mob. As they marched, their thrill was almost sexual. Their momentum was almost orgiastic. He knew they were beyond reason. They were beyond sense, primitive, beyond stopping. They became like subhuman animals of false vengeance, exorcising the baseness of their beings at a level so low that it nauseated the human sensitivity of the Blacks to whom they felt superior.

Luke pictured them reaching the church, firing it, trampling the simple graveyard with glee and vulgarity, and then torching the trees and the fence. He saw them planting and firing the symbolic cross. He saw them lay waste to God's sanctuary and the one hope for the poor Blacks of whom Luke was a part. Luke Powers now had to speak to these same poor Blacks this bright and warm Sabbath morning.

So he stood in the ashes of the Congregation's hope. Looking at them, he thought of the Preacher who had been trapped inside the blazing church while evidently trying to save it. That same Preacher had called on Luke to preach this day. He was suddenly frightened and intimidated by the task.

"What shall I say?" he shouted to his gathered brothers and sisters. "What shall I say! Fear not, Brethren, for your enemy is gone? I cannot for he is near. From this place and this hour he is gone but his horror remains."

The mournful assembly hushed at his words, eyed him. His emotion laden voice floated forth like the ash of the church in the wind. "They came to destroy our hope, and yet have vanished from our sight. Like a shadow in a dark alley, we cannot see them. Yet we know they are near. They remain fearful of the light of God's truth. They are waiting again to hide in the darkness of night and their sin. Then they will venture forth again in violence against us.

"They leave behind other shadows in their path. The shadows of our hopes we now sense as ashes at our feet. The shadows of a man who stood as a giant among us. The shadows of our terror in knowing we are Black. Shadows of ourselves. Shadows."

Luke's head fell at the hopeless emptiness of his words. His heart felt the pain the people reflected. His anger wept in the compassion in his heart for all his brothers and sisters suffering with him. As he raised his head and scanned their faces, just a touch of light green caught his eye from the burned hulks behind them. Just yesterday those black hulks had been the greening trees of early June.

"But these!" he shouted. He rocked to the tips of his soot-blackened toes and seemed to lean over the top of the crowding audience. "These are the reflections of what was. Shadows of the past. The past is gone but will remain in our hearts. We cannot help but hold on to that past. Shadows will trail behind in the sunlight of new hope. We must cast such light on tomorrow so that each among us will stand as a bright new beacon of hope to come.

"We must seek out the evil hiding in the dark alleys of life. We must cast this new light upon those shadows so they never again dare to transgress upon us. We must come together as one common force against all who would deny us our humanity. For when we cast our shadows together, we become as one."

Luke paused, dropping to his heels as his voice dropped to normal, then slowly to a barely audible cadence. He half turned, squinting a sidelong look at his whole race, there represented by a handful of Black hurt. He continued.

"Unlike shadows, we are not obliterated by dark. Unlike shadows, we have substance. Unlike shadows, we have humanity. Unlike shadows, we have hope. Unlike shadows, we have life. Unlike shadows, we have each other. We have love.

"This love, not the hate of the White Shadow, is the root of our power and the assurance of our eventual victory over those who would oppress and destroy us."

"Amen, Brother Luke." The aroused crowd pulsated as the meaning of Luke's words sifted through the cleavages within their grief and found seeds of hope to nurture.

"Brothers and Sisters. We have Jesus to teach us of that love."

"Amen!"

"Brothers and Sisters. We must not mourn the loss of this church for what is a church? Is it a building which can become in one short moment but a shadow? No! It is love. It is humanity. It is caring and sharing. It is the strength of Jesus with us. With you. With me. We are therefore the church. And as long as we believe and stand together as brothers and sisters, we will survive this kind of evil and rise to the power within us."

"Amen"

"And what about our Preacher? Was he but a simple man who soon becomes a shadow of the past, a piece of dust? No! Our preacher was a man who lived with us and will live with us long after he is with Jesus. His thoughts, his words, his ideas were and are our future and our hope."

"Amen, Brother Luke."

"I will not eulogize our lost Brother, for we will do that tomorrow. At that service in his memory as well as now, I will know in my heart that he is not lost to us. He is not a mere shadow of the past for part of him we carry with us as I speak to you now.

"And what I say he would have said if he were standing here in my place. No. He is not but a shadow. Nor, Brothers and Sisters, are we. Far from mere shadows, we are more akin to these mighty trees which have burned around us. Look! See them. They have suffered, as have we. They too are now black, as are we. But they are not dead. Mark my words this day. They are not dead. Soon you will see new green shoots coming from their blackened hulks.

"And like them, we too shall soon send forth new green shoots of faith. Like them, our hope has been torched and is but a shadow of what it was. But it is not just a shadow, for that hope will return just as those trees will. Someday.

"We are like those trees in yet another way, for those trees are made up of rings. Most of you are farmers. You know the land. You know the trees. You know this is true. Each tree grows one ring in one season. Each represents a strength or weakness within the tree itself, depending upon how good or poor the season was. And each is strengthened with new roots spread hungrily in this Georgia soil. Each root is matched by a branch, itself gaining rings of time.

"We too have such rings which shape who we are. We too branch out according to the strength and direction of our roots. In those rings we find our identity. We have a ring for being Black, some for being young, another group for the loves we have shared. And yes, we have weak rings for the hates and fears we have harbored.

"Then there are rings for each of our talents. Like each tree, each of us has a special group of these rings with which we are each marked as special, unique. We are therefore of value to someone, to ourselves, to the God who created us, to Jesus who loves us. We are each special.

"Peel the bark away from the black oak or the white birch and you cannot tell which is which, for they look much the same. Under the skin so do we. With all humanity we stand equal. But still each of us is unique. Each us is different. Each of us is special. But we are still all the same, all human. And in that there is hope. The preacher understood this. He preached this to us and that is his legacy. He was and remains one of our rings. He tended us, encouraged our growth, caused rings of experience and understanding to flourish within us.

"He cared for these trees and us. With the hand of God on his shoulder he assured their health and ours. He protected their roots and ours, so that like the trees we could stand tall and straight together. And the roots of those trees intermingled, and their branches touched. They joined together as one. They became shade for the hot summer day, or protection from the cold winter's wind.

"So, like those trees our roots intermingle. So, like those trees our branches touch. So, like those trees we become one in common with humanity, as brothers and sisters in Christ.

"Just as the intertwined roots of these blackened trees now promise new shade, new protection, new beauty in coming years, our roots promise new hope for us. We do not lose the preacher. We do not lose the trees. We do not lose the church. I am not lost. You are not lost. Look around you. Look at each other. Touch each other and you will know the truth of what I am saying.

"On the surface, here, under the hot Sunday sun then, we may appear but shadows. Yet, below the surface of this ashened clay, our roots prosper. And so, brothers and sisters, shall we. Amen."

Luke looked into the stunned sea of faces before him. He could not immediately discern whether the glistening eyes were moist with tears, bright with hope or reflecting an excitement his words may have provoked. He caught Aggie's eyes staring back at him and recognized in them her love. Her intent gaze made him again aware of himself and he looked to his own body. He was soaked clear through from sweat and tears. He felt elated and shaky and tired yet energetic all at once. He raised his eyes once again to the congregation and realized that they had not moved at all. Not a word or sound come from them. They simply stared those glistening stares he had caught with his final "Amen". They stood still like that a moment more and Luke hung his head in abandonment of the apparently false hope of success which had come to him from Aggie's loving eyes. He told himself then that even with all the power and emotion he could summon for the occasion, had failed to give them the hope of which they so despaired.

Then someone in the crowd uttered a simple "Amen". Luke looked up. The looks in their intense stares were transforming into a common unity among them. A faint, shadowing translucence pervaded the Black faces and imparted a strange light of hope and understanding. Never before had Luke witnessed this among his people. Someone started a spiritual in a deep baritone. Others joined in. The whole congregation started swaying and stomping and bellowing out their hope and grief and agony and cheer in an exorcism of emotion catharized by Luke's words.

Then Luke knew that they would hope again. He felt that something within him had awakened. It combined the talents he knew he possessed with a new and inexorable depth of understanding and empathy. He allowed himself as well to hope. He knew he had found a vocation to help his people.

Then Aggie came from the crowd. She sang and swayed her way toward him. Moist, dancing eyes greeted his and her head came to rest on his shoulder. Like most in the Congregation, Aggie lived one day at a time and did not fully understand Luke's message. But the rich and powerfully delivered sermon had made her feel hopeful, even good despite the tragedy they had faced together.

Aggie knew that Luke had listened to her as well. She felt as close to him spiritually now as she had physically and emotionally in their union at the pond a few days before.

As her head coveted the inviting pocket inside his shoulder next to his dark-skinned neck, she thought of his analogy of the shadows and pictured their shadows as one. She experienced a deep sense of contentment with her life. A shudder enveloped her in passing, and her grief passed with it.

CHAPTER 19

Old Shadows, New Beginnings

"Luke! No! Please! You can't! You mustn't! It isn't your fight. It isn't our world. It's theirs. The Whites. They're the ones that started this thing. Let them finish it."

"Aggie, Sweet, Dear Aggie. I've tried to explain to you what Nazism is, what the Nazis are doing to the Jews.

"I know that. I can't help that. I feel sorry for them, but they're all White. They're all the same. What business has any Black man with them? None!"

"Do you know why the Nazis are trying to annihilate the Jews?"

"To get rid of them. Let them all kill each other off if they must. It's not our concern, I tell you."

"But it is, Honey. You're so wrong. The Nazis are slaughtering the Jews because they say Jews are not pure White. They are not Aryan with blue eyes and blond hair. How many of our Brothers and Sisters have blue eyes and blond hair?"

"None, but---"

"But nothing! If the Germans win this war and take over the United States, what do you think will happen to us?"

"They can't win. They're too evil."

"Ah, but haven't you told me that the Whites right here in Georgia are evil also? Haven't we seen that evil? Haven't we experienced it? Compared to the Nazis, let me tell you, they are as saints at the right hand of God. They do as they do not as monsters like the Nazis, but through ignorance and fear. The Nazis are deliberately murdering thousands, maybe even millions of human beings they consider inferior. They call themselves the 'Master Race'. At the very least that alone shows their intent to place all other races in slavery. Is that what you want?"

"Of course not, Luke. But why must you go?"

Luke struggled again to explain his position on this issue as an American and a Black man. He needed Aggie to see it from his viewpoint and from his belief in the equality of all men and from his faith.

But Aggie ignored any issue which she thought threatened her security. So she refused to see the logic, the values, the reason in what Luke was saying. Yet, Luke knew that with or without her approval, he must join the fight against the Nazis.

Luke began learning of the Nazis when he was fourteen and Aunt Crystal brought him day old newspapers from one of the White homes where she worked. The news became more prolific and condemning after Pearl Harbor. Now, two years after America entered the battle, the press had inflamed Luke and many young Blacks to become involved, to act.

At eighteen, Luke struggled internally with choosing to fight and wanting to be a minister. He needed to choose the right approach for protecting and furthering the human principles in which he rooted his whole philosophy. The immediate threat won out. He concluded that right now his words would do little good against the maniacs threatening the world. If those words were to have a chance of helping change the future, he must now protect his right to deliver them through a more urgent action. He must join the Army. He must fight. Only after he had made this decision did he tell Aggie.

Over the past two years since the church had burned and the Preacher had been slain, she had heard him preach many sermons on the plight of the Jews, relating it to the conditions of Blacks in the United States. But still she could not accept his thesis, for it contradicted the basis of the dream in which she already existed. Now she feared in her heart that if Luke left to fight this war, he would never return to her. That would shatter her entire world. But she knew that she could not change his mind. He was leaving, and soon.

///

"Stand straight, nigger! Put them eyes front!" The sergeant eyed Luke with intense hatred and an air of superiority such as Luke had seldom encountered. Most of the other recruits in this Des Moines reception station were standing easy, smoking and joking. Most of the other recruits were White.

The few Coloreds in the room silently huddled together in a corner with a look of bewildered terror blanketing their faces. It had not occurred to Luke to join them when he processed through to wait for his physical. He immediately moved into the larger crowd of White faces. Feeling neither estrangement nor inferiority nor fear, he had tried to strike up conversation.

The sudden blow to his lower spine flung him forward through the group and he sprawled bloody faced on the reception room floor. Luke drew his hands beneath his shoulders and pushed up. He shook his head to clear it and winced from the pain in his spine.

The sergeant kicked him in the side, screaming "On your feet, you Black bastard." He kicked out again. Luke looked for and rolled away from the second kick. Backing away spider style from the Sergeant, he scrambled to get his feet under him and stood. He did his best to control and conceal his pain. Hoping it did not show on his face, he looked into the eyes of the squat little man in khaki and brown shoes who was standing directly in front of him.

The sergeant spread his legs. He put his hands on his hips and his jaw jutted pompously forward. He raised his round, big and half bald head to meet Luke's eyes. "Don't they teach you anything but how to pick cotton down on the farm, Boy?" The sergeant reared back and pumped his fist into Luke's stomach.

Luke flinched, feeling an awful wave of nausea. But he remained standing. He forced away the teary blink which would have broken his concentrated stare into the sergeant's eyes. He was determined not to show weakness before this bigoted fool.

The sergeant slowly pulled back and rubbed his knuckles with his other hand. A look of surprise briefly eclipsed the hate in the Sergeant's eyes. He glanced around. Everyone was watching the tall Black stand straight and taught. Blood trickled from his nose as his eyes rolled down to the face of his stumpy antagonist.

The Sergeant felt rather than heard the sneer oozing from the group. He knew they were all green, all a little scared. By attacking a mutual enemy, he meant to intimidate them further without affronting or alienating them. It was a ploy which he had used before. But this big Black stood his ground with more than just dignity. He seemed to communicate an actual sense of equality and command which the sergeant had never seen a Black exhibit. He thought of his inevitable loss of face. He knew he must break this Black or lose the recruits for whose training he was to be responsible.

"That's right, nigger. Look at my face." He tried a new approach. "Look good and never forget it. I am Sergeant Cooke. Your body and soul, if you have one, belong to me, to do with as I please for the next eight weeks, or until you quit. You want to train with the Whites? You too good to associate with the nigger scum you come from? Fine. Done. You may be too good to go with your own kind, nigger, but in my outfit, you're nothing but brown shit. And you will get every shit detail there is. And if you survive, which I doubt, I will see that you get nothing but shit for the next three years. Now get out of my sight!"

Before any response from Luke further damaged his control of the situation, Sergeant Cooke turned on his heel to move away in his pretentious strut of false dignity. He knew for all his harsh words and feigned bravado that he had lost round one with this Black. But round two, well he suddenly knew he would also be a casualty of round two, for as he turned, the training officer, Lt. Henderson, was facing him.

"Well well, Sergeant Cooke. Starting your training a little early this cycle, aren't you?"

Sergeant Cooke snapped to rigid attention. "No, Sir. The nigger got smart, Sir. Just maintaining discipline, Sir."

"You mean, the *recruit* got smart, don't you Sergeant?"

"Yessir, that is, it was that Black sonofabitch there, Sir."

"Of course, Sergeant. I understand perfectly. I would not for the life of me burden you with having to work alongside the likes of him."

"Thank you, Sir." Sergeant Cooke spoke the words but knew Lt Henderson's meaning. He had forgotten for a moment that the LT was a "Nigger lover". He vowed to be more careful in the Lt's presence.

"Consider yourself relieved, Sergeant. Report to the Orderly Room and have orders cut for your transfer."

"Begging the Lieutenant's pardon, but where to, Sir?"

"How about the South Pacific? I understand there are a lot of little yellow men over there you can hate with impunity. They're not Black but still should suit your mentality just right."

"But, Sir, What —-"

"Dismissed."

"You can't do that, Sir. You're not the C.O."

"I just did it, Boy!" Luke snapped to attention as the word echoed from the vaguely familiar officer's mouth. But the Lt was not yet addressing him. He was waiting a moment for the sergeant to complete his grand and stiff exit. Then stepping in front of and turning full face to Luke for the first time, he commanded, "Soldier!"

Luke suppressed a broad grin and kept his eyes as noncommittal as possible. He responded with a "Yessir."

"Get yourself in there for your physical. Get yourself cleaned up. Get yourself to the Orderly Room right after." Lt Henderson turned and left the room without so much as a flick of the eye to show any recognition of this Black. But Luke knew who the Lt was, and his heart raced with the excitement of seeing Freddie for the first time in just over ten years. He tried to picture the little boy who Luke's Grandmother carried away in the middle of the night. He superimposed the image over the face of this tall, redheaded and commanding officer. Then humiliation crept in and he was not sure he wanted Freddie to recognize him or ever find out who he was. They had not written in several years. Luke did not know where Freddie had been or what had happened to him. He had heard nothing since shortly after Freddie's baby was born. He was not even sure the child had survived. As he had wondered often, Luke wondered now whether Freddie had married his Martha or finished his time at the military school. He wondered whether the pressure of his unhappiness had driven him to some lesser livelihood.

He must have finished, thought Luke, for he has to be only twenty-one, and he's an officer. I am an ignorant Black country boy already insulted and bleeding in his Army. He must never discover who I am, at least not while he can remember what happened today.

Luke did not feel at all like he had won a victory over Sergeant Cooke. As he moved through the door to the medical exam area, he was more humiliated than he could ever recall. He was shaking inside and hurting in his back and side and face. It had taken every ounce of self-control he possessed to pull himself to full attention against the pain. He knew that for eight long weeks he faced literal hell from people like the Sergeant. He absolutely would not call on Freddie to help. It had to be up to him. And it had just begun.

The actions of Sergeant Cooke humiliated him. But being rescued by a White officer was even more humiliating. Apparently, the Officer did not recognize him as a long-lost friend. He feared that Cooke's abuse was like praise compared to what lay ahead of him.

Although a doctor was present, most of the examiners appeared to be enlisted orderlies running troops through rote tests for urine, blood sugar, rupture, hemorrhoids, heart disease, inflamed throats, rickets, tapeworm, enlarged testicles, venereal disease, or lice infection. As they moved from one test station to another, most of the Whites joked their way through the lines of naked men being poked and prodded and punctured with needles.

For the Blacks it was different. White recruits and orderlies alike gawked, laughed, grabbed at the Blacks with lewd derisive comments, either implying that they studded their women like so many animals, or reversing that, asking why they had so little manhood when everyone knew how a "Boy was hung".

For nearly an hour, Luke tolerated the abuse along with his Brothers. He smiled his most condescending, derisive smile at the perverse antics of his tormentors. For Luke it was not debasing because he felt personally degraded. He knew from experience to expect this kind of treatment. His self-esteem forced such trashy and low taunting to roll from his back. Rather, it embarrassed him as a man, for he still found it difficult to believe that men could behave so. He was finding out some things about life that Aggie had often tried to relate but he had been too stubborn to accept. He was again seeing the baseness of his fellow man coming through. He had always found this baseness difficult to either intellectualize or accept.

A roar of laughter on the other side of the room brought not only Luke's attention but that of the doctor in charge. Luke saw one of his Brothers, broken by torment, cowering in a corner, covering himself with his hands and crying. Luke had enough. Without thinking, he charged across the room and knocked two orderlies sideways while yelling at their inhumanity. He drew back to smash the face of a White recruit who continued to taunt the victim of their perverse humor. But the strong White fingers of the doctor clamped a restraining but gentle hold on his wrist. The doctor's voice was close to his ear.

"Easy, Son." he said. "Keep yourself clean. Calm. Let me handle it." The soothing voice settled Luke almost instantly, and he regained control. Although still panting in the aftermath of his anger, he relaxed his arm and stepped back. Then a booming "Attention" ricocheted across the room from the same doctor whose gentle voice had quieted him but seconds before.

"You Negroes." He was quick to diagnose the center of the problem and moved to eliminate it without emotion. "Get dressed and report back to the waiting room. You're done here." Turning from them in a way that left no room for any response other than obedience, he faced the White recruits and continued. "The rest of you get back to it," he said. "Now, move!"

Before Luke could move, the doctor reached out again and grabbed his arm. "Wait," he said. For the first time embarrassed by his own nakedness, Luke paused in the changed atmosphere. He eyed the doctor. "What." he spoke somewhat coldly as he tried to cover his embarrassment with his own bravado.

"I'm sorry, that's all. And I'm ashamed for what they did to you people."

"I am ashamed for all of us, Doctor. As human beings, we should neither dispense nor receive such treatment." Luke jerked away his arm. He gathered his clothes and dressed. The doctor stood motionless during the whole time, his eyes following Luke, his mouth half open. Luke knew that most in the room heard his comment. But he was sure that they did not hear the doctor's apology. He knew that the eyes of all who heard, like those of the doctor, were watching him as he dressed and walked to the door. He shuddered because he knew that they would be in training with him for at least eight weeks.

Luke realized that he was in deep trouble, but he could not fully accept the reasons. He had acted with humanity; they had not. He was right; they were not. But Luke saw at last that this was not the issue. He realized for the first time how different he was. He was different in his Blackness from his White brethren, and they would not let him forget it. He differed from his Black brethren in the way he spoke and faced and handled life. He realized that this also might estrange him from them. He feared that in this White World, his ideas and actions might well get his brothers in the trouble they had spent the better part of their lives avoiding. Unless he struggled to hide and suppress that difference, Luke reasoned that today's trouble was just the beginning. However, he was not sure he could do that without compromising what he believed and had lived all his life.

Luke briskly walked through the waiting room, looking nowhere but to the door in front of him. Clearing that, he turned and disappeared from view around and behind the building. There, his courage melted into shaking sobs. He thought of Aggie and home.

After he composed himself, Luke moved toward the Orderly Room. He followed the line of temporary barracks-like structures. He noticed that they already peeled from the haste of their construction of green southern pine at the beginning of the war. He finally came to one marked Battalion Headquarters and entered, hat in hand. He stopped just inside the door.

He had no paper, no pass, nothing but his word that the Lt ordered him to report to the headquarters. He did not even know why he was there and felt that he might very well be heading for a third major humiliation in less than an hour. He turned and started to push the screen door outward to escape.

"Hey, Soldier! Hold it!" Luke froze, his hand still on the door. His back to the clerk behind the desk, he waited motionless. He tried to decide whether to run or turn. He sighed and mentally kicked himself for not having the courage to dash through the door, then turned to face the green-clad clerk.

"What are you doing here? Where's your pass? Let me see your pass."

"I---"

"Come on, Recruit. Speak up!"

"I'm Luke Powers. I just got here this morning. I-—"

"Then you belong in reception. It's three buildings back."

"No, I, uh, I'm supposed to see the Lt."

"Which Lt? You know how many damned lieutenants we have running around here? What're you supposed to see him for?"

"I don't know. I'm just supposed to."

"You don't know. I should've figured. Don't know what this army's coming to. Filling up with ignorant kids that don't even know where they are or why. Who told you to come here?"

"He did."

"Who did, dammit. We going through that routine again?"

"No. I mean, Lt Henderson did."

"Ah, yes. Lt Henderson. Very good. Now at last we're getting to the bottom of this mystery of the misplaced recruit." The man's words were sarcastic but his voice was full of humor. Luke realized that the assault was not personal like it was with Cooke. Luke Looked at the nearly empty desk and the coffee cup sitting there in its own spill. The ashtray was running over with cigarette butts. A crumpled Lucky Strike pack was on the floor by the wastebasket. Noticing the cocky angle of the clerk's hat, Luke judged that the whole scenario had to do with boredom, unyielding boredom on the clerk's part. He wondered if the clerk had known that this would be his fate when he joined the army. He felt empathy with the man and relaxed.

"What's your name?" Luke ventured.

"Corporal Saunders. You don't talk like any Negro I ever met. Where you from Powers?"

"Georgia. Just outside of Dawson."

"Naw."

"Yeah. Really. How about you?"

"Me? I think maybe I'm from nowhere, been sitting here behind this desk for so long. Actually though, thinking back, the state of New Jersey comes to mind. Ever hear of it?"

"Does sound familiar. Yep. I believe there is such a place. Up North some isn't it? Though a bit cold this time of the year."

The two men bantered a while longer. Luke relaxed more and more, and the corporal was glad to have someone with whom to break the boredom.

"Used to drive through Dawson. When I was a kid, we'd go that way on the trip to Florida."

"You drive now?"

"Naturally."

"I've never been in a car."

"Really!"

"Yep. Never. But I did get to ride in the back of one of those big trucks to get here."

"Honestly? You've never been in a car? You really are from Dawson, aren't you?"

"Said I was."

"Well, look, Powers. The Lt isn't here right now. What else you supposed to do?"

"I don't know. The Lt told me to come right here after my physical."

"You wouldn't have met up with some sergeant named Cooke, would you?"

Luke looked at Corporal Saunders. Was he a friend of Cooke's? Was this new friendship to end before it had even begun? Luke decided not to answer.

"Well, did you?"

"Why?"

"Never mind. Well, it's just that word's all over the post on how this big nigger--sorry-- Negro faced him down in reception this morning. Plus, he came in here madder'n hell. To tell you the truth, I'm kind of glad to see him go. I had a sneaking suspicion he would make my life miserable." Luke just listened, fidgeted a little and wondered how or even if he should respond.

"You are the one, aren't you?"

"What makes you think so?"

"They said the guy was huge and spoke clear as a college professor and had a deep voice. They said he literally stared the little fart down and didn't even flinch when Cooke popped him in the stomach."

"Do you know when the lieutenant will be back?"

"Shouldn't be too long. Look, if you have got nothing else to do, sit awhile. Have a cup of coffee."

"Here? Now?"

"Sure. Why not?"

"How long have you been in Iowa, anyway? I mean, Colored folks are not generally invited to drink with White folks where I come from, if you know what I mean. Is it accepted here, I mean, is it okay?"

"Well," Saunders replied, "like I said, I'm not from Georgia. The Lt does it all the time, so Iowa must be different. Anyway, the lieutenant is."

"I'm not surprised."

"That Iowa is different?" Saunders responded as he handed Luke a cup of dirty looking coffee.

"No. That the Lt does it all the time."

"Really? How come?"

"Never mind." Luke thought better of divulging to anyone his previous and close relationship with Freddie. It crossed his mind to suppress the old, undisciplined manner in which he usually spoke. Until he was sure of his footing, he thought to keep his mouth shut. He changed the subject. "How long have you been in Des Moines, Corporal Saunders?"

"Got in a couple of days ago."

"A couple of---. I figured you must have been here a long time. You seemed so, well, bored with your job and all."

"I am. Already. I'm not a clerk, I'm an infantryman."

"Then what are you doing here?"

"I came in from Italy, via the hospital. Got shot."

"Where?"

"Italy."

"No. I mean where on your body did you get shot?"

"Ain't saying. Just did. All I know is leave it to the Army to get me a sit-down job now of all times." Saunders grin communicated his meaning to Luke, and they both laughed.

"Anyway," Luke came back while setting the coffee on the desk, "I think I'll pass on this coffee. This part of the country still tends to frown on certain transgressions of tradition, if you know what I mean."

"Damn right, nigger! What're you doin' here?" Sergeant Cooke stood at the open door. "Get outa here before I kick your ass out." The sight of Luke rekindled the rage and frustration Cooke had built in the reception room. But he did not have time to carry out his threat, for shortly behind him was Lieutenant Henderson.

"Powers! Get into that room there." He pointed. Luke glanced at him, then Cooke, and moved quickly to Freddie's office. He stopped inside the door, listening. Freddie continued, but in a soft, slightly sardonic tone, "Well, Sergeant Cooke, I trust you have the papers I asked for?"

"Yessir."

"Good. Then you are leaving us soon?" "Yessir."

"Have any idea where you're going?"

"Uh, No sir, Lt."

"Why, you're going right where we agreed this morning. Remember?"

"No, Sir."

"The C.O.'s waiting for you, Cooke. I'm sure he'll refresh your memory. I already briefed him on why you have made this request."

"Yessir." Cooke placed the papers in Freddie's outstretched hand. Freddie countersigned and endorsed the request, then handed them back to the sergeant. Without a word or salute, Cooke pivoted and left the Orderly Room.

Luke shifted his attention to the room and its contents. It was not what he thought an officer's office should look like. It was clean as he had suspected it would be. However, the walls were yellowing hardboard once painted white on the upper half. The lower half was that dirty putrid army green commonly called "gang green" among the troops. The desk was not old but it was cheaply constructed. It had an army green blotter on it. A picture of a woman and a little boy about five was framed in gold. Two boxes on the desk were labeled "IN" and "OUT". The "IN" box was full, the "OUT" box empty. A third one, separate and nearly buried, was marked "HOLD". Luke's feet felt the waxed linoleum floor as he turned at approaching footsteps. *Now,* he thought, *is the time. I wonder if he will remember me? I wonder if I should tell him?* Luke kept quiet for the moment.

Lt Henderson stepped through the door and closed it. "Hello, Luke" was all he said before his wide smile impinged his ability to speak.

"Gosh, Sir. I was afraid you didn't remember me."

"'Sir' is for out there in the fun and games world, Luke. When it's just the two of us, I'm still Freddie to you. What the hell are you doing here? I never figured you to enlist like an ordinary mortal."

"You really haven't changed much, Sir, uh, Freddie. A lot bigger, but the same."

"Same with you. Has it really been what, ten years?" Each seemed to want to embrace but appeared hesitant to move to the other. Suddenly a stillness filled the room. The small talk was behind them. Neither could think of what to say.

The circumstances under which they had first met no longer existed. Now one was a green recruit. A Black in a White man's Army, he had already been in trouble twice before his first day was over. The other was a White officer who had grown up in an environment full of privilege, always with shoes in a world made for his kind. Yet the bond existed. They could both feel it. Neither wanted to damage that bond. Finally, Freddie motioned to a chair. "Geez, Luke, forgive my manners. Sit down. Tell me what you've been up to."

"Growing up, I guess. I've done a lot of that in the last few hours."

"We mature fast in the Army, if we are to survive.

"That's a fact. Did you ever finish school?"

"In a manner of speaking, Freddie. Mostly, after the six grades in our 'modern' one room school, I taught myself."

"Really? Judging from your English, you must have done a pretty thorough job."

"I had some help from my Uncle, and from the local Preacher until the Klan killed him in a raid a few of years ago and---"

"Killed? Does that stuff really go on?"

"Not all the time, Freddie, but it got worse after the war started. Let's not talk about stuff like that. You're the one whose history is lost. Imagine, little freckled Freddie, orphan of orphans, now an officer in the United States Army."

"Yup. How about that?"

"C'mon, Freddie. Tell me the whole story. Last time I heard from you, you were a brand new father with your senior year at military school in front of you, and Howard had just been transferred to Hawaii."

"I really haven't written you since then?"

"Nope. I used to read your letters so often I memorized them. So I should know. And I wrote six or seven times after that but got no response. I finally quit. But I'll tell you, Brother, I never quit thinking of you."

"I know. You'll never know the thousands of times I've thought of you, too."

"So, what happened to you? I really want to know. Did you ever marry the girl, uh, Martha? What'd you name your boy? What ever happened to Howard? Is he a General by now?"

Freddie leaned back in his swivel chair and placed his freckled hands behind his red hair, fingers linked. He smiled, glad for an audience who would appreciate his story without a lot of preliminaries, glad to have his friend back. "Well," he started, "It's a long story. Lots happened, and I don't know what to tell you first."

"Start with what you named your boy and go from there."

"Oh, right. Jeff. Jeffrey Henderson."

"Henderson? Wasn't that your real last name? I'm surprised."

"I'll get to that. Now, you want to hear my life's story or not?" Freddie half smiled and a little wink passed across his brow. He lit up a Camel, exhaled and started in. "Got through my senior year at school easy enough. But without Howard around it was almost impossible to get away, and I didn't see much of Martha or Jeff. I was pretty lonely and pretty much a loner throughout. But I did well in my studies and was lucky enough to get some cadet command experience. Howard was still watching out for me even from Hawaii. He arranged for me to go on to the Citadel.

"Trouble with that was I would have to continue to live the lie and be away from Martha and Jeff. And I didn't want that. Howard still refused to even consider my going to another school, and I really thought a military career sounded OK. There were some jobs opening up, but they weren't good enough for a guy right out of high school with a wife and baby to support.

"I got away during the Easter break. Martha left Jeff with her mother---did I tell you she moved back home?---and came to Charleston over the holiday. We talked and argued for two days running and finally decided that I should accept the appointment to the Citadel. She insisted on it. Said she had lived without me to that point. Considering what the Citadel could mean to the two of us, she thought she could tolerate a couple of more years."

"But you would be, let's see, a junior, in your third year, or a senior?"

"Doesn't matter. Lots of things happened to change my plans that summer and fall. The first thing was my picture in the paper."

"What?"

"Let me tell you, that was really strange, hard to believe. I got the appointment, like I said. I was getting ready to go to Charleston for the summer. You have to report early the first year, for orientation, testing and stuff like that. Anyway, the Atlanta paper published my picture for the class of '44. I was at school about three days when I got a letter from my mother and father saying they wanted to see me."

"Your parents? You mean your real parents?"

"Yeah. How about that? I had not heard from them since the day they left me to go job hunting just before I met you. I had long ago assumed they were dead. It was the easy way out for me, I guess, because the only other thing that I could see might have happened was that they deliberately deserted me. I could not accept that, especially considering the trouble I had with my stepfather."

"But, Freddie, if they didn't desert you, how come they suddenly knew where you were and contacted you after all that time?"

"The picture, Luke, in the paper. It had my name, and I had started using my full name including Henderson. I guess in a way I did that to give myself some identity. It's a cinch I wasn't really a Sloan.

"Anyway, they saw the picture and read the name and knew where I was. They called the school, but I was in intense orientation and they could not get the call through. They thought they'd come to the school and see me in person. Then they decided that that might prove too great a shock all at once. They assumed I should have time to prepare myself and thought I might not want to see them. So they wrote the letter, telling me they loved me, searched for me all those years, and wanted to see me.

"To tell the truth, Luke, it really got me going. I simply did not believe that they could have been looking for me and not found me. That meant that they would have had to file with the courts and the police. My description and name would have been in the missing persons file for anybody to find. It took six months for my adoption by the Sloans to become official. I thought that in that time they should have been able to locate me. I mean, how many police stations are there in Atlanta?"

"Well, why didn't they, and how'd they come to lose you in the first place?"

"You won't believe me if I tell you. The answers to both questions are too incredible to be true. Let me tell you the reason they didn't find me. I confronted my Stepfather with what they said, and he admitted it was true. He said he did it for my Stepmother and that she did not know about it. He said that they were sure my parents were dead or he would never have done it, but that made little sense. I guess that's the reason he was so willing to pay for my education and all, considering what he'd done. Don't you think?"

"Freddie, you haven't told me what he did."

"Oh. Yeah. He bribed the police to keep my name off the list when it came down from the Juvenile Court. The Court waited for the police to find my parents. When they didn't the court declared me abandoned. And they didn't find my parents because they weren't looking. In a way that sonofabitch stole me. He actually kidnapped me. Incredible isn't it? And you know the funniest part? I almost found my parents before I went to the Sloans and didn't even know it. But I'm getting ahead. Isn't this incredible? I still don't believe it all, I swear."

"So how did your parents come to lose you in the first place?"

"Well, according to my Dad, he and Mom took a bus to Augusta because he'd heard about a job there. The two of them would be caretaker and housekeeper to some wealthy guy and live on the grounds of his estate. This guy asked them to come for an interview or something. Anyway, Dad had been out of work for about four months and was desperate. The mill had closed. I guess I told you that before. Anyway, they got the job, only the man wanted them to start right away. So Mom told Dad to go ahead and she would catch the bus back to Atlanta and get me."

"So why didn't she?"

"She got mugged and robbed in the ladies' room at one of the bus stops. This is really far-fetched, I know. It's so crazy I believe it. Or I maybe I believe it because I want to, because they have been so swell to me and to Martha and Jeff. But like I was saying, Mom was in the hospital unconscious for days. They didn't have any idea who she was because the mugger stole her bag. Some attendant or someone at the bus station found her later, I think. Anyway, the bus driver apparently didn't even miss her.

"After she regained consciousness, she told them who she was, and they got in touch with my Dad through his work."

"Yeah, Freddie, but what about your dad? Didn't he wonder what had happened to his family?"

"Sure he did, that is, after a week. See, Mom and I were not supposed to even be in Augusta for a week or two. And we didn't have a phone at the house in Atlanta, plus he didn't want to take a call at the boss's house, being so new. So Mom said she would call only if she ran into trouble or was delayed or something. He didn't get a call and assumed everything was fine.

"Oh, I forgot. She was supposed to call once, on Sunday. The man they worked for was going to the country or Washington or something for the weekend. So Dad could use the phone. He told Mom he would hang around the house at about 2:00 in the afternoon. Mom was supposed call and tell him when she would be coming home. But then she didn't call.

"At first, this upset Dad a little. But he figured maybe she didn't call because she was on her way. When she didn't show up, he really started worrying. He called our old Landlord in Atlanta, and the man said the house was empty and that Dad owed him rent, so he would rent it out. When the man said the house was empty, Dad assumed that Mom and I were on our way. He told the man to go ahead and that he would send him the rent as soon as he could."

"But your Mom had not been there?"

"No. Remember, that was the day I went home and found that they had rented the place. Just two more days, and I would have been there to greet them. But by then I was in the alleys in Atlanta."

"In two more days? You mean, when your mom came to, and they called your dad?"

"Yeah. He dropped everything and headed for Atlanta through that little town where they robbed Mom and she was waiting for him. I forget the place. After what the Landlord told him, he had the double worry of collecting his injured wife and getting to Atlanta as fast as he could to find me. He used his boss's phone to call the Atlanta police to start them looking for me. He even called some of their friends, but most of them didn't have phones. When he could not find me that way, he asked his friends to spread the word and for all of them to keep their eyes open. He also told them what bus he would come in on."

"Then the police were looking for you?"

"Yeah. The whole time you and I were together, and before. Mom and Dad thought they looked for months, but actually, they quit about three days after I got to the Sloans, thanks to my stepfather. Here's the strangest part. You remember how we ran from the guy in the warehouse?"

"I'll never forget that."

"Remember the police whistles? The hands grabbing at us? Well, apparently they weren't chasing us because of what we stole. They had spotted me. I matched the description, and they wanted to get me for my folks."

"C'mon, Freddie. How can you know that?"

"No, it fits. It really does. My folks said that about two weeks after they called the police, they got a message from them that a little boy matching the description of their son had been spotted running toward Niggertown---sorry Luke---with a Colored boy. They said they tried to catch him but he got away. My folks said that was the last they heard. Finally, they went back to Augusta. They had to or my Dad would lose his job. But they called the police department in Atlanta once a week for several weeks. They even went to the police in Augusta to see if they could help. Nothing seemed to, but they kept trying different things over the years. Later, after they saw my picture in the paper, they headed for Sloan's. That was when they found out why they had not had any luck."

"That is fantastic, Freddie. And great, great news. I really am glad for you. How can you have anything to do with Sloan after that?"

"Sloan's dead. He was killed at Pearl Harbor. As a matter of fact — and this was about the only lucky thing to come from the whole fiasco — he was packing to go to Pearl when the Hendersons located him. He had been there about a year when the attack came."

"And so you and your folks got back together?"

"Sure. In a way. I mean I was already grown up with a wife and kid of my own. But we have become good friends and done a lot of sharing. I love them a great deal and must admit I feel better about myself and my own worth since I found out what happened. They help look after Martha and Jeff when I'm overseas. Actually, Martha and Jeff are in Iowa, now. Hey, Luke, we've got to arrange for you to see them. I've changed Jeff's name to Henderson, and he is very happy to have his grandparents. All's well that ends well, or something like that."

"But you still haven't told me why you are not in school, Freddie."

"Well, I stuck it out a year. But it was a lot rougher than I thought it would be. I don't mean the school. I mean being away from Martha and Jeff, and I needed to get to know my parents."

"So you quit after your first year?"

"Not exactly. I started my second year. But then Pearl Harbor happened, and we entered the war, and I got word that my stepfather got killed at Pearl. That wiped out all obligation I had to anyone named Sloan, and I was a one third beneficiary of his will. It wasn't much, but it was enough to convince me I could get married and provide for my child. Some of the other cadets were quitting to join and fight, so I did too. I went home for a while, married Martha, and we were going to rent a little apartment. But the city was filling up with military types, and the price of things was going up. So we moved to Augusta to live with my folks."

"When did you join? How come you're a Lieutenant if you didn't graduate?"

"Well, I joined about six weeks after Pearl and eventually ended up a Platoon Sergeant because of my military training. We wound up in the desert in North Africa and somehow I got a Field Commission. That's another story which I will share with you someday over a beer. Just let me say that a purple heart and a trip back to the States accompanied the Commission. So here I am, a Second Lieutenant in charge of training for the Battalion because I have combat experience. Also, because I have a southern background. Mostly, I think because they needed volunteers willing to train Negroes. If I'm lucky, I'll leave with one of these training companies one day as a Platoon Leader, or maybe their XO.

"Meantime, I have a lot of time with my family, so I'm not kicking, believe me. You've just got to come meet them, Luke. I know you'll be crazy about Martha. She and my parents know all about you already, at least until you were about, what, thirteen? You've got some catching up to do yourself."

Luke marveled at his friend's story. Freddie's bearing, sense of authority and easy-going projection of command impressed him. Luke was sure he was a good officer and hoped he could serve near Freddie or even be in Freddie's Company. Freddie interrupted his thinking.

"It will have to be some other time, though, Pal. You've got to get to supply and draw your gear. The rest of the recruits should be through with the hurry-up-and-wait routines of reception and on their way over there now. Cm'on. I'll point you in the right direction."

Freddie came around the desk as Luke stood. "I always knew you'd make it, Luke. Look at you," Freddie said as he laid to rest the last barrier to their old trust. Placing his hand on Luke's shoulder, he squeezed as he took Luke's other hand in a firm grasp of his shake. "You'll never know, Luke, how good it is to see you. I really wanted this chance to talk to you in private before we have to assume the public role the Army has selected for us.

"Listen to me closely, Luke. You're like my own brother but once beyond that door you — you in particular I'm afraid — are in for some hard times. I remember how you feel about people. How could I forget. You showed me by saving my life- — "

"And you by saving mine, Freddie. Don't forget that."

"Well, anyway, we're like brothers. But as I was saying, most people from whatever race don't share your view. Your size, your bearing, your wit and education will single you out. The Negroes will look to you for leadership, but a lot of the Whites will — and I'm ashamed to have to say it — they will fear you, resent you. They, some of them, will come after you like Sergeant Cooke did. Not many. There are more decent White people than you might think, from North or South. But it only takes one at a time to make your life miserable or constantly push you toward trouble."

"I know. It didn't take me too long to figure that out."

"Well unfortunately, I won't always be around to run interference for you."

"And I wouldn't want you to if you could. I'll learn to handle it. I've handled things like that before, some worse."

"I'm sure. I just felt like I needed to say it, so you'd understand. I will keep my eye out, but I don't think it would be a good thing if some of those types we're talking about found out we're friends."

"I know."

"But Luke, I am the Training Officer, which is a good cover. If you ever need anything, even just to talk it out, you know where a friend is. And I may just send for you occasionally, just for old time's sake."

"Thanks, Freddie, for saying that."

"Better make it Lt Henderson from now on, Private Powers. No slip like 'Freddie' would help beyond this door.

"Yessir." Luke snapped out the word with a wide grin. Freddie smiled back and grabbed a pad from his desk.

"Here. Just in case the rest of your Company is ahead of schedule, give this to the Supply Sergeant and he'll catch you up in no time." Freddie walked Luke to the door, taking care to move officially and to his front. Pushing the door slightly open, he pointed across the courtyard in front of the Orderly Room and said, "Take this note ten barracks down and across the yard, Private. That's the Negro Company Orderly Room. Ask for Sergeant Sampson. He's the toughest, fairest, best sergeant I ever met. He and Corporal Saunders served with me in Africa before I got hit and Saunders went to Italy. Anyway, I've had you assigned to Sampson's company. Tell him I sent you. He'll make sure you're finished in time for chow. Questions?"

"No, Sir."

"Dismissed, Private."

With a final "Yessir", Luke moved through the screened door. Looking back, he grinned and nodded a farewell to Saunders then quickly stepped out toward his new home. His head was high and there was a bounce in his step. Freddie was after all still Freddie, and men were after all still men. Some noticed color, like Cooke. Some did not, like Saunders. The army seemed to have both, and Luke found this normal. Luke knew he could handle it as he reached the Company Supply Room.

CHAPTER 20

First Stroke of the Brush

Aggie found herself at the pond. It was a place she had not frequented in the weeks since Luke left. Before arriving, she wandered endlessly from place to place, measuring the ache in her heart. She wondered if she would ever get used to Luke's absence. She hoped against hope that he would get a furlough before they shipped him overseas. She completely digested his letters in her mind as her hand massaged their ragged pages in the pocket of her apron.

Aggie wandered through the church grounds where until just last month Luke was preaching. She wandered through the woods where they met so often to talk, study, be with each other, make love. She walked the deserted clay road that stretched through the Georgia peanut, cotton and bean fields. In Aggie's imagination, this road also led to Luke. Finally, with the ache in her body and soul telegraphing the old shadows, she arrived at the pond. Her feet found the softened moist clay. She sat next to the mirroring water where her memories and her dreams had begun and always returned.

Aggie remembered her first time at the pond long before she met Luke. She was listening for dogs. She remembered the many times she heard them and tensed as the sound drew near; she relaxed as the memory faded. *How silly I was*, she thought. Still she felt a tremble of her old fear. She recalled the dogs again. In her mind's eye, they rounded the pond on both flanks as though to come after her. Then thoughts of Luke at the pond took over. She remembered first meeting him there and had to laugh. *He was so angry, and so handsome, oh, so handsome, even if I could only see him from the waist up. I sure thought his skinny body was beautiful. If I hadn't been so scared myself I'd have gotten an eyeful that day, all right.*

Aggie felt longing as her mind filled with images of Luke's full body first seen at the pond three years later. Her mind drifted back to that first confrontation, that first summer. *That was some summer*, for sure, she mused. *Those were some days. My Luke, my Luke.* "God!" she voiced in agony. "Where is my Luke? What am I going to do?" *Will he ever come back to me?* This was a question she might think but dared not voice. So she turned. Her frowning mouth and sad eyes accompanied her melancholy toward home. The sun was near setting and nothing could keep her alone near the pond that time of day.

The next day was only the fourth Sunday out of the last two years on which Luke did not preach. For the Congregation, Luke could preach better than any man they knew whether ordained or called. LeRoy Powers was always available to help or listen or coordinate projects needed by one member of the congregation or another. But now it was different. In those four Sundays everything changed for Aggie.

Before he left, Luke always insisted on preaching on the old church site whenever the weather permitted. In bad weather they gathered in an old barn on one of the farms abandoned during the depths of the depression. The men in the congregation built rough benches for both places.

They had cleared the ashes and debris at the church, but trash and weeds were now invading the trodden footpaths between those rough pews. The whole congregation hoped to rebuild this year, but with the war, they moved that hope to "someday". It was two years since the destructive Klan shadows invaded the church. Now the boys went to war, or to the Northern factories or Atlanta to build things for war. The young girls worked in the fields or had jobs in town with the White folks. They did chores White sons had once done before going away to fight the Nazis. To Aggie, the church was a symbol of Luke, a "someday". By nature and temperament and experience, Aggie did not like "somedays". She much preferred her own version of "now".

On this Sunday, one "someday" to which Aggie never gave much thought, was a "now". Aggie disliked major changes even when Luke was present. They terrified her even more in his absence. They compounded her dread. Luke's absence itself was the most pronounced of the changes she was enduring. Yet this only marked a beginning. There were others. The last Sunday that Luke had preached had been the last Sunday of Yesterday. This Sunday belonged to another time.

Aggie feared that the temporary Preacher the menfolk hired would soon replace Luke in the congregation's heart as he was now doing in the pulpit. The memory-stained clay in front of the bleachers at the church remained empty because the Preacher had routinely moved the service to the old barn. "More like a proper church," he said. But the small barn offered Aggie no support or sense of worship. Nor did it seem to for the Congregation whose church was ashes.

This was the first Sunday afternoon when Aggie finally accepted that Luke was gone. Whose arm would Aggie hang on this Sunday afternoon before the dreaded tomorrow? How would Aggie ever get used to sleeping alone in a room? She had moved out of the crowded shack which had sheltered her for sixteen years and went to live with the Powers. She left Sammy and Jason to their overburdened mother.

Now she had Luke's room and that should have been some comfort. She slept in Luke's bed surrounded by his books. The trunk in the corner held his clothing and all his personal and private things. She explored and examined them over and over. It did not help; she was still alone. It was as though his ghost were present, but not her Luke.

Then, tomorrow. *Oh, tomorrow*, she thought, as the Preacher's unheard words passed by her. She had to get up at four in the cold and dark. She would have to dress and eat and go with Mrs. Powers to a White woman's house to work. Aggie had never been in a White woman's house. She knew they had fine and fancy things. She saw such things in the worn out Sears catalog LeRoy had gotten for Luke so many years before. She had looked at all the finery Luke would get her someday, and these things became as much a part of her dream as Luke himself. Now he was gone, the worn catalogue was tattered and frayed, and she must go to a real house. She must see actual things she would probably always want and never have. She would have to clean them and care for them. She would do it for a White woman. This woman would probably curse and hit her and work her extra and cheat her if she could. Aggie knew that this would happen because Luke was gone.

The hard and cramped bench in the body-heated barn-church was as discomfiting as Aggie's mood. The droning platitudes of the new Preacher and the hot noonday sun made it even worse. Aggie was miserable. She was the worse for believing strongly that this misery was all there was left to her life. True to her prophecy, the afternoon social was no better for her and the night was lonely and sleepless. Finally tomorrow, the dreaded tomorrow, came.

"Aggie." Crystal Powers finally gave up calling from the kitchen. She climbed the loft ladder and shook her young charge's shoulder. "C'mon, Chile. Get out of bed. We've got to get going. I can't be late with Miz Harmon's breakfast."

Aggie stirred slightly and pulled the worn quilt tighter around the top of her head. Far from dissipating, Aggie's misery built during the sleepless night in dread of the very moment now upon her. How she wished she could be by the pond or on the road or even in the churchyard right then. Instead, she was being prodded and scolded by Luke's Aunt. How she wished she were with Luke.

But Crystal was unrelenting both in shaking her and talking. "Miz Harmon has to do some shopping this morning, and she says she got to be there when the doors open. Y'all hear, Girl?" Crystal tugged the covers off and pulled at Aggie's arm as she talked on. Her future niece totally exasperated her. Aggie's refusal to rise after being called several times forced the big old woman to laboriously move her bulk up the narrow ladder through the trapdoor. She did so only when absolutely necessary and never without extreme effort and complaining. With a mixture of fear tinted with mirth, she remembered the day the sheriff got caught in that same opening. She did not climb the ladder at all after the sheriff's visit until forced to do so to clean the room before Aggie moved in. Crystal feared that she might also become a victim to the trapdoor's inadequate size.

Dropping Aggie's arm, Crystal looked around at the room she had worked so hard to make nice for her future niece-in-law. Aggie's clothes were littering the floor by the bed. Books pulled from the orange-crate shelves were lying at random on the table and floor. Luke's trunk was open in the corner with his clothing and personal things jumbled and spilling from it. What she saw thoroughly disgusted Crystal. She resented the girl's total disregard for the fact that she was making Crystal late. *Look what that girl has already done to Luke's room*, she thought.

Crystal kept her opinion of Aggie to herself. She even kept quiet when LeRoy suggested she get Aggie this job and have her move in with them. "We've got to look out for Luke's girl," he said. "Ain't no good going to come of her getting into trouble." Crystal listened and realized that LeRoy was right. Her husband continued, "Now, Luke's gone for maybe two, three years, and Aggie is ripe and ready. She is and so pretty and all, them young bucks around here're going be all around her."

Crystal snorted and pointed out that most of those young bucks were in the army. But still she knew he was right. There were older men both Black and White to whom Aggie represented something desirable. When LeRoy countered by naming several teens not yet in the army, Crystal knew that he would prevail.

Knowing Luke and Aggie as he thought he did, LeRoy doubted seriously that they had risked much beyond serious touching. He mistakenly reasoned that this was mostly Luke's doing. He knew that Luke did not want any children to take care of until he had the education he wanted. *With Aggie it might be different,* he thought. He often saw the way she would flirt with and excite Luke. Long ago he learned from Luke's Grandmother of the incident at the pond on Luke's thirteenth birthday. Still, LeRoy knew what Aggie meant to Luke. Despite all the weakness he saw in her and all the unhappiness for Luke this generated in him, he felt she balanced Luke's strength and will. He convinced himself that she was good for him.

For Crystal, there was a different view. To her Aggie was a lazy, self-centered and immature dreamer who wandered through life dependent on others. She always seemed to complain about anything and everything unusual. She seemed easily flustered by change. She feared strangers, even strangers of her own color. She especially feared men.

Crystal knew Aggie flirted with Luke and easily assumed those flirtations often led to intimate involvement. She thought she might even know the exact day they had first made love. She often recalled the week before Luke first began preaching just before his sixteenth birthday. Crystal knew that Aggie assumed all other men were potentially another Elkins or her father. So many times Aggie all but said so in the last month as she fought Crystal's decision to send her to work in the White man's world.

Yet it was because of this very set of impressions of Aggie's character and personality that Crystal decided to take Aggie to work with her. She felt the exposure to the Whites through a good and gentle woman like Elizabeth Harmon in the controlled routine of a household would help Aggie change her views. She thought this might be just the thing to conquer Aggie's inordinate fears of Whites, people and of new circumstances and change.

She also believed that at seventeen, Aggie ought to at least know what hard work was and learn the satisfaction of accomplishment. It amazed her that Aggie's mother had taught so little to her daughter even with the burden of cooking and cleaning all those years. She could only assume that the woman gave up in the face of Aggie's fears, stubborn selfishness and complaining. She just let Aggie drift as she apparently wanted to. In facing that, Crystal vowed to use the time Luke was away to turn Aggie into a woman who would prove a proper wife for a preacher and leader of his people.

With her mind reeling with this recall and resolve, Crystal moved again to the side of the bed. She reached down and took Aggie's sagging arm and gave it one last jerk. Aggie tumbled onto the floor. "Get this right, Girl. If y'all is going to marry up with my Luke, y'all is going to learn some things about taking care of a man besides just sharing his bed, and I is going to teach you." She pulled Aggie to her feet and snatched off her nightshirt. "And the first thing I is going to teach you is how to rise and shine without making ol' Crystal here huff and puff her way up that ladder every morning. Now, y'all get yourself something to eat and come on. I is leaving here in about eight minutes. If y'all ain't with me, y'all ain't eating tonight. Ain't nobody living under my roof what ain't earning their own way." Crystal turned to the ladder as she spoke and eased her way through the opening as she finished. But Aggie stopped her halfway down with her words.

"You can't do that. And you can't make me work. I'll go back to my mamma's house."

"Fine, Chile." Crystal twisted her head and looked Aggie in the face. Her cheeks flushed with exertion and a rare flare of anger at the girl's insolence. "Y'all go on and go home. Only if y'all do, I is getting Miz Harmon to send my Luke one of them letters telling him how y'all refused to help his Aunt Crystal while y'all is sleeping in his bed and eating his food. Then that letter will tell him how y'all run away from his bed after he done told you to stay there while he was away."

"You wouldn't dare."

"I sure would. I is telling you, Girl. Either y'all learn to be a proper woman for my Luke, or I is going to make sure he never comes for y'all. And I'd be just as glad of that, if y'all must know. Now!" Lowering her massive body the last few rungs to the floor below, Crystal strutted with incredible dignity across the porch to the back door. Aggie stood over the ladder and watched her. Just before she stepped inside, Crystal turned again and looked up at the girl. "Y'all got six minutes left, Girl. That's all." She went into the house.

Aggie sat on the edge of the bed. Suddenly, her misery was compounded by a feeling of being trapped. Her silent fear was that Luke would never come home from the war. Now she had the new fear that if he did, he would no longer love her. Until Crystal's last chilling words that thought had never occurred to Aggie. Its dismal effect on her thrust her from the present and her dream into imaginings of a world without Luke. It nearly shattered her. She forced the thoughts from her mind and grasped desperately for the old dreams built on "ifs" instead of "whens". "If Luke were here," she voiced through her tears, "he wouldn't make me do this. Let her write her old letter. Maybe Luke will come home and tell her to leave me alone." With that, Aggie crawled back under the covers.

Crystal finished getting ready then stood at the bottom of the ladder for a moment. Finally shaking her head, she started the long walk to town.

/ / /

When Aggie awoke, she found herself soaked and her bedclothes drenched. She felt hot even as a chill coursed through her. She had been dreaming that Crystal sent the letter to Luke, who wrote back to Aggie telling her he did not love her anymore. She cried for Crystal to give her another chance, but Crystal refused to even acknowledge her presence. She wrote to Luke but got no answer. She went home but, working hard as always, her mother did not even see her. In desperation, she went to the pond to think. There the dogs came at her from the woods. As though she was not even in their way, they charged after a coon which scooted between Aggie's legs. Then Elkins rose from the pond and told Aggie that he had waited a long time for her. She screamed in abandoned terror as the dead man dragged her down into the pond. She woke up as the last gasp of air in her lungs escaped. She yelled "Luke, Luke" as she woke, soaked and certain that she was dead.

In a panic but relieved to be alive, she was suddenly terrified of the bed. Still screaming for Luke, Aggie slipped into her dress and practically leaped down the ladder. No one was around. A cool breeze off the creek greeted her. Nervously she looked through the screen door into the kitchen. Because of the time Crystal had lost that morning, the breakfast dishes stood stacked by the sink, unwashed. She called for Uncle LeRoy. He was not there. She checked the small barn.

The mule and wagon were not there. Then she remembered that LeRoy worked the night shift in the lumber mill. The mill was running twenty-four hours a day to keep up with the demand for government orders. The mill owners had hired a Black crew for the twelve to eight shift because Whites would not take the job without double pay. Luke had worked there beside his Uncle for a while before enlisting. She remembered resenting the mill even though they set aside the earnings of both men for Luke's education. The work at the mill meant that Luke was going to bed right after dinner so he could be up in time for work. After working all night at the mill, Luke would do his chores so there was very little time in Luke's life for her in that last six months. Now, she reflected, there was none.

Thinking about this, and the dream, and the things Crystal had said, Aggie suddenly felt abandoned and more than a little bitter and frightened. She started to run home. But she hesitated as she remembered home as she had seen it in the dream.

Suddenly, as though by rote, as though controlled by a force outside of her, she turned and went into the kitchen. She cleaned it in a near frenzy. The dream so haunted her and drove her and dominated her that she did not even realize that she was cleaning. She seemed to observe two girls. One industriously worked and sung in a worn old country kitchen. The other ran and ran, with a vacant stare of suppressed terror burning a path before her bleeding and racing feet. Soon the girl working at the sink finished and moved on to other chores. But the running girl remained just there, just out of reach, going nowhere, and looking worse with each passing moment.

Aggie was on her knees scrubbing the floor when LeRoy banged through the back door and dissipating the image of the running girl with his presence. Aggie started at finding herself on all fours with a scrub brush in her hand.

"Hey, Gal. What y'all doing home?"

Aggie looked at him for a minute, trying to collect herself enough to come up with an answer. Finally she said, "Felt kind of sick this morning, Mr. LeRoy. Miss Crystal left me here. Now I feel better and I thought I'd clean up a bit."

"Looking mighty good, Hon. Where'd y'all learn to clean like this? I thought your mamma done all the cleaning at your place."

"Mostly, yeah. But I've watched her lots of times and helped some. It isn't hard to learn, just a little tiring." *I'll get used to it* Aggie thought and realized that she had accepted the changes in her life which she had been fighting for a month. She immediately began reforming the dream. It now accommodated the changes, and they became a part of her as though they had always been there. She completely forgot the terrible nightmare. In her mind she was cleaning Luke's and her home just as she had countless times in the imaginings upon which she survived. Aggie felt some happiness for the first time since Luke had told her he was enlisting. She thought of other things which she should do. "You want some breakfast, Luke, uh, I mean Mr. LeRoy?"

LeRoy smiled at her, fully hearing the slip of her tongue and wondering if Luke was ever out of her thoughts. "I sure would, Hon. Been hard at it over there at the mill. Say, Chile, y'all just call me Uncle LeRoy. That 'Mister' stuff makes me feel like an old man."

Aggie laughed a little laugh and shoved the scrub bucket off into the corner with her foot. "I'll whip us up a mess of grits and some fresh eggs. I'm half-starved myself. Now that I'm feeling better, I mean." Aggie set a pot under the pump, filled it and set it on the woodstove. Taking up the frying pan she had just scrubbed, she cracked four eggs into it and watched as the edges slowly turned white.

"Better chuck a log in that stove, Chile, if you want them grits to cook right. Might want to lift them eggs off for a minute or two, come to think on it, until the other is near done. It takes them grits a spell." LeRoy sat at the table, elbows on its oilcloth cover. His old and battered corncob pipe glowed softly.

"Right, Uncle LeRoy. I plan to do that next, you see." Stoking the fire, she took a good handful of grits and tossed it in the water. She ignored LeRoy's admonition on the eggs. They sizzled and began smoking. She grabbed a turner and scraped them up from the ungreased pan, breaking each yolk as she flipped them over, then took them out. She went back and stirred the grits, finding it both watery and lumpy. Quickly she threw in another handful of grits as a wider and wider grin creased LeRoy's tired face. The grits cooked to a tough lumpy blob just about the time the eggs, long off the stove, reached room temperature. Aggie dished out a gob of grits on each plate and set one in front of LeRoy. "Doesn't look quite right, does it?" she said.

LeRoy could contain his amusement no longer. Laughing out loud, he reached up and pulled Aggie to him, wrapping his big arm around her shoulder. Squeezing, he pronounced the meal fit for a White man. "But," he added, "no self-respecting Colored would touch it."

With a twinge of panic at LeRoy's rough and friendly caress, Aggie suddenly caught the joke and laughed. She felt strangely happy and did not mind at all the gentle fatherly affection shown by this man. Smiling at him, she set the plates aside and laid some fruit and cold biscuits out on the table. "Worked all morning on these," she smirked. "Eat it up, and with no more jokes about my cooking, or I'll tell my Luke on you."

"Do that, Aggie, and I might just tell him what a great job y'all does with grits and eggs for breakfast."

To her own surprise, Aggie smiled and laid her hand alongside the old man's stubbly cheek. "Let's keep that to ourselves, shall we? At least until I've had a little more practice."

"Depends. Y'all planning on practicing on me?" They both laughed again and finished the biscuits.

At this Aggie knew she was home. She knew she would do whatever either LeRoy or Crystal told her to until Luke himself took her away to a home of their own. She was again where she belonged, in the present, with one day at a time, and stronger people in control of her. The hogs got the grits. The first brush strokes across the canvas of reality was mostly a cautious yellow. They hid the part of life which Aggie could not bear.

CHAPTER 21

Mortal Men

The training was behind him. The long staging and lay-over in England were over. Corporal Luke Powers huddled in the landing craft, wet and frozen and terrified. He was struggling to keep his composure as he kept his squad close, ready to disembark on the Normandy Beachhead. The surf was running wild and the craft plowed and bounced through the waves, hitting bottom then riding high. Luke was thankful that his hope of being in Freddie's Company was realized. He needed Freddie to be there, with him, encouraging him. He focused on the moment, on his men, on what he and they must do any minute.

It was a rough landing, hitting the bottom a half mile from the beach. They plunged forward from the craft, struggling and screaming through the rough surf. That they made it amazed them. They splayed prone on coarse sand among barricades, rocks and bodies. They pulled their heads down with their hands and waited for a shell to hit them. The bombardment was all around them. Fear and disorientation dominated their minds and souls. Luke raised his head and counted his men. All but two from the craft had survived. Looking further, he saw Freddie and thanked God.

Freddie rose and yelled to his Platoon to follow. He half ran, half crawled from cover to cover as he inched his way forward. Luke roused his squad and followed. The other squads followed. The bombardment continued. They had to take out the bunkers and stop the guns.

The battle raged on the rest of the day and into the night, but eventually the German resistance broke. The beach and the bluffs above were theirs. It took several days to finish gaining control. Then they started pursuing the Germans.

Days blended together for them in constant motion as they pursued the enemy force, now in full retreat. Luke was not sure how many days passed before the Battalion was pulled back. Another Battalion relieved them and they finally could rest.

When the Germans evacuated Paris, Luke's Battalion was among the first to march into the city. Huge French crowds greeted them and welcomed them and coddled them. Luke and Freddie and the rest had a full week of R&R in the homes and night spots of Paris. Hot showers, long periods of sleep, good food and wine brought them back to sanity. And there were women. Luke wrote to Aggie and passed on the women. Freddie wrote to Martha and did the same.

Then they moved out again, taking part in the giant army's push toward Germany. At first the front was well in front of them, but they closed with it as they approach the Ardennes.

/ / /

Luke had plenty of time to think if his mind could focus through his exhaustion and fear. It seemed an eternity since his last shower, last good meal, last cigarette, last night in Paris. But at last Platoon Sergeant Luke Powers could afford private thought. For the moment, he could risk letting his mind retreat into the shadows of the past. He dwelled on things and places and events that were. He steered his mind away from the danger and boredom of the present, away from reflections of a future which may not exist. He drifted back to the good old days when he was a trainee, when the powerful Platoon Sergeant Sampson was riding him and grooming him and training him and mothering him. He had tried to find reason in both the training experience and in the prejudice he had witnessed from other companies against him and his brothers.

Luke recounted in his mind the two nights he and Freddie played civilian against all orders by going to Freddie's home in Des Moines. He remembered being welcomed by the warm and open Martha and the jabbering five-year-old, red-headed Jeff. He remembered the cozy sense of abandon he shared with all of this family. He now considered them his family almost as much as he did his own aunt and uncle. In a different, an entirely different way, he considered them family almost as much as he did Aggie.

Luke recalled Aggie, as he inevitably seemed to do no matter what else might be in his mind or going on around him. He reflected on his last visit home with her with mixed feelings. He had experienced those same feelings the night of the visit itself. It had been but one day and one night and a long pull in the back of the loaded and smelly highway bus. He had discovered immediately upon leaving the Post that his uniform earned him no privilege which his color did not cancel. In deference to reality, he automatically moved to the rear among the exhaust fumes and his Brothers.

Luke compared the headache he had when the bus finally stopped in Dawson with the one he was experiencing there in his foxhole. He decided the former was worse. He smiled at this. He had thought for some time that nothing could be worse than what the present held. *Perhaps*, he thought, *that headache seemed worse because, after eight weeks of separation, Aggie was not at the bus station to meet me.* Instead, LeRoy and his same wagon and his same mules came to town to take him home. LeRoy made good use of the trip. He stopped at Ol' Tom's for some trading and supplies. So there was little room for even the simple duffle bag Luke hoisted across the tailgate. The trip home was bumpy and full of chatter. But LeRoy avoided Luke's questions about Aggie the whole way. He finally saw that LeRoy seemed a little upset by something that Aggie had done. He decided not to press it but wait and find out from Aggie directly.

Then they arrived. Aggie was standing on the road by the fence at the edge of the farm where LeRoy reined in the mules. Slapping Luke on the shoulder, he said, "There she is, Boy." He gently shoved Luke, who jumped clear and ran to take her in his arms. Her smile pleased him as he approached and her eyes seemed to dance as he saw himself reflected in them. This was what he had hoped for.

What he had not expected, however, was her intermittent detachment. She seemed to drift away from and back to him as the evening then the night wore on. He still could not account for the sudden glaze in her eyes which seemed to block him out. This only lasted a moment each time but startled and concerned him every time it happened.

There in the foxhole with his body so tired yet aching for her now, he recalled her elaborate preparation. It was almost as though she was playing a game before receiving him inside her. When they finally joined, it was late. They were in the barn, away from the house and his sleeping aunt and uncle. He fantasized that this union would melt away what was troubling her. He hoped she would be fully and completely his once again. Yet even in their union she seemed to be acting, to pretend a passion which she did not really feel. Then without warning she would come alive in his arms. She would respond fully and completely to his lovemaking. This excited and compelled him as never before. But when in response he reached the height of his pleasure, he would come down with the feeling that she was again mechanical, detached, just playing a game.

When he left the next morning, he was just as confused and he wondered how he might leave after just one day without a big scene. But though with a look of sadness and a shadow of grief, Aggie calmly rendered a goodbye which to Luke seemed short. On the whole walk to the bus station he felt that he should have sought just one more kiss and held her to him. He should have asked her directly during the night what was bothering her. Luke believed that she was unaware of her strange behavior. He was afraid that Aggie would not be able to share her fears and feelings with him. This bothered him through all the months since then. It was what was bothering him now, and again he tried other memories to push this discomfiture from his tired mind.

He remembered the good times in Paris after the Normandy landing. He would never forget the landing itself. He tried to reject that memory too. Its death and noise tried to take over and blot out the comforting memories he worked so hard to keep. Banishing Normandy from his mind was difficult for that time was so much like today. This time, this place was about some pistol toting four star pushing with tanks to break the stalemate and get on into Germany.

Luke hoped that it would soon be over. But now, as though that future may not happen, Luke did as Aggie would and lived only for the moment. He wanted to create fantasies from his memories that would make life tolerable. He did not want to look to tomorrow. Enemies — the basis of his ever-present fear — differed from Aggie's. In his opinion, Aggie's enemies were self-created. He had always considered her greatest enemy to be herself and her view of things. He recalled countless occasions when he would tell her this. He vaguely recalled his argument with her just before his 16th birthday when he first told her he would be preaching. This argument had involved much the same idea. He said then that it was not what was real, but what she perceived as real that mattered. He knew that if her perception was ugly and violent, she would be afraid and withdrawn and that it would eventually destroy her.

Yet now Luke fully understood what compelled Aggie to think as she did. He finally knew why Aggie fantasized the world as she did. For the first time and for many more behind and in front of him, Luke feared for his own mortality. In conceding this, Luke thought he at last appreciated the motives for Aggie' attitude the last time they were together. *She fears for my mortality, too,* he thought, *and as my dear Aggie would, she is already creating a substitute dream which would exclude me as though I never existed for her.* With this revelation, Luke added another fear to his burden of fear. *What if she becomes so involved in the other dream that I'm longer a part of her reality?*

He rejected the thinking into which he had drifted and his mind returned to Paris. But as though Paris was a part of it, Normandy crept back in. His fears resurfaced. He realized that for all its noise and blood and motion and confusion, Normandy was tame compared to the present. *Consider,* he thought. *I did not think I would die in that place, or on that blood-smeared road in and out of Paris. My God,* he almost preyed silently, *I did not even think it when I saw most of the squad blown away by mortar attack last week. I was sick, but not as afraid as I am now. When did this happen to me? When did I become so afraid?* As he asked this so openly, the answer flashed its pestilent image before him. He knew that he had first known mortal fear when the enemy killed Sergeant Sampson.

He tried to emulate this man's power. Sampson had fearlessly browbeaten, shoved, cajoled and inspired his troops to hard fighting and survival. This man, whom he all but considered indestructible, had his tough Black head blown off not five feet from Luke just three days before. At that moment, *God help me* admitted Luke, *I was too afraid to even move, let alone help others who also were afraid or hurt or dying.*

Ironic, Luke bitterly thought to himself, *that I should be promoted to Platoon Sergeant the very day I first knew mortal fear. How utterly like life that I became too afraid to lead. I became responsible not just for the lives of a ten-man squad, but for a whole platoon. And for this I was promoted? How morbidly twisted,* he mused, *that while Sampson was alive for me to follow, I commanded only ten. Now that I no longer have him for strength, I must lead over thirty.* Luke was again overwhelmed by his thoughts and the fears. The knowledge that over half of those for whom he was responsible were replacements compounded those fears. He had little confidence in these green privates from backwoods or central city ghettos.

These young boys were drafted late in the war to fill the ranks, and they were even more frightened than he. He also knew of their resentment at fighting for "Whitey," just as Aggie resented and did not understand his doing the same thing. He sought for a way around his fear. Ironically, he again adopted Aggie's way as the only way he could bring himself to shoulder the responsibilities he knew he must. He had to learn to bear the burden by viewing time only as "now".

However, it was thoughts of Aggie which most confused and bothered him. But it was also these that helped to save Luke from failure through his own fear. And it was only when he allowed tomorrow to gain an edge on the line of his thoughts that the mortal fear returned to the surface to defeat him. But it was there, constantly, ready to take him over into death. Guarding against it became his preoccupation, his source of drive, the basis for the new face of command he showed to his men.

So there Luke dwelled in that "now" space in his foxhole with his radioman, waiting. He waited for a call to move out, or an artillery round to end it all, or both, or neither. He knew it did not matter, really. All that mattered to Luke was now, and his men, and the moment he was in, as he supplanted each thought by another and that by another, always returning to thoughts of Aggie, dear Aggie, a shadow of things that were.

Feeling a hand on his shoulder, Luke looked up into the face of Captain Henderson. "Hello, Freddie." They had discarded formal titles almost entirely. They abandoned most of the military pomp about the time they hit the Normandy Beach. It was useless to them and a burden easily discarded. But Luke was the only enlisted man to call the Company Commander by his first name. Freddie returned the compliment.

"How're you doing, Luke? Anything happening up here?"

"Nothing."

"Same down the line. Might soon, though. I've told Lt. Johnston to be ready. Word is we'll be moving at dawn."

"Freddie, what about Johnston? He's, uh, between us, about as green as they come."

"Then you'd better watch out over him, Luke."

"Hell, Freddie. I'll take care of the Platoon, but he's an officer. Not only that, he doesn't seem to like commanding a Black platoon."

"Well, he'd best learn. I'll talk to him about it again. Take care of yourself, Brother Luke. We've got to go home together, just like we came. Keep your head down."

Luke seldom saw Freddie appear so cautious and could not recall his friend ever calling him "Brother" before. The edge of the future was clawing again at his present. Mortal fear was edging around his loins. His voice cracked just slightly as he spoke, but apparently Freddie did not pick it up. "Do you know where we're going, Freddie?"

"Where? Not really. But it'll be Patton leading, though. And we all know what that means. I would say the Big Push is on. We'll probably be trying to link up with Monty for the Push to Berlin, although, between you and me, I doubt we'll see that city before the war's over."

"Why not, Freddie? That's where we've been trying to get ever since we hit the beach."

"Yeah. I know. Got a butt?"

"No. I'm out. Hey, McCathrey. Any cigarettes?" The radio man passed two toward Luke. He and Freddie lit up and Freddie talked on in between drags.

"Rumors are that Ike will let the Ruskies have Berlin. Politics."

"Crap. They're nearly as bad as the Germans."

"Yeah, well. But with the concentration camps in Poland and Czechoslovakia and all being in their control now, and with so many Ruskies slaughtered near the Straights and Leningrad-— Hell, I don't know why. Guess I'm trying to justify it in my own mind. Anyway, it's just rumors. What do you hear from Aggie?"

"Actually, she seems pretty good. The war created jobs. You know she's been working ever since just after I left for basic."

"Yeah. She still working for the same---?"

"Harmon. And of course, most of the hate back home these days is aimed at the Germans and the Japanese. So I guess life has been a little better for her, if I can believe her letters. You know, Freddie, she still has never mentioned the war or my being away or even missing me. She talks in her letters like everything was perfectly normal. It gives me an eerie feeling sometimes, but at least she seems relatively happy. How're Martha and Jeff?"

"Seem fine. Last I heard they were still with my folks and Jeff seems to like school. Damn letters never seem to say much, do they."

"Nope. Sure don't. Do you hear from your parents?"

"Yeah. Got a letter with the last mail as a matter of fact. Dad had a heart attack about a month ago, but I guess it wasn't too bad or the Red Cross would have let me know. It's a crying shame that we're over here fighting this damn war to protect them and it still takes a month for us to find out what's happening. Hell, he could have been dead and buried by now. I guess that's the main thing. I'm afraid that something will happen to Martha or Jeff, or my parents, too, and I won't even know."

"You going to try and get home, I mean, to be with your Dad?"

"I've thought about it Luke, but with the Push coming, well, I think Dad would rather I'd stick it out here. What do you think?"

"I think you ought to try to get home. What the hell. We're all just fodder, anyway."

"I can't look at it that way. If I were just a grunt, it would be different. But being a Company Commander, and so many of these boys are so young and green, I don't know. There are damn few of us left with any combat experience. On the one hand, I've had enough and want to go home. You know that. But on the other hand, somehow I would feel like a rat. Only I'd never get a chance to do it again, to fix it if I left and the Push came."

"It's tough, Freddie, I know. Actually, it's kind of funny. You're only, what, twenty-three? I'm just twenty and we're the old men in this war."

"Yeah. Too many killed. That's all. Too many lives ruined. Let's don't talk about it. Maybe I will go." Freddie's voice trailed low as he spoke, and he ground the cupped cigarette out on the sole of his boot and field stripped the butt. "I could try to call home first," he said. "I've been thinking I might try to get one of those overseas hook-ups. I understand the Red Cross can do that."

"Might try. But mainly I guess we've all got to believe this will all be over soon, and then we can all go home."

"Do you believe that, Luke. Really believe?"

"I don't know. Lately, Freddie, between you and me, I try not to think about anything beyond the next minute or two. I've got to tell someone what I've been thinking. It's driving me-—" Whatever his words might have been, Luke's never finished, for a dreaded and familiar whine interrupted and drowned out any intent to complete his thought.

"Oh oh. Sounds like the bastards are starting with the big guns and mortars again," yelled Freddie over the din. "Get your men ready. We could move any minute."

Miles away across the charred, open earth the night sky was showing a false and sporadic dawn. They could hear vague thumps signaling the man-made aura of coming day. A moment after, the screaming residue of regurgitated lead and shrapnel and missile plummeted downward toward Luke's platoon and the Allied line.

Freddie squeezed Luke's shoulder as he pushed himself to a crouching position. He patted McAthrey on the helmet and started up out of the foxhole. Luke tapped his palm on Freddie's back in the ritual exchange which had become a silent testimony to their immutable bond. "Luck" Brother. See ya," he threw at Freddie, and started redirecting his attention to the war in front of him.

"You bet, Brother. Keep your head down and---" The rest of Freddie's softly spoken sentence was drowned out by the deafening wail of an approaching mortar shell. Explosions in front and behind them strafed the foxhole with dirt and debris. Silence fell again, except for the distant thumps with their telltale foreglow. Luke turned to McAthrey to check the radio before organizing the move of his Platoon. He heard Lt. Johnston calling his name from somewhere down the line. He called to McAthrey and moved in his direction.

A large, jagged fragment of metal or rock protruded from McAthrey's neck. His eyes stared back at and through Luke. He did not respond. "Goddammit, Freddie. They got him. They got him, too."

Freddie paused just over the edge of the foxhole. "Christ, Luke. Doesn't it end? They got Saunders yesterday. Most of them are gone---" Again the scream of the artillery shocked the two friends into motion. Luke instinctively knew from the pitch of the whining missile that it would be another close one. Freddie suddenly saw it coming. He grabbed Luke's field jacket. He jerked him face down into the bottom of the foxhole and jumped in on top of him.

The shrieking death coming at them tore at the ears and the mind. In a final desperate surge of strength, Freddie threw himself completely over Luke's torso. The impact bounced Luke clear of the dank and smoldering earth by an inch or more just as Freddie landed on him. The impact drove him forward face down into the putrefied soil and its concussion rendered Luke senseless.

When Luke was again aware of being alive, he tried to reckon where he was, what was happening. It was still dark. He could not hear the artillery booming. Silent shadows of moving men surrounded him. Behind them in the distance, the sound of tanks creaked through the woods. Luke felt wet and heavy. He squirmed his hand down to the wetness by his sides and tried to push up. It was then that he felt the pressure on his back.

"Freddie?" he whispered. "Freddie! You OK?" He got no response. Pushing hard with his left hand, he rolled back to the right and scooted forward. Hot pain blasted up his body from his left leg as he shoved himself free. With thoughts of his friend blunting the physical agony of his own body, he twisted back to face Freddie. "Hey, Freddie, c'mon, get up, we gotta get outa here." He reached out and shook his C.O.'s shoulder. There was no resistance to his motion.

Freddie's eyes were closed. His helmet was pushed forward and to the right. It glowed wet in the predawn haze of light that was erasing the blinding blanket of night. Luke's eyes focused on the red tinge in the light playing off of Freddie's head. A constriction in his chest surged toward his throat as he struggled up over his friend.

The horror of what he saw sent shock waves surging in hot chills from his burning, smoke-filled eyes down his spine. A suppressed scream grabbed his throat and aimed for his chest, only to collide with the rising and ominous constriction there. His premonitory fear smashed into the convulsive reality his senses now delivered to him.

The back of Freddie's head appeared gone. "He's dead. God, he's dead." Luke screamed a hollow, resounding grief-filled agonizing scream. He collapsed across Freddie and froze. Unable to react further and shocked as he was, one tiny, alien question screamed out loud from his numbed senses. "Goddam you, God, How can you be, and this be?"

Then Luke lost consciousness again. He drifted half between images of the Freddie that had been until a moment before, and the Freddie that wasn't Freddie anymore lying beneath him. So intense were his erratic nightmarish thoughts that he could almost feel himself rise and fall over the heaving chest of his best friend beneath him. The image of two boys lost in the shadows of a dark alley long ago flashed in the dawn and the dirt and the blood. Luke, still feeling the rise and fall beneath him, knew it was real. He imagined Freddie's hot breath on his face. In unconscious response, Luke laid his blackened Black hand on the dirty red stubble of Freddie's chin. He cried softly. At last he reached a point where he might calm the turmoil of terrible emotions within him. A weak wave of moist heat touched his palm as his hand slid toward the earth.

His bloodshot eyes popped open. He moved his hand back, waited. Again he felt the warm caress of air. *I've got to get ahold of myself*, Luke thought. But no. It was real and recurring. The rise and fall beneath him, although nearly imperceptible, continued.

"Medic!" Luke shouted and danced to his feet. "Medic!" he screamed through his agony and crumpled to the ground with the stab of pain from his mangled leg. "Medic," he mumbled over and over as he sat helplessly by Freddie in the dawning dreariness of the War's next day, the first day of the Battle of the Bulge.

CHAPTER 22

Random Strokes

Aggie was still working for Elizabeth Harmon two years after Luke left, and she reformed her dreams to accommodate Luke's absence. Christmas was over. All were waiting for 1945 to start. She was in a routine now that was a comfortable blend of her fantasy world and every-day reality. Even though she considered it the Holidays, she was at work. She needed the money for her future with Luke and Mrs. Harmon need the house cleaned and the dog bathed.

"Aggie, Dear. Please bring Rufus in now for his bath." Aggie hated bathing the dog, a chore she had to do once a week. Elizabeth Harmon insisted on it. Aggie liked Rufus, for the giant Labrador had become very close to her. The dog was even a fixture in the dream world house existing now in Aggie's mind. But she dreaded bathing it. She reluctantly learned to adjust the fantasy she held of life to accommodate and assimilate changes like bathing the dog. Aggie deftly, if unconsciously, integrated change in the pattern of her life. Her dreams of Luke and the world he would create for her already existed in her mind. The dream she was living was her reality. And Rufus had become a part of her reality.

Certain elements of true reality she rejected outright. While she pretended that men did not exist, she excepted LeRoy, the kindly father of her dream. She excepted her brothers, who were but boys. She excepted Luke, who was the basis of the dream itself. She pretended that Elizabeth Harmon did not exist, and that Elizabeth's house was really hers. Like Rufus, the things and shapes and smells of the house became part of the dream.

Intensely, she developed this fantasy. By the end of the first year in the Harmon household, Aggie totally replaced the dream. The old elements she had stolen from the Sears and Roebuck catalogue she replaced with the finer, more opulent and more tangible things of this fine White man's home.

She fully believed that Luke was just at work and would be home in the evening. On that basis she allowed her fantasy to take on new intensity. Nearly everything she did, she did in her fantasy's context, her world. In her mind, she cleaned her own house. When she prepared the Harmon's meals, she pretended they were for Luke. She believed she was not even caring for the Harmon children and dog, but her own.

All of this she kept a secret even from Luke, even from herself. So when faced with an unpleasant chore like washing Rufus, she simply accomplished it while in her mind doing something else entirely. Rarely was she conscious of doing it. Soon she imagined that it was Luke washing the dog, and she was just helping.

Each week during the ritual, she did the chore while silently scolding Luke for not doing it right. Taking over to show him how, she would bathe the dog. Each week almost the same words and motions came from her mouth and hands as she performed this task. Aggie used similar rationale in most unpleasant or ill-fitting parts of her life to make them fit neatly in her dream. To the world she seemed happy, if somewhat detached and to herself.

She impressed everybody with her quality work. Believing as she did that it was for Luke, she accomplished all her tasks quickly and correctly. To Crystal's surprise and relief, Aggie got so good that Crystal left her on her own and moved to a neighbor's house. This way she was taking advantage of the opportunity to double the meager income offered Southern Blacks for domestic work.

Aggie also impressed Elizabeth with the quality of her work, her appearance and demonstrated respect. Aggie's humility and articulation also impressed her, as it was rare for the Coloreds with whom she had contact. She grew genuinely fond of the girl. In her fondness, she rewarded Aggie beyond the pittance she received for her formal duties. She gave Aggie dresses not up to the latest style. Aggie taught herself to sew and was soon altering them into a fine wardrobe for herself. With Mrs. Harmon's permission, she borrowed selected books from the library and subscription magazines. In addition, Mrs. Harmon started giving Aggie small pieces of costume jewelry and such things as old dishes, small furnishings, discarded curtains and various knickknacks and household items.

Aggie evaluated each new acquisition. When it fit her fantasy, she squirreled it away in boxes in her loft room or stacked it neatly in a corner. That which she did not want went to her mother or Aunt Crystal. It was an arrangement which suited Aggie well. It allowed her to learn the skills she continuously needed in her fantasy and to save both money and goods she saw as custom-made for her own home. Considering the Harmon house to be hers, the paradox of it all was how she still accepted and saved so much from it for the home in her dream.

She offered none of her money to the Powers, and they never expected her to. Nor did she frequent the stores and social places where she might spend it. She was too fearful to venture beyond the walls of her dream. That dream encompassed only the Powers and Harmon homes. The result was the accumulation of almost all her wages, nearly two hundred dollars in the first two years of her employment.

So Aggie bathed Rufus each week without complaint. She made sure she was quiet, efficient and agreeable in Mrs. Harmon's non-presence. She allowed Mrs. Harmon to exist when there was something free to get or wages due or books to borrow. Aside from some clothing and a quilt, Aggie used none of the things Elizabeth gave her. Instead, she arranged them in her mind in the fantasy house in the fantasy world where she was living with a fantasy Luke built on the shadows of things that were.

There was an exception to this pattern. One day, Mrs. Harmon gave her a small, square tin fruitcake box. She kept the letters from Luke in that box. Letters from Luke were in Aggie's mind like getting a personal message from the Almighty, for they represented the reality of the fantasy in which she lived.

Luke knew of Aggie's fear of the world. He tried desperately from his foxhole to keep her love and help her know that he would come home. He wrote cheery letters full of hope. He often recounted humorous incidents. He told her about some of his exploits in the war. In the quirks of her mind, she allowed these letters to exist as treasured moments from her lover who was far away. She struggled with those letters coming from trenches in Europe, for she denied that Luke was in any danger.

The cumulative results of these letters on Aggie's imagination offered both needed hope and the rationale for allowing war's reality into her dream. Luke became like God to Aggie. When she occasionally realized where Luke was, she assumed he was invincible. In her mind, he was in absolute command; he overwhelmed the enemy with his intuition and courage. Therefore, she need not fear for him. It was that simple for her.

As time went on, she saw Luke as taller and stronger. This provided confines to the fantasy which made Aggie more and more resistant to any event outside of its realm. There was a big problem which she did not recognize in all of this. Luke might come home one day and not fit into her dream of him at all. He may never come home. In either case, her dream was in danger.

Aggie did not hear from Luke for nearly three weeks, but his last letter described his promotion to Platoon Sergeant. Attempting to explain what that meant, he described the structure of a platoon and how thirty men were in his care. As he often did, Luke also wrote about his best friend. He told how Freddie had made Captain and was now his Commanding Officer. Aggie did not connect Freddie with the Freddie about whom Luke told her years ago. Luke mentioned his childhood friend to her only a few times as they grew up, when he tried to puncture her stereotype of Whites being all bad.

But Aggie's mind rejected anything she heard which countered her own deep fear. Knowing this, Luke never told Aggie that Captain Freddie Henderson was Freddie Sloan, or even that he was White. To Aggie, Luke and Freddie were a team of Black giants single-handedly winning the war, with Luke the de facto leader of the Allied Forces. She envisioned hosannas at his victorious appearance on the field in his medal bedecked uniform as he stood astride a jeep. She imagined that, by his commanding presence, he caused the enemy of White, blond and blue-eyed masses to cast aside their weapons in sheer awe of his presence.

Aggie was unprepared for the telegram she received at Mrs. Harmon's. Her mail was routed there because of the lack of mail service to the Black farms in the district. It was just before lunch that week after Christmas, 1944. Aggie would be free in another half day for her evening fantasies. A knock on the door caused her to utter a small curse. She intensely disliked answering the front door, for it opened to unforeseeable events and an unfamiliar world. Often, she became flustered by visitors, especially White, male visitors who might be on the other side of the door.

"'Scuse me Missy, but I has dis here tel'gram fo' a Miss Agatha Lonstrom. She be home today?"

"That's me. Give it to me!"

"Dis yo' house?" The youngster's eyes widened at the incredible thought. Aggie smiled secretly, enjoying the fact that the boy should assume this. Thus reinforced, she took the telegram and closed the door in the face of the expectant lad. Empty-handed and disappointed, the boy turned from the front porch. He muttered under his breath about uppity rich niggers being worse than Whites.

Aggie read the address on the envelope and a mixture of curiosity and fear seeped through her. She did not understand what a telegram was. That she had never received one before was cause enough for her to fear it.

"Who was it, Aggie, Dear?" Mrs. Harmon came into the hall to find Aggie staring at the envelope. She was leaning lightly against the closed front door with a kind of detached look about her. A quizzical look of slight fear was just discernable in her quiet black eyes.

"Just a boy, Mrs. Harmon."

"What did he want, Child?"

"It was a telegram, Ma' am. For me."

"Oh, how exciting. Let me see it." Elizabeth reached out to take the envelope, but Aggie drew back.

"It's for me, Ma'am. Me."

"Oh, well, of course, Aggie. What does it say?"

"I haven't opened it yet."

Elizabeth Harmon became impatient and the tone of her voice harshened slightly as she countered. "Well, do so, Aggie. I want to see what it says." As if prompted to action by the sharpness of the words, Aggie suddenly ripped the flap open and pulled its threatening contents loose. Under the watchful eye of Elizabeth, she wiggled two fingers around the telegram and slowly unfolded its halves, wondering why it got this White intruder so excited. Aggie glanced at the whole of the strange looking message, then seeing the name Powers jump from the page, read it intensely.

REGRET INFORM YOU PLT SGT L POWERSRASN 1006792

WOUNDED IN ACTION 16 DEC '44 ARDENNES FOREST X

EVACUATED MIL HOSP PARIS X

CONT ARC INFORMATION ON CONDITION X

TIMING TRANSPORT HOME X IF AVAILABLE X

FOR CDR X FIRST ARMY USA

Aggie handed the telegram to Mrs. Harmon and watched the older woman read the message. "What does it mean?" she asked, but she knew full well its meaning as she felt a sense of crumbling within her. Tears were rapidly forming in her eyes, blurring her vision as tears also gathered in Elizabeth's eyes.

To Aggie the message could not be true. But there it was. It did not fit. But cold and precise like a knife, it sliced through her world. Its truth would violate the basic premise, the foundation, the myth of Luke's invincibility. But she could not deny the harsh black words on the yellow paper. They instantly fragmented her dream.

"Oh, My Dear Child." Mrs. Harmon's arm instinctively enveloped the girl. Aggie swayed with the touch but did not notice it. "I'm so sorry. I'm sure it's just a minor thing."

Aggie heard nothing over the roar of "wounded in action" that permeated all the conscious and unconscious cells of her brain. Bit by bit they attacked the complex illusions upon which she pinned her existence.

"You must be brave," continued her comforter, but fear and grief overcame Aggie. She grieved not for Luke, but for his image, not for his injury, but for her dissolving dream. Luke, the living, breathing, warm and human person who had left her for the last time over a year ago, was somehow not now whole. He was suffering pain in a place where she could not go to him and comfort him. He was not what she pictured. What she pictured was a shadow of his being. It was a cross between the Luke that was when they were together, the Luke that she had created in his absence and the Luke in the telegram. They all whacked away at her life, murdering her, destroying her.

Overwhelmed, Aggie slipped from Mrs. Harmon's arm to the floor. The simple telegram shattered her fantasy world. Mrs. Harmon tried to support Aggie but lost her to the hallway's carpeted and nonpersonal grip. Thinking of needing help and where to get it momentarily quelled a sense of panic rising in her. She stepped across Aggie's limp form to the front door. Flinging it wide, she called and called again, "Crystal," and abandoned entirely her grace and breeding as she scurried to the gate and almost trotted next door.

Crystal met her at the door. She was already moving through it, responding to the panic in Elizabeth's voice. "Aggie has fainted," Elizabeth blurted between breathless heaves. "Her Luke was hurt in the war." She grabbed at Crystal's hand and pulled her heavy former housekeeper down the walk as she chattered. "She got a telegram and, oh, it's just awful. And right in my hall she just slipped right out of my, oh my, she's just lying there and what shall we do?"

Elizabeth spewed forth six words for each long stride with a rapidity equal to her movement. Her hand tugged at Crystal's strong arm. Urgently they moved together faster and faster through the gate, down the walk, in the gate, onto the porch.

When they got to the front door of Elizabeth's house, they pushed it open to find Aggie gone. On the floor of the hallway lay the telegram. Rufus was barking in the kitchen. They followed his voice, looking for Aggie.

"Aggie!" exclaimed Crystal as she swung her body through the kitchen door.

"Why, Aunt Crystal. How nice. Are you going to join us for lunch?"

"Aggie?" Crystal paused, flat-footed just inside the doorway. Elizabeth was peering over her shoulder at the bewildering girl by the sink. "You all right, Chile?"

"I'm fine. Shouldn't I be?"

"But the telegram---"

"Oh, that. That's just a mistake. The Whites just wanted to scare me. But they can't fool Aggie. I know my Luke is fine. I know he is. Nothing can happen to my Luke. Why, he's in charge of all those men. He'll tell me it's all right when he gets home this evening."

"But---"

"Besides, Luke is too important. They wouldn't let anything happen to him, even if he is Black. And there's Captain Henderson. He's Luke's best friend, you know. And he isn't about to let anything happen to his best friend, even if the Whites would. I suspect our people will watch over each other."

Crystal was amazed. She was amazed at the way Aggie dismissed the telegram. She was amazed to discover that Aggie thought Freddie to be Black. She was amazed to hear Aggie say that Luke would be home for dinner. And she was confused.

Was Aggie really living in such a crazy dream that she would believe what she just said? Crystal was suddenly more frightened for Luke than ever. She thought, if this was what Aggie has become, what would Luke return to? What if he was so badly injured that he required constant attention and long convalescence? What if he were a permanent cripple? Would or could Aggie take care of him? Could she really be so weak that she could totally ignore the pain and danger to the very person in the world whom she professed to love the most?

Crystal's amazement gave way to fear, to disgust, to anger, and then to compassion. She convinced herself that Aggie's delusion was just something that she felt for the moment to shield herself from the shock of it. *Or* thought Crystal, *to shield me, to protect me.* With this new explanation, her heart went out to the girl. She moved to her to perpetuate the false sense of safety as though she accepted what Aggie had said. But then she stopped. She looked back over her shoulder at Elizabeth's expression.

The two women looked at each other and back to Aggie, whose dark eyes were rimmed with a reddened glaze contradicting her words. Her skin was flushed and moist. Her hand shook as she went about trying to finish preparing the lunch. Then the facade crumbled, and Aggie threw herself into Crystal's arms and screamed, "Why'd they have to kill my Luke? What am I to do?" Her speech gave way to deep, heaving sobs. Then, without loss of one heartbeat, she straightened, dried her eyes and smiled at them. "Heavens," she exclaimed, "What is the matter with me to say such a thing? Why, Luke will be home this evening, just like always."

Crystal grabbed Aggie and hugged her close, patting her gently on the back. Now she knew that Aggie was in deep danger. What Aggie said when they first entered the kitchen was too real, and no pretense would shield her from pain. This terrified Crystal. She was terrified because she did not know what to do for Aggie. She was terrified that Luke might be dying. She was terrified that she had failed to protect and care for Luke's Aggie while he was away risking it all for them. She knew Aggie needed more help than she could offer or they would lose her. "Miss Elizabeth," she said as she cradled Aggie, "Please, Ma'am, send for the doctor. Get a boy to fetch my husband and the wagon. I've got to get this girl home."

Elizabeth responded immediately. She was glad to have someone else take charge, take responsibility for this most disconcerting event of her life. She moved quickly to help and countered with an offer to get out her car as a faster way to get the girl and the tragedy out of her house, out of her mind. Grabbing her keys before Crystal could argue, she said she would have the doctor meet them at the Powers' place and disappeared through the back door.

Within moments they were on the road to the farm. Aggie lay motionless, full of tense silence in Crystal's arms. Elizabeth wheeled the big Packard back and forth down the clay road, trying to avoid the ruts and potholes more easily navigated by LeRoy's mules and wagon.

The bouncing auto affected Aggie's condition not at all but it jarred a dawning in Crystal's mind. She began to understand Aggie's mutterings, packrat habits, dreamy attitudes, demonstrated fears of change. All these things fell at last into a pattern.

Crystal cowered from her realization. She was ashamed of the way she had misread the girl as a selfish and lazy person over the past two years. She knew now that only Aggie's perception of Luke's strength and protection kept her going. Once Crystal saw this, she grasped the root of Aggie's reaction to the telegram. Her heart melted in love and pity for the poor, lost girl. She felt a deep shame for her own callousness and failure to comprehend and help Aggie before it was too late.

By the time the sedative wore off, the two women could relay word from the Red Cross that Luke would be fine and would be home sooner than even Aggie suspected. And he would not have to go back.

"I know," was Aggie's calm reply, and her mind instantly reassembled the dream and wiped the scars from her consciousness. In a fit of relief and pity, Elizabeth Harmon told Aggie to rest until after the New Year holiday and even offered to pay her for the time. Aggie nodded acceptance without comment.

CHAPTER 23

The Letter

The heavy white cast contrasted with the pasty faded brown of the foot protruding from it. It clashed with the thinning, weak looking thigh attached to it. Luke's unmistakable head topped the jumble of white sheets shrouding his brown torso and limbs. Luke's eyes sometimes closed, then opened and looked off toward the open window. They rolled in pain and anticipation. His exhausted mind sought enough coherent thoughts to compose the letter his attendant Red Cross worker was scribing for him.

He did not know where to begin, for there seemed to be no beginning. Was it when he woke up in this all white, sterile corner of the ward? Should he first ask the unanswered question about Freddie? Should he start by first telling Aggie that he was fine when he was not? Could he say he would be home soon when he had no idea how long he might be there? In that white bed in that white room with that White nurse, the only hint of color was he himself. Where should he begin? Before he could begin, he knew that he could not. He knew he must have some answers about Freddie before he could put his life in order. Yet they only said "later, rest now" to his queries.

How can I rest, he thought, *until I know about Freddie? How can I rest*, he punished himself, *not knowing whether Freddie died in trying to save me? How can I rest,* passed through his mind as an irony, *when Aggie probably spends every night sleeplessly waiting to hear?* He knew he could not, but he knew he must. He saw himself in the mirror beside his bed. The white exaggerated his color all around him. It sickened him to a graying hue. Rubbing the constant itches on his chest, he felt the bumpy rows of ribs where once muscle and firm strong flesh was dominant. He knew he was wasting away because he could not rest. He knew he must rest. But how could he?

The Red Cross worker lowered her pad and pulled the glasses from her face. Although she had seen it a thousand times since coming here to work, there was something more profound, more poignant, very different about this one. It was not that he was Black. Usually, the casualties were Black. It was not the extent of his injuries, for by most standards they were minor. She could not blame it on his wasting away when he should recover, for she had seen that many times. She knew that it was a battle of time for each casualty to come to grips with himself before the real healing could begin. She knew the things it was not, but she could not discern what that difference was.

She reflected, as the eyes rolled in front of her from this once powerful, now frail head. She recalled his mumblings about someone named Freddie, about someone named Martha, about a girl named Aggie. The name Elkins screamed from him when he fell into fitful sleep. She realized that first on his lips was nearly always Freddie. She wondered at this from day to day, and finally determined to try and ease his mind with that knowledge.

She knew about Freddie, yet had not told Luke. She was afraid to. She was afraid because the doctors told her he was not strong enough to take the shock. So she resorted to her normal pleasantries. She took her pencil and tried again to get him to write the letter he had been trying to for days. But she could not do it. For today, she finally discovered what it was about this casualty that was different.

Her visit began in the usual way. She pushed aside the white muslin curtain and took the uncomfortable army green chair from the wall. She pulled it to his bedside. She gently touched his arm and received the usual smile from his sleepy face. After that smile, he turned his eyes away from her and looked toward the window. As usual, any coherent thought was hers. So she gently badgered and cajoled and teased and touched and rubbed his bony chest and patted his hand and mopped his damp brow and moistened his lips from the cup on the nightstand.

His response was always that haunting smile, a mumbled thanks, a quickly returned squeeze of gratitude from his big Black hand. Then he again looked out the window, away from her, always away from her. She knew he was not really looking out the window. He was looking into himself.

On impulse, she got up and lay the pencil and pad on the nightstand. Picking up the chair, she moved around the bed and sat it down. She was now between Luke and the window where his attention always seemed focused. Their eyes met, locked and remained without flinch or waver. It was there that she finally knew what was different. She sensed fright, then awe, then fascination, and finally power.

Then she realized that the fright, the awe, the fascination were hers. But the power was his. It amazed her that such power could come from the eyes of a suffering man like him. By all outward signs he was dying, wasting, turning inward with hopelessness. And she realized that it was not his injuries that this broken man was struggling with, but rather not knowing how those whom he loved were faring.

She saw for the first time in her life a level of selflessness which put her own self-sacrifice in being here to shame. That was the power that she saw. She knew that she must tell him what she knew of Freddie. And she knew that he would not only handle it, but that it would make him better. She was sure that weak in the body as he was, the strength of his spirit would carry him with the knowledge. The peace which comes from knowing, even knowing the worst, would outweigh the pain inherent in the knowledge itself. And so she began.

"Sergeant?"

"Huh?" Luke's eyes remained constant but caught those into which he had been staring.

"Luke." Can I call you Luke?"

"Sure. OK."

"Luke, I---"

"What can I call you?"

"Me? Miss — No. Millie. My name is Millie."

"Nice. I like that."

"Luke, I must tell you something."

"What?"

"You must promise to tell no one I have told you, for they all told me not to."

"What's it about?"

"You promise?"

"What's it about?"

"It's about Freddie. But you must promise."

Any information about Freddie could wipe away part of the quagmire of thought which had infected his brain. He focused to receive the news. He felt sure the rest of his life hinged on this. He must know if his life was his because Freddie was dead. Then he could decide what to do with it, or even if it was worth keeping. He promised.

"First. Well. He is alive."

"Sweet Jesus. Thank you." Just the trace of a tear softened the pale red border accenting the faded white of Luke's deep, black centered eyes. A sigh escaped from his emaciated chest and his head rolled back on the pillow. He broke the entrancing gaze which he had locked upon Millie when she came between him and his window to the world. The incredible change in his physical appearance heartened her and set off the white swaddling of his bed. He suddenly seemed huge, radiant, alive, healing.

But she had given the best, if not the only good news first. Now she must give him the bad. "Luke. I must be honest with you. I decided to tell this just a moment ago. I saw your strength and knew you could take it. I must tell you the rest."

Luke tensed. His eyes locked again on hers. A shadow of foreboding tragedy flickered there for a moment. Then a resolute look of the need to know the truth replaced it. Squirming with the fear of his reaction, but knowing she could not turn back, Millie continued. "He is in a coma, Luke, and critical, but---"

"Will he die?"

"He is stable but making no progress. The injury to his head, you see, took, well, uh---"

"It took part of his brain, didn't it?"

"How do you know? My God, Luke. How can you just say it?"

"I saw him." The words were the faintest whisper, issued from another new body, this time a deathly gray. He was shaking and sweating so profusely that even the edges of the white cast turned gray with the moisture. They sat for a moment. Both looked out the window.

When Millie looked back, there was no more gray. The brown was back. His eyes turned once again on her, frighteningly on her, commanding her as no words could to tell all she knew. She began without hesitation, without regard to consequence, to do just as his eyes commanded.

"They brought him in the same ambulance as you. I don't know if you remember wrapping his head with a bandage soaked in water, but you did. That was the only thing that kept him alive, but it also caused terrible infection. The medic swears he did nothing but stop the bleeding in his back and limbs, that his head was wrapped already."

"Go on." Luke's voice was steady, although barely audible.

"At first, they assumed the worst of his wounds were those treated by the medic. But the Doctors removed all the bandages from him in surgery. It was at the field hospital, not here. When they uncovered the hole in his skull, they figured he was a goner. They could not figure out why he was still breathing. They treated the peripheral with sulfa and got him to a B17 which was being used to move injured back from Germany to Paris. He actually beat you here by three days."

"And he's still comatose?"

"Luke. Listen. They do not give him much chance. He is too torn up. One of the fragments severed his spine and lodged in his brain."

"God, Millie. Don't." Luke was quaking as tears threatened his long-dry eyes. Then they streaked down the red and yellow and black abyss marking his now stark and strained face. He knew enough. Yet she still spoke.

"Luke. all right. But listen to one more thing. Please. It's important. Luke, he spoke once." Luke reacted to the words with a sinewy attitude that belied the faded strength of his body. But his voice lacked the vitality his body had just telegraphed. It was as though his strength was just an illusion. It was a last ashen flimflam of something that was not really there. But his eyes said it was. They said the strength remained. They signaled to Millie to continue where his words could not. "In his one lucid moment, oh, days ago, Luke, he said only, 'give Luke the letter.' He said it three times, but they did not know what he was talking about. But I found a letter in his things. He addressed it to you. It must be the one." Millie pulled the letter from inside her sweater and slipped it into Luke's quivering hand.

He looked back at her with his wet eyes and a husky thanks slipped through his thin and pale lips. His eyes closed as though in sleep, but he clutched the letter close to his breast. He did not move, yet his breathing was regular and light, not that of a sleeping person.

Millie watched him for a moment more, then decided he wanted to be alone. Standing over him for a moment with her hand lightly on his arm, she finally pulled the curtain on its overhead pipe around his bed. Then she left.

Luke was silent a moment more. He suspected that Millie was gone, but he wanted to be sure. He could not be certain how much longer he could contain himself. He thought to himself, *the news of Freddie is better than I expected. Freddie is alive. But, with brain damage, will Freddie ever be Freddie again?*

It was long after sundown. The faint shadows of streetlights beyond the window dimly illuminated the white dark of the sterile room. Luke awoke and remembered the letter. He deliberately avoided thinking of it when Millie left. He was afraid to read it then, afraid that he might not be able to stand what it said. But he was calmer now. And it was blessedly near dark, and reasonably quiet on the ward save for the constant sounds of others in pain in their sleep. *So now,* thought Luke, *if I can get the light right on it, now is the time.* He tore it open.

Dear Luke,

I think of all the letters I have written to you starting in just such a way, and know that if you read this one, it will be because it is the last. I sense that I shall die soon, although I cannot say why.

It is just some dark foreboding which started to settle over me yesterday when Sampson got it. I knew that only Saunders and I were left from the North Africa Squad that was mine just before I got my bars. Only three, out of eleven of us, counting Sampson. He was my Platoon Sergeant then, too, as you know. He trained me and cared about me just as he did about you.

I, too, care about you. I have always loved you as the brother other circumstances denied me, and always regretted that the world in which we *live should require that, even as children, we had to be apart.*

It is ironic that it took a war to give us time to really know each other, and that war should separate us forever when our bond is strongest. Yet I know it is about to.

You will live, Luke. You must. For I have learned that despite society's judgements to the contrary, because I am White and you are not, you are worth ten of me to the humanity we both believe in and want to serve. Knowing this gives me some comfort even as I face death, for I know you will live.

I cannot exact promises from you. Because we are as close as we are, I cannot share these thoughts with you in person. So I must write this last time and trust in you to do that which I ask. I know you will try.

First, promise me you will live. Promise me you will return home and go to college and become a minister to mankind. I wrote Martha and told her I want to set up a trust for your education. It will be waiting for you whether or not I am there. Use it for me, Luke, to equip yourself to do what God intended you to do. If you do, my life will have been worthwhile.

Second, go see Martha and Jeff. Tell them for me. Don't let the Army tell them. And watch out for them. Tell Martha I want her to remarry. She is so beautiful and so good, and I do not want Jeff robbed of a real father as I was. Tell them that, Luke.

Finally, don't let them ship my body home. It would only prolong the agony for those I love. Make them bury me here, quickly and finally. I think I would like to be buried in Paris. We loved that city, didn't we?

One more thing, Luke. Remember me. You saved my life a couple of times when we were kids and I never really got to return the favor. But we had a special friendship, anyway. That was better than anything except Martha that ever happened to me. Remember me, Luke.

I Love you Brother

Freddie

Luke wanted to tell Freddie that he had the letter, that he had read the letter, and that Freddie, too, must live. But then he sensed a kind of darkening of the shadows in the room. A morbid culmination of all his pain and suffering from every corner of his life overtook him in a premonition of death. He felt the last breath from the battered body of his friend. He believed Freddie had lived only long enough for Luke to read the letter and commit himself to the promises. Beyond tears, beyond emotion, he was full of resolve to honor every single thing Freddie had asked of him. He resolved to be the minister and leader Freddie wanted. Luke stared into the blackness of the night until his thoughts turned inward to dreams. Sometime later, several days in fact, Freddie died. Luke never knew when. But he thought he did, and he would never forget.

CHAPTER 24

Seeking Luke

Even though Freddie wanted Luke to tell Martha in person of Freddie's death, the United States Government sent the traditional telegram to the Henderson household in Augusta. Martha expected it, but this did little to soften the pain of its harsh and final words. Martha was certain the telegram would come since Freddie's last letter to her. The earlier news of his injury only delayed the inevitable for her. Still, Martha expressed none of these fears to the Hendersons or Jeff. The Hendersons had shared little time with their son since rediscovering him, so his death seemed unjust. Martha tried to believe the announcement of his injury would be the only manifestation of her fears. She still hoped that Freddie would come home. But her premonitory feeling remained, and Martha knew why. Freddie's last letter haunted her into believing that Freddie would die.

Although Freddie spoke of his death in his letter to Luke, Martha had not seen that letter. He did not speak of death in his letter to her. Throughout Freddie's involvement in combat, his letters mentioned loss of this friend, that leader. Intermittently through most of his writing, he continued to express the hope that their sacrifice would produce for mankind peace and justice. But this time, in this last letter, he omitted these things. He did not even mention the war except in the vaguest passing comments. Instead, he filled it with his longing wishes to be home and safe and at peace with his family.

Nor had the letter asked how the family was or responded to questions and news Martha had written to her husband. Instead, he entreated her to watch over their child and take good care of herself. Most ominous in the letter were instructions to set up a scholarship fund for Freddie's friend, Luke. Martha wondered at the specificity of the instructions compared to the vagaries of the rest of the missile. She thought about this. *Why would Freddie mention such a thing in such detail if he were coming home, where he could do it himself?*

From the receipt of the letter until the agonizing notice of Freddie's injury, Martha endured her forebodings. She tried to deny them with rationalized hope and incessant, silent prayer. Perhaps by the grace of those prayers, that agony was not overly prolonged. The curt announcement of Freddie's injury reached her expectant hand a few short days after the mailman brought Freddie's confusing scrawl.

Even the most pessimistic among humans harbor deep within themselves a faint hope that things will turn out better than circumstances show. It is this root hope that encouraged Martha to reject in disbelief bad news even when she expected it. Martha was not a pessimist. She was an aggressively alive person full of love for other people. She instilled in those with whom she came in contact a kind of zest for carrying on with life and living. Despite the evidence and the worry, Martha worked at remaining hopeful that Freddie's injuries might heal, and that he might still come home to her.

At the same time, she began almost unconsciously to forge ahead without him. Deep within her she felt an emotion of defeat in direct conflict with the well of hope that was always such a part of her. So the second telegram was not a surprise. But it was final. It quenched the hope and confirmed the fear. It brought forward the suppressed grief.

But grief did not overwhelm Martha for long. Martha believed that life would continue. She almost immediately set about trying to master her grief. She sought some way to surmount it and make herself worthy of what Freddie would have wanted of her. She tried to move on and care for and explain to and console her child as best she could. She prayed for spring to come early so she might use the inspiration of its burst of life in her own renewal process.

Luke came to see her five months after the news of Freddie's death. Martha was planning a new life for herself and her family. It was the May for which she had prayed, and her grief was under control. Late in the afternoon, Luke called the house to say that he was in Augusta. He asked if it would be convenient for him to stop by. "Absolutely," Martha told him.

Luke's bus ride from the hospital to Augusta was difficult. It was his first time off the hospital grounds since his injury. Although his mangled leg was relatively straight and recovering its strength, it still bothered him. It hurt, especially when he needed to walk on it too much or when he was hot or overly tired. The day he travelled to see Martha and Jeff, it was all of these. Still, he was eager to make the trip despite the pain. Going to Aggie should have been his preference and something which he thought would make the pain more endurable. But he knew he could not go to her and the future she represented. He must first satisfy his feelings about Freddie and the past. So he chose on this first weekend pass to go to Augusta instead of Dawson.

Luke could not find a taxi near the station. It was only after a difficult and painful three blocks that he found one with a Colored driver willing to take him on as a fare. The driver showed his dismay that the address Luke gave him was in the White section of town. But he reluctantly agreed. In about fifteen minutes, the taxi pulled up in front of a medium size brick house. Its short Georgian columns looking rather pretentious on an undersized front porch. A white picket fence surrounded a neat, shaded lawn in front of the house. It all seemed picture-book clean and unreal for Luke after the slightly shabby sterility of the hospital. Even more so, he thought, after the reality of the foxhole. He pictured the decaying artistry of Paris, the blood of Normandy. He envisioned the stoic tradition of England, the raw newness of the training camp, and the red dust of home. They now seemed unreal as he took in the reality of this charming little home surrounded by the fresh green of spring.

Luke reached across the seat of the taxi and retrieved the small Valpak he was carrying. As he handed the cabbie the fare, he thought of the man's probable poverty. Luke slipped him an extra quarter as he got from the cab. He offed a thanks across his shoulder, then stood for a moment at the gate. He was not sure he had the courage to proceed up the walk and face Martha. The words of Freddie's letter were stenciled on his mind. The last ominous moments of peace with Freddie before the mortar attack were etched on his heart. The conflict between those things lived surreptitiously in between. Luke was afraid he could not find the words to truly express what he felt. He needed to give comfort and hope. He needed to receive forgiveness from Martha, whose reason for living he felt he had taken by allowing Freddie to die for him.

Finally, with the pallor of his skin reflecting panic in his heart, Luke tripped the latch on the gate and forced his legs to move him painfully up the walk. The front door opened before he reached the step. He saw Martha step out under the porch roof. The columns which seemed to frame her fit in with the dignity she presented. Luke's pace quickened. He felt an unexpected calmness growing inside him and smiled at Martha.

Then Luke was close enough to see Martha's eyes, and he knew it was all right. He knew she accepted Freddie's death as he could never do. He knew she was ready to move on with healing and life. As he mounted the steps to the porch and held out his hand, Luke felt a sense of confidence that Martha would remarry as Freddie wanted. He lost some of his fear of telling her that this was Freddie's wish.

It was a plaintive and melancholy visit. The meal and long evening with Martha, Jeff and the Hendersons forced Luke into a precarious awareness of his own pain and confusion. He became even less sure of who he was and where he should be. He described Freddie's heroism to Jeff and saw the pride in the boy's eyes where he had expected to see resentment. Somehow this all made Luke feel worse instead of better. Martha seemed to sense this, and her words expressed a deep-seated urgency in their attempt to relieve Luke of the terrible guilt he carried.

From Martha, Luke heard words of life and living and anticipation and optimistic expectancy. They further intensified both his burden and his need to live up to everything that Freddie had implied in his simple letter.

Suddenly Luke was ready to go. He had intended to remain the night. He had gotten by the actual first meeting. He had endured the discussion, the emotion, the initial pain of recounting for them what Freddie had said and done. Because of these things, Luke felt too tense and exhausted to wake up in the morning and be with Freddie's family again. He knew that his intense guilt at causing Martha and Jeff to lose Freddie had eased, and for that he was grateful. But in its place, or perhaps finally allowed to surface, Luke found other guilts. He felt guilty because he felt unworthy of Freddie's faith in him. He knew Freddie should not have died for that faith. He felt guilty about being with the Hendersons his first time off the post when he should have gone to Aggie. He knew he could not have gone to Aggie, even if he had not gone to Augusta. That made him feel guilty, too.

Luke constantly worried about Aggie. He felt that something was terribly wrong that was beyond his ability to right. These feelings worked against the fear he found growing within himself. He dreaded going to her and hearing her before he conquered the confusion he was experiencing. He wondered why he did not expect the same accepting comfort and sharing which he experienced at the Hendersons. He wondered if he had deliberately chosen this visit instead of one to Aggie for that reason.

Despite the improvement in his physical injury, Luke wondered if he might not still be too vulnerable in his mind and heart. He did not believe he could cope with the puzzling uncertainty at home which Aggie's letters had telegraphed. So Luke left the Hendersons and went back to the hospital. He concluded that he had a great deal more sorting to do before he was ready to set aside those perpetual and sharp-edged shadows of things that were.

The bus pulled out of Augusta about midnight. Luke sat in the very last seat in the rear without thought or resentment or an awareness of its symbolic significance. It was where he preferred to be, alone. There he could be with his thoughts. The sounds of shifting bodies, the smell of smoking and exhaust, the groans and snores of sleeping people were in front of him. The rumble of the engine vibrated the seat beneath him. Out the window, darkness was punctuated here and there by an unimportant star or a temporary, fleeting shadow exposed by a distant light. That was all. He silently partnered with the rhythm of the noises.

In the dark and motion of a night rider moving down a black, un-seeable road, Luke struggled to come to terms with himself and his life. He began with the guilts he felt. In his mind he thought again of the brave and comforting Martha. He agonized over the sacrifice Freddie made and the gift of hope Freddie's scholarship fund offered. These thoughts made Luke feel both more guilty and more inadequate.

He remembered his condemnation of God and His wisdom on the battlefield as Freddie lay mortally wounded in his arms. He hadn't yet known of the gift Freddie had already assured. He remembered his own wasting away in anxiety in the Paris hospital. He remembered his terror that Freddie had died so he might live. And he remembered the letter which confirmed his deepest fears and provided the basis for his deepest regrets. He struggled to accept that this letter gave him the opportunity for a future in which he could be the leader Freddie had hoped he would be.

Throughout the trip, Aggie was never far from his mind. But he did not analyze her behavior, question her strange letters, condemn her or feel conscious guilt at his fear of seeing her again. He just thought of her. She was just in his mind and heart. She was a part of him as he wrestled with his heart there on the bus in constant, droning motion, in the night.

Confusion permeated all this. No resolution to the conflicts within him materialized, so he could not say to himself, "That's it, that's settled." Without that, he found no relief, no peace in the simple act of sleep. Exhausted as he was though, he remained wide awake. But his tired mind eventually stopped trying to piece together all that had happened. It stopped working to recall the things that were. Instead, it moved to those circuitous realms of random impression men and women experience when monotony casts its hypnotic spell upon them. So Luke's mind was finally freed from its dwelling in self-recrimination and guilt. After months of pain, he finally thought about what his soul may offer.

Luke considered the purpose for his life and the God of whom he had once been so sure. If, he concluded, there was a purpose for the talent he possessed and the pain he endured, then guilt should not be worthy of him. He recalled the first day he knew he wanted to be a minister. His preacher had just died in fires born of hate and fear. It had been he who had offered comfort and hope from the tragedy to his congregation. *Why, then,* he asked himself, *can I not call on that faith to help me handle this as I could do then? Why, when the tragedy is mine should I feel so helpless, yet when the tragedy is someone else's I can glibly find words that help them?* Even as he reflected on this, Luke knew that it was so much drivel. The tragedy at the church was his as well as the congregation's. Certainly Freddie's death did not touch him alone. Luke was simply making one of his speeches, and he felt ashamed of it. His mind went silent again, and he heard the noises within the bus once more.

Luke did not know how much time had passed before his next lucid thought. His eyes closed, he supposed himself asleep. But something in the hinterland of his mind, perhaps not even there but in his heart, kept trying to work its way loose. It forced its way into his consciousness so he would face it, admit it, deal with it. Luke again slid into thoughtless semi-slumber. That something saw its chance, and it worked its way into Luke's brain. The minute it did, Luke was fully awake, sure that he had come across the real reason for his guilt and his shame.

I am afraid, he thought almost aloud. *I really am. Still. Six months after leaving the battlefield, I am afraid. And I have known I was afraid and wanted Martha to tell me I did not need to be. I am fearful of having Aggie see me full of fear, and so I am afraid to go home. I am afraid that I cannot be what Freddie wanted me to be, so I feel guilty. I even resent his dying and leaving me to carry on under the burden he has given me. But why am I so afraid?*

Again, Luke succumbed to the hypnotic rhythm of the bus, and let his mind slip back into emptiness. He hoped to capture more of the thought which he finally realized had been working its way toward fruition through the entire day.

Even before he asked why he was afraid, he knew why. He admitted that he had known all along. He was afraid because he was alone, as alone as a man can be. He was alone because he had lost his faith in God. He challenged his faith when he cursed God and demanded to be told how what he was experiencing could be. He denied his faith when he did not receive an answer.

Luke knew that his fear and confusion were complicated by Freddie's written admonition to live, to become. Luke surmised that he would need his faith to do as Freddie asked. He was afraid that if he did not become a minister and a leader of his people, he would probably lose Aggie too.

As the night slipped by full of shadows of things that were, random realizations and coherent conceptions played their game of hide and seek within Luke's mind. Then, from the quagmire of his thoughts, the truth emerged. But that truth lent no solution to Luke's dilemma by the time the bus reached the hospital. He could not just recall his faith by admitting that he had lost it. Without his faith, he doubted that anything planned by him or for him in that lost past would ever be a part of his future.

Instead, he realized he would need to discover the fundamental answer to the question he had posed in such agony to God. Without that, without some reason beyond himself, he could not again believe that God was just and loving. If he could not believe that, from where would he draw the strength he would need to become what Freddie and the world expected of him?

There is no flash of light to clear my head, he thought as he dragged his tired and aching leg through the rain to the ward. *I simply must go on. I must face what I must face and wait and see. Perhaps I must also pray that I can understand and so have my faith restored.* That resolution was not enough, but it was all Luke could handle. He was tired in his bones and in his heart. He still could not figure out why he was alive while his best friend was dead. The trip to Martha's was to have been the beginning for him. It was to have been the final chapter on the past, so he could go home. Instead, it resurrected self-doubt. It made him grieve all over again at the losses: Freddie, Sampson, and all the others who would never come home. Luke knew he had to face the grief and conquer it. He had to find his way home in a way that would honor what Freddie and the others had given. But it would have to wait until tomorrow. He was too tired this night for any further thought.

CHAPTER 25

The Reality of Going Home

Although more rested and excited about getting out of the hospital, Luke still had not resolved his conflicts some two weeks later. But with new strength and a whole summer ahead to think, he was beginning to feel that life might just begin again. At least the war was finally over for him.   He saw nothing left to do but make peace with himself and try to rebuild his life. He thought this as he stood at attention on the parade ground of the hospital where he had been recuperating for six months. It was an award ceremony typical of those held weekly for veterans injured but recovered enough to be publicly honored by their country. He was pleased for he knew that the next thing was release and going home.

He had left the hospital only one time when he visited the Hendersons. That had begun the healing process only by reopening the wounds in his soul for a fresh cleansing. He still carried some of his guilt over Freddie's death and suspected that he might always. He felt that he still would need to try to come to terms with it before he could go on with his future.

Luke thought of the visit to the Hendersons again as he had in one form or another almost daily over the last two weeks. He still knew of nothing more he could say to Martha which would ease her or Jeff's pain. He knew words would still be needed. He also knew that they should be shared with Aggie and not Martha. But he still was very disturbed by Aggie's behavior. He could not understand why she had not been to see him but hoped and prayed that she would be there today for the ceremony and for him.

Luke's discontent and confusion continued to soften just by a touch of hope. The first step would be getting home. He needed to be in familiar places with people whom he loved where he could be himself and share without guilt. Perhaps the day by day activity, the ordinary things of life without the intensity of the last two years would heal him. He had to believe that patience and prayer would bring the answers he felt God had denied him. Then perhaps he could recover his faith. As Luke thought this, he knew his faith was returning already for he had consciously sought an answer from God and acknowledged that God might have had a purpose in all that had happened.

Luke kept his ear tuned to the activity on the parade ground as he let his mind travel inward. When his mind discovered his returning faith, the jump in his heart induced a roar in his ears that returned him totally to the present. Suddenly aware of a crowd before him, he scanned the faces for Aggie. Instead, Martha's eyes seemed to find his and he swelled inside and smiled at finding her there. She had come all the way from Augusta to see him. She had chosen to show him that she was his friend and that Freddie's loss could be overcome because Luke was her friend, too. And Luke felt a touch of what had become an unfamiliar emotion. Luke felt a touch of joy.

A measurably more poised and confident looking Luke shifted his eyes back to the sea of faces in search of Aggie. When he saw his aunt and uncle and not Aggie, the joy subsided in the face of his disappointment. She had not come. She was not even there to see that Luke had healed and was once again whole. Perhaps she simply no longer cared. Luke retreated again into his mind keeping only his ear in touch with the world.

Eventually the ponderous procedure for decorating the rows of injured men and women ended. The brass departed and the band stopped playing. This door to the past was closed. As the soldiers began disbursing, Luke saw his aunt and uncle coming across the hot, green parade field toward him. Although his leg was hurting from the strain of supporting him for two hours, he stood and waited for them. His eyes searched for Martha, but she did not come from the crowd.

Then LeRoy and Crystal were there hugging him and helping him and fussing over him. This might have been embarrassing if Luke had not been so hungry for their close warmth. Their reunion was accomplished with tears and laughter, and with the puffing of Crystal. As she reached and embraced her nephew more puffing ensued. Luke and LeRoy led her away from the thinning crowd. Luke looked over his shoulder one more time for Martha before the rush of the present enveloped him.

Finally they reached the door of the hospital ward. The first excitements and tensions fell away and they were as close as they had always been. There was a moment to think, to question, to feel that closeness and the bond of each to the other. There was time to ask.

"Why isn't Aggie with you?" Luke's Aunt and Uncle exchanged strange and strained looks and responded with questions as to how Luke was feeling and when he might be released.

"I'm fine. Just a slight limp. But where is Aggie? I really need to know. Now."

"She just couldn't come, Luke."

"That's no answer and you know it. You came. It is surely much harder on you than her. Is she still with you?"

"Yeah."

"Then she's sick?"

"Well, no. That is---" LeRoy stumbled around trying to answer. He did not himself fully understand why, anymore than he understood Aggie's strange behavior in the seven months since the telegram had come. During all that time, Aggie had not once referred directly to Luke's injury. When he or Crystal did, she would freeze in whatever she might be doing. Then she would turn and leave the room or continue to speak of Luke as being just at work, home soon, and the things she must do before he arrived. It was as though the whole war and Luke's absence did not exist for her. Yet she had shown signs at times of knowing fully that Luke was in the hospital. Mention of his name would bring tears to her eyes. She would become disoriented, withdrawn, defensive and finally retreat to her room. Sometimes she literally remained in that room for days without contact with either LeRoy or Crystal. Then without warning, Aggie would be back working in the kitchen. Once they had found her standing on the back porch calling to Crystal to hurry so they would not be late to Mrs. Harmon's.

But Mrs. Harmon herself had become frustrated with the changes in Aggie who became undependable. She constantly daydreamed and suffered emotional outbursts. Mrs. Harmon told Crystal not to bring her back. Crystal made excuses to Aggie as to why she need not go on this day or that. Eventually Aggie simply removed the idea of working in a White household from her pattern altogether.

So neither Crystal nor LeRoy had any idea of what was going on in Aggie's mind. Instead each hoped that once Luke came home, Aggie would abandon the terrible fears and thoughts which seemed to be destroying her. They prayed she would fall back into the pattern of the old Aggie that Luke had loved so much. But they also realized that Luke might be too late or too changed himself for that to happen. They were determined to prevent the two from marrying until they were fully satisfied that both were settled and had put the agony of the last two years behind them. They needed to be sure that Luke and Aggie still shared the love they once had after all.

These thoughts, this worry, and their final determined action were in LeRoy's mind as he tried to answer Luke's question. Yet he could not find the words. Crystal interjected.

"Luke, Honey. I think it awright. I think she goin' be awright. But she been through somethin' terrible since y'all got yo'self hurt. We tryin' to 'splain it to y'all. Is there somewhere we can go, private like, and mebbe just talk?"

Luke felt a constriction in his gut. He had half expected to hear that Aggie was ill and thought perhaps that this was what he had just heard. But he could not be sure. He could fathom no other reason for her not to be there with him now.   Yet they had denied that she was sick, then hedged. He had to hear, had to know. "You all hungry?"

"Could eat."

"There's a little cafe just off the Post. We could catch the Post bus to the gate and walk over to it."

"Can y'all walk that far on your leg?"

"It isn't far, and the leg's okay. Really. I've gotten good treatment."

"Well let's go, then."

The cafe was a yellowy kind of hole in the wall catering to colored soldiers from the hospital with a little money looking for a quick beer or a quiet corner. But it did serve food of sorts. Luke had never seen it before as he saw it while bringing his Aunt and Uncle to it. Suddenly he did not want them to eat there. "Come on" he said. "Let's find somewhere else."

"No, Luke. Really. This'11 be fine."

"It's so . . . dirty."

"Has y'all eaten here before?"

"Yeah, but---"

"Well, y'all is lookin' no worse for it, so let's do some sittin', grab somethin' light and get on with the talkin' we needs to do." They moved to a shabby booth in the back corner of the room. Crystal eased her bulk onto the hard bench and hefted herself by pushing on the plain wood table. She slid sideways to the wall. LeRoy sat beside her, with Luke on the opposite side. They looked at each other, but no one found the words to start.

A young girl in a dingy smock approached the table. She looked at Luke, then to the older couple. "Beer around?" she asked.

"Two beers and a Coke, Missy," Luke replied, he but was interrupted by Crystal.

"You drinkin' Coke, Luke?"

"Well, no, but---"

"Then make it three beers, Missy," Crystal said. LeRoy and Luke both looked at her, startled.

"Why, Crystal Powers. When did you take up beer?"

"I ain't. I just feels the need to celebrate. 'Sides,

I'm thinkin' I need it. Now hush up."

What might she need it for, thought Luke as the constriction in his gut tightened its hold once again. He was anxious to hear of Aggie. But still no one spoke. The beers came. They were drunk in silence. Another was ordered, along with some fried potatoes and, a gamey piece of pork with greens. All three of them bowed to the meal. They looked back and forth at each other from under their eyebrows. They heard only the clinking of their own forks and were unaware of others in the diner.

LeRoy pushed his plate away and pulled the old cob pipe from inside his denim jacket. As he struck fire and began the lighting, Luke leaned across the narrow table and caught the end of his cigarette in LeRoy's flame. Crystal waved the waitress to them and ordered dessert. Still no one spoke.

But the tension was easing. Coffee came. A comment from one or the other about the food being good after all was generally accepted with agreement. Luke said he liked Crystal's chops better. LeRoy quickly agreed and puffed a little faster while Crystal indicated that she certainly hoped so.

LeRoy said, "That little gal o' yours has come to be a mighty fine cook too, Luke. Mighty fine." The other two looked at LeRoy, waiting for him to say something else. "She does good at keeping up the house too, while your Aunt here is out working."

"Isn't Aggie working anymore?"

"Well, no. Miz Harmon don't need her no more now that I'm back there," threw in Crystal.

"I thought you were working next door."

"Oh, I is. I is. But they ain't 'nough work at either place to keep me goin' so now I'm doin' both. But I ain't bathin' Rufus. Fo' sure."

"Who's Rufus?"

"He's the dog. Miz Harmon's. Aggie used to bathe him once a week. But Miz Harmon's boy John is bigger now and he done take that on himself. To tell Y'all the truth, Aggie done better at it, but---"

"Yeah. A little truth would help about now. Isn't it about time you told me why she isn't here?"

"Ain't no need to get lippy, now, Luke. Y'all may be de big sergeant and war hero, but I is still your Aunt and still bigger than y'all." A touch of softness in her voice took the edge off the words, but the look in her eyes signaled to Luke a tinge of hurt, some heavy burden and the need for patience. He sat quietly but reached across and took her arm. They shared a common and lightly held glance. A tear just showed itself in the old woman's eye but was quickly lost in a flurry of blinking as Crystal began talking again.

"Truth is, she's better off at home and is doin' a fine job there keepin' the place together while me and LeRoy is workin' the mill, the fields an' the White folks' homes. Why, Aggie, she's keepin' up with the goat and the milkin'. She's feedin' the chickens and tendin' the hogs most days on top of cleanin' the house and doin' the wash."

"Then why, really, is she not here, Aunt Crystal?"

"Well, she---"

"You are more like my mamma than my aunt. You know me better than anyone alive except maybe Aggie, and that's a maybe. That leaves you to tell me. You need to tell me straight out. Because I think I know."

"You, uh, do?"

"I think so. I just can't seem to say it."

"Me neither."

"Me neither."

Luke struggled for a way to begin. "I recall the day I got shot. Not the shooting part, but what I was thinking. You know what I was thinking?"

"'Bout your Aggie?"

"Well, yes, in a way. She certainly was never far from my thoughts. But specifically, I was thinking of the way Aggie has of living for the moment, of making the moment fit what she thinks life is, instead of what it really is."

"My, she does that, all right."

"Well, anyway---"

"Luke. How long you know that 'bout Aggie?"

"Years. We used to talk about it all the time. I used to try to tell her life was not the horrible thing she created in her mind, that her perception of it was what made it seem so bad, but---"

"If life could be what she thinks it is now, we'd all be better off."

"What do you mean?"

"She won't allow no pain. She won't hear no bad news. She won't listen to what things is really like. She just makes up somethin' else." It was the first time LeRoy had been able to say what he thought Luke needed to know before he got home.

Crystal knew there was more. "Ain't all, either, Luke. If we tries to tell her somethin', anythin' that ain't already in that head of hers, she up and goes off by herself, 'times for days."

"What were you trying to tell her?" This truly shook Luke for he had always been able to settle Aggie down if he could not change her mind he could at least convince her that her way might not be the best for the two of them.

"Luke. Y'all ain't gonna believe what I'm sayin' but from what I done see these last months, she never let herself know y'all been gone at all. She ain't never admit y'all been hurt in the war. She done make up some Luke outa her mind or somethin'. She's been livin' there in your room with that make—believe man since y'all done left."

"But that's ridiculous. I've written and she's written back. It's true she never mentioned the war but she talked of you, of her work, of the things she was getting for when I get home and we get married." Even as Luke said it, he was realizing that what his aunt and uncle had said made sense. It accounted for the tone of and omissions in her letters which had disturbed him for so long. A sudden chill went down his back as he thought of the last time he was home just after basic and before Europe. He recalled the strange and unaccountable way she had behaved toward him. *My God,* he thought. *Just as I feared. She was already dreaming and I had already changed too much to fit the dreams.* He pulled his thoughts away from the realization and caught the eyes of his aunt and uncle bearing down on him. He saw curiosity and fear. Most of all he saw love for him.

He cleared his throat and spoke to break the spell and learn more. "I'm still not sure," he started, then stopped. He thought then he knew he had to go on. He knew he had to hear it out loud. "I'm still not sure why she did not come with you."

"Luke, if she believe y'all ain't never left, an' if on top of that she 'fraid to leave the house, how y'all think she's goin' to get in that ol' wagon then that big bus and travel for two days to get from there to here? Far as she is concerned, here just ain't. It's not here. Where she is, is all there is, long as she's there."

"My God!"

"I'm so sorry, Luke. We just didn't know. Y'all told us nothin' 'bout her strange way before y'all left. We thought she, well, were just a little lazy and mebbe a little scared. We tried. We loves her, too, ya know. Really we tried." Luke now knew that Aggie was in a bad way and that his Aunt and Uncle blamed themselves for her condition. But he could not help feeling that if he could go to her, love her and talk to her, he could break through the shell and she would be Aggie again. He must, he knew. For even with the worry and doubts that went with the memory of her, that memory was a sustaining force within him since Freddie's death. He considered all that he must do with his life for himself, for his people, and to keep his promise to Freddie. Every thought, every plan, every move, even his new search for faith, had to be for Aggie, as well as him. He could not now conceive of it being him only. He just could not and would not. He knew he must go to her and said so. But to his surprise, he got an argument from both LeRoy and Crystal. "But why not? If anybody can replace that shadow of me, it's me. I've got to try."

"But Luke, Honey. That shadow ain't y'all no more."

"What do you mean?"

"That shadow is a seventeen—year—old barefoot boy what ain't hardly ever been off the farm. He's lighter than you by mebbe thirty pounds. He talks much higher, and well, he don't limp."

"My limp's getting better all the time."

"Even so. Y'all don't know. Y'all ain't see how she's been. She's afraid of men and y'all a man now. She see you limpin' that way and she may just turn around and go in the house and never come out. I'm just tellin' you, there have been times---"

"She wouldn't. Maybe she'd be just thinking I got a little hurt at work. Lord, she's seen me with a broken foot and stayed with me."

"No she ain't, said LeRoy."

"What do you mean?"

"As far as she is concerned, that never happened. Far as she is concerned, every bad thing that ever happened to her ain't happened. I'm tellin' you, Luke, y'all don't know."

"But that's incredible!"

"I know" offered Crystal. "We done prayed 'bout her, tried talkin' with her. We done give in to her time and again. Since the telegram sayin' y'all be comin' home, we been tryin' to get her to come with us to see y'all here."

"And she said no?"

"No, she didn't. That what I'm sayin'. Instead she say it's silly to go. She thinks y'all ain't here. She thinks y'all's there with her."

"Then, don't you see, I should go and be there with her."

"By and by, maybe. Not now," said LeRoy. "The way I see it, when y'all come home y'all better not be limping and y'all better not be leaving again. If y'all come home to that girl y'all's going to have to come on her terms. Otherwise, I think y'all's going to lose her before y'all even has a chance to get her back."

Luke leaned back in the booth and slipped his hurting leg straight out under the table. He rolled the empty beer can back and forth in his hands. He stared intently at the foggy reflection it held of the lonely light bulb hanging behind Luke from the old gas jet fixture on the yellowy and peeling wall.

He considered and reconsidered what his aunt and uncle had just said and slipped a little lower in his seat. He felt the ache in his body and soul for Aggie and for faith and for new life and considered again. He knew there was no decision to be made today. His feeling that he could solve the spiritual or emotional problems Aggie carried by the sheer strength of his calling, pushed hard against the force and finality of LeRoy's words. It was pulled by the fact that he knew he had changed and was struggling for his own spiritual life, his own identity. It had been a long time since he had the courage to use that inner force to lead or convince anyone of anything.

During that time Freddie had died. Aggie had pulled away from life. He had been shot and the world had changed.

But then he prayed that the changes in the world would make it easier for him to be the person, the minister, the leader that Freddie and the others wanted him to be and that Freddie had made him promise to be. He must have Aggie with him to be that person. Or must he? Was Aggie now the Aggie he had left, any more than he was the boy who had left Aggie? It was so long ago. It was before the war and growing up had happened to them both. Had Aggie grown up? Luke suddenly knew that these thoughts and not thoughts of Freddie had dominated his mind during his visit to the Hendersons. He had seen in Martha the strength he hoped Aggie would display. He had seen in her the will to leave the past and go on. He knew Aggie would need that kind of strength if they were to have the life together he had searched for during his recovery. As Aggie obviously needed his strength, he knew he also needed hers.

This need gave him resolve. Even in the face of Crystal and LeRoy's objections, he decided to try to get discharged from the hospital as soon as possible.   He even dared hope for Monday. He decided that regardless of what his aunt and uncle said, it was time to go home, to face life and Aggie. It was time to start putting the future back together again.

He had to find his own way home. LeRoy and Crystal could no longer do it for him. He had to find home in his faith and in Aggie. It was the only way and it promised to be a long way home.

CHAPTER 26

And Like Shadows, These Things That Were

It was the morning Luke came home. He faced the summer sun rising in the east and his long shadow stretched out behind him.

Luke stopped a moment in the dusty red street of long ago and reflected on how little things there had changed. The faces of the children were different and some of them wore shoes. But that was about all. Ol' Tom's looked about the same. Most of the men on the front porch wore the same faces. The rusting, antique Coca Cola cooler looked as though it had sat there on the weathered and splitting porch for so long that to move it would cause disintegration. Luke limped slightly to the spot in front of the store where Elkins had knocked him down and stomped his ankle. He stared at the dirt and conjured for a moment the feeling of pain he had endured that day. Then he knew that the pain was real and that he could not walk on home as he had planned.

When the doctor released him, he cautioned Luke to remain off the leg as much as possible for at least another three or four weeks or risk a permanent limp. The leg had felt so good and the limp had been so slight when he left that he had thought the man wrong. Now only half a mile from the bus station from which he had lugged the big duffle bag, his leg was exhausted and hurting again. He had to sit.

"Hey, Tom." He greeted the storekeeper.

"Who dat?"

"It's me, Luke Powers."

"Powers! Dang me if it ain't. Where y'all come from, Boy? I thought y'all in de army."

"I am. Home for a while."

"Well, come on up here and sit a spell. Share a Dr. Pepper like de old days." The invitation was just what Luke was waiting for and he limped up to the two steps leading onto the porch. Reaching out to grab the old porch post, he pulled himself up on to the worn boards as his hand released its hold on the duffle bag. Luke was sweating with the walk and pain.

"Lookin' a little peaked, Boy. Dey don't treat y'all good dere in de army?"

Luke grinned. "Treating me fine, Tom. Just a little soreness in my leg and a little too much walking for one day, is all."

"Dat de leg what got hit? Unnerstand y'all was saved by some White fella. Hard to figger." Luke went tense, then remembered that folks at home may not understand about Freddie. He relaxed, forced a smile and took a pull on the Dr. Pepper Tom handed him.

"Actually, it was my brother and he died in the process."

"I's sorry to hear that, Boy. But I didn't know y'all had no brothers." Tom leaned over and brought a match to Luke's cigarette.

"Got four in Atlanta."

"Which one save y'all?"

"Wasn't any of them. More like what you might call, maybe, uh, a soul brother, a very close life-long and dear friend."

"I thought he White."

"He was."

Luke took another pull on the Dr. Pepper and watched the perplexed and changing expression on Tom's face. He knew that Tom had spent a lifetime outfoxing, lying to, conning and cheating when necessary the Whites in the area in order to avoid being outfoxed, lied to, conned and cheated, and perhaps murdered for the fun of it. He knew Tom could not understand. But he needed to tell someone. He needed to be true to himself and not hide the fact that a White man had been closer to him than anyone else in his life except Aggie. This testified to his belief in humanity and he knew it was time to begin practicing that belief again.

"Must o' been some special kind o' man. Y'all sure dere weren't just a tinge o' Colored back yonder in him somewhere?"

Luke laughed a good laugh and Tom and the others joined in. The men had begun to pull their chairs around Luke's and pump him with questions about the army, the war, the world. Luke warmed to the interest and began spinning the web of his words. He recounted in small brush strokes some of the battles and incidents of his adventures. He slipped deeper into his tale. He told of his fighting side by side with Whites, and with their mutual support. He told of sharing meals, latrines, foxholes and R&R when they could get it.

The second Dr, Pepper remained unwanted and uncorked in the cooler and the famous jug kept being pulled from behind the counter. The talk became looser and freer and Luke's tale-spinning more rampant. The pain in his leg was either forgotten or subdued and eventually he stood unsteadily. He said his farewells to the group. Dragging the duffle, he started on down the road toward home.

Traveling in the mild heat of the late morning with the head of the stump liquor bringing an ache to his own, Luke finally stopped on the lonely road and sat for a minute on his duffle. He looked around at the familiar landscape and noted with a grin that it too had changed little.

The bad fields were still bad, while the good ones were showing signs of the life of early summer.

The spot where he was sitting took on an even more familiar look. Inspecting it closer, he found beneath the weeds of neglect the bare trace of an old footpath.

To the left, through the woods and across the creek was his home. To the right the path crossed White man's fields and ended up at the pond. Luke turned right.

Splashing in the murky waters of the pond which had witnessed so much of his growing up, Luke felt like a boy again. He got his fill of whooping and splashing. He settled down to float on his back and recall.

In a few minutes he climbed from the pond. Just as he had so many times before the war, he removed and threw away the army green skivvies and tee shirt and fell back in. He lay there and remembered his thirteenth birthday and Aggie. He thought he saw her coming. Naked as he was he pulled himself to a standing position in the water to greet her. But it was not her. It was no one.

Suddenly he wanted to be home. The games were done. It was high noon and his shadow had disappeared. Life was waiting.

In a few moments he was dressed. Somewhat damp and fully sober, he started on his way back up the nearly invisible trail of his childhood, back to his past, forward to his future. Now was the time. The time had come.

When Luke arrived at the back of the cabin there was no one around. The mules were gone and the pigs were asleep in the sun. The screen door was swinging gently in the light breeze. No special sounds were there. Luke walked forward and started to call out. Then he stopped. *I can get to my trunk,* he thought. *I can be in a pair of coveralls and out of this uniform before any of them see me. Just like old times.* It occurred to him that Aggie might like that better too, so he slipped onto the porch and grabbed the ladder.

Working his way upward, he popped his head into the loft. There she was filling his eyes and heart and raising a hot chill in his back and groin. She was lying before him on the bed with her soft black hair and quiet, smooth skin. Luke could see that she had filled out, that she was anything now but a child. The room itself reflected everything she had written to him. It was full of nick knacks and linens and dresses hanging on nails. His trunk was tucked in the corner by itself with nothing else near it. It was open.

Barefoot now with his combat boots lying at the foot of the ladder, Luke crept across the old floor. He silently slipped his shirt and pants off and reached for the strap of overalls just visible among the clothing in the trunk. He pulled it to him and the pants came free. Just then the trunk lid slammed, sending a loud whapping sound reverberating through the room. Aggie sat up, startled. She saw him standing there naked with Luke's pants in his hand. She screamed.

He was in a panic. She continued her hysterical sobbing and screaming despite several minutes of trying to convince her that it was Luke she was screaming at. The overalls proved much too small and he simply slipped back into his khaki uniform pants. He did not know what to do. She kept screaming for him to get out, get out. Leave her be. She said that he had better be gone before her Luke got home, or Luke would kill him.

"But I am Luke, Aggie," he implored, trying to hold her and calm her. Nothing seemed to work. He finally retreated and went to get her some water.

Luke pumped one last time and the glass overflowed. He let go of the pump handle. He set the glass down and grabbed a towel to swipe at the water now covering the drainboard.

It was then that he noticed the screaming had stopped. Grabbing the glass, he stepped to the back porch and looked up to the trap door, listening. He could not believe what he was hearing. Aggie was singing quietly to herself in the loft not two minutes from uncontrolled screaming and crying. Luke crossed the kitchen to the living room and sat down. Drinking the water himself, he placed his head in his hands in confusion and wonder. He sat there daring not to move which might set off his Aggie again.

"Hello, Luke, Honey. You're late."

"What? Aggie?"

"No matter. I took me a nap and slept a little too long. I'll start dinner any minute. We've got to hurry, though. Our Aunt and Uncle are coming to have dinner with us tonight." Aggie turned to leave.

Luke sat there half out of the chair. He was astounded, unbelieving and not knowing what to do. Aggie kept talking as she moved into the kitchen. Not quite able to hear, Luke moved to the door frame and watched and listened. Aggie chattered on, fussing a little at this or that as she worked. "And Luke, you really should try not to be late. You've been late too much lately, and I get worried. And today just before you got home, there was a strange man in my room. Truly. He was trying to steal some of your things. I screamed and he ran. Didn't you hear me? It was just a few minutes ago. I don't like being here by myself during the day. I think we should get a dog, don't you? I'm partial to Labradors, myself. No telling who might come here while you're working the fields.

"Why are you working the fields anyway? You make plenty from your preaching. Why not stay home with me during the day? Luke? Answer me! Why are you looking at me like that? You look like you don't believe me. Truly, there was a man in my room. Now you either get me a dog or stay home, hear?"

"I'll stay home."

"What?"

"I'll stay home. Being with you is all I want right now anyway. I love you, you see."

"Luke?"

"I'm home."

Aggie slid to the floor. Luke stood frozen above her. The screen door continued its slight sway in the breeze. There were no other sounds. Inside Luke's head however, sounds from far away and long ago meandered and mixed their way through his subconscious. They were the sounds of splashing waters and a gentle girl's voice. "I can't read," it said and, "Give us something to hope for." There were the roaring sounds of fire in the night, the rolling, clanging sound of a trashcan lid winding down like a spinning coin losing its momentum and settling in the alley. There were the sounds of barking dogs and running feet. There were policemen's whistles and admonitions of a preacher on a Sunday morning.

Then there were profanities and the embarrassed sounds of field hands in an army reception station. There were the first sound heard from Freddie the man, and his last too. The soundless words of Freddie's last letter now reverberated in Luke's mind.

Luke's eyes focused on the prone form lying at his feet and he sank to his knees and leaned over her and laid his head on her breast. He slipped flat beside her. Then he heard a special sound which he did not at first recognize. When he recognized the sound he was startled, for it was the sound, the real sound, of crying. So Luke raised himself up to look for the tears in Aggie's eyes. Those eyes were on him now, full of love and recognition. But they were dry. And Luke knew that it had been his own tears that he had heard.

Aggie's arm slowly encircled him and she said, "I have waited as you asked. I had begun to think you might not come. I have waited." Then there were more tears from both and without shame. Neither heard the mules pulling a wagon into the yard. Yet each heard or felt the other's heartbeat and Luke knew he was home. And he knew Aggie would be all right at least for now. Luke knew that "Now" would have to do for the moment.

///

Through the bright days of summer, the war ended and the White troops came home to ticker tape parades and small town celebrations. They were rightly honored for the work they had done and the sacrifices they had made. The country began a post-war boom that was like nothing ever seen before.

The Blacks went home in the back of the bus. There were no honors and what they found at home was what they had left. All the shadows they had left behind were there to greet them.

But Luke was already home. He was with Aggie. He was again working the farm because it was the time of year when all had to work to make sure the crops were in and next year's income would be secured.

Luke took advantage of the endowment he had received from Freddie and renewed his dream of college. He applied to several he knew would consider a Black candidate. Some rejected him because he did not have a high school education. Others overlooked this because he had served with distinction. The government did not help because the government did not yet provide the G.I. Bill to most Black veterans, especially in the South.

But to Luke the biggest challenge that summer was not finding a school. It was Aggie. When he came home, Aggie seemed to totally emerge from the fantasy shell which had provided her sanctuary during Luke's absence. But Luke was concerned about how she might react when she faced more change. Moving away to go to college might re-submerge her in her fantasy world. He was afraid he would lose her again. He strongly believed that considering what she had been through and the way she had coped with it, she could not suddenly just be whole again.

Luke knew that his Aunt and Uncle would offer severe resistance to his marrying her and taking her away if they were not satisfied that she would still be good for Luke. Although he knew this would be a decision he would make with Aggie, he also knew that he loved them and literally owed them his life. He vowed to do everything he could to honor them by listening to them and considering their views. He knew he could not marry Aggie without their approval. He had to prove to them and himself that such approval was warranted.

The shadows of things that were, the shadows of the past blend into the soul of each of us to influence and shape who we will be and how we will act. Luke and Aggie's shadows also took what form they might in their minds and souls. Those shadows for Aggie represented fear and the way she had coped by withdrawing into fantasy.

But Aggie continued through the summer to be the Aggie that Luke knew and loved. As time passed that summer without Aggie having any more delusions, Luke gained more and more confidence that she would be alright.

He recognized that this had to be a matter of faith for him. He believed he was prepared for and capable of helping Aggie stay in reality if she did show signs of slipping back into her dreams.

For better or for worse, their past was done. Luke and Aggie married that summer. With the confidence in each other born from their love, they planned together to go away to school in the fall. A whole new way of life would begin for both of them. Day by day it would add other shadows. When life once again changed direction Luke was certain that these changes too, would become but shadows of things that were.

And like shadows, those things that were, are. They are always there for all of us. It is just that we cannot see them until the light shines in a certain way. But they remain, always. Luke knew this and prayed that Aggie would come to know and accept this as well.

About the Author

Ted Baldwin was born before WWII in San Pedro California and grew up travelling America. He has lived in all regions from the northwest to the deep south, from southern California to New England, in the Midwest and Mid-Atlantic.

Throughout his travels Ted has been and remains a dedicated observer of the peoples and cultures of America's diversity, giving him a wide perspective on the strengths and problems of this unique nation.

This foundation is demonstrated in the realistic depth of character, conflict and hope in Ted's series of books revolving around the racial and cultural conflicts this nation has faced since the Civil War. But although pegged to an historical narrative, this series of novels is not just another history book. They are about character, struggle and the human spirit which Ted believes will ultimately bring the divergent peoples of this nation together. The characters are inspiring but all too human. They are racially and culturally diverse resulting in both internal and external conflict. Their trials and triumphs are easy for any reader to identify with.

Ted lives with his wife of fifty-three years in Central Pennsylvania.

www.ingramcontent.com/pod-product-compliance
Lightning Source LLC
Chambersburg PA
CBHW060347260626
47160CB00006B/2231